NOTHING BUT MURDERS AND BLOODSHED AND HANGING

Mary Fortune (1833-1911) was the author of hundreds of detective stories as well as hard-hitting journalism. Born in Belfast, she married in Canada and emigrated to Australia in 1855 with her young son and an assignment to write about the gold rushes. There she gave birth to a second, illegitimate son, George Fortune, who became a career criminal. In 1858 she made a bigamous marriage to a policeman, and what she learned from him, along with her own experience of life in the goldfields and in bohemian Melbourne, provided source material for the police procedurals she began writing in the 1860s. These stories make up *The Detective's Album*, serialized for forty years in the mass-circulation *Australian Journal*. Fortune published under pseudonyms, thereby shielding her identity and earning a precarious living even when she was jailed for drunkenness, or had no fixed address. Her true identity was almost lost forever, but dedicated research has revealed an extraordinary woman and her story.

"The themes of marriage, murder, and gendered violence resonate with contemporary concerns. The writing is beautiful, complex, and thrilling . . . From the small towns of the goldfields to the arid yet lush landscape of the outback, and back to society living in Melbourne, these stories will enthral you."

— CANDICE FOX

"With their twisty plot lines, freewheeling social observation (low to high and back again), and their ornate, sometimes almost wacky Victorian narrative style, Mary Fortune's detective stories comprise a unique and compelling contribution to early crime fiction."

— PETER DOYLE

Mary Fortune shares her street eye view of a chaotic public world with that quintessential representative of modernity, the detective, as she shares some of his defining characteristics— his minimal private life, his sharp eye for human types, and his simple faith in decent values to guide him th   ral uncertainties of a fragmented moral world, wh always as they seem.

— JUDITH BRETT

ABOUT THE EDITORS

LUCY SUSSEX is a novelist and literary historian. Her fiction includes *The Scarlet Rider*, a novelized account of her search for Mary Fortune; many of her short stories are collected in *Matilda Told Such Dreadful Lies: The Essential Lucy Sussex*. She is also the author of *Woman Writers and Detectives in Nineteenth-Century Crime Fiction* and *Blockbuster! Fergus Hume and The Mystery of a Hansom Cab*, and the editor of a collection of Mary Fortune's journalism and memoirs, *The Fortunes of Mary Fortune*.

MEGAN BROWN is a literary historian and teacher. She wrote her doctoral thesis (University of Wollongong) on Mary Fortune and has since contributed chapters to academic books and published scholarly papers on various aspects of Fortune's work. She teaches science and nineteenth-century literature, and has drawn on her wide-ranging interests in researching colonial-era figures such as botanist/novelist Louisa Atkinson and surgeon/polymath Thomas Young Cotter.

Lucy Sussex and Megan Brown are the co-authors of *Outrageous Fortunes*, a biography of Mary Fortune and her son George (2025).

Nothing but Murders and Bloodshed and Hanging

*Stories of crime and detection by a
pioneering Victorian mystery writer*

MARY FORTUNE

Edited and introduced by
LUCY SUSSEX & MEGAN BROWN

VERSE CHORUS PRESS

First published in 2025 by Verse Chorus Press
Portland, Oregon, USA
www.versechorus.com

'Mary Fortune: A Biographical Sketch' © 2025 Lucy Sussex.
'An Introduction to the Stories' © 2025 Megan Brown.
The work of Mary Fortune is in the public domain.
This edited selection © 2025 Lucy Sussex, Megan Brown, and Verse Chorus Press.

All rights reserved. Without limiting the rights under copyright reserved above, no part of this book may be reproduced, stored in or introduced into a retrieval system, or transmitted in any form or by any means (digital, electronic, mechanical, photocopying, recording, or otherwise), without the prior written permission of the copyright holder or the publisher, except by a reviewer, who may quote brief passages in a review.

Cover image: *Mrs. Brentford was standing with the loaded revolver in her hand, as the door fell in with a loud crash*, wood engraving, published in the *Australian Journal*, 3 October 1868. Courtesy, State Library of Victoria.

Cover and interior design by Steve Connell | *steveconnell.net*

Library of Congress Cataloging-in-Publication Data

Names: Fortune, Mary, 1833?-1911, author. | Sussex, Lucy, 1957- editor. | Brown, Megan (Literary scholar), editor.
Title: Nothing but murders and bloodshed and hanging : stories of crime and detection by a pioneering Victorian mystery writer / Mary Fortune ; edited and introduced by Lucy Sussex & Megan Brown.
Description: Portland, Oregon : Verse Chorus Press, 2025. | Summary: "A selection of Mary Fortune's crime stories, which comprise the first detective fiction series written by a woman. Set in the outback, on the goldfields, and in the burgeoning metropolis of Melbourne, her stories offer a vivid account of life and death in colonial-era Australia. Fortune tackled subjects such as murder, armed robbery, bootlegging, and sexual violence with a frankness unprecedented for a woman in the 19th century, in styles ranging from melodrama and Gothic horror to social realism and what is now termed noir"— Provided by publisher.
Identifiers: LCCN 2024049753 (print) | LCCN 2024049754 (ebook) | ISBN 9781959163091 (trade paperback) | ISBN 9781959163107 (epub)
Subjects: LCGFT: Detective and mystery fiction. | Short stories.
Classification: LCC PR9619.2.F67 N68 2025 (print) | LCC PR9619.2.F67 (ebook) | DDC 823/.8--dc23/eng/20241214
LC record available at https://lccn.loc.gov/2024049753
LC ebook record available at https://lccn.loc.gov/2024049754

CONTENTS

Mary Fortune: A Biographical Sketch 7

An Introduction to the Stories 13

The Dead Witness 23

Down by the Yarra 37

Traces of Crime 53

The Midnight Watch. 63

Lost in Town. 79

The Dead Man in the Scrub 91

Eaglehawk, the Bushranger of the Pyrenees 101

The Hart Murder 113

The Convict's Revenge 139

Our Last Crushing 159

The Stolen Deed 169

Killed in the Shaft 197

Bridget's Locket 213

Constable Dyason's Defeat 237

The Phantom Hearse 245

The Prison Brand 271

An Amateur Detective 293

Notes on the text and illustrations, credits 310

'I'm sick an' tired ov yer stories! It's nothin' but bloodshed and hangin' and murther wid ye from wan week's end to another, until I'm a'most afeared to go to sleep ov a night at all, at all!'

Mary Fortune, writing as W.W.,
from 'The Queen of Diamonds'

MARY FORTUNE: A BIOGRAPHICAL SKETCH

Mary Helena Fortune was many things, some of them quite contradictory. She was a woman living in the nineteenth century, an era which idolised 'the angel in the house,' the domestic, passive, conventional woman. Fortune was anything but. She married and had children, but her second child was illegitimate and her second marriage bigamous. She was also a professional author—and a prolific one, writing poetry and drama as well as in prose modes ranging from the Gothic novel and romance to journalism in which she observed her times acutely, critically, and from the female viewpoint. Elsewhere, she wrote convincingly from a male perspective, in *The Detective's Album*, the longest early crime serial, which made Fortune a major writer of what we now call the police procedural—something all the more extraordinary because she was a woman at a time when her gender excluded her from the legal and police professions.

Fortune was also a woman of mystery in multiple ways. She concealed her identity as well as her gender by publishing under her initials and under pseudonyms. Her publishers guarded her privacy, at first because she wanted it, then increasingly because she and her son George were disreputable—he became a career criminal, serving prison sentences for bank robbery and safe-cracking.

She was born Mary Wilson, in Belfast in 1832, the only child of George Wilson, engineer, and his wife Eleanor Atkinson, who died a few months after her birth. Father and daughter became a family of two, following his work around Ireland. She would recall Ireland and its people fondly,[1] but that period of her life ended in her fourteenth year with the onset of the Great Famine. She and her father crossed the Atlantic to Quebec, where they continued their itinerant lifestyle, with Wilson working for the booming railway system.

She married while still a teenager. Her husband was Joseph Fortune, aged 25, a surveyor from an Anglophone Loyalist family. The pair married in 1851 in the Eastern Townships of Quebec, near the American border. In March 1852 they had a son, Joseph George Fortune. Soon afterwards George Wilson left for the goldfields of Australia.

A wife in the nineteenth century was dependent on her husband, at

---

1 The care with which she reproduces the idioms and speech patterns of the Irish immigrant characters in her Australian stories pay tribute to this.

MARY FORTUNE: A BIOGRAPHICAL SKETCH

risk particularly if she were widowed, or if her marriage broke down. George Wilson, a canny Scot by heritage, took steps to ensure that at the worst Mary could re-join him a hemisphere away. What exactly happened in her marriage is not known, but in 1855 Mary took sail first to Scotland, then Australia, while Joseph Fortune remained in Quebec. If the marriage had failed, the pair could not legally divorce under Quebec law; nor would Mary have got custody of her son. If George Wilson had left her the means, then she took the opportunity. Most likely she took her child and ran—or rather took the trains her menfolk had helped build across the American border, from whence she could not be extradited, and from there sailed back across the Atlantic.

In Scotland she met literary folk, and obtained a commission to write about the Australian goldfields for the English magazine the *Ladies' Companion*, before sailing south. After the long voyage and reuniting with her father in late 1855, she wrote radical poetry instead. This gained her publication under her initials in the *Mount Alexander Mail*, one of the first newspapers established on the Victorian goldfields; the paper even offered her a sub-editor's job (quickly withdrawn when the editor discovered 'M.H.F.' was a woman).

On the goldfields, George Wilson ran a store within a tent, surrounded by the frantic, often dangerous world of mining. He and Mary and her son lived among people who ranged from gentry to former American slaves to old lags (convicts transported to Australia). Crime was rife. This world impressed itself upon Mary: she would soon write about real-life murders and the common activity of producing and supplying illicit liquor. She describes a real-life police raid on sly-grog sellers in Taradale in 1856, but how much Wilson and Fortune were involved is unknown.

Around this time Mary became pregnant; she gave birth to her second son in late 1856. The family continued their itinerant life, travelling from rush to rush. In 1858 they were in Kingower (famous for a monster nugget discovery) when her eldest son died, aged five. Later that year Mary married Percy Brett, a young constable in the Mounted Police.

From Brett she would gain the knowledge to write police procedurals, although the marriage did not last long. Brett may have discovered that Mary was not a widow, as she had claimed on their marriage registry form, and that her second son was illegitimate. For seven years the pair disappear from the historical record, then in 1865 Brett resurfaced in New South Wales. His subsequent life would include being taken hostage by the celebrated bushranger Ned Kelly. Mary remained in Victoria, where she began writing for the *Australian Journal*, a new weekly (later monthly) magazine that rapidly gained a large readership. Three of her poems and a short, fictionalized goldfields memoir, 'Recollections of a Digger,' appeared in its first five issues, all but the first of the poems credited to 'Waif Wander.' But her real breakthrough was still to come.

The first issue of the *Australian Journal* (2 September, 1865) had included the initial instalment of a police casebook, a newly popular form comprising invented police memoirs written as a series of stories with a detective as narrator. The earliest examples were the work of English writer William Russell (from 1849), which evolved from crime melodramas into deductive mysteries and were hugely popular and influential. Casebook stories blurred fact and fiction, with the pretence of authenticity. The first known Australian example was 'Recollections of an Australian Detective,' a 13-part series published anonymously from September 1863 in newspapers in Victoria, New South Wales and Tasmania. It featured true crime narratives, lightly fictionalised. More purely fictional examples followed, among them the story in the *Australian Journal*'s debut issue, a crude melodrama titled 'The Shepherd's Hut; Or, 'Tis Thirteen Years Since: Being Memoirs of an Australian Police Officer.' The anonymous writer was lawyer James Skipp Borlase, a recent arrival from England.

Fortune knew enough to know that his story lacked authenticity and sent in her own submission to the series, 'The Stolen Specimens,' cheekily borrowing Borlase's anonym, 'An Australian Police Officer.' The *AJ* quickly grasped the potential and commissioned her and Borlase to write further stories under the series title *Memoirs of an Australian Police Officer*, which led to some outstanding stories by Fortune, including 'The Dead Witness.' The series ground to a halt the following year, however, when Borlase was sacked for plagiarising Sir Walter Scott.

Fortune continued writing for the magazine—serialised non-crime novels under her Waif Wander pseudonym—but only returned to crime stories in 1867, while working as a housekeeper in rural Victoria. Seeking a casebook motif that would ensure her continued employment as a writer, she came up with *The Detective's Album*, whose underlying conceit is that the storytelling detective is recalling cases from his career while leafing through an album of mug shots—photographs of the criminals he had brought to justice.[2] Fortune's employment of photography as a device in fact preceded its formal adoption by real-life police and

---

2 See, for example, 'The Convict's Revenge' in this collection: 'It is the portrait of this cold-blooded young criminal that is before me in my album as I write . . .'

penal authorities in Victoria. As 'W.W.' she would write more than five hundred stories for the *Album* over a forty-year period.

In addition to the stories for *The Detective's Album*, Fortune wrote journalism in the style of a *flâneuse*, observing the streets both as herself and in the persona of a detective, so she was also a pioneering female journalist in Australia. During this period her personal life became fraught. In 1869, after a move to Melbourne, she was imprisoned for a week for public drunkenness. It was not an isolated instance. Two years later her son George was arrested for stealing a hat; we don't know if this was youthful hi-jinks or because he needed it, but it resulted in him being sent to one of the 'industrial schools' established in Victoria under the Neglected and Criminal Children's Act of 1864.

George would escape, re-offend, and get imprisoned again, graduating from a reformatory school to prison proper. From him, too, Fortune would gain material for her stories, since George belonged to the larrikin sub-culture: a rowdy youth movement that shaded into violence and crime. There is also evidence that Mary, who cultivated relationships with the police for story ideas, became an informer, a 'fizgig.' In 1874, while George was incarcerated, she even figured in the *Police Gazette*:

> Information is required by the Russell-street police respecting Mary Fortune, who is a reluctant witness in a case of rape. Description: – 40 years of age, tall, pale complexion, thin build; wore dark jacket and skirt, black hat, and old elastic-side boots. Is much given to drink and has been locked up several times for drunkenness. Is a literary subscriber to several of the Melbourne newspapers. Stated she resided with a man named Rutherford, in Easy Street, Collingwood.

This is the only known description of Mary Fortune.

She now found writing in the persona of a detective, her son's enemy, too difficult, and for several years turned to another series, the *Navvies' Tales*. Even while personally in dire straits, she also found new markets, using her Irish background to write for the Catholic diaspora audience, for example, despite being an Ulster-born Protestant.

When George was released she took up *The Detective's Album* again. She also began writing short police stories, of a cop on the urban beat, for Melbourne's *Herald* newspaper. In 1879 the paper hired her as part of a move to attract the female audience; it seems she became their first women's editor. Sadly, this new venture ended when her

MARY FORTUNE: A BIOGRAPHICAL SKETCH

two worlds, professional and personal, met. She interviewed her son George while he was in Pentridge Gaol, on Boxing Day 1879, and though the account she wrote for the *Herald* was lightly fictionalized, she was sacked.

While George had periods out of jail, he never really broke free of the criminal milieu—his mother was similarly devoted to writing crime. In the 1880s she wrote for syndications, which brought her a larger audience. George gained fame, albeit ill-fame, when in 1885 he took part in the most notorious bank robbery in nineteenth-century Melbourne. He got five years, and when released in 1890 soon led a gang of safe-crackers in country Victoria. That got him another ten years. His mother wrote many stories about recidivists, how they might be reformed, and how the police conspired against them, through fizgigs and entrapment.

In 1899 George was released once more and tried for a new life in Tasmania, but was soon in and out of jail again, before gaining another ten-year sentence. He did not help matters by apparently picking a prison lock, which led to a further sentence. His health suffered as a result of periods in solitary, in icy conditions, and an unsuitable prison diet. He developed kidney disease and died in Hobart hospital in 1907.

Mary's one surviving letter discusses her son's impending death. She was now old, and her eyesight had deteriorated. The *Australian Journal* had printed her *Detective's Album* for forty years, but now they took it away from her. Mary was denied the newly introduced old-age pension for not being able to demonstrate her sobriety (a necessary proof of good character). She spent months in what was effectively a workhouse for the aged before her pension was granted.

It is recorded that she was also granted an annuity by Alfred Massina, the proprietor of the *Australian Journal*. When she died in 1911, she was buried in the Massina family plot, at Springvale cemetery. Her grave was unmarked, however, and not even an obituary marked the end of her long career, which had gained her enough pseudonymous fame that a horse and a greyhound were named after Waif Wander. When W.W.'s pioneering work was rediscovered, it created a mystery: who was the woman behind the lively journalism and pioneering police procedurals? It took much sleuthing over decades, by various researchers, but finally her life and work can be revealed.

LUCY SUSSEX

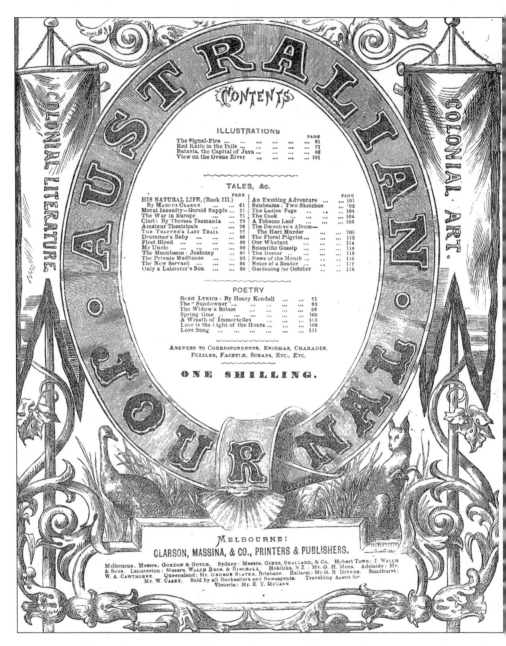

Cover page of the October 1870 issue of the *Australian Journal*, featuring 'The Detective's Album—The Hart Murder' as well as an instalment of Marcus Clarke's *His Natural Life*, which was serialized between March 1870 and June 1872. Courtesy, State Library of Victoria.

AN INTRODUCTION TO THE STORIES

When Mary Fortune arrived in Australia in 1855, bound for the gold-fields, she first stepped into a frontier town. European settlement of Melbourne was barely twenty years old. The city was noisy, chaotic and largely unformed. She found the trains dirty and inferior, the wooden stations inadequate, and 'Elizabeth-street' nothing more than a mass of glutinous clay with scattered houses. It all compared unfavourably 'coming from lands where art and science appeared to have perfected themselves in the production of such conveniences.'[3] It wouldn't be the last time she questioned her decision to travel to Victoria, and yet there she remained, a witness to the rapid physical and social change that took place in Victoria over the next sixty years. Luckily for us she wrote about it, extensively.

Even without considering the quality of her writing, the details of Mary Fortune's life would mark her as a figure of historical interest, because she provides both first-hand and fictional accounts of one of the most important periods of Australian history. However, it is the nature of her writing that gives her a unique place in history. Middle-class women were excluded from the public sphere in the 19th century. They couldn't hold positions of power, they couldn't vote, and they were expected to stay at home and care for house and family. These societal expectations generally restricted women's writing to domestic subjects. Mary Fortune's work defied all these conventions. Her wide experience of crossing continents, living in the gold fields and being a single mother trying to make ends meet in a colonial city meant that Fortune's writing was anything but domestic. There was, she noted, 'nothing of the namby-pamby elegance of ladies' literature in our stirring, hardy, and eventful life in the early goldfields.'[4] And there was nothing namby-pamby about Fortune's writing. One of the first pieces of writing she published while she was living on the goldfields was a poem with radical republican ideas. Later a vast portion of her work was crime fiction, sometimes touching on taboo subjects, often quite graphically.

The *Australian Journal*, a periodical miscellany based on the

---

3 Waif Wander (W.W.), 'Twenty-Six Years Ago; or, The Diggings from '55,' *Australian Journal*, September 1882.
4 ibid.

AN INTRODUCTION TO THE STORIES

well-known *London Journal*, began in September 1865 and in its second issue published Fortune's poem 'To My Little Son on his Birthday' under her initials, M.H.F. This was followed by several romances written under a new pseudonym, Waif Wander. But she quickly realised that stories about crime were more popular and took up that genre using another pseudonym. As we know, she had the credentials for writing crime. It is possible the editors did not know at first that a woman was writing the crime stories they published. The editors informed potential contributors of the success or failure of their submissions through a column in each issue entitled 'Answers to Correspondents.' As well as notices addressed to Waif Wander, for a few months the editors also, separately, addressed notices to 'An Australian Police Officer'—the title we now know she used for her submissions to the anonymously written casebook. They must have found out eventually, but by that time her stories were so popular they turned a blind eye.

The sheer quantity of crime stories Mary Fortune wrote made it a real challenge to select the ones we have included here. In addition to the over five hundred stories she wrote as W.W. for the *Detective's Album* series in the *Australian Journal*, she wrote other crime stories under her more conventional Waif Wander pseudonym, as well as stories for the early casebook by 'An Australian Police Officer,' and two series for Melbourne's *Herald* newspaper—one called *Police Stories*, the other *Sketches of the Force*. She also wrote various one-off feature stories and serials for high-profile Melbourne and Sydney periodicals; 'Bridget's Locket' is one example.

This collection contains at least one story from each decade of her writing, and covers a broad range of crimes, but most importantly each of these stories illustrates something about Fortune's life, displays innovations that she introduced to the genre, and develops her recurring themes. There are more stories from the beginning of her career than the end—while she remained remarkably consistent, forty years of producing crime stories month in, month out, inevitably meant they became rather more formulaic towards the end of her life.

Nevertheless, *The Detective's Album* remained one of the drawcards for readers of the *Australian Journal*. When Fortune's loss of eyesight prevented her from completing her stories, *The Detective's Album* disappeared from its pages, but there must have been a reader backlash, because the publishers urgently sought a replacement writer. In his memoir, Ronald Campbell describes how he came to take over the writing of *The Detective's Album* in 1922. By this time Fortune

AN INTRODUCTION TO THE STORIES

had been dead for eleven years; the publishers had repeatedly tried and failed to replace her, leading them to reprint some of her earlier stories as a last resort. When proprietor Alfred Massina interviewed Campbell for the job he explained that the current writer, A.C. Eiseman, had to be replaced because he 'found the strain of turning out a 10,000 word detective story every month too much.'[5] Yet Fortune had done this for forty-one years.

What is it about Fortune's work that keeps drawing us back to it? For one thing, she has a distinctive voice—unique for a woman writer in the nineteenth century. And her stories are always intriguing, her plots inventive. She is often funny, slyly referential and self-deprecating. There are certain issues and themes that she feels strongly about and she returns to these frequently. She would also react to comments from readers and critics and was not beyond settling scores in print even while guarding her anonymity. The sheer force of her personality is plainly exposed in 'A Women's Revenge; or, Almost Lost':

> I have been told by some that I tell horrible stories, and by others that I am not sensational enough; and I have personally come to the conclusion that I shall tell just such stories as I please, and that those who do not like them need not read them; and so I begin, always with this understanding.'[6]

'The Dead Witness' leads off this collection. Part of the casebook series entitled *Memoirs of an Australian Police Officer*, it is the most anthologised of Fortune's stories, but the combination of its being one of the very earliest detective stories ever written by a woman and the quality of the writing make it an essential inclusion here. Like several of the stories we've included, such as 'The Midnight Watch,' 'Eaglehawk: the Bushranger of the Pyrenees' and 'Bridget's Locket,' it is set in the Australian bush. At this stage of Australia's history, writers still had a love-hate relationship with the bush, often describing it in terrifying, gothic terms. This tendency is more pronounced in women's writing; women of European heritage often found the Australian landscape completely alien. Fortune, however, sang its praises. She opens the story saying that she can 'scarcely fancy anything more enjoyable to a mind at ease with itself than a spring ride through the Australian bush.'

---

5 Ronald Campbell, 'An Editor Regrets' (unpublished manuscript, Louise Campbell Papers, Fryer Library, University of Queensland).

6 W.W., 'A Woman's Revenge; or, Almost Lost,' *Australian Journal*, February 1871.

AN INTRODUCTION TO THE STORIES

As well as being a pioneering work of crime fiction, 'The Dead Witness' exemplifies Fortune's embrace of technological innovations to drive her plots: the then cutting-edge technology of photography functions both as a plot device and a method of solving the crime. As noted earlier, the concept of a photo album of criminals' 'mug shots' underlay her *Detective's Album* serial, before it was even in use by the police themselves. The device of the detective working 'undercover' was another innovation in this story.

'Traces of Crime,' the other story from the early *Memoirs of an Australian Police Officer* series included here, is set in the Victorian goldfields. Fortune's experiences in the goldfields were so foundational that we have included four goldfield crime stories in this volume. In her memoir she describes her first impressions vividly:

To fall asleep and dream dreams that change as quickly as the forms of an unsteady kaleidoscope, and to awaken with a bewildered feeling that you are not yourself but must have changed places with some other identity, must be a sensation akin to that I experienced when I opened my eyes in the morning after my first sleep on the diggings.[7]

The gold rush experience challenged individuals not only personally but collectively. It changed the social fabric of Australia. The people who came searching for gold were of many nationalities, from diverse backgrounds and different social classes, and, surprisingly, most of them were literate. The moveable canvas cities of the early goldrush years created a temporary egalitarian space where everyone mixed together in ways that would have been unthinkable anywhere else at the time.

Despite the assault on the senses Fortune experienced upon her arrival, she grew to love the time she spent moving from one diggings to the next. 'Traces of Crime,' 'The Dead Man in the Scrub,' 'Our Last Crushing,' and 'Killed in the Shaft' convey her intimate understanding of how the diggings worked and the kinds of characters you would encounter. These stories were, like their author, breaking new ground and taking advantage of a moment in time when the traditional rules of society were in flux. It was the only way a woman could possibly have established herself as a crime writer for a major literary periodical.

It's worth keeping in mind that while we are now used to reading

---

7 Waif Wander (W.W.), 'Twenty-Six Years Ago; or, The Diggings from '55,' *Australian Journal*, January 1883.

AN INTRODUCTION TO THE STORIES

crime fiction detailing police procedure or detectives going undercover, the police force was a relatively new entity when Fortune wrote these stories. In England the police force was established in 1829 and the detective force in 1842. Victoria did not officially establish a police force until September 1853. Although it takes a long time to solve the crime and there is an element of chance involved, the clue that mounted trooper 'Mr. Mark' preserves proves vital in 'The Dead Man in the Scrub.' In 'Traces of Crime' the detective goes undercover and uses ratiocinative methods as well as a quasi-forensic approach — all elements of crime fiction more usually associated with the Sherlock Holmes stories that Arthur Conan Doyle only began writing almost thirty years later.

In 'Killed in the Shaft' the crime is solved within the mining community; rather than detective ingenuity the emphasis of the story is on Fortune's recollections of that time and place. She appreciated the chance a man had to be his own master: 'We worked hard, it is true, but we worked each for himself, and at the beck of no master; and what a difference does that simple fact make in the strength of the most willing muscles in the world.' She loved experiencing a sense of freedom that had nothing to do with money: 'All the gold that we ever drew from the earth's hiding places would never buy anything like the happiness of those old days.'

'Our Last Crushing' gives readers a detailed description of the extraction of gold from quartz crushing, as well as additional insight into some of the contrasting characters of the diggings: August the gentlemanly, quiet, hard-working and handsome Swede, in contrast to Jack, the raw-boned, vulgar Scotsman, who has filthy habits and is 'one of the biggest lushingtons to boot.' The crime is a different one in each of these stories and each crime is solved in a different way.

Contemporary readers may not have known that W.W. was a woman, but we can now enjoy the little clues to her gender and side jokes about her, as it were, authorial cross-dressing. Writing as her alter ego detective Mark Sinclair, she plays up the cross-dressing nature of the writing process.

> First I folded my margin down, and then I selected a pen, and dipping it in the ink, wrote manfully, 'The Detective's Album, by W.W.,' and having done so much, I laid down the pen and lay back in my chair to admire the well-known heading.[8]

---

8 W.W., untitled story [aka 'Arch Leslie's First Yarn'] in the *Detective's Album* serial, *Australian Journal*, June 1878.

AN INTRODUCTION TO THE STORIES

'The Stolen Deed' is written with the same tongue-in-cheek attitude. Although the solving of this crime is a serious business, the story includes elements of farce. Detective Sinclair becomes a figure of fun to a landlady when he borrows her Sunday finery to disguise himself as a woman when meeting with an extortionist, who turns out also to be a man dressed as 'a would-be woman.' Fortune takes the joke further by setting their meeting in Fitzroy Gardens, which was well-known at the time as what we would now call a gay beat.[9]

While cross-dressing from male to female was not exactly an everyday theme in contemporary fiction, Fortune also writes about the somewhat less unusual practice of female-to-male cross-dressing. 'Eaglehawk the Bushranger of the Pyrenees,' set in the Victorian Alps, has particularly homoerotic overtones as the ostensibly male bushranger kisses the body of the male policeman. The story itself may have been fictional, but the inspiration of the female bushranger dressed as a man was taken from reality. There have been a few female bushrangers in Australian history, such as the infamous Mary Ann Bugg, who partnered Captain Thunderbolt dressed as a man and riding her horse astride.

Fortune's stories also frequently highlight themes that were widely debated at the time. In 'Down By The Yarra'—a story that she tells the reader is inspired by a real case (research in contemporaneous broadsheets suggests that it was, and that it was never solved)—she depicts the rivalry between 'town' and 'country,' a dispute that twenty years later played out publicly in the popular literary magazine the *Bulletin*, which staged a battle in verse between the poets 'Banjo' Patterson and Henry Lawson over the merits or otherwise of life in the bush. In 'Down by the Yarra' the argument is between city and country policemen, and the city police take over the narration from Mark Sinclair. In describing the crime, the narrator also comments on various social issues. Fortune's description of police rounding up drunken homeless people on the banks of the Yarra suggests this was something she had witnessed (or was she perhaps sometimes one of them?), saying they were 'easy prey' and needed to be read a 'lesson in decency.' She leaves no doubt as to her opinion of the practice. The police narrator also describes the morgue as a disgrace, taking up an issue that was then widely debated in the press. There is also mention of the number of women pulled out of the Yarra who had committed suicide—another sad indictment of the state of Melbourne society at the time.

---

9 Fortune also includes a quip here about a hungry Sinclair needing to 'refresh the inner man.'

AN INTRODUCTION TO THE STORIES

The most notable social issue to which Fortune draws attention in her stories is a very personal one, however. Her son George was in trouble with the police from a young age, and it is not a stretch to imagine that he was also a street urchin or *gamin*, to use her word. These neglected and troubled boys are depicted in her stories as worthy but misunderstood. They are shown being helpful to the police because they have so much inside knowledge: 'I'll back a Melbourne street boy against all the detectives in town to run a regular fox to earth.' She writes a happy ending for the street kid Jemmy Dace in 'The Stolen Deed' as a kind of wish fulfilment for her own son (her description of him is based on that of George Fortune).

A less serious rewriting of George can be found in 'Constable Dyason's Defeat' in which George Lathorp (whose mother is a widow) and his friend Sam set out to make a fool of the vain Constable Dyason. By this time the real George was in jail for his part in a notorious bank robbery in Melbourne, and this farcical story reads like a soft form of revenge (with some more cross-dressing to top it off). It may even have been based on a true incident that involved Edward Huxley, a Melbourne larrikin (whom George probably knew) setting a trip wire for the police. Just as she valorised the *gamins* of Melbourne, Fortune also valorises the larrikins. She tells the reader: 'I am, and always was, very partial to boys, and inclined to take their part, even when I must acknowledge they scarcely deserve it.'

There are two other stories in this collection in which Fortune imagines a better future for her son. 'The Prison Brand' revolves around the difficulties ex-convicts experience trying to stay out of trouble after their release from prison. Not only do the police actively seek to rearrest them, but other ex-prisoners try to draw them back into crime. Fortune wrote a number of stories advocating a move out of the city to the country as their only chance to escape recidivism. We know that George tried moving out of Melbourne, but unfortunately it didn't save him; he was rearrested in the country for crimes he committed there. 'The Amateur Detective' was written only a few months before George died in gaol in Tasmania. By this time Fortune knew he was ill and would never leave prison alive, and here his mother imagines a different future for him—the burglar in the story helps solve the crime and uses the reward to relocate to South Africa.

'The Amateur Detective' also brings together some of Fortune's other recurring preoccupations: her absolute disdain for snobbery, the aristocracy and the self-proclaimed 'upper ten' of Melbourne society. She would only admire someone's class if they were educated and had good principles, like Charles Crawford in 'Killed in the Shaft.' She

AN INTRODUCTION TO THE STORIES

is at pains to point out that: 'in the early days at least—almost every member of the mounted police force was well born and educated.'

Australian historian Margaret Anderson has accused Fortune of being unrelenting and judgmental [about women] in a superior middle-class kind of way,[10] and there are certainly a significant number of her stories in which this is the case. Nell Parsons in 'Lost in Town' is a prime example. She is depicted as driven by greed and with no redeeming features. However, Fortune was equally unrelenting in her portrayal of men and often depicted women as undeserving victims of male violence. Moreover, some of her most memorable characters are admirable women, such as James Parsons's widow in 'The Midnight Watch.' She is loyal and determined to track down her husband's killer and acts as an amateur detective helping Sinclair to solve the crime. (It is in this story that Fortune also introduces a theory that would later become a cliché of crime fiction, namely that a murderer often returns to the scene of the crime: 'drawn by the strange fatality that makes guilt hover round the very spot it ought to avoid.')

In 'The Hart Murder' Sinclair misreads the squatter's daughter, Mary Crawford, as merely indolent and self-centred. She proves him wrong and joins the ranks of admirable women, after passing to Sinclair a note containing information that solves the crime. To his credit he acknowledges her help and rewards her with a handsome pair of gold bracelets fashioned in the shape of handcuffs and with an inscription beginning: 'To the fair detective.' Fortune thus gives us one of the earliest female detectives.

The main character in 'Bridget's Locket' also takes on the unusual role of female detective, setting out to solve the mystery of her friend's disappearance despite being discouraged from doing so. She leads the investigation from the beginning to the end, demonstrating loyalty, determination and kindness in carrying out her quest.

In 'The Convict's Revenge' Sinclair's disdain and lack of concern for the snobbish squatter's daughter Ann Rath leads to her abduction and gang rape. The story highlights the way society and the justice system failed women, often treating them like children requiring supervision and protection, leaving them without the skills to protect themselves. Sinclair's shame at his behaviour and failure is a moral lesson. Fortune,

---

10 Margaret Anderson, 'Mrs Charles Clacy, Lola Montez and Poll the Grogseller: Glimpses of Women on the Early Victorian Goldfields,' in Iain McCalman, Alexander Cook, and Andrew Reeves (eds.), *Gold: Forgotten Histories and Lost Objects of Australia* (Cambridge University Press, 2001), 225-249. It is unclear whether Anderson had read a wide range of Fortune's stories when she wrote this article; many of the stories had still to be rediscovered and most could only be found on microfilm.

AN INTRODUCTION TO THE STORIES

as a lone woman, knew how important it was to rely on herself for protection and in this case her use of a pseudonym allowed her to expose the issue. Without employing a male voice she would not have been able to write this story.

The last story to mention is different again and further illustrates Fortune's considerable range. The investigation into the seemingly supernatural 'The Phantom Hearse' becomes entangled with the common colonial pastime of illegally distilling spirits (a practice about which Fortune quite possible had intimate knowledge).

Her detective character speaks for Mary Fortune in 'The Midnight Watch' when he tells us

> I like to be puzzled; and the detective instinct has grown so strong with habit, that to perceive there is a secret is to give me an insatiable craving to find it out.

He could well be speaking for the editors of this anthology, who have been puzzling over Fortune and her extraordinary stories for many years. We hope you enjoy exploring the puzzles in this collection.

MEGAN BROWN

THE DEAD WITNESS

I can scarcely fancy anything more enjoyable to a mind at ease with itself than a spring ride through the Australian bush, if one is disposed to think he can do without any disturbing influence whatever from the outer world, for to a man accustomed to the sights and sounds of nature around him there is nothing distracting in the warble of the magpie or tinkle of the 'bell bird.' The little lizards that sit here and there upon logs and stumps, and look at the passer by with their heads on one side, and such a funny air of knowing stupidity in their small eyes, are such everyday affairs to an old colonist that they scarcely attract any notice from him, and even should a monstrous iguana dart across his path and trail his four feet length up a neighbouring tree, it is not a matter of much curiosity to him; and a good horseman, with an easy going nag under him, and plenty of time to journey at leisure through the park-like bush of Australia, has, to my notion, as good an opportunity of enjoying the Italians' *dolce far niente* as any fellow can have who does not regularly lie down to it.

Something like all this was coming home to me as I slowly rode through the forest of stringy bark, box, peppermint, and other trees that creep close up to the bold ranges which divide as it were into two equal portions the district of Kooama. I had passed fifteen miles of bush and plain without seeing a face or a roof, and now, having but a mile or two before making the station to which I was bound, I loosened the reins and let my horse take his own time. While, however, I thoroughly enjoyed the calm tranquillity of nature so unbroken around me, and felt the soothing influence more or less inseparable from such scenes, I cannot exactly say that my mind was enjoying the same 'sweetness of doing nothing' as my body. My brain was busily at work, full of a professional case, on the investigation of which I was proceeding; still, thoughts of this kind cannot be said to trouble the mind, being as enjoyable to us, I dare say, as the pursuit of game to the hunter, or the search for gold to the miner.

The facts of the case were shortly these: A young photographic enthusiast, in search of colonial scenery upon which to employ his art, had taken a room in a public house at the township of Kooama, in which he had arranged his photographic apparatus, and where he had perfected the views taken in trips to all the places within twenty or thirty miles that were likely to repay the trouble. The young

THE DEAD WITNESS

fellow, who was a gentlemanly and exceedingly handsome youth of barely twenty years of age, became a general favourite at Kooama, his kindness to the children, especially in that out of the way township, endearing him to all the parents.

Well, one day this young artist, whose name was Edward Willis, left Kooama, and returned no more. For a day or two the landlord of the house where he had put up thought but little of his absence, as he had upon more than one occasion before spent the night away on his excursions; but day after day passed, and they began to think it singular. He had himself expressed an intention of visiting some of the ranges to which I have alluded in search of some bolder 'bits' of scenery than he had yet acquired; but otherwise they had not the slightest clue to guide them in any attempted search for the missing youth. His decision to leave Kooama, if he had made one, must have been sudden, as nothing was removed from his room. Camera, chemicals, plates, and all the paraphernalia of a photographer's handicraft, were still scattered about just as he had left them.

A week passed away—a fortnight—consumed in guesses and wonders, and then came a letter from his mother in Adelaide to the landlord, inquiring the son's whereabouts, as they were getting uneasy at not hearing from so regular a correspondent. Then it was considered time to place the thing in the hands of the police, and I was sent for.

As I was proceeding through the bush then, at the leisurely pace I have described, I heard the loud crack of a stock whip ring out like the sharp report of a rifle between me and the ranges to my left, and shortly after I heard the sound of rapidly advancing horse's hoof strokes, which was echoed and re-echoed from the rocks at either side of the horseman's route. The sound came nearer and nearer, and at last a young man, mounted on a half thoroughbred, and attired like a stock driver or overseer on a station, galloped into the road which I was following a few yards behind me. Here he pulled up, and was soon by my side. The freemasonry of bush travellers in Australia would scarcely admit of one passing another without speaking, on a road where one might journey for twenty miles without meeting a soul; so there was nothing singular in my addressing the new-comer with all the freedom of an old chum.

'Aren't you afraid of breaking your neck, mate,' I inquired, 'coming down those ranges at such a pace?'

'Not a bit of it,' he replied; 'but at any rate I'm in a devil of a hurry, so had to risk it.'

'Bound for Kooama, I suppose?'

'Yes, I'm for the police station, and if I don't look sharp, it'll be pitch dark before I get back, so I must go on; good bye! I'll meet you again, I dare say.'

'Stay! 'I shouted, as the young fellow made a start; 'I might save you a journey, as I'm a policeman myself, and am just on my way to Kooama. Is there anything wrong your way?'

The young horseman looked at me rather suspiciously, as, of course, I was in plain clothes. I dare say he did not half believe me.

'Well,' he said, 'it's nothing very particular, and if you *are* going to the police station, policeman or no policeman, you can tell all I have to say as well as I can, if you will be so kind, and I shall get home before sundown yet.'

I assured him that I was really connected with the force when he told me his errand to the camp.

'There's been the deuce of a talk at Kooama about a young picture-man who's been missing for a couple of weeks, and some think he's come to no good end. Now, I know myself that he has been on our station since he came to Kooama, for I saw him taking views over the range there, but I thought nothing of that, as it was when first he settled at Dyter's, and he has been photographing miles away since then. This afternoon, however, about ten miles from the home station, the cattle (we're mustering just now) kicked up such a devil of a row that I couldn't make it out until I concluded they had come across the scent of blood somehow. Sure enough when I came up to the mob they were bellowing and roaring like mad ones round a spot on the grass that must have been regularly soaked in blood, as it is as red and fresh-looking as possible. What made it more suspicious to me was, that the place had been carefully covered up with branches, and no one would ever have noticed it, only the cattle had pawed and scraped the dead bushes quite off it. Heaven knows what might have caused it, or whether it was worth mentioning; but it's not far from where I saw the poor young chap. I thought I would run down to the camp and tell Cassel about it.'

'Have you mentioned it to any one else?' I inquired.

'No,' he replied; 'I haven't seen a soul since.'

'Well, don't say a word, like a good fellow: it's very strange that I should have met you; I'm Brooke, the detective, and I'm on my way to Kooama about this very business. Will you meet me at sunrise tomorrow morning, and take me to the place?'

The young man readily promised, and I found that he was the son of a squatter whose station (called Minarra) was situated at the other side of the Rocky Ranges to which I have so frequently alluded, and

THE DEAD WITNESS

then we parted, and spurring my horse to a more rapid pace I soon reached the police camp at Kooama, and got my horse stalled and my supper, as well as all the information I could from Constable Cassel before I turned in, which I did at an early hour.

There are a good many fellows—no matter in what anxiety of mind they may be—who are able to forego it all when their usual bed-time reminds them of sleep, and they seem to shake off their troubles with their shoes, and draw up the blankets as an effectual barrier between them and the world generally; it is not so with me, I usually carry my perplexities to bed with me, and roll and tumble, and tumble and roll, under their influence, unless some happy idea of having hit the right nail on the head in my planning soothes me into resignation to my fatigue. So it was on the night in question; nevertheless, the sun was only beginning to shake himself out of the horizon when I met the young squatter at the appointed place, and together we proceeded to the indicated spot on Minarra station.

Over the range we went, and three or four miles through the primeval forest beyond, and my companion, well acquainted with the land marks on his 'run,' stopped before what appeared to be a few decaying branches fallen from a near gum tree. 'This is it,' he said, dismounting and removing the dead boughs, 'I covered it up again yesterday.'

Well, there was very little to see, a patch of blood-stained grass—the colour was very evident still—and nothing more. I looked round to see if perchance there was a view to make it worth an artist's while to visit this spot, and soon perceived that from the very place where we stood a photographer might catch a 'bit' of truly beautiful and entirely colonial scenery. At a distance of perhaps two miles the range over which we had come fell abruptly down into the plain in a succession of sheer faces of rock, while at the foot of what might be almost termed the precipice that terminated the whole, a deep gorge or gully ran almost directly at right angles with it, up which the eye pierced through a vista of richly foliaged and fantastically gnarled trees and huge boulders of grey granite, altogether forming a scene that could scarcely fail to attract the eye of an artist.

The sun was up above the trees now, and, closely scanning the ground at my feet, I perceived at a few yards distance a something that caught his brightness and reflected it, and stooping I picked it up; it was a small, a *very* small, piece of glass, and just such glass, too, as might have been used in a camera. But near the piece of glass, which was not far from the blood spot on the grass, I found, too, what I had been searching for, which was the triangular marks of the

THE DEAD WITNESS

camera stand, which I thought it barely possible might be visible. The holes were indented deeper into the grass than the mere weight of the instrument would account for, especially two of them, the third was not so visible. We covered all up again as carefully yet as carelessly as possible, and after having again cautioned the young squatter to be silent, I parted with him for the present, and made the best of my way to Kooama.

An hour or so later, I was very busy in the deserted room of the young artist, of which I had taken possession, and into which to avoid disturbance I had locked myself. I was quite at home among the poor young fellow's chemicals, &c., as I happen to be a bit of an amateur photographer myself, and I have found my knowledge in that way of service to me on one or two occasions in connection with my professional duties already. The table and mantelpiece were littered with unfinished plates; they were leaning against the wall, and against every conceivable thing that would form a support for them. Naturally supposing that those last taken would be most *come-at-able*, I confined my search at first to the outside pictures, and before very long I fancied I was repaid for my trouble.

My idea, it will readily be guessed, in searching the plates at all, was the one of finding a face or a view that might possibly be a clue in my hunt for the missing youth, or for the murderer, if murder had been done. Nothing would be more likely than that some chance encounter in his excursions might have resulted in a portrait, the original of which, if discovered, might be able to give some useful information.

Well, I found more than I hoped for. I lighted on a plate, only parts of which had 'come out' under the after process, and which was rubbed in several places, and had evidently been thrown aside as worthless. There were two or three duplicate copies of the same view, and among the perfected and most clear pictures which the artist had laid away more carefully by themselves, was one apparently valued, as in case of danger of damage it was 'cased' properly. It was a truly beautiful bit of entirely Australian bush scenery; a steep, rocky bank for a background; at its foot, a still, deep waterhole reflecting every leaf of the twisted old white-stemmed gum trees that hung over it and dipped their heavy branches in its dark waters, and to the left a reach of bush level, clustered with undergrowth on the slightly undulating ground, and shaded here and there with the tufty foliage of the stringy-bark. It was an excellent picture, every leaf had come out perfectly, and the shadows were as dark and cool as shadows could be, while the tone was all that could be wished; nevertheless on

THE DEAD WITNESS

comparing this with the unfinished and imperfect one on which the artist's art had failed, my eye rested on a something in the latter which made it a hundred times more valuable to me.

In the shade of a heavy bush at the opposite side of this still, deep waterhole, there was the faint outline of a crouching human figure, an outline so faint and so shrouded in the obscurity of the faulty plate, that very likely no eye but that of a detective would have observed it, and it is more than probable that the poor lad whose art had fixed it in its place was quite unaware of its being there; but by the aid of a powerful microscope I made it out distinctly. We all know with what perfectness to every line of its object the camera fixes its light copies, even in the greatest failures as to perfect shading and tone, and there I had this crouching and malignant-looking face peering from behind a shadowy bush, as recognisable as if he had been photographed in a Collins-street or George-street studio. Steadily I set to work reproducing this hiding figure, magnifying and photographing by aid of the good camera the young artist had left behind, and I succeeded at length in completing a likeness quite clear enough for my purpose; so after taking possession of the plate holding the view of the bush waterhole, I put it and my likeness into my pocket, and locking up the room, once more sought the camp.

The likeness of the missing youth himself was given to me by the landlady of the public house: he had given it to her a few days before he took his last walk in search of subjects for his art. Poor fellow! he was very handsome and very youthful-looking: a white, sickly, noble face, with large black eyes, and a profusion of curly black hair forming a frame to a high broad forehead. I felt sick at heart as I looked at it and thought of his empty home and the red pool of blood on Minarra station.

It was late in the day when I got thus far in my search, and I was rather glad that my young squatter acquaintance did not turn up at Kooama that evening, as he had intimated an intention of doing, for I was likely to require his assistance, and did not care to trust his young gossiping propensities with my secrets any longer than was absolutely necessary.

Early on the following morning, however, he rode up to the camp, and I so arranged that we should be left alone together. 'I don't know your name, my young friend,' I was commencing, when he interrupted me.

'My name is Derrick—Thomas Derrick.'

'Well, Mr. Derrick, I am sure I need not tell you upon what a serious job I am engaged, nor that it is your interest, as well as that of the

THE DEAD WITNESS

public at large, that no crime should go unpunished; all this you know as well as I do; but what you do not know as well as I do, my dear fellow, is how very little will interfere with a search such as mine, and give a criminal a chance of escaping with impunity. All this I tell you because I am going to ask your assistance, and to beg that while you are affording it to me you will keep as secret as the grave anything that may pass between us until I accomplish my object, or fail in the endeavour to do so.'

The young man promised faithful secrecy, and then I laid the picture of the bush waterhole before him.

'Is there any such place as that on your run?'

'To be sure there is; it's in Minarra Creek, about half a mile from where we found the flock.'

'I thought it likely, and now I am almost sure you will be able to tell me who that is,' and I handed him my copy of the hiding figure. He looked very much astonished, but replied immediately—

'It's Dick the Devil!'

'And who is Dick the Devil?'

'A crusty, cantankerous old wretch; one of our shepherds. Do you think *he's* in it!'

'Oh, of course, we are all abroad as to that yet; where does this Dick live, and what does he do?'

'He minds a flock, and lives at an out hut ten miles from the home station.'

'Alone? or has he a hutkeeper?'

'Well, he's by himself this long time; he had two or three hutkeepers, but at last we were obliged to give it up—no one would live with him.'

'Could you manage to get me in there as hutkeeper without exciting his suspicion.'

'You! of course I could, he's always growling about not having one; but you could never stand it.'

'No fear of me, it won't be for long at any rate.'

Fancy me that same afternoon metamorphosed into a seedy tired-looking coon,[1] accompanying the young squatter to Dick's hut, where he was going, or appeared to be obliged to go at any rate, with rations in a spring cart. Dick was within sight, letting his flock feed quietly foldwards, and his young employer led me to him.

'Now, you old growler, I hope you're satisfied! here's a hutkeeper for you, and I hope you'll keep your ugly temper quiet for one week at any rate.'

I should have recognised my man anywhere, sure enough; the

villainous scowling face of the hider in the photograph was before me, and so determined a looking scoundrel I had not seen for a long time, familiar as I was with criminals. He was an elderly man—about fifty, perhaps—low sized, and strongly built; his years told on him in a slight stoop and grizzled, coarse hair that but added to his rascally appearance, and his character was but too plainly traced in his low, repulsive forehead and heavy, dark beetling brows. I could have almost sworn he was an old hand the moment I set eyes on him.

'Thank ye for nothing, Tom,' was his impudently given reply; 'you didn't send to town for a hutkeeper for me, I'll swear.'

'Well, you're about right; I met him as I was coming over with your rations, and as the poor fellow looked tired and hard up, I thought I'd give you another trial.'

'You be d——d,' was Dick the Devil's thanks, as the young fellow turned away with a 'well, so long, mate!' to me.

'Well,' said my new mate, turning to me, 'if you'll give me a hand to round up the flock, I'll get 'em all the sooner in, and then we can have a good yarn. I'm d——d if I'm not glad to see a fellow's face again; curse such a life as this, I say!'

''Tis a slow one; I'm blessed if it ain't,' I replied, doing as he wished; 'have you no dog?'

'No, I haven't,' he snapped out at me like a pistol shot, with such a look, half of terror and half of suspicion, that I was convinced about his dog there was something more to be learned.

After the billy was slung and the tea boiled, and the mutton and damper disposed of, Dick and I sat down in the still calm twilight outside the bush hut, and while puffing out volumes of tobacco smoke from dirty, black pipes managed to mutually interest ourselves, I dare say.

'Things are looking d—— bad in the country now, mate,' rapped out Dick.

'You may say it,' I replied; 'I've tramped over many a hundred miles without the chance of a job.'

'Where did you come from last?'

'Oh! I came from everywhere between this and Beechworth! I stopped at Kooama last night; there's a devil of a talk there about some murder.'

'Murder!' said Dick, with a sort of a gasp, and a short quick look at me; 'what murder?'

'Some poor devil of a painter or a picter-man, or something of that sort.'

'Oh, d—— them! they don't *know* he's murdered?'

THE DEAD WITNESS

'I see you've heard about it then. Yes, I believe you're right. I think he's only missing, and they *guess* he's been made away with.'

'Let them guess and be d——d to them!' said the hardened wretch, and I thought fit to drop the subject.

'Oh, my lad!' thought I to myself, 'if you only guessed who is sitting beside you, and what his object is here, wouldn't there be another pool of red blood under some tree in the Australian forest, eh?' and then I looked at my neighbour's muscular frame and determined criminal countenance, wondering in a battle for life and death between us should I be able to come off victor. Certainly, I could at any moment lay my hand upon my trusty revolver, and dexterity and self-possession might accomplish much with the handcuffs; but let a fellow be ever so little of a coward, he must feel a *little* at being so entirely isolated and so self-dependent as I was at this moment. Far out before us lay miles of almost level grass, dotted with tall-stemmed trees and patches of undergrowth. There wasn't a living soul within miles and not a sound save as night fell the scream of the distant curlew, that came, I guessed, from the vicinity of the black waterhole in the Minarra Creek, and I could not help picturing to myself the stillness of that night-gloomed water, its heavy, overhanging foliage, and the white mangled face that *perhaps* lay below it. Altogether I was not sorry that Dick showed no disposition to prolong the conversation, but soon turned in, and I followed his example, not, however, without placing my revolver under my hand, and when I *did* sleep it was, as the saying is, with one eye open.

According to a concerted arrangement between me and my young assistant, the very earliest morning brought him to the hut at full gallop. His greeting to Dick was rather abrupt.

'What the devil's the reason you're running your flock up to the rock springs every day, Dick? Connel complains you don't leave him half enough for his sheep, and here's a waterhole close under your nose.'

'Well, the cursed flock always head up that way; they're used to it; and it's d——d hard work to turn a thirsty mob when you've got no dog! in fact, it's impossible.'

'What the deuce have you *done* with your dog? you had a first-rater.'

'Done with him?' replied Dick, vindictively; 'cut his throat! He was always giving me twice the work with his playin' up!'

'Well, you'll have to get another somewhere; at any rate take the flock to Minarra waterhole in future.'

'I can't myself,' was the response.

31

THE DEAD WITNESS

'Your mate will lend you a hand for a day or two, as the water is not far away, and the flock will soon get used to it.'

I had been watching Dick as closely as I could, without being noticed by him, during this colloquy, and could easily see that he was much dissatisfied with this arrangement, but he could make no excuse, as the want of water was beginning to be complained of on all the surrounding runs, and so we headed the flock in the direction of Minarra waterhole.

There was no opportunity for conversation on the way, as Dick and I were far apart, and the sheep were feeding quietly all the way; but when we neared the water, and the flock—which, by the way, showed no anxiety whatever to go in any other direction—had mob by mob satisfied their thirst, and were scattering out over the near pasture, I approached the waterhole, and, sitting down in almost the very spot where poor young Willis must have placed his camera to take the view I had in my pocket, I took out my pipe and commenced cutting tobacco for the purpose of filling it. All the time the sheep were drinking I could see that Dick was very uneasy. He kept away entirely, but when he saw me taking it so coolly he drew up slowly.

'D—— queer place to sit down, that,' he said; 'you'll be ate up with mosquitoes.'

'No fear,' I answered; 'I'm thinking the mosquitoes have something more to their liking to eat down here.'

'Down where?'

'Oh! about the water! What a devil of a lot of ugly things must be down at the bottom there, Dick! it's very deep.'

I couldn't see the wretch, but I *fancied* his face was growing pale, and although I daren't look at him, neither durst I trust myself with my back to him, so, affecting an air of nonchalance I was far from feeling, I got up and faced him while I affected to be searching in my pocket for matches, my hand in reality clutching the revolver.

'I wonder if that picter-man ever *took* this place?' I added, 'it would look first-rate.'

Dick's face flushed up with fury, he could stand the strain no longer.

'D—— the picter man!' he roared, 'what the —— are you always talkin' about him for?'

I looked at him with affected surprise,—'You get in a blessed pelter over it, mate! Anyone but me would be suspicious that you'd done it yourself!'

'And if I did —— to you?' he said, with a face fearful in its hardened ferocity. 'And if I *did*, you couldn't prove it—you've no witnesses!'

While he was saying this, half a dozen bubbles rose to the surface of the water directly in front of us, followed by more and more; and I do not know to this day what unaccountable influence it was that as Dick ceased speaking urged me to seize him by the wrist, and, while pointing to the bubbles before him with the other hand, to whisper in reply,—'Haven't I?—Look!' for, of course, I had no more expectation of the awful scene that followed than has my reader at this moment.

A fearful, dripping *thing* rose to the surface—a white, ghastly face followed—and then, up—up—waist high out of the water, rose the corpse of the murdered artist!

It remained for a second or two standing, as it were, before us, with glaring wide-open eye-balls turned toward the bank on which we stood, and then, with a horrible *plump*, the body fell backward, the feet rose to the top, and there the terrible thing lay face upward,— staring up, one might fancy to the heavens, calling for justice on the murderer!

As I saw this awful sight, my grasp on Dick's wrist relaxed, although unconsciously I still pointed toward the white dripping terror; until it settled, as I have attempted to describe, and then Dick the Devil, with a wild cry that I shall never forget, threw both his hands up to his head and fell heavily to the ground.

To tell you how I felt in these few moments is impossible. I was horror-struck. In all my experience of fearful and impressive sights, I never felt so completely stunned and awed. But it did not last long with me; for, of course, reason soon came to assure me that it required no supernatural agency to cause a corpse to rise from the bottom to the top of a waterhole, although the accounting for the way in which it had thus arisen would not be so simple.

With but a glance at the prostrate form of the insensible wretch beside me, I fired off one barrel of my revolver as a signal to young Derrick, who had promised to hang about; and I had soon the satisfaction of hearing in reply the echoed report of that young man's well given stock-whip, and it was not long before he came galloping down to the side of the hole.

It may be supposed that this young fellow felt even more horrified than even I, more accustomed to deaths and murders, had done, and after I had shortly explained to him how matters stood, I do not think we had two opinions about the guilt of the still insensible old miserable. Be that as it may, I was heartless and unfeeling enough to handcuff him, even while he was unconscious, not choosing to risk an attempt at escape. And then we sprinkled water over him, and used all the means within our power for the purpose of restoring him.

THE DEAD WITNESS

At length he sat up, but his first glance falling again on the floating corpse, he struggled to his feet, crying—

'Oh, my God! Take me out of this! Let me out of this!'

And, one on each side of him—he partly leading—we followed him three or four hundred yards, where, under the shade of a tree, he sat down weak as a child.

'I can't go any farther,' he said,—'You'll have to take me to the camp in a cart.'

'Where's all your bounce now, mate? 'I could not help inquiring, as I handed him a drop of grog out of a flask I carried.

He put it tremblingly to his lips and drained it, and then, with a heavily drawn breath, replied—'It's in h——!'

This was awful, but he did not give us time to think, for he immediately, and without any encouragement, added, 'I'm goin' to tell you all about that lot while I'm able, for I feel all rotten like!'—and then he added again—'like *him*, down below.'

We did not speak, either of us, and he went on—'One day, that chap came pictering up yonder, and my dog playin' up as usual, runnin' the sheep wrong, he got me in a pelter, and I outs with my knife and cut his b—— throat! The young picter chap sees me, and runs to try and save the dog; but he was too late, and he ups and told me I was a villain, and a cruel wretch, and all sorts, and I told him I'd cut his too if he gave me any more of his jaw, and when he went away I swore I'd be revenged on the cheeky pup. I watched him that day down at the Minarra waterhole, but couldn't get a good chance, and then he went home to Kooama. Well, about a week after, he was pictering down yonder.'

Here he pointed in the direction of the blood marks, and I nodded, saying, 'I know.'

'You know!' he said, turning to me with something of his old ferocity; 'how the d—— do you know anything about it?'

'I know all about it,' I said in reply; 'I will finish your story for you when I go wrong, you can set me right.'

He looked at me stupidly—wonderingly. 'Who are you?' he asked.

'I am Brooke, the detective.'

'Oh!'—Dick the Devil drew a hard breath.

'Well, he was taking views with his camera near that tree there, where you covered the blood up with the bushes—you know, and you stole behind him—'

'Yes,' interrupted Dick; 'When his head was under that black rag.'

'And you struck him with something that stunned him.'

'It was a waddy,'[2] said Dick.

34

'And the blow struck the camera also, capsized it, and broke it to shivers.'

'Jest so!' added the wretch, a hideous glee lighting up his ferocious countenance; 'and then I took out my clasp knife and nagged his pipe, jest as I did the dog's, and I axed him how he liked it, but he couldn't tell me!'

'Oh, you *awful* devil!' cried young Derrick, whose face I had remarked becoming paler and paler until I gave him a nobbler[3] too, or I positively believe the poor fellow would have fainted.

'And then I carried him all the way to the hole on my back, and I got a rope and I rolled it round him in good knots, and then I tied the rope to a good sized boulder, and I rolled him and the boulder to the bottom together! But tell me now,' he added, sinking his voice to a whisper, 'how did he get up again? How *ever* did he get up again?'

Of course, this we can only surmise, the rope might have got damaged in the roll of rock and body down the bank, and remaining attached to the feet, had given below, and given until it allowed the unfastened part of the corpse to reach the surface, and then slackened more from the rock below until the feet also were able to find the surface. This is the most likely solution of the difficulty, for the rope, when the corpse was removed, was still found attached to both the body and the rock.

Dick the Devil was punished for his crime, but where and when, it is unnecessary for me to state.

First published as 'Memoirs of an Australian Police Officer, No. V: The Dead Witness; or, The Bush Waterhole' in the *Australian Journal*, 20 January 1866, with no byline.

NOTES

1   *a seedy tired-looking coon*: the detective is attempting to present himself as a man who has been tramping through the bush looking for work, and Fortune is evidently employing "coon" here in its sense of "a rustic or undignified person" (Collins Dictionary), without any racist connotations.
2   *waddy*: an Aboriginal Australian pointed club made of hardwood used as a weapon or as a throwing stick in hunting. The word comes from the language of the Darug people of Port Jackson, Sydney.
3   *nobbler*: here, a drink of spirits from his flask.

DOWN BY THE YARRA

'Look here, mates' (it was Tom Corrigan told the story one night, when I was down 'reporting' at head-quarters)—'Look here, mates, you may talk and yarn until you are tired, about your bushrangers and your murderers up-country, but, *by dad*,[1] we can bate 'em in town for all that.'

'I b'lieve you,' interjected Conway, during the necessary removal of his pipe to see what interfered with its want of agreeability; I say agreeability for want of a more expressive word, and if you can find a more expressive term than *dis*agreeability for the humours of a pipe that will not draw—that is to say, a term more adapted to the understanding of a confirmed—I dare not say inveterate—smoker, well, 'I'll lave it to you,' that's all.

'I'm sick of your confounded detective yarns,' snapped he. 'We may drag our lives out here widout thank ye. An' for what? An' what bether is a detective in town than a crusher,[2] I'd like to know?'

'Who the mischief are you calling crushers?' almost shouted our old friend Sam Rinder.

'An' what the deuce have you to say about town detectives?' inquired Sullivan, hastily. 'Bedad, it's only too glad you'd be to get the chance yourself!'

'You're a lot of queer fellows, you town chaps,' said I, Mark Sinclair, with some idea of throwing oil on troubled waters, 'if you had the up-country work for one month, you'd be blessed glad to come back again, to walk up and down in a civilised neighbourhood on patrol, instead of riding half a dozen hours through the bush, on the look-out, when every tree may hide your grave.'

'Fine talking!' ejaculated No.—.

'Now, look here, mates,' again said Tom Corrigan, 'I'll lave it to vote; let us town chaps tell Sinclair one or two of *our* yarns, and lave it to himself to settle which bates which. Sure I know he's a jontleman.'

I beg you, dear reader, to believe that the sarcasm contained in those last unqueened* English words was not, by any means, lost upon me; but what was I 'among so many?' This was, however, *inside*; outside, it was 'Oh, I'm quite agreeable, Tom,—only I'd rather leave it to the vote.'

'Vote be it, then,' almost simultaneously exclaimed Conway,

---

* *Un*queened, in contradistinction to 'Queen's English.' [*footnote in the original—Eds.*]

DOWN BY THE YARRA

Corrigan, and half a dozen others, who were sitting around the table, smoking, and listening like sensible fellows as they were.

Well, it was put to the vote, and the lot fell upon Corrigan, who was to 'bate' any of the up-country detective stories by a town one; 'an' if he couldn't do it, there was three or four more would try a hand at it.'

I don't suppose the idea that it was one against a dozen or so ever suggested itself to my worthy mates. I don't think that it ever entered their heads for one moment that they were displaying a very laudable *esprit de corps*, and yet it was so undoubtedly; *only*, that while each felt an anxiety to suppress the superiority of 'up-country,' there was scarcely one of them but would have 'hanged, drawn, and quartered,' metaphorically speaking, his neighbour—if he had dared.

'Go on, Corrigan,' from all sides.

'Wait a bit'—with a removal of the pipe, and a careful examination of its contents—'Wait a bit, mates, and don't hurry a chap. I haven't quite made up my mind yet *what* story I'm to tell.'

'The swamp murder,'[3] was the cry from two or three mouths.

'*That* case wouldn't redound much to your credit,' I let out before my reason had time to assert itself.

What a storm I brought about my unfortunate ears, to be sure! Corrigan, Conway, No.—, and even 'dacent' and kindly Sullivan himself opened such a volley against me, that I began to seriously think of a pressing engagement I had with the superintendent himself.

'Oh bedad, it's a pity we hadn't Misther Sinclair in town that time! Poor fools! what good are the town police at all, at all?'

'Divil a sacret it would have been if his lordship had been in it. Ha ha!'

'I'll lay my head again a turnip that he'd a got another medal, boys!'

Now this was too bad altogether—flesh and blood could not stand it. Many of my readers will, I trust, recollect what an ass I made of myself about that so-called 'Medal Case,'[4] and if I live to be a hundred years old, I'll never forgive that same No.— for his too blessed good memory.

Nor shall I forget my friend Sullivan's kindly interference, or how he softened matters down, by flattering Corrigan's story-telling abilities, until the same Corrigan was the very first to insist upon the feelings of the 'visitor' being respected, and silence being kept 'in the camp' while he told his 'shtory.'

'There isn't a man of ye here knows anything about it, only Sullivan, so ye needn't gammon[5] ye do,' he began, 'for ye're nothing after all but a pack of new chums, an' this I'm goin' to tell ye of only happened two years ago, afther all.'

DOWN BY THE YARRA

'I'm four years in the force!' cried No.— viciously, bringing down his clenched fist on the table.

'Not in the *town* force, mate,' calmly observed Corrigan, who, as the hero of the hour, took some considerable authority upon himself. 'Maybe you forget that you spent three of them four from one counthry station to another, bedad, for all the world like 'possum, gainin' his livin' from one three to another.

'You be — ,' amiably responded my friend No.—. (I'll put the number in plain figures if ever he ventures to allude to the medal case again.)

'Look here, I'll put it to the vote again,' I interjected, 'if another man interrupts Corrigan, he's fined a bottle of brandy.'

'Done,' on all sides. So, with a preparatory 'hem!' our good Corrigan began—and, by way of parenthesis, I may observe that you quite possibly think it high time that he *did* begin.

'Well, as I said before, it is about two years ago, an' one day, about five o'clock in the evenin', I was on duty on Prince's Bridge. It was a terribly hot day, and I was heartily wishing to be relieved, when I saw a woman comin' slowly along from town way, an' stoppin' every now an' then to look over into the Yarra, as she might be watchin' the boats, or the like.

'Well, you see, I was so tired of drays and conveyances of all sorts, and people passin' by on business and pleasure, and everyone carin' as little for me as I did for them, that when that woman stopped near me an' looked from the Yarra into my face, I was kind of glad, you see— anything to pass the half hour or so I had to wait before I was relieved.

'"It's a fine afthernoon, so it is, ma'am," I said, "an' ye seem to take a great interest in the wather."

'If I live to the age of Methusalem, I'll never forget the look she gave me. "Have *you* any interest in the Yarra?" she asked me, drawing herself up against the parapet of the bridge, as if she was prepared to fight, and grasping her dress in her right hand as she spoke, as though she were crushing some enemy to death.'

Another parenthesis. My friend Corrigan was an educated man, and as capable as you or I of speaking English correctly; but only in moments of excitement, when old memories caught a firm hold of him, did he forget the vernacular in which, to please his less fortunate mates, he ordinarily indulged.

'I looked at her from head to foot as she asked me the seemingly silly question; but the strange wild look in her eyes almost, but not quite, prevented me noticing in what attire she was clad. I saw a dress of some black material, a dark, heavy cloak, that fell almost to her feet,

DOWN BY THE YARRA

and a white face, surmounted by something of crape in the shape of a
bonnet; and I saw that her hair was wavy and of a pretty glossy brown,
but uncared for and neglected, as if she had little thought of either life
or loveliness.'

'Oh, bother your grand phrases; get on with your story, if you have
one to tell.'

I am happy to say there was a general cry of 'shut up!' and Corrigan
was permitted, through his scowls, to continue his story.

'We weren't all born in Australia; nor, thank heaven, on the "other
side"[6]—ahem!—and it so happens, never mind, mates, I said, as if she
had little thought of life or loveliness, and I say it again, eh?'

There was not a dissentient—thanks to the recollection of the fine.

'"Have *you* any interest in the Yarra?"

'"Interest, ma'am! Certainly. There's the boats I like to see spinning
along, and the water running so glitteringly in the sunshine, and—"

'"And the broken, dead reeds you gather from it to decorate the
Morgue," she interrupted, with a curling lip.

'"To hear you talk, one would think we liked to gather up the
drowned people out of the river," said I.

'"And so you do," she said, sharply—"so you do, every one of
you; it's your most delightful pastime. What do you think one of your
precious mates said to me here on this very spot, last night, when I told
him I was homeless, and asked to be directed to a lodging? What do you
think he said, eh?"

'"Lord knows!" I answered.

'"Yes, the Lord *does* know, and, thanks be to heaven, such words
are recorded where a river of policeman's tears won't wash them out.
'Put yourself in *there*!' your precious mate said—'put yourself in there,
where it would be for the peace of decent folks if every one of your
likes was; an' more,' he added, 'if the liftin' of my finger was to save one
of ye from drownin', I wouldn't lift it.' Oh, you are a pretty lot, you
Melbourne police!"

'This wasn't very flattering, mates, was it? but I didn't mind it at all,
for I saw that the poor woman was in trouble of some sort or other, and
trouble is not apt to speak too politely.

'"I hope, at any rate, you won't take such bad advice," I said to her.
"No matter what trouble is over you, don't let it drive to suicide, which
is not only death to the body, but the loss of the soul."

'As I spoke, she was looking once more dreamily over the bridge
into the far below water; but when I stopped, she turned and replied,
emphatically,

'"Do not fear; you or yours shall never have the pleasure of drawing

DOWN BY THE YARRA

me from among the river reeds—a dripping and white death."

'Even as the words left her lips, a little ragged lad walked quickly from the other side of the bridge, and addressed the strange woman. What he said, I could not hear, for he spoke in a rapid whisper, but I heard her reply, in a tone which I thought betokened surprise,

'"Down by the Yarra, did you say? Why there? Why am I to go there?"

'"I don't know, ma'am. That's all I was to say."

'The stranger passed her ungloved left hand across her forehead when the boy left her, and in so doing, gave me an opportunity of observing that the plain gold ring encircled the usual finger, and that, instead of a plain keeper, she wore a peculiar and beautiful ring, with a heart formed of small diamonds on the back.

'"At any rate, she can't be very hard up while she wears that ring," I thought, watching her black-robed figure slowly and most gracefully moving to the other side of the bridge.

'She walked hesitatingly, I fancied, and even paused to look once more down over the bridge, before she commenced to descend the wooden stairs that lead down to the back of one of the boat-houses at Princes' Bridge. Just at this time I was relieved, and the last thing I saw as I passed, barrack-ward, were the black garments of the strange female as she flitted past the green wattles down by the Yarra.

'Perhaps the subject would not have obtained a second thought from me had it not been for an order issued on the following early morning. You know what a nest of iniquity is down by the Yarra in these days, and even two years ago the place was the nightly haunt of the vicious and vile. The order I allude to was to the effect that every man or woman found among the wattles, on the bank of the river, was to be arrested, that a lesson in decency might be read to them at the City Police Court.

'Well, I was one of a party told off on this particular duty, and the fog was but beginning to lift off the Yarra when we commenced our raid. The dew was lying heavy on the long grass at the back of the scrub, and at every step we brushed it off, each leaving a trail behind him as though in a light fall of snow.

'It was an easy task ours on that particular morning. Lying, helplessly intoxicated, with empty bottles around them, or just waking up, cold and trembling, with the debauchee's horrible thirst, and the misery of disease in their bones—it was the easiest matter in the world to lead the wretched beings to the watch-house. Men and women—dirty and degraded, ragged and bloated, some quietly, some profaning the morning air with the most horrible language—they were marched over Princes' Bridge in bands, and yet our task was not completed.

41

DOWN BY THE YARRA

'I walked along by the river while some of my mates beat up the scrub, or watched to prevent any escape by way of the swamp, when all at once the scene on the bridge, on the previous evening, was recalled to my mind by the sight of a portion of a black dress that I fancied I saw at a little distance from the river-side pathway.

'There was indeed a black-robed figure lying under a spreading bush—a figure lying upon its side, restfully, as if in peaceful sleep. The folds of the dress were carefully disposed around the form of the woman, who lay there, and that it was indeed the lady who had, on the previous evening, paused on the bridge, one glance convinced me.

'She lay upon her right side, with one hand so carefully placed beneath her cheek that even the small black crape bonnet I had noticed was not displaced half an inch. Her dress and mantle were glittering almost with the heavy dew, that lay like frost on the herbage around; and upon the dress, naturally stretched out, and lying with outstretched fingers, was a small, delicately formed left hand, as white as death could make it.

'Yes, it was death, mates. There was no breath passing between the blue lips that were half-parted, as though to let it escape. The heavy eyelids were blue and stiff, and as lifeless as the dark dress that clung around her form movelessly was the heart that I felt the evening before to be heavy with care. The stranger was dead.

'And how? The first thing I noticed after I had recognised death was that the left hand bore but one ring. The plain gold circlet still guarded the dead finger, but the very uncommon and handsome ring I had observed on the bridge was gone. A little closer examination, too, brought me a fresh discovery. Upon the dress, lying partly under one of its folds, was an empty phial, labelled "Laudanum," so close to her hand that it might have escaped from it at the commencement of that last terrible sleep.

'I was astonished, as well as grieved. Oh, you needn't laugh, Tom, as if a fellow had no feelings at all because he chops and murders the Queen's English to please the like of you. I was, as I said, astonished as well as sorry, because from the way in which she spoke of her determination not to give us what she called the satisfaction of pulling her out of the Yarra, I never dreamed she would go down by its side and commit suicide after all.

'However, our business was plain in the matter. We had to remove the quiet figure, in its black robes, to that disgrace to our authorities, the Morgue of Melbourne. Oh, you may make as many faces as you like at me, Mark Sinclair—and I'll defy you to make yourself uglier than nature made you—but I don't care if every man jack of the said authorities

DOWN BY THE YARRA

was listening to me saying it. The morgue of our city is a crying disgrace to every one of us, and I never help to carry an unfortunate corpse into it but I feel ashamed to think that human beings should be treated so like dogs. It is not much comfort for a fellow, either, to remember that the world treated them worse than dogs while they were alive, or to be certain that, as far as treatment received when they are carried into that wretched hole, they care for it no more than you and I do for what happened to our grandmothers.'

'Talkin' av grandmothers,' here interrupted a raw Irishman, just landed from the sweet town of Cork—'talkin' av grandmothers, I have a fine story I could tell ye, b'ys, about me grandmother be the father's side. She was from Kerry, an'—'

'Bad luck to you and your grandmother too,' interrupted my respected mate, the relator of the present sketch. 'Maybe, if she'd been to the fore, she might have larned ye manners. Would you be kind enough to let a chap finish wan story before ye shtart an another?'

And my friend Corrigan relapsed into what his satirical mates were wont to term his grand language.

'Now, I suppose Mr. Mark Sinclair won't acknowledge that to be a case at all equal to any of his fine ones; but wait a bit. The inquest, or rather the *post mortem*, proved that the woman had not taken a drop of laudanum, but that she had been chloroformed to death. Yes, it was rather a strange thing, was it not? But the doctors were unanimous that the woman had been kept under the influence of chloroform until death supervened.

'Here was work for the town detectives. Sullivan, there, wore himself to a shadow plotting and scheming to get some sort of idea how to set to work; but I had the best chance, and I kept it, eh, Sullivan? There was the ring, which none of them saw but me, and there was that little boy that gave her the message on Princes' Bridge. I should know him among a thousand, and my first look-out was for him. If I could find out who sent that message, I should not be far from the secret, I fancied.

'Well, I spent all my own time nearly in hunting among the little *gamins*[7] of Melbourne. What funny chaps those same little ragamuffins are, to be sure! And even if they are *not* ragamuffins, but decent little b'ys going to school, with a bag of books, and a "clane" collar, an' the like, I'll back 'em against any young scamps between this and Nova Scotia for cheek and divilment of all descriptions. Some of them will scamper off at the very first sight of a "bobby"; more of them think no more of aiming straight at the white cap cover, with the prohibited "shanghai,"[8] than they do of stealing a bunch of grapes out of Paddy's Market; and more of them, bedad, they'll look up in a policeman's

DOWN BY THE YARRA

face with as innocent a look on 'em as if butter wouldn't melt in their mouths, an' say "Yes, sir," an' "No, sir," to every word you say; an' only for a chance look you get at some young divil stickin' his tongue in his jaw at you, bedad you'd think 'em as innocent as lambs.'

'My dear fellow,' here I thought it advisable to interfere with, 'You're getting into your brogue again, and we'll never get at the end of your wonderful "case".'

'Maybe not so fast as *you* got at the end of your medal case, mate, but when we do get at the end of mine, it might be more satisfactory.'

'Oh, not another word I'll say till you're done!'

'And show your sense. Well not a tale, or tidings could I hear of the young lad that brought the message to the strange female on the bridge; and I was getting disheartened from inquiring right and left, without any result, when I heard something at a time when I least expected it. I was on patrol on the very same beat, viz., Prince's Bridge, one moonlight night, when the poor dead lady had been about a week buried, and was looking over the bridge at the water shimmering in the moonlight, when a step ceased behind me. I turned and saw a young man, very respectably dressed, who seemed inclined to speak to me.

'"I've been away from town since the fifth," he said, abruptly, "and just now, at Mellon's public, I got hold of an old *Argus*, with something about an inquest in it. Can you tell me anything about it?"

'"If you've read the account, you know as much as I can tell you," I made him answer; "but what makes you take any interest in it—did you know the party?"

'"I don't know—wasn't there something about a laudanum bottle being found—a laudanum bottle with Tyrrel's label on it?"

'"Yes—but Tyrrel declares he never sold a drop of laudanum within a month of the date, and his assistant says the same. We haven't been able to discover who the poor woman was, or where she came from; in fact, the whole horrible affair is enveloped in mystery."

'"Look here—the very day before the body of that female was found, *I* was Tyrrel's assistant, and only stopping in the shop to put the new hand in the way of the place, for I was going up to see my mother at Carisbrooke. *I* sold two ounces of laudanum to a female who answers to the description in the newspaper, so there is the laudanum accounted for."

'"Tell me what the woman to whom you sold it looked like," I said.

'"She was rather tall, and very pale; she was dressed entirely in black, and I noticed on her wedding-finger a plain ring, and also one which appeared to be of real gems, for it sparkled in the light of the gas like stars."

DOWN BY THE YARRA

'"It was night then when you sold the laudanum?"

'"At about eight o'clock on the evening of the fourth."

'"Was the woman good-looking?"

'"Very handsome, but deadly pale; and I don't think I ever saw a more graceful or lady-like figure. She said she had been accustomed to taking the drug for years, to ease pain to which she was subject; so I did not hesitate to give it to her, but I put my own private mark on the label, and I could swear to it anywhere."

'Well, here was a perfect description of my lady of the Yarra, and yet I did not believe that she had bought that laudanum for the purpose of destroying herself. There were some among us who laughed at the doctors and the verdict of murder against "some person or persons unknown," but I was not one of them, and I felt certain that foul play had been done down by the Yarra.

'Having questioned and cross-questioned the young chemist, I made an appointment with him and we parted. Certainly, the information he had volunteered appeared to be of but little service to me, but as things eventually turned out, his evidence was of incalculable benefit to *my* case.

'It never rains but it pours, they say, and who should I fall in with on the very next day, in Swanston-street, but my young gentleman of the raggy jacket, that I had been in search of for days.

'"If you please, sir," he said, "some of our lane boys told me you wanted me; I've just come back from Kilmore, sir."

'"Aye? And what were you doing at Kilmore, my hearty?"

'"Minding cows for a man, sir, and he gave me the sack."

'"Not before you deserved it, I'll be bound. But why didn't your lane boys tell me where you were when they knew I was chasing the town for you?"

'"Please, sir, they thought you might be wanting me for something bad, and they wouldn't split[9] on me."

'"No, I'm blowed if they would," I said, "for ye're a nice lot to hang together. But now do you know what it is that I do want of you?"

'"No, sir."

'"Do you remember bringing a message to a lady in black, one day last week, while she was standing looking over the bridge and talking to me?"

'"Of course I do, sir. I brought it from a gentleman down by the Yarra, and he gave me sixpence for doing it. He was a tall, fair-haired gent, sir, and he said he'd wait for the lady by the Yarra, about a hundred yards from the boat-house."

'"Tell me exactly what he said to you."

DOWN BY THE YARRA

'"He said to tell the lady on the bridge that P B was waiting for her down by the Yarra, and that it was a matter of great consequence to them both."

'"Did you ever see that gentleman before or since?"

'"Never, sir."

'"Well, look here, my man, you know that lady was murdered down by the Yarra that same night—there's a fine reward offered, and if you can find out that chap for me, I'll give you such a whack of money as you never had in your life before. It'll be the making of you, that's what it'll be, only you find out that fellow."

'To see how the little chap's eyes brightened cheered me up. "After all," I thought to myself, "after all, I'll back a Melbourne street boy against all the detectives in town to run a regular fox to earth—that is to say, a chap that wants to lay close—for the telegraph is nothing to the sort of freemasonry they have among them."

'"I'll ask Bill Drummond," said the lad, quickly. "Bill waited for me at the back of the boat-house while I ran up the stairs, and he might have seen the gentleman since."

'"Do, my boy; and if you hear anything, come to me at the bridge at seven o'clock to-night"; and off like a shot went my youngster on his voyage of discovery.

'"He lives back of seventy-five, Park-street, sir," saluted me at seven precisely. "Bill Drummond saw him at the theatre on Monday, and he was so tight that Bill followed him home, to get some of the money he was shying[10] about."

'"How did he follow him?"

'"The gent rode in a cab, sir, and Bill whipped behind.[11] Oh, it's all right, sir."

'Well, I gave the little cove half-a-crown on account, and set him and his mate to shepherd[12] the gent at the back of seventy-five, Park street. Of course, I meant to have my own finger in the pie, but was quite as determined to let no one else have one unless I couldn't help it. That is, none of my mates, you know—for, independent of the "glory and honour of it," I was thinking mightily of the reward, and not a little about the poor lady who had spoken so bitterly to me on the last night of what, I have no doubt, had been a most miserable existence.

'By the way, Sinclair there is twisting his mouth. I suppose he thinks I didn't show any considerable *nous* in scenting out traces of the murder by the banks of the Yarra. It may not have been very clever of me, certainly, to meet accidentally with the young chemist, or my little *gamin* of the lane, but they didn't do it all, you see. Many a fine hunt I had personally after the occupier of back of seventy-five, but for many a day

46

DOWN BY THE YARRA

I could learn nothing whatever of him or his belongings. He went little out except at night, and then seemed to loaf, alone, into the theatres or saloons of one sort or other; for I never could hear or see that he made a friend or acquaintance among the crowds he frequented. He appeared to drink deeply, and to stand it like a barrel; his name was Clayton, and he had a "Mrs. Clayton" at home, and that was about all I could learn of him. Perhaps you may think I ought to have arrested this man on suspicion, and I dare say I ought to have done so. He was the last person who was supposed to have held any communication with the murdered woman, and to my own certain knowledge he had inveigled her down to the banks of the Yarra by a strangely worded message; but as I told you before, I was on my own hook, and determined to hold on until I had something more certain to work upon than the knowledge of Clayton's whereabouts.

'At last my patience was rewarded. I followed my man to the Coliseum one evening, and was a witness of a rather stormy interview between him and a young woman of seeming respectability, but of apparently a most violent temper. I was standing near the door and in uniform, when he sauntered in with a cigar in his mouth. The young woman appeared to have been following him, for she was close on his heels, and just as they passed me, she seized him by the coat and arrested his progress.

'"You may as well stop," she said, excitedly, "for I tell you I won't be humbugged any longer by either you or Ann Reilly. I tell you what it is, my man, I have some fine suspicions of you. Where is your wife? I saw Ann in Collins-street, the other day, in a full suit of black belonging to her, and a ring on her finger that might do for a duchess. Come, fork out, Mr. Clayton, or as sure as you stand there, I'll tell the first policeman I see all I know and all I guess."

'"For mercy's sake, Ellen!" he gasped, in a sort of choking whisper, "don't talk so loud, and come round this evening. Ann and you can arrange it between you."

'"Arrange it!" she sneered. "Perhaps you and she might arrange it too well. Where's your wife, I say? I want to know, and I'm determined to know—and more than that, I'm determined to get the money I advanced Ann. Do you think it likely that I'll go short while you and she are flashing it about in silks and diamonds? Not likely!"

'"Hush! you fool. Come up in the morning, when I'm at home, and I give you my word we'll come to some settlement."

'"Well, I'll be there, believe me; but I give you *my* word that I won't go alone—I don't want to be murdered, neither down by the Yarra, or elsewhere."

'You may believe, mates, that I pricked up my ears at this

DOWN BY THE YARRA

conversation, and blessed my stars over and over again that I should have turned into the Coliseum that night. As he walked quickly away from the girl I stepped up to her and laid my hand on her shoulder. "You're quite right not to trust them, miss," I said. "And you'll take *me* with you to the back of seventy-five, Park-street, tomorrow morning."

'"What do you mean?" she exclaimed, turning as pale as a ghost.

'"Only that I overheard every word you said to Clayton just now, and that if you don't immediately tell me all you know of the affair, as well as all you suspect, I'll arrest you as an accomplice in two twos."[13]

'"Oh Lord!" she cried, "I don't know anything, and I'm willing to tell you what I think. But do you think he *did* murder his wife? Good heaven, although I said it, I don't think he's so bad as that!"

'I needn't, however, give you word for word of the story she told me when I got her into a quiet room; the substance of the matter I can give you in my own way.

'The girl's name was Ellen Glynn, and she had come out in the same vessel with Ann Reilly, the present "Mrs. Clayton." Clayton and his wife were cabin passengers in the same ship, and during the course of the voyage Clayton had become infatuated with Ann Reilly, who was an excessively handsome and very genteel-looking girl. Mrs. Clayton would seem to have been a neglected wife all throughout, and perhaps it was no wonder, for Ellen said she was one of those dreamy, thoughtful, delicate women who seem to live in a world of their own, and careless of the doings of this. Ellen said, too, that she had money in her own right, and that she was in deep mourning for her last relative, a fond and devoted father.

'"She didn't seem to care when her husband engaged both Ann and me as servants on our landing in Melbourne," the girl said, when she was telling me the story. "Indeed, I don't think she took enough of notice of Clayton to see how things were going on, until I myself could not stand it, and gave notice that I was going to leave, and then all at once her eyes seemed to be opened. I never saw anything like the flashes of fire that seemed to fly from her eyes, as she ordered Ann Reilly to leave her house that instant. She seemed like one just woke out of a sleep to see some horrible sight staring her in the face."

'"And what happened then?"

'"I'll tell you what happened. Clayton took his wife by the shoulders and turned her out of doors, and Ann Reilly laughed at it."

'"And what then?"

'"I packed up my things and went too, threatening to summons Ann for my money if I didn't get it the next day. You see she hadn't a penny when she left home, and she being an old schoolmate of mine, I shared

48

DOWN BY THE YARRA

with her, on the promise that I was to be paid out of her first wages."

'"And when did all this happen?"

'"Yesterday was three weeks."

'"Why that was the very day of the murder!" I exclaimed.

'And I remembered the poor lady on the bridge, and no longer wondered at her bitterness. It must have been very hard to bear. It was not strange that she looked so yearningly at the river, although she had no thought of drowning herself from her earthly troubles under its calm waters. Many a time I long myself to see the shadow of the Cratloe Hills fall across my dear old mother's cabin in far away County Clare, but well I know that 'tis not for me, by's.

'"Not an hour we'll lose, my girl!" I cried, jumping from my seat. "Morning is one thing, and to-night is another. Come, Ellen, we must have this nice pair in the lock-up this very night; so you must make up your mind to an earlier visit to 'Mrs. Clayton' than you intended."

'It was not a pleasant task for the girl, and I was obliged to go to her mistress and partially explain, so that she should get no blame for remaining out. Bob, there, went with us, so he can verify the rest of my story.

'We laid our plans as we walked toward Park-street. It was almost a certainty that Clayton would remain in town until a much later hour than the one which would find us at his residence, and we thought it would be better to get what we could out of the woman before he came home, and then arrest him on his arrival. Ellen was left a little way down the right of way, while Bob and I went boldly up to the door and knocked.

'It was promptly opened. Doubtless the wretched woman thought it was her paramour who sought admittance. No sooner was the door opened than I pushed inside, closely followed by Bob, to the utter astonishment of Ann Reilly, who seemed for a moment completely paralysed with terror at the sight of the police uniform.

'"What do you want?" she screamed at last. "Go out of this, I tell you! How dare you push into a woman's house in this way! What do you want here?"

'"We want you," I made her answer; "and if you don't make less noise about it, 'twill be all the worse for yourself. I arrest you, in the Queen's name, for being an accessory to the murder of Mrs. Clayton."

'I needn't tell any one of you, mates, that the greatest criminals are often the biggest cowards, and a bigger one than Ann Reilly, *alias* Clayton, never existed. She supplicated for her liberty in the most abject terms—she offered to give up to justice the very man who had committed murder at her instigation, and she declared, with the most solemn asseverations, that she would do everything in her power to hang him,

49

DOWN BY THE YARRA

if we would only let her go free. The love of woman, eh, Mark?

'We listened to her wild ravings—Bob and I, that is to say—after cautioning her in the usual manner; but at last we admitted Ellen, and, at the sight of her old schoolmate, our prisoner fell on her knees before her, and begged her to plead for her; and she actually wound up by directing us where to find the diamond ring I had noticed on the finger of the lady on the bridge, declaring that Clayton had drawn it off and brought it straight to her on the very night of the murder. It was a sickening sight, I tell you, for of all things out, I hate the very look of a coward.

'At about twelve o'clock, Clayton himself returned. He had been drinking heavily, but was one of those persons upon whom spirits have no exhilarating effect. He stared stupidly from one to the other of us, and when the handcuffs were clasped upon his wrists, he fell, in a helpless sort of way, into a chair near him. All at once he looked toward Ann Reilly, and a sudden sense of his position seemed to flash into his mind.

'"May the curse eternal rest upon you!" he cried, lifting his manacled wrists up over his head, as if he would have felled her to the ground; "you have ruined me here and hereafter! Here and hereafter!" he reiterated, rising to his feet and waving his clasped wrists still above his head. "It was my hands that did it, but *you* are the murderer, for I knew not what I did, and God knows it. What could I do with the devil at my elbow always—always, by day and by night—urging me to kill! Oh, may the heavy curse of heaven rest on your head, Ann Reilly!"

'And as the last word escaped his lips, he fell to the ground in a state of insensibility.

'I don't think that a single one who knew the real state of the case regretted that Clayton escaped the fate that would surely have awaited him. He never recovered from the shock of the arrest and the fit which succeeded it, but died the same night, in his own bed, at the back of Park-street. During his last hours, he didn't "babble of green fields,"[14] but he murmured a woman's name incessantly, and his last words were,

'"Down by the Yarra."

'During my pretty long career as a peeler, both here and in the old country, I am sure I never performed a duty with more pleasure than I did upon the day when I stood behind the police van that conveyed Ann Reilly from the Court House where she was sentenced to the gaol. She made a full confession, even to the elucidation of the laudanum mystery. She had purchased it in a suit of Mrs. Clayton's clothes, so that it might be supposed that a suicide had been committed, and it was she who suggested that the empty phial should be placed near the dead woman's hand.

'Oh, how she screamed, to be sure, when "Imprisonment for life" was delivered, and with what vile epithets she saluted the judge himself and every one in her vicinity, as despair changed her hopeful pleading into the fiercest rage! And there's my story for ye; what do ye think of it?'

'Why, that we've had quite enough of it.'

'What became of your little ragamuffin?' asked Mark Sinclair.

'Bedad, there isn't a better boy in Melbourne. Out of my reward, I rigged him out like a prince, and got him a comfortable billet in Bourke-street. He often comes to see me. But go asy, ye haven't the best part of the story yet. Sure ye all know that Bob there is going to be married next week. Who do you think it's to? Why, Ellen Glynn, if you plase; so if nothing came out of that night's chase but that, we did some business anyhow.'

'Well, as you're getting into your brogue again, Tom, I see that the story is really done, so I vote that we count the fines.'

'Sorra[15] fear of your forgetting the bottles, mate; but I say, Sinclair, can you beat that with any of your detective yarns?'

'I'll try next month, at any rate, Tom, and if I don't, may I be fined half a dozen instead of one.' So we shall see.

First published in the *Australian Journal*, June 1870, as part of the *Detective's Album* serial, under the byline 'W.W.'

NOTES

1 *by dad*: usually spoken and written as *bedad*, as elsewhere in this and other stories); a mild Irish oath (euphemism for 'by God').

2 *crusher*: (abbreviated form of beetle-crusher); someone with large, flat feet; in this context a policeman walking a regular beat (cf. UK: flatfoot)

3 *The swamp murder*: Fortune often claimed her stories were based on real cases that had been covered in the newspapers. In 1869, Bridget Lynch was found strangled in the swamp behind Melbourne's Military Barracks. Three men would separately be charged with the crime, but the prosecution collapsed in court.

4 *that so-called 'Medal Case'*: see 'The Medal Case,' published in the *Australian Journal*, 1 June 1867, before W.W.'s *Detective's Album* series began in November 1868. It bears no author byline, but mentions characters from stories in the series.

5 *gammon*: pretend.

6 *the "other side"*: England, perhaps?

7 *gamins*: street kids.

8 *the prohibited "shanghai"*: a catapult.

9 *split*: inform.

10 *shying*: throwing.

11 *Bill whipped behind*: i.e., he jumped and held on to the back of the cab.

12 *shepherd*: tail, follow.

13 *in two twos*: in an instant (Irish usage).

14 *he didn't "babble of green fields"*: as the dying Falstaff did in *Henry V.*

15 *sorra*: in this context, an emphatic negative, so: 'No chance of your forgetting the bottles . . .'

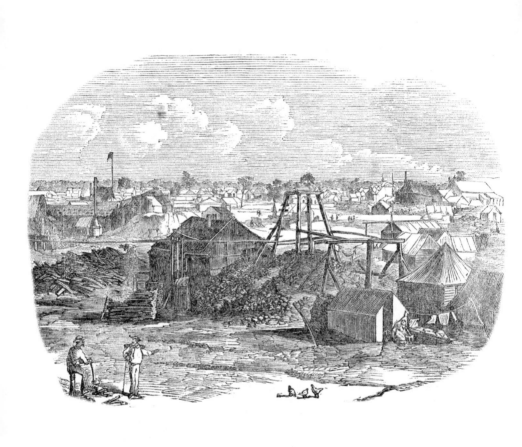

TRACES OF CRIME

There are many who recollect full well the rush at Chinaman's Flat. It was in the height of its prosperity that an assault was committed upon a female of a character so diabolical in itself, as to have aroused the utmost anxiety in the public as well as in the police, to punish the perpetrator thereof.

The case was placed in my hands, and as it presented difficulties so great as to appear to an ordinary observer almost insurmountable, the overcoming of which was likely to gain approbation in the proper quarter, I gladly accepted the task.

I had little to go upon at first. One dark night, in a tent in the very centre of a crowded thoroughfare, a female had been preparing to retire to rest, her husband being in the habit of remaining at the public house until a late hour, when a man with a crape mask—who must have gained an earlier entrance—seized her, and in the prosecution of a criminal offence, had injured and abused the unfortunate woman so much that her life was despaired of.

Although there was a light burning at the time, the woman was barely able to describe his general appearance; he appeared to her like a German, had no whiskers, fair hair, was low in stature, and stoutly built.

With one important exception, that was all the information she was able to give me on the subject. The exception, however, was a good deal to a detective, and I hoped might prove an invaluable aid to me. During the struggle she had torn the arm of the flannel shirt he wore, and was under a decided impression that upon the upper part of the criminal's arm there was a small anchor and heart tattooed.

Now, I was well aware that in this colony to find a man with a tattooed arm was an everyday affair, especially on the diggings, where, I dare say, there is scarcely a person who has not come in contact more than once or twice with half a dozen men tattooed in the style I speak of—the anchor or heart, or both, being a favourite figure with those 'gentlemen' who are in favour of branding.

However, the clue was worth something, and even without its aid, not more than a couple of weeks had elapsed when, with the assistance of the local police, I had traced a man bearing in appearance a general resemblance to the man who had committed the offence to a digging about seven miles from Chinaman's Flat.

TRACES OF CRIME

It is unnecessary that I should relate every particular as to how my suspicions were directed to this man, who did not live on China-man's Flat, and to all appearance, had not left the diggings where he was camped since he first commenced working there. I say 'to all appearance,' for it was with a certain knowledge that he *had* been absent from his tent on the night of the outrage that I one evening trudged down the flat where his tent was pitched, with my swag on my back, and sat down on a log not far from where he had kindled a fire for culinary or other purposes.

These diggings I will call McAdam's. It was a large and flourishing goldfield, and on the flat where my man was camped there were several other tents grouped, so that it was nothing singular that I should look about for a couple of bushes between which I might swing my little bit of canvas for the night.

After I had fastened up the rope and thrown my tent over it in regular digger fashion, I broke down some bushes to form my bed, and having spread thereon my blankets, went up to my man—whom I shall in future call 'Bill'—to request permission to boil my billy on his fire.

It was willingly granted, and so I lighted my pipe and sat down to await the boiling of the water, determined if I could so manage it to get this suspected man to accept me as a mate before I lay down that night.

Bill was also engaged in smoking, and had not, of course, the slightest suspicion that in the rough, ordinary-looking digger before him he was contemplating the 'make-up' of a Victorian detective, who had already made himself slightly talked of among his comrades by one or two clever captures.

'Where did you come from mate?' inquired Bill, as he puffed away leisurely at a cutty.

'From Burnt Creek,' I replied, 'and a long enough road it is in such d—— hot weather as this.'

'Nothing doing at Burnt Creek?'

'Not a thing—the place is cooked.'

'Are you in for a try here, then?' he asked, rather eagerly I thought.

'Well, I think so; is there any chance do you think?'

'Have you got a miner's right?' was his sudden question.

'I have,' said I taking it out of my pocket, and handing the bit of parchment for his inspection.

'Are you a hatter?'[1] inquired Bill, as he returned the document.

'I am,' was my reply.

'Well, if you have no objections then, I don't mind going mates

54

with you—I've got a pretty fair prospect, and the ground's going to run rather deep for one man, I think.'

'All right.'

So here was the very thing I wanted, settled without the slightest trouble.

My object in wishing to go mates with this fellow will, I dare say, readily be perceived. I did not wish to risk my character for 'cuteness by arresting my gentleman without being sure that he was branded in the way described by the woman, and besides, in the close supervision which I should be able to keep over him while working together daily, heaven knows what might transpire as additional evidence against him, at least so I reasoned with myself; and it was with a partially relieved mind that I made my frugal supper, and made believe to 'turn in,' fatigued, as I might be supposed to be, after my long tramp.

But I didn't turn in, not I, I had other objects in view, if one may be said to have an object *in view* on one of the darkest nights of a moonless week—for dark enough the night in question became, even before I had finished my supper and made my apparent preparations for bed.

We were not camped far enough from the business part of the rush to be very quiet; there was plenty of noise—the nightly noise of a rich gold-field—came down our way, and even in some of the tents close to us, card-playing, and drinking, and singing, and laughing, were going on; so it was quite easy for me to steal unnoticed to the back of Bill's little tent, and, by the assistance of a small slit made in the calico by my knife, have a look at what my worthy was doing inside, for I was anxious to become acquainted with his habits, and, of course, determined to watch him as closely as ever I could.

Well, the first specimen I had of his customs was certainly a singular one, and was, it may be well believed, an exception to his general line of conduct. Diggers, or any other class of men, do not generally spend their evenings in cutting their shoes up into small morsels, and that was exactly what Bill was busily engaged in doing when I clapped my eye to the hole. He had already disposed of a good portion of the article when I commenced to watch him: the entire 'upper' of a very muddy blucher boot lying upon his rough table in a small heap, and in the smallest pieces that one would suppose any person could have patience to cut up a dry, hard, old leather boot.

It was rather a puzzler to me this, and that Bill was doing such a thing simply to amuse himself was out of the question; indeed, without observing that he had the door of his tent closely fastened

TRACES OF CRIME

upon a warm evening, and that he started at the slightest sound, the instincts of an old detective would alone have convinced me that Bill had some great cause indeed to make away with those old boots; so I continued watching.

He had hacked away at the sole with an old but sharp butcher's knife, but it almost defied his attempts to separate it into pieces, and at length he gave it up in despair, and gathering up the small portions on the table, he swept them with the mutilated sole into his hat, and opening his tent door, went out.

I guessed very truly that he would make for the fire, and as it happened to be at the other side of a log from where I was hiding, I had a good opportunity of continuing my espial.

He raked together the few embers that remained near the log, and flinging the pieces of leather thereon, retired once more into his tent, calculating, no doubt, that the hot ashes would soon scorch and twist them up, so as to defy recognition, while the fire he would build upon them in the morning would settle the matter most satisfactorily.

All this would have happened just so, no doubt, if I had not succeeded in scraping nearly every bit from the place where Bill had thrown them, so silently and quickly, that I was in the shelter of my slung tent with my prize and a burn or two on my fingers before he himself had had time to divest himself of his garments and blow out the light.

He did so very soon, however, and it was long before I could get asleep. I thought it over and over in all ways, and looked upon it in all lights that I could think of, and yet, always connecting this demolished boot with the case in the investigation of which I was engaged, I could not make it out at all.

Had we overlooked, with all our fancied acuteness, some clue which Bill feared we had possession of, to which this piecemeal boot was the key? And if so, why had he remained so long without destroying it?

It was, as I said before, a regular puzzler to me, and my brain was positively weary when I at length dropped off to sleep.

Well, I worked for a week with Bill, and I can tell you it was work I didn't at all take to. The unaccustomed use of the pick and shovel played the very mischief with my hands; but, for fear of arousing the suspicions of my mate, I durst not complain, having only to endure in silence, or as our Scotch friends would put it, 'Grin and bide it.' And the worst of it was, that I was gaining nothing—nothing whatever—by my unusual industry.

I had hoped that accidentally I should have got a sight of the

TRACES OF CRIME

anchor and heart, but I was day after day disappointed, for my mate was not very regular in his ablutions, and I had reckoned without my host in expecting that the very ordinary habit of a digger, namely, that of having a 'regular wash' at least every Sunday, would be a good and certain one for exposing the brand.

But no, Bill allowed the Sunday to come and go, without once removing what I could observe was the flannel shirt in which he had worked all the week; and then I began to swear at my own obtuseness — 'the fellow must be aware that his shirt was torn by the woman, of course he suspects that she may have seen the tattooing, and will take blessed good care not to expose it, mate or no mate,' thought I; and then I called myself a donkey, and during the few following days, when I was trusting to the chapter of accidents, I was also deliberating on the 'to be or not to be' of the question of arresting him at once, and chancing it.

Saturday afternoon came again, and then the early knock-off time, and that sort of quarter holiday among the miners, namely, four o'clock, was hailed by me with the greatest relief, and it was with the full determination of never again setting foot in the cursed claim that I shouldered my pick and shovel and proceeded tentwards.

On my way I met a policeman, and received from him a concerted signal that I was wanted at the camp, and so telling Bill that I was going to see an old mate about some money that he owed me, I started at once.

'We've got something else in your line, mate,' said my old chum, Joe Bennet, as I entered the camp, 'and one which, I think, will be a regular poser for you. The body of a man has been found in Pipeclay Gully, and we can scarcely be justified by appearances in giving even a surmise as to how he came by his death.'

'How do you mean?' I inquired. 'Has he been dead so long?'

'About a fortnight, I dare say, but we have done absolutely nothing as yet. Knowing you were on the ground we have not even touched the body: will you come up at once?'

'Of course I will!' And after substituting the uniform of the force for the digger's costume, in which I was apparelled, in case of an encounter with my 'mate,' we went straight to 'Pipeclay.'

The body had been left in charge of one of the police, and was still lying, undisturbed in the position in which it had been discovered; not a soul was about, in fact, the gully had been rushed and abandoned, and bore not the slightest trace of man's handiwork, saving and except the miner's holes and their surrounding little eminences of pipeclay, from which the gully was named. And it was a veritable

TRACES OF CRIME

'gully,' running between two low ranges of hills, which hills were covered with an undergrowth of wattle and cherry trees, and scattered over with rocks and indications of quartz, which have, I dare say, been fully tried by this time.

Well, on the slope of one of the hills, where it amalgamated as it were with the level of the gully, and where the sinking had evidently been shallow, lay the body of the dead man. He was dressed in ordinary miner's fashion, and saving for the fact of a gun being by his side, one might have supposed that he had only given up his digging to lie down and die beside the hole near which he lay.

The hole, however, was full of water—quite full; indeed the water was sopping out on the ground around it, and that the hole was an old one was evident, by the crumbling edges around it, and the fragments of old branches that lay rotting in the water.

Close to this hole lay the body, the attitude strongly indicative of the last exertion during life having been that of crawling out of the waterhole, in which indeed still remained part of the unfortunate man's leg. There was no hat on his head, and in spite of the considerable decay of the body, even an ordinary observer could not fail to notice a large fracture in the side of the head.

I examined the gun; it was a double-barrelled fowling piece, and one barrel had been discharged, while very apparent on the stock of the gun were blood marks, that even the late heavy rain had failed to erase. In the pockets of the dead man was nothing, save what any digger might carry—pipe and tobacco, a cheap knife, and a shilling or two, this was all; and so leaving the body to be removed by the police, I thoughtfully retraced my way to the camp.

Singularly enough, during my absence, a woman had been there, giving information about her husband, on account of whose absence she was becoming alarmed; and as the caution of the policeman on duty at the camp had prevented his giving her any idea of the fact of the dead body having been discovered that very day, I immediately went to the address which the woman had left, in order to discover, if possible, not only if it was the missing man, but also to gain any information that might be likely to put me upon the scent of the murderer, for that the man had been murdered I had not the slightest doubt.

Well, I succeeded in finding the woman, a young and decidedly good-looking Englishwoman of the lower class, and gained from her the following information:—

About a fortnight before, her husband, who had been indisposed, and in consequence not working for a day or two, had taken his gun

TRACES OF CRIME

one morning in order to amuse himself for an hour or two, as well as to have a look at the ranges near Pipeclay Gully, and do a little prospecting at the same time. He had not returned, but as he had suggested a possibility of visiting his brother who was digging about four miles off, she had not felt alarmed until upon communicating with the said brother she had become aware that her husband had never been there. From the description, I knew at once that the remains of the poor fellow lying in Pipeclay Gully were certainly those of the missing man, and with what care and delicacy I might possess I broke the tidings to the shocked wife, and after allowing her grief to have vent in a passion of tears, I tried to gain some clue to the likely perpetrator of the murder.

'Had she any suspicions?' I asked; 'was there any feud between her husband and any individual she could name?'

At first she replied 'no,' and then a sudden recollection appeared to strike her, and she said that some weeks ago a man had, during the absence of her husband, made advances to her, under the feigned supposition that she was an unmarried woman. In spite of her decidedly repellent manner, he had continued his attentions, until she, afraid of his impetuosity, had been obliged to call the attention of her husband to the matter, and he, of course feeling indignant, had threatened to shoot the intruder if he ever ventured near the place again.

The woman described this man to me, and it was with a violent whirl of emotional excitement, as one feels who is on the eve of a great discovery, that I hastened to the camp, which was close by.

It was barely half-past five o'clock, and in a few minutes I was on my way, with two or three other associates, to the scene of what I had no doubt had been a horrible murder. What my object was there was soon apparent. I had before tried the depth of the muddy water, and found it was scarcely four feet, and now we hastened to make use of the remaining light of a long summer's day in draining carefully the said hole.

I was repaid for the trouble, for in the muddy and deep sediment at the bottom we discovered a deeply imbedded blucher boot; and I dare say you will readily guess how my heart leaped up at the sight.

To old diggers, the task which followed was not a very great one; we had provided ourselves with a 'tub,' etc., and 'washed' every bit of the mud at the bottom of the hole. The only 'find' we had, however, was a peculiar bit of wood, which, instead of rewarding us for our exertions by lying like gold at the bottom of the dish in which we 'turned off,' insisted upon floating on the top of the very first tub, when it became loosened from its surrounding of clay.

TRACES OF CRIME

It was a queer piece of wood, and eventually quite repaid us for any trouble we might have had in its capture. A segment of a circle it was, or rather a *portion* of a segment of a circle, being neither more nor less than a piece broken out of one of those old fashioned black wooden buttons, that are still to be seen on the monkey-jacket of many an Australian digger, as well as elsewhere.

Well, I fancied that I knew the identical button from whence had been broken this bit of wood, and that I could go and straightaway fit it into its place without the slightest trouble in the world—singular, was it not?—and as I carefully placed the piece in my pocket, I could not help thinking to myself 'Well, this does indeed and most truly look like the working of Providence.'

There are many occasions when an apparent *chance* has effected the unravelling of a mystery, which but for the turning over of that particular page of fatality, might have remained a mystery to the day of judgment, in spite of the most strenuous and most able exertions. Mere human acumen would never have discovered the key to the secret's hieroglyphic, nor placed side by side the hidden links of a chain long enough and strong enough to tear the murderer from his fancied security, and hang him as high as Haman.[2] Such would almost appear to have been the case in the instance to which I am alluding, only that in place of ascribing the elucidation and the unravelling to that mythical power *chance*, the impulse of some 'inner man' writes the word *Providence*.

I did not feel exactly like moralizing, however, when, after resuming my digger's 'make-up,' I walked towards the tent of the man I have called Bill. No; I felt more and deeper than any mere moralist could understand. The belief that a higher power had especially called out, and chosen, one of his own creatures to be the instrument of his retributive power, has, in our world's history, been the means of mighty evil, and I hope that not for an instant did such an idea take possession of me. I was not conscious of feeling that I had been chosen as a scourge and an instrument of earthly punishment; but I *did* feel that I was likely to be the means of cutting short the thread of a most unready fellow-mortal's life, and a solemn responsibility it is to bring home to one's self I can assure you.

The last flush of sunlight was fading low in the west when I reached our camping ground, and found Bill seated outside on a log, indulging in his usual pipe in the greying twilight.

I had, of course, determined upon arresting him at once, and had sent two policemen round to the back of our tents, in case of an attempted escape upon his part; and now, quite prepared, I sat down beside him; and, after feeling that the handcuffs were in their usual place in my belt, I lit my pipe and commenced to smoke also. My heart verily went pit-a-pat as I did so, for, long as I had been engaged in this sort of thing, I had not yet become callous either to the feelings of a wretched criminal or the excitement attendant more or less upon every capture of the sort.

We smoked in silence for some minutes, and I was listening intently to hear the slightest intimation of the vicinity of my mates; at length Bill broke the silence. 'Did you get your money?' he inquired.

'No,' I replied, 'but I think I *will* get it soon.'

Silence again, and then withdrawing the pipe from my mouth and quietly knocking the ashes out of it on the log, I turned towards my mate and said.

'Bill, what made you murder that man in Pipeclay Gully?'

He did not reply, but I could see his face pale and whiten in the grey dim twilight, and at last stand out distinctly in the darkening like that of the dead man we found lying in the lonely gully.

It was so entirely unexpected that he was completely stunned: not the slightest idea had he that the body had ever been found, and it was on quite nerveless wrists that I locked the handcuffs, as my mates came up and took him in charge.

Rallying a little, he asked huskily, 'Who said I did it?'

'No person,' I replied, 'but I *know* you did it.'

Again he was silent, and did not contradict me, and so he was taken to the lock-up.

I was right about the broken button, and had often noticed it on an old jacket of Bill's. The piece fitted to a nicety; and the cut-up blucher! Verily, there was some powerful influence at work in the discovery of this murder, and again I repeat that no mere human wisdom could have accomplished it.

Bill, it would appear, thought so too, for expressing himself so to me, he made a full confession, not only of the murder, but also of the other offence, for the bringing home to him of which I had been so anxious.

When he found that the body of the unfortunate man had been discovered upon the surface, in the broad light of day, after he had left him *dead* in the bottom of the hole, he became superstitiously convinced that God himself had permitted the dead to leave his hiding place for the purpose of bringing the murderer to justice.

It is no unusual thing to find criminals of his class deeply impregnated with superstition, and Bill insisted to the last that the murdered man was quite dead when he had placed him in the hole, and where,

TRACES OF CRIME

in his anxiety to prevent the body from appearing above the surface, he had lost his boot in the mud, and was too fearful of discovery to remain to try and get it out.

Bill was convicted, sentenced to death, and hung; many other crimes of a similar nature to that which he had committed on Chinaman's Flat having been brought home to him by his own confession.

First published as 'Memoirs of an Australian Police Officer, No. IV: Traces of Crime' in the *Australian Journal*, 2 December 1865, with no byline.

NOTES

1 *hatter*: a miner working on his own, without a partner.
2 *hang him as high as Haman*: in the Book of Esther, Haman was a high-ranking official at the Persian court who built a 'gallows fifty cubits high' on which to hang a Jew, Mordecai, for failing to bow to him, but who was hanged on it himself instead.

THE MIDNIGHT WATCH

I don't think I was ever out in a hotter day in Australia than the one of which I am about to write. The sun had been pouring down streams of fiery light that made me thank my stars I was not in 'Force' uniform, though, as it was, the heat burning through the tweed coat upon my back made it feel as if it was cast iron and was rivetted upon my body. My poor animal felt the fatigue and almost insufferable heat quite as much as I did, I dare say; while the flies, those tormenting nuisances of bush life, nearly drove both him and me mad.

Very beautiful in early morning is the green scattered 'bush' of Australia. A thousand beauties may be freshly discovered, as it were, at every fresh mile of travel. In one spot, grand, crooked old trees lean caressingly over some tortuous and glistening creek, or stand sentinel over their own still reflections in the placid waters. Early birds call to each other from scented, golden wattles, or wash themselves in the shadow of the old gum trees upon the edge of the creek. If it is the season for the stately magpie, he utters those delicious gurgles of music that cannot be compared with the notes of any other bird in the wide world, or stalks proudly over the grassy slopes, as if he really believed he and his were 'monarchs of all they surveyed.'

Later in the day, too, when the thermometer stands no higher than one hundred and three or four, or so, one may yet enjoy a ride through the glades of our eastern forest. The screams of the cockatoos are discordant, no doubt, but how enjoyable it is to catch a glimpse of them hovering over some tall tree or resting upon a bough, with outspread wing, swaying themselves to and fro, in very enjoyment of pure life. Cawing crows are nasty things, too, and suggestive of something that one doesn't at all want to come in contact with; nevertheless, their feathers are so glossy and black, and the clear blue sky, unflecked by a single cloud, throws their *wishing* wings out into such bold relief above the green tree tops, that one cannot but try to forget their disagreeable habits and admire them as a part of a very Australian bush scene.

Well, I cannot be sure that you will exactly know what I am driving at, but I am coming to the point. After assuring you that I admire and enjoy the beauty of bush scenery as much as any one, when it is really admirable and enjoyable, I defy any man living to picture to himself or to endure a more detestable ordeal than a ride through that very same beautiful bush scenery on the sort of day it was when my story commences. Over a long, broad, treeless plain, we will say, with the sun burning up every blade of grass dry and brown, and pouring down upon your miserable head; or on a lonely track, where only now and then a tree comes aggravatingly near the road, to make you wish for shade, if it were but for one moment; I say aggravatingly, for I do think that, with respect to shade, those same Eucalypti are the most aggravating trees in the universe.

Fortunately, I was in no hurry upon that particular day. I was returning from the successful accomplishment of a troublesome piece of police business, and was only anxious to get to my destination for the night and over the seemingly interminable day of heat I had just passed through; but had I been upon the most urgent business in the world it would have been next to impossible for my poor horse to have galloped many miles at a stretch, with the thermometer standing so high as it did that day.

Poor Vino! I fancy I see her now as we neared the lonely bush inn, where she was as certain as I was myself of rest and refreshment. She was a glossy bright bay, strongly built, and yet a half-blood; although she bore no broad arrow branded on her silky coat, she been in the Force many years. She was a detective's animal, and I had ridden her for most of the seven years during which I had seen colonial service. I do believe that she was almost as good a detective as I was myself; and I am not ashamed to own that her sagacity or instinct, or whatever you choose to name it, gave me many a hint, of which I never found it to my disadvantage to avail myself.

The sun, then, was just dipping below the tops of the trees as Vino pricked up her ears with a glad whinny, and I perceived, away through the heavy box that were thickly scattered over the grassy plain which we passed, the long weather-boarded 'Wallaby Hotel' which was my destination for the night. I had been there before, but in such different guise that I had no fear of mine host recognising me; nor did I much care though he should, save that the usual caution of a detective officer made me prefer secrecy, with a view to some possible future contingency.

As we neared the hotel I perceived a bullock dray approaching it from an opposite direction to that in which I myself travelled, and just as I drew up at the door, the team came also to a halt in front of it; while the driver, leisurely tumbling himself off the empty dray, proceeded into the bar, one might guess for the purpose of obtaining a nobbler.[1] All this was very natural, and there was nothing whatever suspicious about it; but as this man passed Vino, from whose back I had just alighted, she turned her head sideways with a suspicious twist that I well knew, and gave a sniff at the man's back, pretty much as

THE MIDNIGHT WATCH

a dog might do when he happened to come in contact with a person who, his instinct told him, was not to be trusted.

This was quite enough for me; and as I threw the bridle over the hook, I took a closer survey of the bullock driver. He was a young, fair-haired and soft-featured man, certainly not more than twenty-seven years old, dressed in the usual careless dress of a teamster; and the expression in his face was of listless dreaminess — in short, just such an expression as one might expect to see in the face of a man of little intelligence who passed most of his time on the monotonous roads of a bush country.

As I entered the bar he asked for a pint of ale, and receiving it, sat down on a bench that ran along the wall, and seemed absorbed in imbibing it, and in gazing listlessly out at his bullocks. Casting but a glance at him as I passed, I informed the landlord of my intention of passing the night there, and requested that my horse might be carefully attended to.

I have already spoken of my tweed coat. I was dressed in a suit of tweed, and to all appearance might have been a comfortable farmer or a country storekeeper on my way to or from transacting some business connected with my livelihood, at the not very distant large township.

'It's been a terrible hot day, landlord,' I observed, as I availed myself of the drink I had ordered.

'Frightful, sir,' he replied, glancing at the thermometer that hung in the bar behind him. 'At two o'clock the glass stood at one hundred and twelve, and I say that's too hot for any white man.'

'Or a black one either,' I answered, seating myself carelessly. 'Well, will you see about my animal, if you please? By and by, when I get a bit cool, I'll go out and see that she's all right myself.'

The landlord left to see after Vino, and I remained sipping my brandy and water, and slyly watching the bullock-driver, who still kept silence opposite. His eyes seemed to be fixed upon the belt of forest which skirted the grass at a little distance; and had it not been for the entire absence of any intellectual appearance of face or expression, one might have fancied he was engaged in trying to solve some knotty problem, to the entire forgetfulness of everything around him.

At this moment a female entered the bar. I am not one to forget faces readily; it is my trade to remember, and I recollected having seen the very same face when I visited the 'Wallaby,' some eighteen months before. This woman was a quiet, staid-looking person of about thirty years of age, precise in her movements, and rather slow. She was quite respectable-looking, but had not a single iota of the too common 'flashness' of a colonial barmaid.

THE MIDNIGHT WATCH

Very possibly the landlord had sent her in to attend to the bar just then; at any rate, she commenced in a mechanical sort of way to rinse out some glasses, and to polish them in the same mechanical manner, without lifting her eyes, that I could observe, from her employment. My seat commanded a view of both her and the bullock-driver, it is true, but my thoughts were engaged so entirely with the latter that I paid little attention to the barmaid; and she was not one of those obtrusive ones, who, 'for the good of the house,' will insist upon making themselves conspicuous.

My man, however, appeared so completely absorbed in his pint and himself, and manifested so little inclination to move, that at length I turned my regards towards the female. At the moment I did so, she lifted her eyes carelessly toward the door, and something she saw there distended them with some feeling resembling terror, while her cheeks grew ashy pale and her lips rigid as stone; the glass in her hand, too, had almost escaped her fingers, but with a strong effort she replaced it upon the tray and caught hold of the counter, as if to support herself, while she turned a piercing quick glance first toward me and then toward the bullock-man; *there* her eyes rested.

Naturally I looked out at the door to see what had occasioned the strange change in the woman's quiet face. I saw nothing that could possibly have affected her, turn it any way I would. The patient-looking bullocks were standing drowsily under their heavy yokes, directly in front of the entrance, and nothing else was in view save a patch of grassy land over their backs, and farther away the green bush, now beginning to look dimmer that the sun had nearly set and was throwing long shadows beneath the trees.

I own to being completely puzzled, but was beginning to be quite in my element. I *like* to be puzzled; and the detective instinct has grown so strong with habit that to perceive there is a secret is to give me an insatiable craving to find it out.

I could not fancy the barmaid was acquainted with the man, for the gaze she fixed on him was not one in which was an anxiety to discover some trace of an old acquaintance, it was a look with which one might regard a person in some way notorious, to find out what constituted his peculiar difference from other of his fellow men; and yet the woman's eyes still retained that strange terror with which she had first seen the unknown something in her look-out through the doorway.

All this, you will understand, scarcely occupied a moment of time; and after her quick, strange survey of the bullock-driver, the woman sauntered idly, as it were, around the counter and stood in the doorway. She looked first up the road and then down it, and then she looked directly before her. Of course, I could but judge from the movement of her head, as I was now behind her, but whatever she looked at she remained but a moment, and then returned to the bar.

My friend the driver now began to show symptoms of a move. He lifted the long-handled whip which he had leaned against the seat, and went to look out the door likewise, and then he returned to the bar and called for a nobbler of spirit. Tossing it off at a mouthful, as it were, he appeared to have reached some determination, for as soon as he had swallowed it he walked outside and commenced rapidly to unyoke the bullocks.

There was a verandah in front of the public house, and finishing my glass, I strolled out, with my hands in my pockets, to watch my friend the driver in his arrangements.

'They are a fine team, mate,' I observed, 'and in good condition. I wouldn't care if I had such another. Horses are no good in rough bush land, where mine lies. You're going to camp here to-night?'

'Yes,' he answered quietly; 'I did think of pushing on to Cole's Creek, but 'tis later than I thought; and the day's been so terrible hot the cattle's regular baked.'

'I think you're right. There's plenty of feed here, and water, too, I think,' and I moved inside to order supper.

There was no business doing to distract my attention from my chief present interest—the bullock-driver. In that quiet bush inn, dependent upon stray travellers, or perhaps the occasional wasted cheques of a shepherd or a shearer, there was scarcely a movement upon that particular evening, and my supper and Vino attended to, I sat down in the bar and, while indulging in a 'colonial yarn' with the landlord, watched the man outside as he made all his arrangements for passing the night.

He had taken the dray a little farther on before he unyoked his cart, and it now stood almost close to the stable of the house. I saw him drive the bullocks to water, and then fasten on their bells and turn them out. I watched him return and unfold the tarpaulin that lay upon the dray and spread it over it, while his blankets were spread beneath, to form a primitive but accustomed couch. In all this, as yet, I was at fault; but I never believed that Vino's sagacity was, or doubted for a single moment that my watch would be rewarded.

During the time the man was so employed, I often spared a curious glance at the movements of the bar-woman. Her demeanour seemed as calm and unruffled as ever; but I observed that her whole thoughts were occupied with the same object that formed the subject of my watch. She made many excuses to visit the bar, and once, with a glass in her hand, which she still kept polishing with that circular movement that barmen

THE MIDNIGHT WATCH

and maids affect, she went to the door and stood a considerable time, looking intently over toward the now grazing cattle, with an occasional glance at the teamster, as he prepared his bed for the night.

At length he retired under his tarpaulin, and I, too, expressed a wish to be shown my room. It was one of a row of small bed-chambers built in a style frequently to be met with in country public houses, viz., weatherboard, with iron roof, and almost detached from the main building. Each room was provided with a door of its own that opened into the yard—a rather unpleasant arrangement, especially during wet weather, when you require an umbrella to reach the dining-room, but one which exactly suited my plans at that moment.

My room was the very last of the row, and it was within a few feet of the stable that lay between me and the road where the teamster was camped. No sooner had I gained it than I took an opportunity, in the now gathering darkness, of passing out again, locking the door, putting the key in my pocket, and entering the stable, where Vino and another horse were contentedly munching their feed. In the stable was an aperture constructed, as is usual, for throwing out the manure, and this opening was almost close to the dray in which I was interested.

Placing myself in as easy a position as I could, I commenced a watch, for what I should have been puzzled to tell. I was certainly determined to watch the bullock driver; but what I expected to discover was, at that time, as much a mystery to me as what I *did* discover is to you at the moment.

The darkness, as I have said, was gathering; indeed, it had gathered and now there was nothing but a host of clear, bright stars to illuminate it, but not a cloud in the whole magnificent firmament. I waited there quietly until every sound of life had died out of the hotel, and every light was extinguished, and my patience was beginning to be almost exhausted when a rustle of the tarpaulin attracted my quick ear. In the stable's obscurity I could perceive the teamster cautiously emerge from his lair and peer carefully around before he raised himself to his full height from under the dray. Once satisfied, however, that everything was quiet, he started off quickly in the direction of the bush, and I, bounding through the opening of the stable, was on his track as rapidly.

It might have been his bullocks he was looking after for all I knew, for he was proceeding directly toward the sound of their tinkling bells; but if so, why all that caution as he left the dray, and why his anxiety to stay under the shadow of every tree and bush he met? It was to solve that question that I followed his example and kept as much in the shadow as I could; and it was fortunate that I did so, for the man's

THE MIDNIGHT WATCH

haste did not prevent him from stopping occasionally and casting a quick glance behind him, although, strange to say, be seemed to hesitate more as he *neared* the forest than he had done as he left his dray.

It was but a few moments ere he reached the darker bush, and there he paused, out of breath, as I could hear him panting as I stood, within fifty feet of him, behind a huge trunk of some tree, the genus of which I did not trouble myself to note. As he stood there, irresolutely it seemed to me, I was glad to perceive that the moon had arisen, and was beginning to pour long slant rays of brightness through the branches that lay like lances of silver upon the shaded grass, and made the darkness of the bush less obscure.

Slowly, at the lapse of a few minutes, he went on, cautiously creeping and, as it appeared to me, starting at every crackle of a stick under his foot, or every rustle of a branch that he disturbed as he passed.

I followed him as carefully, and once, as I was obliged to hide hurriedly behind a bush as the teamster suddenly stopped, I fancied I saw another shadowy form stop likewise, and likewise hide behind the trunk of a tree at the other side of the man I followed. This rather startled me, and I felt to see that my revolvers were all right, but a moment served to convince me that it must have been all fancy, or the shadow of some waving branch that the night breeze had moved.

The teamster moved onward again, and in a few more steps reached a small open glade in the bush, where the trees were farther apart, and the moonlight, penetrating through the more open distance, lay brilliantly upon a small clear space, near which he stopped suddenly. I was not more than ten yards from him now, but remained in the dim shade of some underwood, while he stood directly in the slant rays of the moon, and I could see every feature of his face, that looked white and wan as that of a ghost in the weird light, contrasted as it was by deep shadows of overhanging heavy dark branches.

He stood like one fearful, staring directly before him; and directly before him lay a fallen tree that seemed to have lain there for years. The patches of grass looked white, like snow, in the moonlight, and so did parts of the fallen log; but directly before the man a broad spot seemed to have been burned, and the fire had blackened and scorched the centre portion of the log, so that it contrasted vividly with the two extremities and with the surrounding lighted grass spots.

I had but barely time to notice these facts, and to wonder what interest they possessed for this man, when he retreated backward as if in fear and fell, rather than leaned, against the rough trunk of an ironbark that must have been anything but comfortable as a support, and there he stopped, with an expression upon his face that I shall never forget,

69

THE MIDNIGHT WATCH

and which the momentarily increasing moonlight rendered almost as visible to me as if it were day. Hie face, that had seemed so expressionless as I first remarked it, was full of terror; every muscle was rigid, and his distended eyes turned in every direction alternately, as if in dreadful expectation. From my first glimpse of that face in the lonely bush I was as sure of the correctness of Vino's instinctive suspicion as if I had seen the crime the man had committed, and if I had been asked to name the crime, I should have answered—'Murder.'

Murder! and where? Was it here on this spot, where the man shook like a leaf, and wiped the sweat from his forehead with a hand that trembled so that it would scarcely hold the handkerchief? Had he come, drawn by that strange fatality that makes guilt hover round the very spot it ought to avoid, until the avenger's hand is stretched forth, and justice is at length appeased?

But in the middle of such thoughts as these I arrested myself angrily.

'You are a fool,' I mentally apostrophised myself; 'a fool, and a detective! Can't a man go into the bush for any purpose but to commit a murder? Suppose he has a "plant" here? Nothing more likely, and everyone knows it isn't safe to carry money about the country nowadays; his own hard earnings, perhaps, and here you are dogging his steps without any cause whatever, save the sniff of a horse!'

This reasoning did not satisfy me, however; I am afraid I must confess that I *wanted* to find this man out a criminal—that I would have been disappointed to see him go and dig up a chamois bag with a few coins of gold in it, and that I would have much preferred clapping a pair of steel bracelets upon his wrists to seeing him go happily on his harmless way, driving his patient cattle, and smoking his short, black pipe to keep him company upon a lonely bush track. I am afraid I must confess that it was so; it is the force of habit, you see, and I do believe I was born to be a detective, it is so entirely my 'vocation.'

As I was thus arguing with and against myself, the teamster seemed to make a strong effort, and raised himself from his leaning position to his feet. Pressing his hat firmly down upon his head, he strode determinedly to within a few feet of my hiding-place, and kneeling down upon the ground began to rapidly remove the soil with his knife, or some small implement he had brought for the purpose. As he did so, a rustle behind me caused me to look hurriedly around, and again I distinctly saw that dark shadow I had fancied before; but this time I kept my eye on it, and distinctly saw it flit past me and creep cautiously to within ten feet or so of the busy teamster, and there, behind a bush, it rested, and leaned eagerly over to watch the man's movements, as if life and death depended upon sight and silence.

THE MIDNIGHT WATCH

I will confess to you that at this moment I was so entirely paralysed with astonishment that, if there had been occasion for sudden action, I could not have used it. The figure that I had watched, and fancied was a creation of my own imagination, now distinctly showed itself to be a female in dark attire, and in the white, anxious face that leaned over to watch the teamster who rooted and scraped out the mould so hurriedly, I recognised the barmaid at the Wallaby.

In the face of all creation what was *she* doing here? What connection was there between this man, who evidently knew nothing of her, and this woman, who left her room to steal into the fearful dark bush to watch a man who was an utter stranger to her?

It was all dark to me, and I was glad when the bullock-driver quickly gathered something out of the hole, and throwing, or rather pushing, the mould in again with his feet, hastily covered up all traces of it, and prepared to depart.

It seemed to me to be a small parcel tied in a bit of calico that he carefully stowed in his shirt, but I was not near enough to notice distinctly, and my attention was distracted by the woman, who still remained leaning over and watching, and so close that I almost fancied I could hear her breathing, although I was careful to keep closely hidden in the thicket I occupied.

Much more rapidly than he had entered it, and with his hand firmly grasping the treasure hidden in his breast, the man left the bush, closely followed by the woman, who flitted from shadow to shadow like a spirit. In the wake of both, I myself proceeded cautiously, much more occupied now, however, with the movements of the singular barmaid than I was with those of the teamster; him I was sure of, he was not at all likely to run away and leave his bullocks and dray behind him; and I was at least certain of knowing when he left; with her it was different. With no clue to the conduct of the man, I was determined to have an explanation of her own that very night, nothing doubting but there was some strange mystery attaching to it which it would be to my advantage to know.

When he had reached the edge of the more dense wood, my man emerged into the open grassy plain and made straight for his cattle, which were scattered at a little distance, grazing in the bright moonlight and ringing their bells with every mouthful they cropped. Quite certain that, his great object, whatever it was, accomplished, he would return to his camp under the dray, I paid no further attention to him but followed the woman, who stood a moment in the shade and looked wistfully after him. Then she quickly skirted the bush until she reached the nearest point of the inn, when she ran with the speed of terror

71

THE MIDNIGHT WATCH

across the short open distance, and disappeared behind the house.

I followed more cautiously; but, as the driver was out of sight, I lost no time in gaining the yard into which my bedroom door opened; there, in the shade of the wall, I stood, and listened and watched for some sign of the woman gaining an entrance to the main building. I did not know in what portion of the premises she slept, or I should have devoted my attention to that particular quarter, but I was like a watch-dog, all eyes and ears.

In a few seconds the darkly clad figure I was in search of emerged from around the very abutting building against which I leaned, and so close to me that before she had time to take one step after I had first caught the moving form, I had a firm grip of her wrist and stopped her.

'Don't be frightened,' I said; 'I am an officer in the detective force, and I want to have a few words with you.'

She did not scream or speak; she was not a timid woman, I knew, else she would not have dared that midnight watch, alone in the bush; that there was some still more powerful feeling than mere animal courage at work in her breast, to make her keep silence, I had no doubt. When I arrested her arm so suddenly, she did not, as I have said, speak, but she shook in every limb like one who had been stricken with ague.

'You need not be afraid,' I repeated quietly, 'there is nothing wrong, only I want some information from you. Go in there,' and as I spoke I opened the door of my room and pushed her gently in. Even then she did not speak; and when I had locked the door, and, as there was no window, lighted the candle, I saw her leaning against the wall, with a face white with terror, and her hands hanging by her side helplessly.

'Sit down,' I whispered, placing a chair for her. 'Is there anyone in the next room?'

'No,' she answered; 'there is no one outside the big house but yourself.'

'Well, now,' I continued, calmly but firmly, 'I want to know what you have been watching that bullock-driver in the bush for?'

'Are *you* watching him?' she whisperingly questioned. 'Do you know anything?—oh, tell me, for mercy sake!'

'It would not do for me to tell everyone my business, you know,' I replied; 'but I tell you I am a detective, and I followed you both to-night, and now I want to know for what reason you watch that man, who seems to be a stranger to you? *Is* he a stranger to you?' I added, as she hesitated and wrung her hands.

'I never saw him in my life before.'

'Explain then—you must do so, mind.'

'If you are a detective,' she whispered, suddenly lifting up her face and looking keenly into mine, 'you will remember James Parsons.'

'James Parsons? A man who disappeared about two years ago, and was supposed to be murdered?'

She nodded.

'He left home with a team of bullocks,' I went on, 'and a heavy purse, to bring a load from F——, and he never returned?'

Again the woman nodded.

'Why, 'twas about two miles from this very house,' I continued, light all at once breaking in upon my bewildered brain, 'that we lost all trace of him. Some one had met him upon the road, and after that he was never more heard of.'

I was looking keenly and anxiously at the woman as I spoke these words rapidly; when concluded, she said faintly, 'I was James Parsons' wife.'

If I had not been accustomed to control all outward semblance of feeling, I should certainly have uttered an exclamation at this moment. It was as if the corner of a mysterious curtain had been lifted, and I was beginning to see a dim but partially illuminated vista beyond, which included a lonely bush track, upon which jogged along a team of bullocks driven by James Parsons, and terminated in that scorched and blackened log near which I had so lately seen the strangely moved teamster digging up some hidden thing.

'I was James Parsons' wife; and this evening when that man came in the door I knew my husband's bullocks. I could swear to every one of them. We reared them ourselves, and I am as sure as I stand here that every one of them this moment would eat from my hand.'

I was silent, as much from admiration of this poor woman's noble courage in the attempt to discover her husband's murderer as from any other feeling, and she went on calmly.

'When the police gave up all hopes of finding James, or any trace of him, I came and took a situation here, in hopes that some day I might see or hear something of the man that killed him! — killed, I'm sure he was; and I'm sure that the man I followed to-night did it, and did it on the very spot where the hand of God seemed to strike him to-night and freeze up his marrow with fear.'

'Well, give yourself no further anxiety, my poor girl,' I said, 'I will dog this man's steps like a shadow, until I prove his guilt, if he is guilty. Meanwhile, say not one word about the events of this night, and as soon as I gain any information I shall see you again.'

'Mind,' she said emphatically, as I opened the door to let her out, 'if you play me false in this, I will find this man out though he died! Now that I have seen the hand that spilled my poor Jim's warm blood, I will

THE MIDNIGHT WATCH

track him until I die myself, or he is hanged!' and she softly closed the door and went away.

I sat down upon the edge of the bed to think; and you will, perhaps, laugh at me when I say that my first thought was a delight in the proved sagacity of my faithful animal, Vino. Well, you may laugh if you like, but it has never deceived me yet, and never will; I feel as sure of it as I do that heaven's air is around me at this moment.

Satisfied that all was well with the teamster, as I could hear the tinkle, tinkle of the cattle-bells still, I laid down in my clothes to snatch a few hours of as sound a sleep as I ever enjoyed. We are used to it, you see; and the certainty that I had fairly got hold of the right end of a clue that would give me credit with my superiors, caused me to sleep well. The sun was but barely up, however, when I arose and hastened to take a look at things outside.

The bar was open, and the woman, as quiet-seeming as ever, was attending to her various arrangements in it. The teamster was busily yoking up his cattle, with the same quiet and listless air I had observed the night before; and, hastily giving the bar-woman a hint to let me have breakfast immediately, I went to look after Vino.

While I was eating my breakfast, I heard the loud cracking of the driver's whip, and the rumbling of the rough conveyance convinced me that he was off. This, however, gave me no concern, as it was far from my intention to let him perceive that I was about to return by almost the same track I had arrived by the previous evening. I was most anxious, of course, to avoid awakening his suspicions.

Half an hour saw Vino and myself upon the road, upon which, however, I proceeded scarcely half a mile when I diverged into the bush, and rode leisurely along, keeping within an easy distance of the road so as to be able at any moment to near my friend the driver. I could hear the crack of the whip in the distance, and even the rattle of the wheels; and satisfied that he was still proceeding, I proceeded also.

It seemed a long forenoon to me, going at the slow pace of the cattle, but everything has an end, and at last the hour of noon arrived, and from the vicinity of the only water within miles, I felt sure that my man would stop soon.

I was right. As I neared the road cautiously I saw that he had selected a shady spot near a waterhole, and was about unyoking his cattle once more. Alighting, I left Vino to graze quietly. She was too well trained an animal to go far away, and then I stole cautiously nearer and seated myself under a close bush to resume my watch. I was anxious about that little parcel he had exhumed, and fearful that he might make a fire and destroy it.

THE MIDNIGHT WATCH

He made no fire, however. As soon as his cattle were turned out he commenced to examine one of his yokes, and a most unusual step it was for a carter, who had two good hours' spell before him, to set to work mending a yoke before he had made the slightest preparation for his noon-day meal. That, however, was what he appeared to be doing, and he chose an old stout log that lay upon the bank of the creek, and leaning the yoke across it, went down on his knees and commenced his repairing.

That was how it looked to me, I say, for I was at some little distance, you know; but his occasional fearful looks around him aroused my suspicions, and I kept a closer eye upon the movements of his body.

Mending the yoke? Bah! he was digging a hole under the log, and simply using the yoke as a screen in case of watch.

'Ah, my man!' said I to myself, 'I have you now; you are simply *re-planting* your parcel, and with a bad conscience, too, or you would not use so much caution.'

A few moments after, and his task was ended, his fast broken upon some cold provisions, and he was lying in the shade, to all appearance fast asleep. I followed his example in that matter at least, after having consulted a pocket pistol and some sandwiches with which I had provided myself at the Wallaby.

The first crack of the teamster's whip aroused me, and I watched his departure with impatience. It appeared an hour ere he had fairly disappeared, and I was at liberty to pounce upon his 'plant,' and to unearth it. I found some difficulty in doing so, but at length I had in my hands the parcel which was so apparently valuable to the bullock-driver. It was tied up with strong cord in a piece of tarpaulin, and had it been a measure of Aladdin's jewels, my fingers could scarcely have trembled more as I undid it.

There was little to reward me, you might have supposed, but I was fully satisfied. An old leather bag, containing some notes to the value of twenty pounds (I remembered these very notes being missing, and known to have been in the possession of James Parsons when he so unaccountably disappeared, and I had the numbers of them in my notebook at that very moment), and a crooked sixpence, which had also been described. That was absolutely all of value the parcel contained, as two or three scraps of belt, shrivelled and burnt, two buckles as of braces, a few brass buttons sadly discoloured, and a few charred and partially destroyed *bones* might seem valueless to anyone, but they were everything to me, and they were *life itself* to the wretched man who had tried to hide them, to his own destruction.

Carefully wrapping them up, and once more securing Vino, I

placed the precious find in my valise, and mounting, rode rapidly along the road after the bullock-team. I had not much to hide now, as I was quite justified in arresting this man with such a strong chain of circumstantial evidence against him. I thought it as well to wait, however, until we reached a house of accommodation not more than three miles off, which I knew we must pass, as a desperate man in the lonely bush had a chance it were as well not to give him.

I soon overtook the dray, and I thought the driver looked rather uneasy as he recognised me.

'You're luckier than myself, mate,' I cried, as I rode up; 'I've been riding in the bush all day lost. I ought to be ashamed to tell it, too, after being in the colony so long.'

'There's a good many tracks hereabouts,' he answered. 'You've taken the wrong one, I guess.'

'Yes, I took the wrong road after leaving the Wallaby, and then trying to cut across the bush I lost myself. If it hadn't been for the sound of your whip I never should have pulled myself up. Are we near any public house?'

'Yes, the Accommodation Inn is only a couple of miles on.'

'Well, I'll go on then; I'm regularly tired. Call as you're passing, mate, and I'll shout.'[2]

So we parted, and as I left I saw a feeling of relief steal over the man's face. Had there been any other road, I should have feared his trying to avoid me; but there was not, so I waited patiently in the bar of the inn until I heard the dray passing, and then I went to the door and called him in.

There was no one in the bar but a man who served; and who supplied the driver and myself with our chosen drinks. I suffered him to swallow his in peace. Poor wretch, I knew he would require all the fortitude it would give him to enable him to undergo the terrible ordeal before him. But no sooner had he finished than the handcuffs were locked upon the hand that placed the glass on the counter, and in another second the other was clasped beside it.

He turned upon me such a look of speechless terror as I shall never forget, and once more I saw before me the same agonised face of the night before during the midnight watch in the moonlit forest.

'I arrest you for the murder of James Parsons,' I said, and he staggered back against the wall, and then fell heavily to the ground.

I assisted him to rise, for he was faint and weak, and the handcuffs prevented him from helping himself. But when he had been seated on a form where he could support himself against the counter, his pale, haggard face grew wild with excitement, and I feared he was going mad.

THE MIDNIGHT WATCH

'Thank God, it's over!' he said. 'It's better to be hung at once than live such a terrible life. I did it; yes, I did it! I killed him, and burned his body.'

'Take care,' I remonstrated; 'every word you say now will be used against you.'

'I want them to be used against me,' he said, loudly; 'I want to relieve myself and die. I met Parsons about two miles above the Wallaby; I was on tramp with my swag, and he gave me a lift. I found out he had money, and coaxed him into the bush, gammoning I knew a fine waterhole to camp at for the night. We made a fire near a log, and while he was putting his billy over it, I struck him with the axe—his *own* axe—right on the back of the head, and he fell into the fire. I piled branches and wood on, half the night, until he was burned to cinders, and then, when the fire died out, I raked up every bit of strap, and button, and *bone* I could find, so that no one could find any trace. I put these into a bit of rag and planted them, but until last night I never had a chance to take them from the spot. Oh, heavens above! it's a fearful thing to be a murderer! I should have had to drag these bones over the world with me; fire or water would never have hidden them! You will find them planted at—'

'They are here,' I replied, laying the parcel before him as he spoke.

He *glared* at it for a second, shuddered as if a keen, cold wind pierced his bones, then he lifted up his manacled hands as if to seek for the hot blood he had spilled and, staring wildly at them for a second, fell back—dead!

I have been in many terrible scenes during my colonial experience of crime, but, among them all, that one often starts vividly into remembrance. The bush inn, with the open door showing the green, beautiful plain, with its dotting trees, the quiet bullocks lashing the flies off lazily on the road, and the dead man, with staring eyes and fettered hands, fallen against the wall, with that terrible look of unspoken agony stiffening into his face!

First published in the *Australian Journal*, 6 April 1867, under the byline 'W.W.'

NOTES

1 *nobbler*: a serving of beer or spirits.
2 *I'll shout*: I'll buy you a drink.

LOST IN TOWN

The following events occurred but a few years ago, and although I am of course obliged to alter names, I have no doubt that many of my readers will remember the circumstances, as reported in the papers of the day.

I was strolling down one of our back streets one day, when I was off duty, and observed a man looking from one side to the other in a helpless sort of way that attracted my attention. There were but few people about, and as the man's eyes rested on me, he hesitated a moment, and then crossed over and addressed me.

But before I go any farther, I had better describe him to you. He was a middle-sized man, about thirty-five years of age, with dark hair and whiskers, and an honest-looking face that had evidently become intimately acquainted with the sun and wind. He was dressed in new moleskins, new tweed coat and vest, and wore a light felt hat on his head.

'You look like an honest chap,' he said awkwardly, 'and I don't think you'd be above giving a poor fellow some advice in one of the most miserable positions he was ever in.'

'You're right there, mate,' I replied, 'what is the matter?'

'Well, it's rather a long story to begin at the beginning; but to cut it short, I've lost my mate,[1] and I've lost his money, and I'm frightened he has met with foul play. We only came to town yesterday, and I haven't been in Melbourne for twelve years, so I'm like a fool in it.'

'Come with me,' I said, turning and leading him into a public house where I was well known, 'you've happened to hit on the right man for your purpose. I'm a detective, and if you think anything has happened to your mate, it's only my duty to help you.'

Well, when we were seated in a private room, and my new acquaintance had sufficiently collected himself, this is the story he told me:—

'My name is Matthew Warren, and I have been knocking about from station to diggings ever since I came to the colony fifteen years ago. At Pleasant Creek, twelve months ago, I fell in with Tom Mason, and we have worked together as mates ever since. We were pretty lucky, so it was easy for Tom to persuade me to come to town with him, when he was coming down for the missis. I never knew a man so fond of a woman as Tom was of his wife; he seemed to live on her letters, though she didn't write half as often to him as he did to her.

LOST IN TOWN

They had been married only two years, and he had left her to go to the diggings.

'Well, we came down, as I told you; and he took me up one of these narrow streets, and into a small house in some back way or other; but as we had had a good deal to drink, I can't remember the place well enough to find it again. I saw the wife, and was awfully disappointed, I remember, as Tom had given me such glowing accounts of her; and I didn't think either that there was any necessity for such a number of friends as she seemed to gather in to welcome him.

'I've always been a cautious sort of chap, and when I saw so much drink going, and so many strangers about, I got a chance, and persuaded Tom to give me his money to take care of. He gave me four ten-pound notes, and I went out for a stroll, as I gammoned, to see about some way of planting them.

'Well, I'll tell you what I did. I walked on a good bit, straight along one street as I thought, and I went into a large and very first-class hotel, I took it to be. Calling for the landlord there, I told him all about the affair, and asked him to keep the money for me. He agreed at once, and I gave him eight tens, four of my own and four of Tom's. There's no doubt the man acted fair and square, for he wouldn't touch the money till he called two gentlemen as witnesses, and they signed the receipt he gave me.'

'But you have that receipt?' I asked, at this stage of the man's story.

'That's the worst of it — I haven't. I went knocking about after that, with an easy mind, knowing I hadn't much money on me. At first, I was trying to find the way back to Tom; but after I called into two or three publics I got too drunk to care for anything. I had a sleep in some bar or other, and when I wakened up and found I had lost the receipt, I didn't care so much for that as that I didn't know where to look for my mate; but just as I was having a livener at the bar, in comes one of the men I had seen at Tom's wife's place, and just as it was getting dark he took me back there.

'Now I've told you nearly all I can swear to, for what happened after is more like a dream to me. We had lots more drink, but before I fell asleep Tom and a man that seemed quite at home there had a devil of a row. It was all about the wife, as I fancied, and some of the most awful language was used that I ever heard in my life. I can tell you no more; only that this morning I found myself lying in a sort of lane, where there were nothing but dead walls on each side of me. I feel as if I'd got some rough usage, that's all.'

'But what grounds have you for supposing that anything may be wrong with your mate, since you left him with his wife?' I questioned.

'Well, I'm not a fool altogether; for one thing, I have lived long enough in the world to know that the lot I was among last night were all off the square. The men were the lowest you can imagine, the women were worse. But I have something else to frighten me—look at that!'

As Warren spoke, he lifted up his coat and exposed a most suggestive mark on the band of his white trousers; it was a distinct impress of bloody fingers—a grip, as though some one had seized him by the belt to drag him off or from something.

'I saw that when I woke up, in the lane, this morning, and was trying to shake the dust from myself. I fancy they have dragged or carried me outside, after some bloody work had been done, and I tell you I tremble for poor Tom.'

'Bah!' I said; 'they may have had a sort of free fight among themselves, and a blow on the nose would make show enough to mark half a dozen pairs of trousers.'

'And what was *I* turned out for? Does it look straightforward?'

No, that it certainly did not. I was obliged to make that reply to myself, whatever I might say to the anxious man. But something must be done, and so many things offered that I was at a loss which to do first.

The money was my least anxiety, for Warren distinctly recollected the landlord to whom he entrusted it saying that he would deliver it to no person but himself, in case someone might illegally obtain possession of the receipt. An advertisement in the *Argus* would doubtless arrange all that; and as we had some hours to spare, I proposed taking the man at once to the office to report the affair.

With the intention of doing so, we went down Swanston-street, and had got near the Globe, when suddenly my companion pulled me by the sleeve with the exclamation,

'By George! that's the place where I left the money!'

You may be sure I was glad that something had turned up connected with the affair at all, and in a few moments we were in a private room, and waiting the landlord's appearance.

Warren was not wrong, the landlord recognised him at once.

'Ah, you've come yourself,' he said, 'that's all right; but as I said I should not give up the money to anyone but yourself, I would not. Your mate seemed to think it very hard that he couldn't get his own money.'

'My mate!' cried Warren.

'Yes, he presented my receipt last night, and said you were gone off on the spree somewhere; but I was determined—and there is the money,'—and the landlord laid eight ten-pound notes on the table.

'I only want your receipt, you know, and the thing is done.'

'Tell us what sort of fellow this mate was, if you please, Mr. F.,' I requested.

'I am in a position to do so, for under the circumstances I thought it only prudent to remark him particularly. He was a short, dark man, with greyish whiskers and hair, wore dark tweed trousers, and a black cut-away coat.'

'Why, that's no more like Mason than the man in the moon!' interrupted my companion. 'Mason is tall and fair, and dressed exactly as I am.'

About an hour after that, you might have seen your humble servant talking to a rakish-looking fellow dressed in a light tweed suit of a fashionable cut, and with a respectable-looking Albert gold chain disappearing into the watch-pocket of his vest. His hat was a stylish-looking felt, his boots of the nattiest elastic-sided—in short, I flatter myself that he was well got up, for it was I, Detective Sinclair, who got him up. The individual was Matthew Warren, and I am certain that even his mate, poor Mason, could he have seen him, would not have known him.

'Now, Warren, you know what you have to do. Our object is to find any one of the men or women you saw at that house. We are convinced they were a bad lot, and that we shall find them among bad people. Your cue is to feign the bushman down for a spree; you have a few notes in your pocket, flash them about *here*, and you will soon have a crew around you. I shall shepherd you like your shadow, mind, and you know how to call me. Now go, and remember that you are entrusted with more than your own life—your mate is in question. Throw every drop of drink away that you can.'

'If they make me drunk this day, may God forsake me!' he said, and turned round the corner to leave me alone.

You may be sure I didn't stand there long. I darted across the street, so as to keep him in view; but if one of you, my readers for seven years, were to have seen me, even you would not have recognised your friend the pseudo-'W. W.' In short, I had donned Warren's attire, and looked the digger to a nicety.

I had left Warren at the corner of Little Bourke-street, and I watched him as he sauntered along Swanston-street, as a man might saunter who had nothing to do but amuse himself. I could not have done it better myself, and I felt proud of my neophyte.

All at once I saw him turn into a public house—how expressive is that title!—a house that I knew to be one of the lowest in town, and, after a little, I also slouched over with the air of a man who had had too much to drink, and called for a glass of brandy at the bar.

LOST IN TOWN

Warren was standing, not far from me, talking to a man that I recognised at once, from his description, to be the one who had taken him back to his mate on the previous night.

'This, then,' I said to myself, 'is the place where he fell asleep and where doubtless they robbed him of the receipt.'

I don't suppose it is necessary for me to say that I knew the man whom Warren was talking to, in other ways than from his description. As soon as I saw him, I saw a noted thief, burglar, and fence[2] of the lowest order, if one dare to say that there are degrees in crime. His name, or his alias, was 'Ben Harris,' and he really was a Jew.[3]

'I want to see a little life,' was what I heard Warren saying, as I drank my 'P.B.'[4] and asked for matches. 'It's all very well for you who have been in town, lord knows how long, to preach to a fellow. But I've been up country twelve years, and I'm —blessed if I don't see a little life now.'

The words were scarcely out of his mouth when the man he addressed observed me. He started—turned white as death—tossed off the drink Warren had ordered and came to my side.

'I want to speak to you,' he whispered hoarsely.

'All right,' I said, 'speak away, there's no one hindering you.'

'Come outside. Good God, it's a case of life and death.'

'A case of brandy,' I said irreverently, 'but come on, I'm half-tight, and nothing will stop me.'

'You're that man's mate,' he whispered, as we got outside the door into the street. 'You know who I mean, Tom Mason?'

'I know nothing but that you're a cowardly lot. *I'll* never go near one of you again. A pretty thing to do with a mate indeed. Spend his money, and turn him out to sleep in the lane. *I'll* never go near one of you again. What'll you have to drink?'

'Oh, for Heaven's sake, man, try and be sober! Why, your mate's dead! Shake yourself!' and he shook me incontinently. 'Shake yourself together, and listen to me! Your mate's murdered as sure as I'm a living man!'

I couldn't act any more. It was a matter of impossibility. Before the man could expect that I had shaken myself together, the handcuffs were on his wrists, and he was staring at me in the imbecile manner of one who has been taken by surprise, and has not been as yet able to collect his senses sufficiently to realize his position.

'Now Ben Harris, you know me,' I said, 'and your only hope of escape is not to hint, but to tell me all you know about this Tom Mason business.'

'Take these off,' he pleaded, 'and I'll take you there.'

LOST IN TOWN

'All right,' I said, 'but you know shuffling[5] is useless. I can have you safe enough in ten minutes, and you know it. Now lead the way.'

Harris went up Little Bourke-street. He turned down a right of way that I recognised at once, from the description of Warren. He opened a little gate in a dilapidated fence, and pushed in the door of a brick cottage. At the threshold he paused and listened, and then he beckoned me, and I entered.

A narrow passage, and at the left hand a door. Harris entered that door, and I followed him. It would not be hard to take an inventory of the articles in that room. There was an empty gin-case overturned on the floor, seven or eight bottles standing on the mantel-shelf, an empty fire-place with a litter of matches burned out on the floor, and that was positively all.

Harris passed on and opened a door leading into a room at the back. He seemed afraid to enter, and paused with his hand on the latch, and looked back at me.

'What ails you?' I asked.

'I don't know,' he said, 'but I know there was murder committed here somewhere, last night. I didn't see it, mind you, for I was drunk, but I saw Nell Parsons this morning, and I *know* there was something wrong.'

'Nell Parsons!' I cried, 'was *she* Mason's wife?'

'Yes. She's been leading him on a string for the last two years.'

'God help him,' I thought to myself, knowing as I did, that Nell Parsons was one of the lowest, most unscrupulous, and notorious women about town. 'Open the door, man,' I said aloud, 'and let us see the worst.'

The worst was a room, as nearly empty as the one we had already passed through. There was absolutely nothing in it but a wretched old dirty mattress, and two or three wretched dirty old coverings upon it. There was no sign of disturbance of any kind, and a door that apparently led to the back was wide open.

'Ben, your own bad conscience has been troubling you,' I said, 'there's nothing here that looks suspicious.'

'If everything had been all right, they would have been all in bed at this time of day,' the man said, and as he spoke he wiped off the perspiration from his face with the sleeve of his coat.

Even as he was speaking, there was a sound at the gate as of some one entering, and Ben seized me by the sleeve and drew me into a sort of enclosure under the stairs. To this enclosure there was a door, which Ben drew after him and fastened. It did not need his warning grip to make me almost hold my breath to ensure silence; but I confess to

84

feeling a great disappointment at seeing, through a chink in the wood-work, my friend Warren enter the room, and look curiously around him. Still I knew that he had some object, connected with our business, in coming, and I felt sure of it when I saw that he had as companion one of the very women I knew as companions of Nell Parsons.

'Why, this is a funny sort of crib,' said Warren, taking the cigar from his mouth and chucking it into the fire-place. 'Surely this is not where you put up!'

'No, but I was sure of finding Nell here. I wonder where she's gone,' and the girl opened the door and called 'Nell! Nell!' several times before she seemed to be assured that the house was empty.

'Well, never mind,' she said at last, 'she's sure to be here before long. I'll go for something to drink.'

I've been in a queer lot of places before now, but I don't think I ever felt so entirely strange as I did sitting in that hole under the stairs, under such circumstances. Of course, you know I had removed the handcuffs from my companion, and I was not afraid, knowing as I did that Warren was so near; but I felt stifling, somehow, and I couldn't account for it, as plenty of air penetrated the place between the boards, even from the open yard.

When the girl went for the drink I called to Warren, who came immediately.

'I knew you were here somewhere,' he said, 'for I followed you to the corner, but this woman picked me up.'

'Manage to bring us something to eat and drink,' was my reply, 'for I've a mate here, and don't go out of call, that's all I want.' And that was all I had an opportunity of saying, before the woman's foot was heard at the door.

I want you to pass over a few hours, and to fancy me still in my hid-ing-place, with Ben Harris within reach of my arm. The man was fairly overcome with fatigue and anxiety, yet I dared not let him sleep, in case some somnambulistic noises should betray us. There was neither sound or light in the house, it being some hours after sundown, and there we waited for we scarcely knew what, waited in silence and in darkness.

At last came the faintest imaginable sound, a sound that I recog-nised as the creaking of the gate, cautiously opened. So long was it before another sound followed, that I thought I must have been mis-taken, when Ben's hand gripped my arm, and I heard a match struck in the very same apartment our lair looked into. I need scarcely repeat that the apartment I allude to was the front one, containing simply the empty gin-case, and the mantel shelf full of empty bottles.

As the lucifer slowly kindled, it lighted up the anxious face of a young woman. She was plainly dressed in a dark dress and small black hat in the sailors' style; but even had I not known the face, it would have been impossible for me not to guess to what class the woman belonged; but I did know it, you see; it was the face of Nell Parsons, who, I need scarcely remind you, was identical with the unfaithful wife of the lost digger, Tom Mason.

With the match, the woman kindled a candle she held in her hand, and then, lifting the light above her head, she peered around every corner of the room. I might have fancied I saw her shuddering, but I am certain I saw her draw a bottle from her dress and lift it to her lips in a long draught. Then she sat down and put the candle in a bottle behind her—sat down on the gin-case, with her face towards us, and with her hands clasped on her lap, and waited for, I could not guess what, with such patience as I have often since wondered at.

And often since I have wondered, and congratulated myself at being the unseen and unsuspected witness of that strangely rigid face, during those memorable hours. For whole moments not a change could be seen in a feature, save those made by the flickering shadows of the draught-blown candle, as it burned on in the corner behind her; and then all at once would come a spasm, as it were, that made the young but dissipated face look hideous, until it was once again hidden by the bottle, out of which the wretched being seemed to borrow strength and endurance.

And then came a cautious step and a cautious tap at the window. The woman got up and opened the door. A man entered and, with a hurried look around him, whispered, 'What a cursed fool you are to leave the light burning this a-way.'

'Maybe you'd like to stop here in the dark,' she said, sneeringly. 'You can now, if you like, in company. Shall I blow it out?'

'No, curse you! Have you got anything to drink?'

'Not a drop, but I'll go for some if you like.'

'No you won't. *I'll* go.'

'Ha-ha,' she laughed wildly. 'You *daren't* stop! Go, then: but where's your cash?'

'In your pocket; hand it out.'

'No I don't, I want all the money I can get for a wake.'

'Look here, woman; don't try any of that game on me! It's as easy to kill a dozen as one, by —— I'll murder you'; and he seized and shook the woman, so that she was incapable of reply for a moment.

Only for a moment, however; the next, her low hissing tones were as audible as if she had shrieked out every word.

'Murder me, would you! and do you think *I* care; only that it would be hateful to me to see your hateful face last in this world, I wish you *would* murder me! If it hadn't been for you, you wretch, if it hadn't been for you! Oh, Tom! Tom!'

Anything like the agony expressed in the woman's tones as she uttered that name, I should fail to describe to you, and they appeared to affect the man, for he spoke softly as he said,

'Look here, Nell! It's too late for you and I to quarrel, what's done can't be undone. Go for something to drink, like a good girl, and I *will* wait here until you come, we want something to give us heart for our work; you know it must be done, and then we'll be off.'

The woman turned to go as he wished, but ere she went, she looked around her at the bare walls, and at the empty fire-place. I fancied too, strangely, that she seemed to look cravingly at *me* as I watched her through the boards, and then she opened the door, and was gone.

I well knew the man she left behind her; he was known to the police as Flash Jack, a man who had been so often convicted as to have become almost a denizen of the gaol. He sat down on the same seat the woman had occupied, and he placed his back close up to the wall as though he was going to encounter an enemy who should not be able to attack him from behind.

I watched his face there until it grew white with terror, until great drops of sweat broke out on his forehead, and gathering strength as they went, rolled at last down into his beard. I saw the terrified eyes of the wretch that seemed to stare into mine, with a horror in them that I have many a time since dreamed of: and then I saw him start forward and shake his clenched fist towards me, as he shouted until the house rang.

'You can't come out, d—— you! You're not able: *I* settled you there! — you, don't be grinning at me, curse you!'

At this moment Harris's grip on my arm showed the man's agony of mind so clearly, that I was fearful he would cry out and discover all. Warren had managed to supply us with food and drink, as I had requested, and there was a bottle of brandy standing somewhere behind me in the hole we were in. With the intention of giving him a drop to keep up his courage, I put back my hand to feel for the bottle. If I were to stay now, and describe to you, or try to describe to you, my feelings at what followed, I should only waste my own time and yours, for you would never realize the one fiftieth part of them.

My hand was back as I have told you, but I was still keeping my eye on the movements of Flash Jack. Searching for the bottle then with one hand, while with the other I grasped Harris's shoulder to caution him, I felt under my fingers the rigid outline of a dead human face.

There are few of us so fortunate as to be unacquainted with the dread feel of death. Almost every one of us can remember with what shrinking we have encountered the dead hand or the dead lips that, in life, we would have given worlds to have held close to us forever.

But the touch of death has even a greater horror in it when it comes to one in so sudden and unexpected a manner as this came to me. I did not cry out, however, or do anything but pass my hand silently over the body of a man who was huddled up at the very far corner of the cellar under the stairs in which we were hiding.

Of course I had no doubt of it from the very beginning; it was the body of poor Mason I had laid my hand upon. Yes, there was the tweed coat, the new moleskins, the long thick beard that Warren had described; and he had doubtless been murdered by Flash Jack and his wretched wife, who had now come to dispose of the body.

My determination was taken at once. I seized the bottle and pushed it into Ben's hand, and then I dashed open the door of our hiding place and stood before the paralysed man like what must have seemed an incarnation of vengeance. He started to his feet, but they refused to support him, and in another moment he was sitting on the box, leaning against the wall, handcuffed, and at my mercy.

'Come out, and lend me a hand here, Ben,' I said then, and immediately Harris crawled out of his hiding-place, with a face almost as white as though he had seen the dreadful thing he had left behind him. As he appeared, the wretched murderer lifted his head, looked at him and shuddered, and then drawing himself as far back into the corner as he could, he stared at the terrible closet as though waiting for what it would next reveal. Evidently the man was suffering from an attack of delirium tremens, in addition to the awful accusations of his own conscience.

I at once dispatched Ben Harris for the nearest policeman, who soon made his appearance. The unhappy prisoner seemed too entirely helpless to attempt an escape; however we set the horrified Ben to keep a watch over him while we two removed the body of poor Mason from under the stairs; it was only prudent to do so, for there was a faint chance that there might still be a spark of life left.

But there was none. As we laid the body down upon the floor of the miserable room, it presented a most pitiable spectacle. In the cramped position in which it had stiffened, with the clotted blood on the fair hair, and dabbling the white rigid face, it was something truly awful to look on. We had laid it just in front of Harris, who stood between it and the prisoner, and I have often since reproved myself for a thoughtlessness that approached the refinement of cruelty, and produced such dreadful consequences.

As I have told you, Harris was standing between the murderer and his victim. When the dreadful object was laid gently down on the floor, Harris uttered a cry and stepped quickly back. Of course his movement removed the only impediment between the dead body and the wretched prisoner, his eyes fell upon it—with a shriek that rang in my ears for many a day, he bounded convulsively to his feet, stretched out his manacled hands as if to implore protection, and then fell forward on his face across the corpse, a dead man.

Talk of chapters of horrors! I never think of these circumstances that I have just related to you without recognising more than ever the truth that there are quite as terrible realities as fiction ever invented. It is very pleasant to read stories all about the rosy side of life, but we cannot be men and shut our eyes to the fact that there is a night side to nature[6] in more ways than one.

And now, as a wind up to this story, I must tell you what happened on Princes' bridge, about the very time of Flash Jack's death. The constable on duty there was pacing to and fro, as is the wont of constables on duty, when a female strolled quietly on to the bridge from townwards. She was plainly dressed, and wore a sailor hat. When she came near the policeman, she paused and looked over the parapet into the river. It was a bright starlight night, but there was no moon.

'You didn't notice anyone waiting about here, did you?' she asked, turning suddenly round to the constable.

'No,' he replied, 'who are you looking for?'

'My sweetheart of course,' she said with a laugh. 'I suppose you haven't heard of the terrible murder in town yet?'

'Murder! What murder?'

'Oh, there's been a terrible to do in Little Bourke-street. They were just finding the body as I left. A poor digger came down to take his wife home to Pleasant Creek, and she and her pal smashed him to death with an axe when he was too drunk to defend himself. A nice wife that, wasn't she? Hanging is too good for the likes of her. Well, I'm tired of waiting here. If any one should ask you if you saw Nell Parsons, tell them that she's gone to join Tom Mason below the boat-house, will you?' and the speaker crossed the bridge rapidly and descended the stairs that led down to the side of the river.

The policeman looked after her in some doubt, thinking the woman's brain was affected; but, bless you, a policeman sees so many strange things and persons, that by the time he got to the end of the bridge,

LOST IN TOWN

and returned on his beat, he had forgotten all about Nell Parsons, only to recall the name when the terrible events of the night became known to him.

A few days after, a loiterer on the Falls Bridge, looking over the crazy-looking wooden railing at the more crazy-looking timbering below, saw a something surged by the rushing water against the wooden pier under the bridge; that something had a sad white face, revealed ever and anon, as the swirling water covered or left it, and there was long black hair waving to and fro like tangled seaweed from some wave-worn rock. It was Nell Parsons; she had gone to meet her husband, Tom Mason.

I think I have finished. It was a very sad heart that Warren carried back to Pleasant Creek; but if he should happen to read these pages, I hope that Time's influence will have been sufficient to prevent his feeling very much at reading the old painful story.

First published in the *Australian Journal*, November 1872, as part of the *Detective's Album* serial, under the byline 'W.W.'

NOTES

1 *mate*: i.e., mining partner.
2 *fence*: someone who deals in stolen property.
3 *and he really was a Jew*: Fortune has no antisemitic intent here; she is remarking that a petty criminal who is Jewish has picked as an alias a name that is also typically Jewish.
4 *P.B.*: pale brandy (so-called because it has taken on a yellowish tint from the cask in which it was stored).
5 *shuffling*: trying to escape by means of trickery.
6 *there is a night side to nature*: perhaps a reference to Catherine Crowe's *The Night-side of Nature: Or, Ghosts and Ghost-Seers* (1848), a popular and influential work about supernatural phenomena.

THE DEAD MAN IN THE SCRUB

Some years ago, at the close of what had been a hot summer, two men who had worked unsuccessfully for some months on a diggings in the Loddon District determined to go and 'prospect' in a scrub some four or five miles off. It was a lonely and out of the way place, far from any road or settlement or whatever, and, as far as the mates knew, had never been penetrated by a human foot. In this opinion, however, a few miles tramp convinced them they had been mistaken; for, after succeeding in making their way through the tangled vegetation for about two miles they came upon a small spot of partially cleared ground, where there were evident traces of man's labour. Two or three shallow holes had been sunk, and at a small waterhole, not far off, the stuff had been evidently cradled. Looking around for some appearance of a home or pathway near this spot—for of course the man or men who had been working here must have had some place to live in; it was not likely workers would tramp that weary scrub twice in the day—they fancied that in one particular place the vegetation seemed to be less dense.

But, seeing no way toward that place, they made one slowly with the tomahawk; and after cutting and untangling hundreds of feet of the mallee vine, they came upon a little white tent, almost hidden in the very heart of the bushes. Here an awful scene awaited them; and if you have not heard something of the same sort yourself, I need not attempt to give you any idea of the sound made by millions of those horrible flies that collect around and revel in the decomposition of any animal life in Australia. Inside the tent, which was quite closed up, a continuous buzz, suggestive of innumerable myriads of flies, met the ears of the horrified mates, who were now quite certain that death, in some shape, inhabited this little white calico home in the mallee; indeed another of the senses already assured them that their fortitude would most likely be severely tried by the sight in store for them. What to do was the question; the tent, as I have already said, was fastened, the door being apparently secured closely inside, while the slight movement one of the men made in ascertaining this fact seemed to disturb the feasters upon the dead; they rose in such terrible clouds that through the thin calico one could see them, as they came buzzing in millions against its sides.

'What are we to do?' asked one.

'Go back to Leggat's and tell the police,' replied his mate.

THE DEAD MAN IN THE SCRUB

'Tell the police *what*, man?' inquired the first speaker, 'for all we know it may be a dog's carcase that's inside.'

His mate shook his head, 'a dog wouldn't stay in a closed tent to die, Bill; but at any rate I wouldn't like to open the place without a policeman.'

'You know the dog might have been chained up; a digger might leave his dog to watch inside, and maybe something prevented his coming back,' observed Bill.

'Maybe,' replied the mate dubiously, 'but at any rate we can't stop here much longer, I can't stand it.'

Bill walked around the tent, and at the back observed a small hole near the wall-plate, which he slightly enlarged with his fingers and so enabled himself to peep into the interior. He gave but one glance, and then drawing back with horror ejaculated, 'Oh God, that's awful!'

'What is it?' eagerly enquired the other.

'Oh, it's a man lying there dead—rotten! Look for yourself, and come away for God's sake! I feel like fainting!'

Well these men tramped back these miles and told me at the camp, and we returned, in a spring cart, to the lonely place. To avoid meddling with the door, I tore up a width of the calico, and entered to witness the most piteous and horrible sight I had seen for a long time. A man, or the remains of what had been a man, lay extended upon the floor, but in such an advanced state of decomposition as to be almost unrecognisable. He was fully dressed, and in good sound digger's clothes: his boots were nearly new, his trousers quite respectable. He had on a blue Guernsey shirt, over a good flannel one, but of course, in consequence of the fearful state of the body, even these articles were not to be identified. The poor fellow lay as if he had fallen out of his bunk, which was close by, one arm under his forehead, but the head, detached by decomposition, had fallen partially away, and not a feature was recognisable; the abundant black hair alone being remarkable. Upon his bunk were good blankets, and in the tent was a billy, and one or two other little cooking utensils; but there was not the slightest appearance of anything to eat, or anything whatever which might have held provisions; not a scrap of paper, not a crumb of bread.

Having observed this, I turned my attention to the fastening of the opening, which in every original tent forms the entrance, and I was astonished to find that it had really been nailed up from the inside; a stone and a few broken tacks still lay upon the ground near it, and I could readily believe that the former had been used as a hammer. The first idea that suggested itself to my professional mind was that of suicide, and suicide most likely induced by want, remembering the

THE DEAD MAN IN THE SCRUB

absence of anything like food in the place; or, that the poor fellow had really died of starvation, and had fastened the door with the hope of preventing his body from being devoured by dingoes before it was discovered.

I had not time to speculate about it just at that moment, however, as my duty obliged me to remove the remains and give information to the coroner of the district as early as possible; and so, with great difficulty, we succeeded in enveloping the remains of the poor miner in one of his own blankets and, after carrying them some distance, depositing them in the cart. A jury was empanelled, an inquest was held, which resulted in an open verdict of 'Found dead,' for the condition of the body rendered it impossible for a *post mortem* to be of the slightest service, and the poor fellow was buried. No one knew anything about him—no person had been aware of a digger being in the scrub, and the general impression was my first one, that he had perished of want.

I say my first one, for I soon altered my opinion, although it was not likely to be of the slightest service to the interests of justice that I did so. Almost as a matter of form, I suppose, I went to remove the tent, which had become the property of Government; it was of so little value as to be scarcely worth the trouble; but I was glad of an opportunity to examine the place at my leisure. Well, there was nothing, absolutely nothing, in the tent but what I have already mentioned, and a match-box under the blankets on the bunk which contained half a dozen matches and, at the bottom, pushed into the smallest space, a small piece, about a square inch, of some woollen material, apparently new.

I did not believe at all that this unfortunate man had died a natural death, I was firmly convinced in my own mind that there had been foul play; and yet, had I been asked to give a reason for that conviction, I must have been silent, I had none to give. Yet, with all that, I looked for traces of murder, just as if I was absolutely certain it had been committed. The door was nailed *inside*: well, supposing the poor fellow himself had *not* nailed it, where did the person who *had*, find egress? Might he not have ripped a seam of the calico, and sewed it again outside? I set to work and examined the seams carefully. The tent had apparently been made by a woman, no man or tentmaker was likely to have taken the trouble to stitch so neatly; and besides the seams were *all* on the inside, except in one corner, where, for about two feet in length, a much rougher seam had been made upon the *outside*.

'Here, then,' I convinced myself, 'the murderer has got out; fastening the door inside, to leave it to be supposed that the man himself must have accomplished it.'

THE DEAD MAN IN THE SCRUB

I pulled down the tent and removed every little article in it, and as they were few, I had soon done and took a last look around before I left. As I have before stated, the scrub was growing almost closely around the tent; and, from the length of time that had elapsed since the owner lay dead inside, the little space was untrodden, and the creeping mallee vine had enwrapped itself over and over, and under and around, every near stick. Examining closely the circumscribed space of the tenting spot, I perceived a portion of a dirty rag of some sort, peeping out from the vegetation, and drawing it forth, I was possessor of a pair of old trousers, which, from the size of the dead man, might have belonged to him; they were of a large size, and he had been a tall man. There was nothing particular about them; a pair of old cast-offs evidently, nothing in the pockets, and no difference in them whatever from any other pair of old trousers in the world, only that from the portion least worn, at the back of the leg, a square piece had been taken for some purpose or other. It was no accidental tear, for the piece had been cut out, and the cut extended across the side seam, where it was quite certain it would not have *torn*. So, interested in these old rags, I carefully folded them up with the rest of the dead man's property, and proceeded campwards.

Months passed on; indeed, I may say years; it must have been nearly three years before I fell over the clue to the death-tenanted home in the untrodden mallee. I had meanwhile been removed, and was, at the time I resume my story, stationed at Walhalla, a prosperous reefing township,[1] and a great improvement upon the old alluvial 'rush': the tent was the great exception, the slab and bark erection most common, while there were many of weatherboard, and zinc roofing. In short, Walhalla was such a mining township as we may see anywhere today. In passing backwards and forwards I had often noticed a snug hut that lay upon my way, or rather I had remarked the clean, bright, good-looking woman who lived there, and as it is our business to know as much as possible about everything and everybody, I was aware that she was the wife of a man named Jerry Round, who worked as wages-man[2] in one of the Companies. There were no children about this hut, but the woman, who might have been some twenty-five years old, was always busy; I think she took in washing.

One day, then, about this time, I was passing this hut early in the forenoon of a Saturday. Mrs. Round was apparently having a grand clean out, and the dust was flying in all directions. I was going straight on as usual, when out of the door came flying a pair of dirty old trousers, which, after passing within an inch of my nose, fell directly upon the pathway before me, and there, as they lay sprawling out, covered

THE DEAD MAN IN THE SCRUB

with the dirt of a week's underground work, I saw upon the knee of one of the legs the identical patch missing from the old pair which I had still safely stowed at home in the camp! I could have almost sworn to it the first moment my eyes lighted upon it; the pattern and colour were peculiar, and I had been too much interested not to have closely marked both; but when I came to perceive that in the patch was the very side-seam of *my* trousers, I had no doubt in the world about it. I stooped down in a puzzled, bewildered sort of way, wondering to myself how that patch came upon these trousers, and what connection it had with the dead man in the mallee, and how it would all end; when, just as I was carefully, and with as little detriment to myself as I could, picking up the pants at arm's length, Mrs. Round herself rushed out in a state of great excitement.

'Good gracious me, sir, I hope you don't think I threw the old things at you a'purpose! I didn't know anyone was passing, and they were in my way while I was sweeping, and so I "chucked" them out! I hope you will excuse it, sir!'

'Oh, you needn't bother your head about that, Mrs. Round,' I replied, still holding the articles in my hand. 'I guessed how it was when I saw the dust flying out of the door; but I was just taking a fancy to this patch here; if you've done with the old trousers, I am sadly in need of a bit of woollen rag to clean up my traps,[3] and this would be the very thing.'

'Lord, to be sure, sir; Jerry wore them down in the shaft until they would hardly hang together, but anything most is good enough for working on them drives.[4] But wouldn't a bit of old flannel be better, sir? I could give you lots of flannel.'

'No, Mrs. Round,' I replied, handing her the trousers, 'these bright buckles of ours want such a lot of rubbing you see, flannel lasts no time, while a piece of that good woollen trousering would be worth twice as much to me; so if you'll just be good enough to rip it off for me, I'll owe you a heap of thanks!'

'And welcome, sir,' she replied, going toward the hut to procure a pair of scissors, and I followed her to the door, holding, when she returned, the trousers while she ripped the piece off.

'It's been a good piece of stuff, Mrs. Round,' I remarked, as she slipped in and out, 'you could not buy such a good bit of trousering on the diggings now.'

'No, sir,' replied the woman, a shade coming over her face, 'it's a bit of a pair that came from England long ago; my first husband bought them before we left home, and many a happy gathering of friends they were at!'

THE DEAD MAN IN THE SCRUB

'Your first husband? is it possible you've been married twice? you're very young for that.'

'Jerry and I have only been married a matter of two years,' she said, adding, with an effort to change the conversation, 'anyone can tell it was a man that sewed this; I expect Jerry put it on while he and poor Jim were working together; it's as hard to take off as if it was nailed on.'

'And where were you then, while Round and Jim were working together?' I asked, guessing at once that 'poor Jim' meant the dead husband.

'I was in New Zealand, sir; they came back to a rush at Carngham, and I never saw him again, he died at Sailor's Gully.'

'And you married his mate?'[5]

'Yes, sir.'

There was the shadow of old memories in the poor woman's face, as she simply gave me this information, and I had not the heart to grieve her by questions that might perhaps excite her curiosity, as well as put Round on his guard; and so, for the present, I said no more. The patch I carried home safely, and found, as I had expected, that it was indeed the very piece which had been cut out of the dead man's trousers, and I was, of course, quite certain that the dead man of the mallee was none other than the 'poor Jim' of Mrs. Round.

What story did Round tell about his death, I could not but wonder; and I thought long about the best means of finding this out; and the conclusion I came to was to ask Mrs. Round herself, and make some reasonable excuse for so doing. So the very first time I went that way, I made it my business to time my walk down the road so that I met her coming from a hole with a bucket of water, and as she set it down to rest herself, I stopped before her for a moment.

'Do you know, Mrs. Round,' I said, affecting an air of great interest, 'I have been puzzling my head ever since I saw you last about your first husband; I believe I knew him; and your mentioning his name as 'Jim' made me almost sure of it. I believe I have seen those very trousers on him a dozen times! You said he worked at Carngham, but he didn't die there, did he?'

'No, sir, the poor fellow died at some little out of the way gully back of Bendigo, him and Jerry were prospecting, and when Jim was taken bad, Jerry had to bring a doctor six miles through the scrub to him. But it was no use, and after he died Jerry brought the news over to me, and bad news it was, I tell you.'

'Well, well! It it is strange how things come about!' I ejaculated, 'when I saw poor Jim last, I had no idea that I should make your

THE DEAD MAN IN THE SCRUB

acquaintance through a patch of a pair of his old pantaloons!'

'It was a sore grief to me, sir,' said Mrs. Round, with a sigh, as she again lifted her pail, 'to hear that he was dead, and without my hand to smooth his blankets, or give him a drink! we were very fond of each other; and—to tell the truth,' she added, lifting her eyes to mine for one moment, 'I don't know how I ever came to marry Jerry at all, for poor Jim never liked him, though he was his mate!'

''Twas instinct,' I repeated to myself, as I proceeded on my way, 'little cause the poor fellow had to like him! I dare say if Mrs. Round liked she could give me a good reason for this wretch murdering the poor unsuspicious husband, so that he might go and inherit his place in the affections of the betrayed wife.'

And so I was going on, thinking moodily over the affair, when my attention was attracted by a great commotion among the deep workings: people were running and shouting to one another, and all were tending toward one place, so, hastening my steps, I went in that direction too, and soon found that a frightful mining calamity had taken place, one of the drives had fallen in! From the men who had escaped I learned that the drive had fallen in only at the further end, and that, warned by the cracking of the timber, all had escaped in time, save one—it was Jerry Round.

I went down into the drive, where every exertion was being made to extricate the unfortunate man from the most terrible position that can be conceived: he was not buried, that would have been a merciful fate in comparison with what he endured, and my heart sickened as I looked at him. The drive had partially collapsed, and two steps more towards the shaft would have saved him; but those two steps he did not get time to make; one of the cap-pieces of the timbering had fallen right across his body, the fallen earth partially supporting it, and partially also covering his body. His head, however, was quite exposed, his eyes protruding in his great agony; and for a few minutes he was even able to speak, urging the workers for God's sake to hasten. But there was no need for that, every man worked as if his own existence depended upon speed; and, indeed, they could not be certain that at any moment farther breaks would not take place in the shaken timbering, and place themselves in the same position from which they were endeavouring to rescue their wretched mate.

A very few moments and he was extricated. But the torture he was enduring had become unbearable before that; he was insensible when they carried him upon a stretcher to his own hut, which was not far away, and where his wife met him, quite unprepared for a sight so horrible; yet she met it with far greater composure than one might

THE DEAD MAN IN THE SCRUB

have anticipated. The medical men who were immediately summoned, declared the case of Round to be hopeless; his internal injuries precluded any expectation of a change, save the last great one; and so Mrs. Round, the doctor, and I watched the bruised and broken remnant of humanity stretched out upon his own comfortable bed, comfortable, alas, to him no longer; but we only watched to see the last faint breathing cease, to return no more.

He was a dark, stoutly built man, his hair and whiskers were black as night; one of his arms, broken in two places, lay in a twisted, unnatural position beside him, and his nerveless head, rolled over helplessly to one side, was covered with blood from a wound upon his temple; from which the crimson drops, still oozing, fell down over his white face, making the whole picture more horrible. Poor Mrs. Round wept silently, wiping, meanwhile, the blood gently from his face, and the death damp from his forehead.

The time was not far off now. By his side sat the doctor, holding his fingers upon the wrist of the dying man; and at that moment he gave me a slight nod, unnoticed by the wife; he felt in the fluttering pulse indications of the last struggle. I was about to try and send Mrs. Bound upon some excuse or an errand, for the purpose of saving her the last scene, when Round opened his eyes, and with a gaze full of consciousness rested them upon the face of his wife.

'Oh Ellen, I am dying!' he gasped, faintly, and with horror, 'I am dying, and I murdered poor Jim!' And with this last confession the last breath went away too. He was dead!

Mrs. Round turned round from her dead husband, and stared at me; some instinctive certainty, I have no doubt, she felt that I had something to do with the truth of these last words, some recollection, no doubt, of our late conversation, and a multitude of old ones, with which I had nothing whatever to do, would be sure to lend their aid in overcoming the poor woman, for the light of life faded out of her white face. She had fainted.

There is nothing that touches so mutually the feelings of a whole mining community as a sudden death from one of those fearful and frequent underground accidents to which their calling is so liable, and which, indeed, the carelessness of the miner himself makes so much more frequent; and therefore Jerry Round was followed to the grave by every man in the place who could manage to leave his employment. Little guessed the mourners how guilty was the poor broken mortal whose shattered remains they followed; and as I watched the sad procession winding away among the rocks and trees, true to the instincts of my profession, I quietly speculated how many of these

THE DEAD MAN IN THE SCRUB

very mourners would be likely to come within my jurisdiction, if the secrets of all hearts were known.

As I was making these heartless speculations, as you may think them, I was smoking a cigar, and leaning upon the fence which surrounded our Police Camp; and the black coffin had scarcely disappeared away on the bush track, when Mrs. Round herself stood before me. Poor little woman, she looked very ill; and was, at the moment I speak of, as calm-looking and nearly as white as if she had already lain down in the narrow, peaceful resting-place to which they were bearing her husband. She impressed me with the idea of *rigidity*. It seemed as if she had hard work to keep herself calm, and, in the effort, over-produced the appearance.

'Mr. Mark, I am going away to Melbourne, tomorrow,' she said, laying her hand emphatically upon my arm, 'I am going, with the few pounds we had saved, home to my friends in England. Before I go it is your duty, before God, to tell me all you know of my husband, Jim!'

'Perhaps it is,' I replied, gently, 'but of what use can it be to harrow your feelings by retailing the crimes of the past? Death has covered them all up now!'

'But death hasn't covered *me* up!' she replied, 'and death hasn't as yet covered up all the thoughts that have no guide unless you tell me the truth.'

I felt that she was right, and I led her into the barrack-room, where my traps were, and there I unfolded the pair of old pants which I had got near the dead man in the mallee, and with the piece she had so lately given me herself I handed them to her. She recognised them at once, said she would have known them among a hundred, from some mending of her own upon them: and then she listened, weepingly, while I told her all about the little tent in the scrub, and its death-tenant.

'And was there no more?' she asked, 'was there nothing else you could have brought? oh, poor Jim! poor murdered Jim!'

'There was this,' I said, giving her the match-box, with the little bit of stuff in it, 'and this,' I added, handing her a lock of the poor fellow's dark hair, which I had cut off, and folded in a bit of paper.

Poor Mrs. Round opened it, and looked at the hair; and then, after all the horrors she had heard, she pressed it to her lips. Alas! it was more than I could have done, had it belonged to the dearest and nearest I had in the world! for it had far more than usual of the smell of death which the hair of the dead always has. How could it be otherwise, considering the state of the head from which I had taken it? The piece of stuff in the match-box, too, how well she knew it!

'I sent it to him in a letter from New Zealand,' she said, 'to show

THE DEAD MAN IN THE SCRUB

him the sort of dress I had bought with the first money he sent me from Victoria!'

And so ends the story of poor Jim; his wife left the next day, as she had said, taking with her all she had left of the young husband she had followed from her home in old England; and that all was an old match-box, a pair of worn and dilapidated trousers, and a lock of black death-tainted hair!

First published in the *Australian Journal*, 3 Aug 1867, under the byline 'W.W.'

NOTES

1   *a prosperous reefing township*: reef mining is the process used to extract the gold that is found in reefs or veins of quartz. It involves sinking mine shafts, from which horizontal tunnels (drives) are dug out to find the gold-bearing rock.

2   *wages-man*: with the rise of the goldmining companies Fortune refers to here, miners were usually paid 'on tribute,' effectively based on the volume of ore they extracted. A wages-man, on the other hand, was paid a fixed wage, which could be more lucrative and was certainly more reliable than that of a miner. They worked in a wide variety of specialist areas in the mines, for example as winder drivers.

3   *traps*: here, an abbreviation for trappings; i.e., the accoutrements of his profession.

4   *drives*: the underground passages that run along the length of a vein or reef.

5   *mate*: in this context, mining partner rather than friend.

EAGLEHAWK, THE BUSHRANGER OF THE PYRENEES

It was in the early and palmy days of bushranging that the outlaw known by the sobriquet of Eaglehawk held sway in the wild ranges of the Pyrenees[1] and held tributary to his unlawful sceptre the wide country that bordered their fastnesses. For two years he had reigned supreme before his wild escapades and bold robberies aroused the tardy authorities to try and follow up his movements, and to offer a large reward for his apprehension.

Little was known of the bushranger in question. The rapid swoop with which he seemed to alight from his eyrie upon the unlucky traveller, which had earned him his rather romantic appellation, and the rapidity with which he generally disappeared from under the very eyes of his intended captors, prevented any particular examination of his appearance; but he was known to be very youthful, and reputed to be exceedingly handsome; and, in addition to these popular qualities, he had never taken life, and he robbed with the courtesy of a gentleman. No wonder, then, that he was a favourite with a certain class of the people scattered over the outlying districts, and that the police found it next to an impossibility to gain even a clue to his whereabouts.

However, orders had come that, by hook or by crook, Eaglehawk must be captured, and four of the most determined men in the mounted Force were told off to join our Station, which was situated the nearest to the usual haunts of the bushranger; and among the rest came Harry Willins, my greatest friend and one of the finest young men that had ever worn her Majesty's police uniform in any one of these colonies.

Harry and I were schoolmates in merry old England long long ago. How very long it does seem to look back to those half-forgotten days! Our very identity appears to have become indistinct as we compare this vivid present with that dreamy far-off past. And yet Harry Willins was but young still, not old enough to feel tired of life, although he had met with trouble on its very threshold.

He had been the 'only son of a widow,' but soon loved a fair young girl better than the faithful mother who had borne him. That young girl had deceived him, and married one who bore but an indifferent character. I don't think that the death of his mother was felt so deeply by Harry as it would have been six months before, for his very soul

EAGLEHAWK, THE BUSHRANGER OF THE PYRENEES

seemed crushed with the bitterness of his first disappointment, and another grief added little to the depth of that already felt. But he was only twenty-one, and a policeman's jacket in Victoria soon softened the memory of the past, although tears still filled his eyes at the mention of his mother: to the faithless girl he never alluded.

There was a sweetness wreathed around 'our Harry's' soft, proud lips that made itself felt by all with whom he was intimate; but it was a melancholy sweetness that calmed and purified. He had the blue eye of a hawk, surmounted by a forehead broad and white, and by masses of golden chestnut hair that, in his merry moods, tossed with every movement like living sunlight. For Harry had merry moods, when all his melancholy seemed cast back into the past; and at such times as these 'our Harry's' laugh was the gayest, and his musical voice the most cheerful, that one could hear on a long summer day.

And it was in one of these moods that he formed one of the cluster of troopers that gathered, laughing and joking and tightening their saddle-girths, in the barrack yard on the morning I have mentioned.

'And now,' he cried, springing into the saddle when all was ready, carabines slung, and holster pipes not empty — 'now, who'll win Eaglehawk and the rhino?'[2]

'I will!' shouted Tom Dalzell.

'Ten to one against you, Tom.'

'I'll bet you the half of the reward that *I* win the bushranger,' was Harry's challenge.

'Done!' cried Tom Dalzell.

And amid laughter and exclamations, off galloped our harum-scarum party. Alas! that 'our Harry' should so certainly have won his bet.

Our destination was an elevated part of the range, where a late report had located the hiding-place of the renowned Eaglehawk. Upon one side this precipitous range was impregnable; upon the other, where the huge rocks were piled upon each other higher and higher, until they overlooked a whole country, foothold might be obtained, and an ascent accomplished with the aid of the luxuriant lichens that trailed, in garlanded greenness, from granite to granite.

It was known that Eaglehawk was single-handed, and the leader of no band. He had never been known to rob in company; and as each man of us felt courage enough to attack him singly, it had been decided that our horses should be fastened up at the foot of the rocks, and that separately we should scatter over the face of the range, and in trying to ascend, cover as much as we could well examine. Of course we looked for his stronghold, feeling confident that the eyrie once discovered, we should be able easily to entrap the Eaglehawk.

EAGLEHAWK, THE BUSHRANGER OF THE PYRENEES

At about fifty yards distance from each other we commenced the difficult ascent, it having been previously arranged that a pistol shot, or a whistle, should the former prove an impossibility, was to be the signal for summoning the whole party in any one direction that might be indicated by the sound.

It was getting toward evening by the time we had reached the ground, at least the afternoon was fast waning; but hoping to reach the summit of the rocks and make our descent with daylight, we lost no time in prosecuting our search.

Harry and I, from a choice of mine, were next to each other. He was on my right hand, and the trooper I have called Tom Dalzell on my left. They both proved better climbers than I did, and I was soon mortified to perceive them both far higher up the steep face than I was myself. Very soon I lost sight of Tom Dalzell altogether, and could but occasionally catch a glimpse of Harry, as, some rugged spot overcome, I paused for breath, and to observe what progress he was making.

I met with occasional plateaus of verdant grass as I ascended, where the giant rocks had parted and where Time had deposited, particle by particle, the rich vegetable mould, from whence at length sprung the tall sheltering trees, and the graceful creepers that tossed many-coloured blossoms over the precipitous crags.

Upon one of these plateaux, at a considerable elevation, I paused, tired and disappointed, having discovered no trace whatever of cave or hiding place, and being leg-weary as well as torn in several places by the corners of rocks and the rough lichens I was obliged to seize for assistance in climbing. Almost simultaneously with the first breath I drew on my resting place, a shot broke the silence of the range, and its echoes rang and repeated themselves in a hundred voices from crag to crag of the grey rocks on its face. An instantaneous look toward the spot where I had last seen Harry, convinced me that it had been fired by him, for a little cloud of light smoke was still hovering around it.

But I had not time to think ere another report, louder and sharper, followed in the wake of the last, and then I saw the form of my friend hanging, as it were, upon the very verge of a cliff that fell down from the limited foothold from whence the shots had rung, in a dangerous precipice of seventy or eighty feet high—a precipice that was only broken by clusters of bushes with twisted stems, or jutting rocks that served as resting places for the bird or the snake. He was hanging over the very edge of the cliff, I have said, but only for a moment, for the next the poor lad had fallen over, and went crashing downward among the stones and bushes, to disappear from life in the covering verdure below.

For a second or two that seemed long to me, every vital power seemed to have left my body. My heart ceased to beat, my eyes looked into a dizzy haze. Was that the same blue sky up among the trees that crowned the range upon which I had gazed but a moment ago? Was this really the same world as it erewhile had been? Was I myself? and was 'our Harry' dead? The dreadful thought nearly drove me mad, and with a wild bound I lessened the distance between my crushed friend and myself by many yards, landing on my feet, when I had done so, at an elevation considerably lower than the one I had previously occupied.

Another bound, and I was scrambling over some loose stones that lay at the foot of a huge rock; another, and I had lost my footing, and was falling helplessly down to almost certain destruction.

What a horrible sensation it was, that headlong fall! I feel it yet; and the gasping breath, and the vain, instinctive clutches with which I grasped the resistless air as my body cleaved it with the speed of thought. And then the terrible shock when my helpless frame was dashed on the soft grass, to be but for one instant conscious of its miserable position.

That last moment was the bitterest of my life. A faintness like that of death was stealing over me, and there, close to my face, lay 'our Harry.' My very hand was tossed helplessly against his side; and, becoming insensible as I was, I could yet feel that *his* warm blood was bubbling over it, and gradually creeping up my arm, as the sleeve became soaked in the stream. It was my last effort to look into the poor boy's face—it was there, close to my own, white and ghastly, with the erstwhile red full lips pale and rigid, and the soft curls tossed roughly over sadly closed eyes. The sight was too much to bear—I remember no more.

No more, until a cold wind, blowing into my face, and making my weak heart shudder, aroused me once more into life, and I tried to rise before I even attempted to recall what had happened. But suddenly the fearful recollection once more rushed into my memory, and I fell back helplessly as a child, and with a sickness at my heart that told of Harry. Poor Harry! It was dark as pitch ; there was not a star in the sky to light even the most faintly, and I could not even distinguish the sky itself from the rocks and trees of the landscape around me.

Cautiously I stretched out my hand directly before me, where I had seen that pale face; there was nothing there but grass, soft and rustling, and dew damp. Had he moved, or been removed? The hope gave me strength to arise, and I groped about on my knees, vainly feeling for the body of my friend.

Had I dreamed it all? Ah! there was a pool of gore *there*, on the velvety grass. Alas! it was no dream. And my mates, where were they?

EAGLEHAWK, THE BUSHRANGER OF THE PYRENEES

Had they heard the pistol shots, and had found Harry? No, they would never remove him and leave me to die helplessly and alone.

Besides, as I recalled it, circumstance by circumstance, I persuaded myself that it was very improbable that any of our party had seen Harry's fall save myself. They had doubtless heard the pistol reports, and would hasten to the point from whence they judged the sounds to have proceeded; but with Harry and myself lying bruised and unconscious down among the clustering wattle bushes, who was to tell them where we were hidden, or to guide them in their search for the lost?

What was I to do? Feeling bruised and weak, I staggered against the trunk of a tree near which I had stumbled, and remained there despairingly, feeling conscious that without assistance I could never gain the camp, and inclined to lie down despairingly upon the cold ground from whence I had so lately arisen. The darkness was so intense that I did not attempt to pierce it, and it was a peculiar sound that caused me to raise my eyes to the dark face of the rock near me.

The sound, that died out instantly, was like the human voice uttering tones of distress; but the occasion of it, or indeed its reality, troubled me little; for as I lifted my eyes I detected the glimmer of a light not ten feet above me. It was filtering out into the darkness through a thick curtain of young wood that grew in crevices of the cliff, and it was a steady light and a brilliant, as one could judge from the brightness of the few rays that streamed out unimpededly beneath the branches.

The sight infused new strength into my bones, for I guessed at once that it was the cave of Eaglehawk upon which I had dropped unexpectedly. 'If my narrow escape from death has gained me one chance of revenging the blood of my poor murdered Harry, I shall bless it as long as I breathe,' I muttered, stealthily making my way toward the spot from whence the light issued.

That Eaglehawk had, suddenly surprised by Harry, fired upon him, I had no doubt; but doubts were about to be set at rest, and I vowed a solemn vow beneath the dark sky of heaven, that peace by day or rest by night I would not seek to enjoy until I had met the wretch, face to face, who had sent the widow's son to so cruel a death.

In a few moments, and without feeling my bruises much, so great was my excitement, I had reached the opening of the cave from whence issued the light, and nothing but the curtain of young trees that guarded the entrance separated me from the secrets of the robber's haunt. How my hand trembled as it clutched the revolver in my belt, and how loudly my heart beat! Would they not hear it in the cave before I was calm enough or strong enough to effect an entrance?

EAGLEHAWK, THE BUSHRANGER OF THE PYRENEES

With but a gentle rustle of the fresh cool foliage and an unechoing step upon the soft granite sand of the floor, I stood within a lofty and arched cave, where such a strange and unexpected scene met my eyes that I drew back horrified, as one who advanced to combat life and revenge, and was met in the face by Death! Such a singular scene, far up on the side of a lonely granite range—in a time-hollowed cave in the very bowels of the rock!

In the centre of the cave stood a bier covered with a white sheet that swept down to the floor, and lay on the sparkling sand in folds. Upon this bier was stretched a corpse carefully covered, all but the head, with linen as white as snow. All but the head, and that was turned toward the entrance, so that I could not see the face; but I could see the six candles that burned around it, and the soft bright hair that caught the light in golden curls as they rested lifelessly upon the pillow.

What was this? All the blood in my body gathered into my weak heart, and my knees trembled like ruffled water in moonlight: alas! should I not know that noble young head with its wealth of chestnut curls among a thousand, though my eyes never rested on his dear face again!

Cruel death! Can the tongue of living man find words to tell of the desolation thou carriest to home and heart? Or, were a hundred volumes written, would the cold mystery of the white seal thou implantest on the forehead of the beloved dead be elucidated? That strange mystery that carries awe into the most loving heart—that terrible immobility that severs, by so great a gulf, the present from the past, as if that past had never been, and the present were but a dreadful dream from which we pray God to awaken!

Yes, it was indeed 'our Harry.' With a rapid step I advanced to look into the face of the dead, and found my worst fears but too well founded. Calm and rigid—cold and white, with drooped eyelids and half-open lips—with the well-known chestnut hair resting gently on a forehead purer than ever—with the too well-known passionless expression of utter 'nothingness' on the well-known features, lay, in the flickering glare of the bier-lights, our kindly Harry, dead!

Before time has seared and rendered selfish and cynical the soft affections of our nature, death in any form seems to wither life in our heart's core. In childhood, it is the bird or the puppy over which we shed our first tears of bitterness, as we feel the blight of the great Destroyer; in youth it is over the friend or the lover that our own heart-strings appear severing. Perhaps, it is well ordained that years should bring callousness of feeling; but I had not yet arrived at those years, and at the first glimpse of that stilly face, retribution and revenge, nay, duty itself, was for a time forgotten, and I felt only that was Harry dead, and that the grief I felt was almost worse than I could bear.

Little I cared for Eaglehawk at that moment—he was utterly forgotten.

With a cry of agony I threw myself beside the corpse, and burying my face on the cold hard bosom I had so often seen panting with full life, I am not ashamed to own that I wept bitter tears. Ah! those merry old school days—the torn jackets and the soiled bands. Ah! those confiding moments of manhood—the warm pressure of the hand and the look of encouragement and affection—was this the sad end of it all?

'Oh, Harry, Harry!' was all of the grief that found vent in words; and at the last utterance of the well-known name, I heard it repeated in a strange and terrified voice, so closely that I lifted my head and looked up.

'Harry!—what Harry?'

The voice was scarcely raised above a whisper, but it sounded loudly and distinctly in the quiet death-tenanted cave. As I raised my eyes, the sight I beheld started me to my feet at once, and the rage that flashed through my veins like a fire, clutched in my hands with a grip of iron on my revolver.

Opposite the spot where I had knelt fell a dark curtain of coarse serge that I had not noticed, and standing with this curtain grasped and held back by one hand was a slender youthful-looking figure, dressed in dark trousers and a loose jacket fastened at the waist by a strong belt. Within the belt were a brace of pistols and a long knife in a sheath. He had a French cap on a head that was small and delicately formed; and the features of the noted robber were familiar and far from unpleasing. Yes, I was sure that my eyes looked into those of Eaglehawk the Bushranger, and it was not because his face was full of a strange fear that my heart beat madly for an encounter; it was that I saw before me the spiller of my friend's young life, and that I burned for revenge on the murderer.

'What Harry?'

'Harry Willins!' I almost shouted, 'your victim, murderer that you are, and may the weight of his innocent blood render death terrible to you! Die, dog that you are—die!'

I raised the pistol I held in my hand as I spoke, and it covered the immoveable figure of Eaglehawk, whose death seemed certain to my delighted gaze. But ere the movement of my ready finger told on the trigger, the revolver was dashed from my hand, and my arm was firmly seized by some one behind me.

Astonished at this unexpected interruption, I looked round to see an elderly woman, of a stout build and with grey hair. She was attired in a plain, coarse dress of black stuff, and her fading hair was partially covered by a cap of linen as white as snow. Every feature of her wrinkled face was working with emotion, and her grasp on my arm trembled as she spoke.

'You denounce the murderer, young man, yet you would emulate his deeds.'

'Mrs. Davidson!' I exclaimed, in astonishment, as I recognised the but little changed face of an old woman who had long been housekeeper to Harry's dead mother; who had nursed the poor fellow in childhood, and shed bitter tears over the disappointment of his youth.

'Mrs. Davidson! how on earth did you come here?'

'And you?' she said, dropping my arm as she looked wistfully into my bewhiskered face, 'I do not recognise you, although you seem to know me, but it is no matter, it is little I care for the living, with my poor murdered boy lying here before me.'

These few words had taken but a moment to exchange, and Eaglehawk still stood irresolutely, as it were, at the entrance; but at the last words of the old nurse he advanced quickly to the side of the bier, as if for confirmation of some terrible fear. Once there his gaze rested upon the calm face of the dead with a growing horror burning in it, as every particle of colour receded from his face till it became as white as the corpse he stood near.

Hesitating what to do, I saw the despair of the lost imprint itself in every feature of the bushranger, and, with a shriek I shall remember to my dying day, he threw himself upon the body and pressed his lips passionately to those of my dead Harry. 'Oh, Harry! Harry! Oh, my Harry! my Harry! dead, dead, dead, and killed by me! Oh, merciful God, wither me from life, for it is too hard to bear!'

'Stand back!' cried old Mrs. Davidson, seizing the arm of Eaglehawk angrily; 'contaminate not the dead by your touch! Wretched creature, have you forgotten that his blood cries aloud for vengeance from the earth where *you* spilled it!'

Until this moment I had remained paralysed with astonishment at the strangeness of the scene, but the old woman's words aroused me once more to a sense of my duty. As she held the outlaw by the arm, and partially succeeded in dragging him from the corpse, I sprang behind him and attempted to pinion his arms while I handcuffed him. He was too quick for me, however. With a wild laugh he wrenched his arm from me, and, seizing the revolver in his belt, with one rapid movement he pressed its muzzle to his heart, and shot himself dead.

No—not quite dead, from his lips, from whence the stream of life gushed rapidly, one word was weakly whispered with a sigh as he fell heavily to the ground. That word was 'Harry,' the name of our poor lost friend he had murdered.

'Explain this strange contradiction, woman, if you are able,' I said sternly, turning to Mrs. Davidson, who looked upon the last gasp of the bushranger with little apparent pity; 'who is this Eaglehawk, who dies with my friend's name on his lips, although his was the cursed hand that deprived him of life?'

'Look for yourself,' she replied, stooping beside the dead outlaw, and lifting the cap from the nerveless head. 'I think I remember you now, and Mark Sinclair ought to know the face of Jane Carlton.'

'Jane Carlton! Good heavens above, do you mean to tell me that Eaglehawk the outlaw is Jane Carlton, the unfaithful mistress of poor Harry!'

'It is even so,' replied Mrs. Davidson hardly, for grief had rendered her almost callous; 'but even she, miserable as she was, must claim a grave; lend me your help to carry her away from this. I cannot bear that even her corpse should contaminate the air made sacred by the precious clay of my boy.'

We carried the corpse into a rude inner cave, and laid it upon a rough bed that stood in one corner; and then the old woman opened a box near the wall, and produced from it a bottle and a tin measure.

'She used to drink wine,' she observed, making an inclination of her head toward the body, 'and I think that you will not be the worse of some, for you look white and ill. Are you hurt much? Can you eat?'

'No, I do not think I am more than badly bruised,' I replied, 'and I cannot eat now'; but I poured myself out some wine, and felt much better when I had drank it. And then I went back to the side of our poor Harry, and wept my fill, while Mrs. Davidson performed the last offices for the wretched girl who had for two years been known as Eaglehawk the bushranger of the Pyrenees.

It was a strange hour I spent there. While the candles guttered and flickered, and flared up occasionally to light up the sparkling mica with which the walls of the cave were thickly sprinkled, and the stilly face of him who would smile again no more—while the cool breeze rustled the branches before the entrance, and crept damply in to lift the soft curls on the dead forehead with a movement so life-like that it startled me—my thoughts were far away among the haunts of our boyhood, where our happy laughter had echoed and blended in the days of old.

'Tell it to me,' I said, as Mrs. Davidson entered and seated herself also beside the dead trooper, 'tell me this strange story which has had so terrible a *denouement.*'

EAGLEHAWK, THE BUSHRANGER OF THE PYRENEES

'It is a short one, and can be related in a few words,' was the answer. 'You doubtless recollect that the husband for whom Jane Carlton deserted our Harry was a wild and unprincipled character. They were but a short time married when he brought her to these colonies, where a few months saw him the associate of robbers, and one of a band of bushrangers that infested New South Wales. He was shot in an encounter with the police, and his miserable wife, who but too closely resembled him in feeling and tastes, fled to this district to escape pursuit. She had worn a man's dress during the whole of their bush career, and it was but one step farther to become a knight of the road herself.'

'But you? How did you become mixed up in the affair?'

'Very simply. When the last of my earthly ties was laid in the grave, I came to Australia, hoping to discover some trace of the boy I had nursed, and whom I loved as dearly as if my own blood ran in his veins. I was unsuccessful, and at last took a situation on a station. Two days ago I was proceeding to it by means of the mail, when the notorious Eaglehawk bailed us up, and robbed the coach. In spite of the dress I recognised at the first glance the well-known features of Jane Carlton, and the recognition was mutual. She insisted on my accompanying her here for the night, and, in the hope of influencing her to abandon so guilty and unwomanly a career, I did so with little persuasion. The rest you know, and here is the end,' and the poor woman laid her head upon the cold bosom of the corpse, and gave way to the bitterness of her grief.

Yes, that was the end. I spare you the legal business connected with the mournful and tragic events of that day; but the secret was well kept, and to this day there are few who know that it was a woman who bore the title of Eaglehawk, the bushranger of the Pyrenees.

First published in the *Australian Journal*, 11 January 1868, under the byline 'W.W.'

NOTES

1   *the Pyrenees*: a low mountain range in Victoria, whose highest point is Mount Avoca (757 m). The Pyrenees Ranges are ca. 90 km northwest and 110 km southwest, respectively, of the former goldfields of Ballarat and Bendigo, and ca. 200 km northwest of Melbourne.
2   *rhino*: money (British slang).

THE HART MURDER

Riding lazily homeward from Barron Township one day, I met Mr. Crawford of Illancarra Station, almost close to the road that turned up to the homestead. You remember Crawford? He was one of the best hearted men I ever met, I think, and had those hearty open manners that reminded English people so much of home that he had acquired the title of Squire Crawford, by which he was known far and wide.

'Hallo! Sinclair, you're not going to pass?' he said—'the day is hot enough for a rest in the house. Where have you been?'

'Only posting a letter.'

'Oh yes, a despatch, with O.H.M.S.[1] on it, of course, and as much of course, with nothing worth communicating in it. Come on up. I declare it's a charity for anyone to have pity on me and give me half an hour's chat.'

'I dare say you do miss Harry,' I replied as I turned my horse's head, greatly to his satisfaction, 'but he won't be very long away will he? How is Miss Crawford?'

'Moping,' he answered; 'but I don't know what you will think of a step I have taken. You know how the house has been going at sixes and sevens since my sister and I had that disturbance and she took herself off? Mary is no more good in the homestead than a statue, and the servants have had fine times of it. Well, I've sent to town for a housekeeper, and I expect her by tomorrow's coach.'

'Where did you get her?'

'Oh, through one of those Melbourne agencies or institutions, or whatever they call them. Something I saw in the paper put the idea into my head. What do you think of it?'

'Hum—think it's a great risk.'

'How?'

'Why, you'll get some cunning creature who will feather her nest at your expense; or some fool who will upset all your household arrangements, and make you glad to give her a ten pound note to get out of your agreement. Or, worse than all, you'll have some very nice amiable widow coming the soft sawder[2] over your heart, and then what will Miss Mary say to a new mamma?'

'So you wind up with thinking that I myself am an old fool, eh? No, no, no women for me; by Jupiter, my sister's jurisdiction gave

THE HART MURDER

me enough of that, and, after all, there are many worse women than her—it was only a little temper.'

'She *was* rather an odd lady, certainly. Where is she now?'

'Blest if I know. But I'm not at all uneasy about her, as she is, you know, independent as far as money matters go. And, after all, she is only to be pitied for her temper and can't, I dare say, help it. I never saw an old maid yet that had not a troublesome temper.'

'Well, I am afraid the exceptions are few.'

To give you some idea of Illancarra and its inmates, I have only to take you homeward with me, after I had parted from the hospitable Squire, and let you share a few of my thoughts. During my short stay I had seen Miss Mary Crawford, a very pretty but very inert young lady of seventeen, who did not care though the whole establishment should go to the mischief, so long as she remained undisturbed to enjoy her novel or her nap in the handsome easy chair she had appropriated to her own especial use in the sitting room at Illancarra. Most thoroughly did this young lady enjoy the *dolce far niente* of her happy existence; her greatest exertion consisting of the arduous formation of a crochet purse or a bit of elaborate wool work. 'Her mother all out,' was the good Squire's only reproof. 'It's no use reasoning with you, my girl, for you can't help your constitution.' But I used to think that Miss Mary would have been obliged to help it if the lines had fallen to her in less pleasant places, and her daily bread had depended on her own exertions.

'I wonder how she will like the introduction of a stranger to her lazy life,' I thought, as I rode campward from the homestead; 'but, of course, it will depend entirely upon the person. If she has sense enough to let Miss Crawford alone, most assuredly will Miss Crawford return the compliment, though the housekeeper should swindle her father under her very eyes.' So you may perceive that Miss Mary was no great favourite of mine.

'But what business is it of mine,' thinks I, as I pulled the *Police Gazette* out of my pocket, and proceeded to open it in search of something more interesting to me personally. I had just received the *Gazette* in company with some other official documents, at the township, and as my horse's pace was a leisurely one, I had an opportunity of looking over its contents as I rode.

And there was something very interesting indeed to a chap with my proclivities—there was a reward of five hundred pounds offered for the capture of a woman, who was more than suspected of the murder of an old lady with whom she had been for years living in the capacity of companion.

THE HART MURDER

The case was one in which an embryo detective could not but feel an uncommon share of interest, independent of the large reward, which was, of course, calculated to increase professional anxiety on the subject. The ungrateful atrocity of the crime—added to the youth and apparent self-possession of the suspected—had created quite a *furore* of excitement in the minds of a sensation-loving public.

Something like these were the particulars. An old lady named Hart had resided for some years in the suburbs of Sydney, apparently on a very comfortable income. She kept a couple of servants and no company, so that the lives of the said servants were uncommonly pleasant, and to their own satisfaction. A companion lived with Mrs. Hart—a Miss Fairweather, the daughter of a deceased friend of the old lady, who placed every confidence in her.

The old lady had been ailing for some time, and nothing could exceed the attention of her companion. It was known that a will had been made in Miss Fairweather's favour; and upon the very morning following the signature of the document, Mrs. Hart was found lying upon the floor of her chamber, dead and cold, and Miss Fairweather was summoned from her room, at an early hour, by the shrieks of the servant who made the discovery.

Her death had evidently been a violent one. There were marks of violent compression upon her throat, and several apparent blows from some heavy blunt instrument on her head. It would seem as if she had been left for dead in her bed, but had recovered sufficiently to try and crawl toward the bell, when death had overtaken the poor victim.

And Edward Marsh, the man servant who had lived with her for fourteen years, had disappeared, along with every available article of jewellery and value the house contained. Of course he was accredited with the inhuman murder, while Miss Fairweather was pitied and condoled with on the loss of so good a friend.

But she had no difficulty in getting possession of all the old lady's property, and converted it all into cash in spite of the advice of the executors. A short fortnight after the open verdict returned at the inquest, Miss Fairweather left Sydney for England, as it was understood, to join some relatives there.

All these particulars were known to me previous to the day upon which I have opened my story; but you will now more readily understand my interest in the reward. The case had taken quite another phase, and, from some communication received by the police at Sydney, the Government reward of two hundred pounds was supplemented by the relatives of Mrs. Hart, and five hundred, in all,

THE HART MURDER

was now offered for the apprehension of Miss Fairweather for the murder of her benefactor, Mrs. Hart.

I was truly astonished at this change in the programme, and wrote that very night to Escott, my old chum, who was at Sydney in the detective force, to give me all particulars. It was natural that I should feel anxious to know them, since the information supplied by the *Gazette* included the fact that Miss Fairweather had not in reality left the colonies for England, but was supposed to have landed at Geelong or Melbourne in male attire.

To post Escott's letters the next day, I started once more for Barron township, and I had occasion to remember that day on more accounts than one. The squire passed me on the road, driving a very fast mare in one of his buggies, to meet the new housekeeper at the coach office.

The coach, however, had not arrived when I started on my return, leaving the squire at Barron in conversation with some of his friends. He overtook me on the road, though, and in rather an odd and unexpected manner; for he picked me up from off the middle of the road, where he found me lying insensible, with a broken arm, and a pretty well smashed skull.

I shall never forget the good man's kindness to me at that time, although days elapsed before I was sensible of it. Illancarra was nearer than the camp, so he and the housekeeper lifted me into the conveyance and took me to the homestead, from whence a messenger was despatched for a doctor with all haste.

I was a favoured guest at Illancarra for several weeks; indeed, it was nearly two months before I left finally. Of course, I had leave from head quarters at first on account of my accident, and afterwards simply because I was performing a very important duty by remaining at the station.

Six weeks had quite elapsed before I joined the small family circle and had an opportunity of inspecting the housekeeper. Of course we had many a talk about her, the squire and I, and I felt rather curious to see if my opinion would at all coincide with his—that is to say, with the constant declaration that he could not, for the life of him, form one of her.

My days of confinement had seemed very long to me, although I had been given possession of one of the nicest rooms in the house, with a view from the window of mountain and plain, that had life in its very beauty, and although my kind host spent hours of every day in my apartment. My attendance devolved chiefly upon an old female servant named Maggie, who seemed well up in nursing.

THE HART MURDER

Many a thought of mine went out to the murderer of poor old Mrs. Hart. I begrudged every day I spent in helpless idleness in my comfortable quarters at Illancarra, and devoured the letters I received from Escott with double avidity. As for the *Police Gazette*, the only item in it which possessed any interest for me was the description given in it continuously of the wanted Miss Fairweather.

I had formed such an idea of her from it in my own mind, that I fancied I could detect her under any disguise whatever. In twenty different situations and dresses I pictured her, but always, or nearly always, in the male attire with which the *Gazette* had accredited her. But, at any rate, her appearance was too decidedly marked not to offer a certain detection to a policeman of any acumen whatever.

'You'll be able to go into the drawing-room tomorrow,' said the squire to me one evening as we sat puffing our cigars at the open window of my room. 'The sooner you get about now the better, I say, and I don't care one rap for old thingumbob, the doctor's, opinion. Besides, I know as well as it you said it, that you are as curious to see Mrs. Bell as ever you can possibly be.'

'Indeed I am,' I said. 'What is she up to today?'

'What is a shadow up to? I never saw such a woman in all my born days. Everything in the house seems to go on well oiled wheels, but you do not recognise the motive power. She must be up at day-break, for I scarcely ever see her interfering in household concerns, or without a book in her hand.'

'What sort of reading does she patronise?'

'Oh, nobody knows. I never asked her. Religious, I should suppose, from the dull look of both herself and the books.'

'It seems my prophecy as to you taking a fancy to the housekeeper is not in a way of being fulfilled. Squire? How does Miss Mary and she get on?'

'I am not a very observing character, Sinclair,' replied the Squire, with a sudden interest; 'but I have noticed that Mary seems to have taken a great dislike to Mrs. Bell. Perhaps I am making use of too strong an expression in saying dislike, but it is so seldom that Mary takes an interest in anything, save her own girlish pursuits, that her suspicious watch of Mrs. Bell is observable.'

'Does the housekeeper observe it, think you?'

'It would be impossible to say with any certainty. There are some persons, Sinclair, who can see without looking, as you very well know; and if Mrs. Bell notices anything in particular, she must be one of those persons.'

'She would be a good detective, then. But, hurrah for tomorrow,

THE HART MURDER

and you shall have my ideas on the matter.'

And tomorrow came, and the afternoon of it found me lolling in a deep, comfortable chair, with half a dozen pillows around me, and the subject of as much fuss from my good host as if I was a confirmed invalid.

My chair was placed near one of the large windows, and under the partial shadow of the voluminous damask that decorated it. Had the position been my own choice, it could not have been better adapted for a post of quiet observation.

My friend Crawford had seen me installed, and Miss Mary had so far exerted herself as to compliment me on my return to health and partial capacity to enjoy life before she returned to what constituted her chief enjoyment of it, viz., the manufacture of some ornamental article in beads and wool, with a novel upon her lap, and her dainty feet on a soft cushion. The new inmate, too, had passed me the time of day, as the saying is, but, abruptly, ere she left the room for some purpose connected with her duties, I presume.

It was a warm afternoon, and when the Squire took himself off on some expedition or other, my drowsy head seemed inclined to take advantage of the softness behind it. There was nothing, to a man of my tastes, at all attractive in the pretty Miss Mary lounging on her sofa. When I had observed the elaborately dressed hair and its scarlet bows of ribbon, the betrimmed *panier*, as it is called, I believe, and, above all, the utter carelessness of my own handsome presence her bead-dropping fingers evinced, I had seen quite enough of Miss Mary, and I fell fast asleep.

I dreamt of a young person with a profusion of very fair hair, with a high broad forehead, and a plump pretty countenance. The forehead was as smooth as a baby's, but marked with a vivid scar close to the hair, high up; and the slight pretty figure was almost too girlish for the twenty-three years that had passed over the sunny head. Need I tell you that my dream was of Miss Fairweather, the suspected murderess of her kind benefactor, Mrs. Hart?

I have told you that Mrs. Bell, the new housekeeper, had congratulated me briefly upon my ability to leave my room, but it was during my weak transition from my chamber to the drawing-room. I had no opportunity of observing her, even sufficiently to pronounce upon her personal appearance; and when I opened my eyes after my nap, and they rested upon the figure of Mrs. Bell, the sight occasioned me a more perfect disappointment than I had experienced for months.

She sat in a rocking chair at the other side of the window and in a position which formed a triangle with that which was occupied

THE HART MURDER

severally by Miss Crawford and myself. A musty-looking book lay upon her lap, and she bent over it thoughtfully, a long thin finger marking the page—a finger of the left hand, upon which gleamed a heavy plain gold ring.

The face and figure of the woman before me was perfectly commonplace in that it was that of a woman, in widow's weeds, of about forty years, and with no pretensions whatever to good looks. She was thin and bony, had black hair that was plainly folded under a widow's cap, and a low forehead, denoting no great intellectual powers.

The silver-rimmed spectacles that rested on her sharp nose were not at all ornamental, and from them to the stiff arrangement of her scanty black drapery, the whole woman was so uninteresting that I was astonished to intercept a look of keen suspicion from Miss Mary's bright eyes that fully bore out her father's idea of her feelings.

'I'm sure the woman doesn't deserve a second thought,' was my opinion as I re-closed my eyes. 'One may read her character at a glance—a stingy, old-maidish because childless widow, with a tendency to hard, cold religion; or, more probably still, a thorough hypocrite. There's no danger of the Squire getting soft there, at any rate, and that's one good job.'

I fell asleep again. I was weak, you see, and not able to indulge in much cogitation. When I next opened my eyes, I did so suddenly and with a start—at what I did not then know—and the changed face and figure of the housekeeper riveted my eyes.

She was sitting bolt upright in her chair—the book had fallen to the ground. Her face was as white as her cap, and an expression of awful fear made her eyes seem horrible behind her spectacles. She was staring at me in such a manner that I, too, lifted myself up, with some idea that there must be a snake about me; or that I must have unconsciously burst a blood vessel, and be bleeding to death before the horrified eyes of the new housekeeper.

'What on earth is the matter?' I cried, looking towards Miss Mary, who was staring first at me, and then at Mrs. Bell.

The housekeeper sighed, in a sort of stifled manner, and then grew scarlet from neck to forehead as she stooped to recover her book. When she lifted up her face and met my eyes over her spectacles, a sort of spasm seemed to pass over her face; it must have been the effort to recover her self-possession.

'What were you dreaming about?' she asked, in the strangest tone of voice I ever heard—a sort of monotone—a voice that ran in a soft, single groove. 'You positively frightened me.'

THE HART MURDER

'How?'

'Did you hear Mr. Sinclair, Miss Crawford?'

'Hear what?' asked Mary, sharply.

'Mr. Sinclair speaking?'

Miss Crawford did not reply, unless an impatient movement which changed her position could be tortured into one.

'Was I really speaking in my sleep?' I inquired. 'I hope I told none of my secrets. What was I talking about?'

She glanced toward the silent girl on the sofa, as if she would be able to contradict her in case she should venture upon telling a falsehood—at least, that was the strange idea her movement suggested to me. 'You were arresting someone, I should suppose,' she answered slowly; 'and you seemed to do it with a will. I should fancy you an unpleasant enemy to deal with.'

'I would run that woman down with as little pity as a bloodhound would follow the trail of a scalping Indian!' I cried, suddenly remembering my dream of the murderess. 'And I believe I shall do it yet—she follows me in my very dreams!'

'You must not excite yourself that way, Sinclair,' said the voice of my good friend Crawford, as he stepped through the open window. 'If you do, we'll have to get the old medico back to you again. What's it all about?'

'Oh, I've been dreaming of that monstrous incarnation of infamy, poor old Mrs. Hart's murderess, and frightened Mrs. Bell almost out of her wits. Is that the *Gazette* you have?'

'Yes—and one of your mates tells me there is something fresh in it about that very case that interests you so. Bynon asked me to hand you the *Gazette*. I met him at the township. By the bye, he's full tilt after some bushranger who is supposed to have headed this way, and wishes you were able to mount again.'

I heard but the first part of my friend's gossip, for the same instant that he handed me the paper the cover was torn off, and my eager eyes were seeking the well-known corner.

Did you ever feel that strange sharp shudder, that the Irish tell us we feel only when some foot is pressing the spot which is to form our future grave? Well, that was the feeling that stayed my nervous fingers in unfolding the paper and caused me to lift my eyes toward my opposite neighbour, whom I had already nearly forgotten.

She was chalk white to the very lips, and bent over her book; although a furtive look from under her very dark eyebrows convinced me that she was both watching and listening. A something which I could not describe to you determined me to set a close watch upon

120

THE HART MURDER

the housekeeper's movements—perhaps it was my sudden conviction that she was in some unaccountable manner interested in mine.

There was indeed something fresh about the Hart murder case, as it had got to be known as; an anonymous communication had been received at head-quarters containing an offer to disclose all particulars connected with the murder, on condition that the writer's name should not be divulged, or any publicity whatever given to the means he should take to forward the said information to the authorities.

Added to this was a statement, that two stations (the numbers of which were given) would be furnished with private instructions regarding this affair.

Now, if ever a man was annoyed at his own incapacity, I was on reading that paragraph. The police stations indicated were none other than the one where I was quartered and the nearest one to it. By the time the *Gazette* was in my hands my trooper mate Bynon was in possession of the interesting telegram, and here I was incapable of stirring in the affair.

From the fact of our particular stations being singled out for private instructions, it was to be gathered that something must have turned up in our neighbourhood in connection with the Hart murder case. Was ever anything so aggravating? Here was the very game, after which I was craving to hunt, running into my very arms, as it were, while I lounged helplessly at Illancarra.

But with the knowledge and recollection of detective duty came the old instinctive wish to deceive; and I laid down the *Gazette* upon my knee, with a sigh as much resembling one of disappointment as I could manufacture.

'Bynon has been romancing,' I observed; 'or doing as I was a little ago, dreaming of the Hart murder, eh, Mrs. Bell?'

'Nothing new, then?'

'Not a thing.'

I could almost see that a load was lifted from that woman's heart, so rapidly the warmth crept to her face and lips, and the rigidity left her limbs and features. Thinks I to myself, 'that woman is in some way interested in that case—there is not a doubt of it'; and from that moment I found myself connecting with every thought of the Hart murder the new housekeeper at Illancarra.

I carefully folded up my *Gazette* and placed it in my bosom, at a moment when I thought that Mrs. Bell was not observing me; and at that time the Squire offered his arm for a stroll on the verandah, as the shadows were growing longer and the afternoon cooler. I was only too glad to avail myself of an opportunity of conversing with

THE HART MURDER

him privately, and we were soon out of earshot of the drawing-room.

'Can you manage to send a messenger to the station for me, Squire, without attracting the notice of your housekeeper?' I asked.

'Of course I can. What crotchet have you got in your head now?'

'Don't ask. You know I was always a queer chap. But how can you give orders, for I don't want anyone to suspect that we have left the verandah?'

'Nothing could be easier. See, there is Bob. I have only to wave my hand to him. There, you see, he is coming.'

I stopped, and from my note book extracted a leaf, on which I wrote in cipher, some requests to my friend Bynon.

'Send him with that as if it were from yourself,' I said; 'and tell Bynon to come over at once and bring the brands.'

As the man approached I resumed my stroll alone while Crawford gave his orders.

'Be sure that he has the note at once,' he added, 'and Bob, don't forget to tell him I want the brands at once. I wouldn't lose that horse for any money.'

'All right, sir,' said Bob, as he pocketed my note, and ran off to saddle a horse.

'There's something interesting in that *Gazette!*' said the Squire, as we resumed our walk.

'There is, and I want to see Bynon about it.'

'But what ails you at Mrs. Bell? One would think you were afraid that she should hear us even talk.'

'So I am. I am open to a confession that I fully share Miss Mary's suspicion of Mrs. Bell. Nothing would surprise me less than to find that she was in some way implicated in that murder, and could lay her hand on the wanted Miss Fairweather at a moment's notice.'

'Nonsense! Upon my word you're a dangerous man to have anything to do with. Fancy, a poor woman not being able to take a situation near you without being suspected of being accessory to a horrible murder! Now, Sinclair, that's what I call carrying the detective spirit altogether too far.'

'Maybe so, Squire. But what do you call that?'

And I indicated by a look the figure of Mrs. Bell, half-hidden in the curtains, eagerly peering at us, as if to satisfy herself of our whereabouts.

'A woman's curiosity,' he replied; 'or an expression of a very favourable impression made by our handsome trooper friend upon my new housekeeper. Allow me to congratulate you, my dear fellow!'

And with his well-known joyous laugh, Crawford turned into

THE HART MURDER

the drawing-room, followed by myself.

The laugh she could not but have overheard seemed to have set Mrs. Bell quite at her ease, and she favoured us by a monotonous anecdote of her earlier days, while she carefully polished her specs with her snowy cambric handkerchief. But, through all her affectation of ease, I fancied I could detect a close but furtive watch of the invalid policeman, who leaned back in his chair with half-closed eyes and a feigned air of fatigue.

We had just finished an early tea, and I had begun to talk of retiring to my room, when the well-known cavalry gallop of my trooper mate's horse was heard coming to the homestead.

'Hallo! there's Bynon,' said our host, getting up to meet him, 'and I'm right glad of it. I hope to goodness he has brought the right brands with him.'

I could not help smiling at the good Squire's determination to please me by throwing dust into Mrs. Bell's eyes as to the real cause of Bynon's visit to Illancarra.

Presently the clatter of spurs and indescribable jingle of accoutrements, to which my heart warms to this very day, crossed the hall and in a few seconds Crawford ushered Bynon into the room, and made conspicuous inquiry about the brands of the mythical horse he pretended to be so anxious to secure. Now, Bynon was a schoolmate of mine, and understood every shade upon my countenance so well that one look into my eyes was enough to let him see there was something behind the scenes. Besides he had a hint in my cipher note, you know.

I asked Bynon to give me his arm to my room before he entered upon his business with the Squire.

'You know this is my first day,' I said, 'and I am not very strong yet, so I am tired.'

And he accompanied me to my room, and assisted me into bed.

'Now for the telegram!' I cried, as he closed the door of my bedroom. 'You might have come straight up, I think, to let a chap know what was going on.'

'You couldn't do anything if I had; but, as far as that goes, none of us can do more than keep our eyes open. It seems that a man was, by the merest accident, observed putting the letter, offering information regarding the murder, under the door of the detective office. They have had the man followed, and lost trace of him about twenty miles off. That's all.'

'What can the man be heading here for?'

'Oh! that is not to be guessed at; but I suppose it will be part of

123

THE HART MURDER

our business to find out. Here is his description,' and he read from a paper he took from his breast pocket, 'Middle-sized and stout, of dark complexion, and with very sleek and glossy black hair. When seen, he was dressed in a suit of gray tweed, and appeared to be about forty years of age.'

Well, after a few minutes conversation, during which we made some arrangements respecting my suspicions of Mrs. Bell, he rose to go.

'I say, have you got a pair of handcuffs with you?'

'Yes,' he replied, laughingly. 'But you are going rather fast, are you not, mate?'

'You don't know what might happen. At any rate, I could put the bracelets on a man if he should put himself in my way.'

'Of course. Well, there you are.'

And he drew the articles from his belt, and tossed them on to the bed.

I lay for some time quietly enjoying myself in the perfect rest of a very comfortable bed. Faint sounds occasionally reached me from the room where Bynon had again joined the Squire. The hearty laugh of the old gentleman and occasionally a more subdued chorus from my trooper friend assured me that they were, in their own way, thoroughly enjoying each other's society.

At last the clatter of accoutrements was once more audible, and finally the joyous gallop of the horse ridden by Bynon indicated his departure.

It was the nightly custom of the Squire to bring to my bedside, with his own hands, the basin of gruel which I had chosen for my last meal of the day. He used to chaff me a good deal about my oatmeal proclivities, and my 'land o' cakes' origin,[3] too, but in a happy way of his own, at which no one could take offence.

Not many minutes after Bynon's departure came the Squire, then, with his dainty china basin full of steaming gruel.

'I tell you what it is, it must be a deuced fine thing to be sick,' he said, gaily. 'No one ever makes such nice stuff as this for me'; and he began to sip a spoonful of the fluid. 'There's nutmeg, and wine, and Lord knows what in it besides. Here, up with it while 'tis hot.'

'Yes, it is very nice to be sick at Illancarra Station,' I said, 'at least while the kind squire reigns over it. Here's to his long life and prosperity at Illancarra.'

And I drank my gruel and said good night to my host.

What a strange sensation is that of going to sleep! I wonder if everybody feels the same just at that moment, or a few moments

THE HART MURDER

before, when the senses are merging into a state of oblivion? I felt a delicious sensation of comfort and warmth pervading my frame some little time after my friend's departure, and gradually my thoughts of the Hart murder, and the unknown man with the sleek hair, and the purse, or whatever it was, which Miss Mary had been crocheting, became strangely amalgamated with Bynon and the Squire and a pair of bright handcuffs that reposed peacefully under my pillow, and I was on the very verge of a sound sleep.

All these sensations were quite legitimate; but all at once an odd throb of returning consciousness—I can describe it in no other words—drove every dreamy thought out of my head with a fierce sense of evil. I cannot tell you how I felt. It was as if I knew I was parting with my senses, in spite of all my efforts; and yet there I lay, staring at the lowered lamp that burned on the table.

I was awake. I felt conscious of that, but it seemed as if insensibility must overpower me. In my efforts, and yet they were only in thought, to resist it, the perspiration actually rolled off my face, and I felt it. So terrified did I become that, with the desperation of a half-revivified body bound in a coffin, I made fierce efforts to sit up in bed, but the only result was a wrench of myself from the pillow and a sharp blow on the nose from the edge of the table, against which I fell.

Looking back from this point of view, of course, I am aware that it was the copious discharge of blood induced by this accident which rendered me conscious of the events that followed. Even as I lay there, incapable of recovering my position, I could feel the warm stream flow from my nose, and with each additional drop that fell upon the carpet a part of the strange incubus that had paralysed my limbs and lain heavy upon my brain evanishing.[4]

As my sense of reflection returned to me, I felt a growing certainty that I must have taken some very powerful narcotic. You know what a wretched feeling one endures who cannot sleep away the effects of a heavy dose of opium. Just so I felt, my powerful resistance of the unnatural sleep producing the cold, death-like sensations that had so terrified me. When at last I was fully lightened, and my brain relieved by the flow of blood, I blessed my stars for the accidental blow that accomplished it.

And I got up, 'fully clothed in my right mind,' to remove from my face the stains, and to obliterate, as well as I could, the marks of any disturbance. Having done so, I returned to my rest, and wondered.

I wondered, in the first place, if I had really been drugged; and, in the second, if so, for what purpose. I wondered if my suspicions of

THE HART MURDER

Mrs. Bell were any sign of an approaching mania for detective work, which was sure to be my especial one if I should eventually become an inmate of the Yarra Bend;[5] and then I wondered what that noise could be.

It was a footfall, as cautious and hesitating as that of a cat. The passage was carpeted, yet, in spite of the velvet shoeing, I could hear every step as distinctly as though it had fallen in my own room; and then the door opened.

Noiselessly—good housekeepers do not allow unoiled hinges in their well-ordered households—noiselessly as any door could possibly do, mine crept slowly back for a space sufficient to give admittance to—Mrs. Bell!

Oh, it was impossible for a practised eye to mistake her, although she was in some measure disguised, and not at all the Mrs. Bell of the day. She had on a loose, dark, shrouding wrapper, up to her throat, and down to her toes, and some sort of hood that shrouded all but her eyes and the lower part of her face.

'What on earth does she want!' I thought. 'But what on earth is that to me? Perhaps she has some particular use for the gruel basin; or has come out of pure kindness, having overheard my movements and feared I was ill.'

Hum! rather a strange way of evincing solicitude, you will think. She deliberately possessed herself of my coat and commenced to rapidly examine the pockets of it. She was eagerly interested, too, in whatever was the object of her search, for, after the first glance toward my bed, which doubtless assured her of my helplessness, her eyes actually scintillated as she grasped the prize she coveted. I don't suppose you will be much surprised to hear that it was the *Police Gazette*.

You will understand my deep interest—I almost held my breath in my anxiety to assure myself that the new intelligence concerning the Hart murder was the object of her search. And it was. I could not be mistaken in the paragraph she perused as she bent over the faint lamp. Every feature was set, as she ran her eye over it, and then let it run rapidly over the room and the few articles of clothing that were lying about.

'She wants more information,' I thought, and I was right—and she got it.

Lying upon the ground, within a few feet of my bed, was a small bit of paper which I had not observed until she pounced upon it like a hawk upon his quarry. You should have seen the woman's face as she read what it contained—it grew like that of a devil! First grew an

THE HART MURDER

ash-coloured horror all over her face, and then it seemed as if all the blood in her heart rushed in a rage to her rigid features, and her very clenched fingers grew scarlet, save at the tips, where the pressure crushed them white.

I was in hopes she would speak in the suddenness of what appeared her raging surprise, but not a word came from her lips until the instant that some recognised terror brought a white reaction once more into her trembling frame. Her fingers lost their power and let the paper go fluttering to the ground, and her figure seemed to sway as she leaned against the wall for temporary support.

Of course, you will understand that all this occupied but a moment or two; and my eye had scarcely returned from following the flutter of the paper to the floor when the housekeeper had disappeared. She closed the door behind her silently, and left no trace of a visit which was better than all the doctor's medicine to my weakened frame.

How I jumped out of bed and grabbed that paper, to be sure—I chuckled to myself as I found it to be, as I had guessed, the written description of the Hart murder man, upon whom the authorities had set a watch, that Bynon had copied for my benefit.

Of course, I needn't ask now what that man wanted in the vicinity of Illancarra—he was facing[6] the abode of Mrs. Bell. There could be no doubt of her interest in the matter of the murder, and yet how clumsy it was of her to drug me for the purpose of getting a look at the *Gazette*. Yes, Mrs. Bell, it *was* a clumsy trick—I could have done it in a far simpler manner.

And what *had* she to do with the murder, then? That was the question I reiterated to myself as I curled myself comfortably under the blankets. Some relation of Miss Fairweather's, perhaps—and a sudden light seemed to break in upon me all at once—who knows but it was the mother of the murderess. How I longed for day to watch her movements; and how pleasantly the sound of my silvery handcuffs sounded under my pillow as I touched them in joyful anticipation.

My sleep, although delayed, was sound and refreshing; and I astonished the Squire by appearing at the breakfast table. To his expostulations, I declared that I felt so much better as to have almost escaped altogether from the invalid list, and that his splendid gruel of the previous night must have worked a miracle.

'Ah, you must thank Mrs. Bell for that,' he said, in his happy way, 'I saw her making it nice for you herself. Eh, Mrs. Bell?'

The housekeeper looked so visibly conscious, that poor Crawford

THE HART MURDER

could not refrain from winking at me. Little guessed the good squatter what occasioned the conscious heat in his strange housekeeper's face.

I saw little of Mrs. Bell during the day, nor did I wish to see her, fully certain as I was that the party whom I expected would not attempt to visit her by daylight. I felt easy in my mind about a watch outside, too, as I knew that Bynon had taken all that in hand, with a full understanding that all of the affair that my state of health would permit me to take was to be left to my management.

Of course, you will believe that I was not strutting about the homestead of Illancarra in the garb of a policeman, but in the attire of an ordinary member of society; and I had occasion to be glad that it was so when I strolled down the front terrace, among the trellises, on that eventful afternoon, and encountered, boldly making his way to the house, a middle-sized man of about forty years of age, attired in a gray suit of tweed, and with the sleekest black hair I ever saw.

'The wanted man,' I guessed, 'for a hundred pounds!'

The man's appearance was that of a well-to-do tradesman or upper servant, and his manner was faultless as he took off his hat to me, and said, 'Good afternoon, sir.'

'Good afternoon, friend,' I returned.

'Might I ask if you belong to the house above?' he inquired.

'Well, yes.'

'You will please excuse me, sir, but I am in search of a lost relative of mine and I have reason to believe that she is in service at Illancarra.'

'In service? There are three or four women employed with the Squire. What sort of woman is your sister?'

'Have you got any new upper servants in the house, sir?' he asked, evading my question by another.

I paid him back in his own coin by inquiring, 'Have you only lost sight of your sister lately, then?'

'Only lately.'

'The only newly employed person at Illancarra is the housekeeper. She has been here but a few weeks.'

'Ah.'

'She is an elderly widow—very faded-looking, and named Bell. Is that your sister?'

'Elderly? Faded-looking?' he repeated, as if astonished. 'I think I must have been misinformed.'

'Very likely, I should think. So your sister is not elderly or faded-looking, eh?'

THE HART MURDER

'I never said I was looking for a sister,' he said, looking suspiciously at me from head to foot; but how could he recognise, in the easily clad, lounging chap of the homestead, that sharp detective, Mark Sinclair? But I was sure of my man—he was the man of the *Gazette*, and I was ready.

'Are you a good shot?' I asked, taking a small revolver from my pocket with assumed nonchalance. 'See if I don't hit that hawk,' and the sharp report rang out a pre-arranged signal to the Squire that I wanted Bynon instantly.

'You didn't, then!' he said, half-triumphantly. 'Not a feather is touched.'

'My hand's out of practice, I suppose,' I observed as the pistol was replaced. 'But what will you give me for some information of that missing relative of yours—sister or what not? I think I know where she is, and all about her.'

The man stared at me in terrified surprise; but my easy, careless air had doubtless a reassuring effect.

'Come down this way,' I continued, leading towards a sort of arbour at some distance down a trellised walk, 'and take a seat while I tell you all about it.'

He followed at my side. The seat I had chosen had more advantage than one for the sort of conversation I intended to hold with the, to me, interesting stranger. There was no egress except by the doorway, and that commanded a view of the road to the police station; besides, it was the rendezvous to which I had arranged with the Squire that Bynon should be sent, in the event of my having occasion to discharge my signal shot.

A rustic seat and a rustic table.

'Go in. You will find it beautiful and cool—it is a favourite seat of mine. And now to business.'

'I don't understand,' he began, seating himself, in a hesitating sort of way, as if he dared scarcely refuse. 'I can't quite see how it is—'

'That I should take so uncommon an interest in your private affairs,' I interrupted.

'Well, yes. You are a stranger to me, and—'

'Stop at that,' I said, leaning against the door post, and watching two horsemen encountering one another on the road. One I knew was the messenger gone for Bynon; the other I was almost delightfully certain was Bynon himself 'How do you know that if I am a stranger to you, you are equally one to me?'

'I never saw you before, that I know of.'

'Nor I you; and yet it is possible that my name is quite familiar to

THE HART MURDER

you, while I only guess at yours.'

'And what *is* your name then?'

'Hum—suppose I give you a hint of your business at Illancarra. You come here on an affair connected with a certain interesting lady named Fairweather.'

The man's face grew stony and white, but he was no coward, and that was the only outward sign of terror he evinced. He was sitting in rather a peculiar position at the moment, and he did not change it as he replied with apparent coolness. One elbow rested on the table, the other upon his crossed knee. The hand of the one on his knee was bent back from the wrist, and on it was laid the palm of the hand on the table. In this way the back of his right hand formed a rest for his left cheek, in which posture he answered coolly, as I have said,

'I never even heard the name. So you are wrong, mate.'

I was standing close to his right side, and the comfortable posture of the man's wrists it was impossible for me to resist. It seemed but a touch and a click and he was handcuffed, and even then the man's nerve never forsook him. I thoroughly admired the fellow's pluck.

'What's the use of gammoning[7] that way, eh? There, that's comfortable, isn't it?' That's what I said as the 'click' sounded in the arbour.

'What's this for?—who do you take me for?—who are you?' he asked rapidly, but he never removed his cheek from his hand, and very funny he looked in that odd position, with the bright steel bands on his wrists.

'Which question am I to answer first? Who am I, eh? Well, my name is Mark Sinclair. Have you ever heard it?'

'The Victorian detective?'

'Ex-actly.'

'What do you want of me—who do you take me for?'

'What do I want you for? Well, I only want that information you offered to the Sydney police respecting the Hart murder—that's all; and, perhaps a little additional about that sister of yours, you know—the housekeeper above.'

'Did you follow me here?' he inquired, with interest.

'No, I did not. You coolly walked to me yourself; and I am delighted to see you.'

'Oh, I see—you have found out, and you are watching—' he broke off suddenly, and for once in my life I felt that I had betrayed too great an interest in my face, and set the speaker on his guard.

'You have no right to handcuff me!' he cried, with sudden passion, 'and, I guess, no authority. How do I know that you are even a policeman.'

THE HART MURDER

'Well, here's one for you,' said my mate Bynon at the door, in full uniform, 'and I arrest you on suspicion of being an accomplice in the murder of Mrs. Hart. Mark, you've been pretty smart here!'

I took the compliment with a pleasant smile.

'No one could mistake the man—the description in the *Gazette* is too evidently his.'

'How the deuce did they come to get me in the *Gazette*?' he cried; 'but I had no hand in the murder, and know no more about it than you do.'

'Ah, that's not a very good comparison. I perhaps know more about it than you imagine.'

'Well, you'll know no more from me,' came angrily from Bynon's prisoner.

'Perhaps you'll think better of that, mate. Bynon, I want another pair of handcuffs.'

'Ha-ha!' laughed he, giving me those he had re-supplied himself with. 'I'll have to send to head quarters for a fresh supply for you. Are you coming down to see our new friend, here this evening?'

'Will it be necessary? Can't you make a clean breast of it, my man, and save both yourself and us a great amount of trouble?'

The stranger stood up, and looked helplessly from one to the other of us. 'What am I to get into it for?' he said. 'I did no murder, and hadn't a thought of murder in my head. It's too bad, so it is.'

'Why make yourself an accomplice by hiding what you know, then? You are poor Mrs. Hart's late servant, and one might expect that, instead of trying to hide her, you would run to the ends of the earth to bring the murderess to justice. The murdered woman was a good mistress to you for many long years.'

'She was all that,' he exclaimed. 'And it was far from my thoughts that it was to be through me going she was to meet with her end. But, dang it all, the very name of money puts the devil into a man's head!'

'Sit down there and tell us all about it,' said Bynon, seeing the hesitating air of the speaker. 'Make a clean breast of it, as Sinclair says, and you'll sleep easier in your bed o' nights. How was it now?'

He seated himself, and with his manacled hands upon his knee and an expression of bitter regret upon his face, commenced the following relation:—

'You know that the old lady had made a will in Miss Fairweather's favour. Well, the very night after the signature there was such a noise of excited voices from the old lady's room that I got out of bed and stole to the door to listen.

THE HART MURDER

'What I overheard interested me so much that I hurried round to the old lady's dressing room, where I knew there was a closet door, behind which I should be in a position to see as well as hear all that passed in the room. Something had occurred to arouse Mrs. Hart's suspicions of Miss Fairweather, and as she was a very violent-tempered woman when aroused, she overwhelmed her companion with every term of reproach.

'"Early in the morning, I shall revoke every word of my will!' she cried."

'"You shall never have the chance, fool!" hissed Miss Fairweather, whose vicious face I cannot forget.

'"I'll settle *your* chance this very moment!" cried the old lady, darting from her bed and seizing a desk, in which I knew the will had been deposited. Then commenced a struggle for the possession of the document, in the middle of which I made my appearance in the room.

'"Edward!" shouted the old lady, who was in her night-dress, "I call you to witness that I wish this will to be destroyed! Not a penny of my money shall the creature ever inherit! I order you to assist me in recovering the paper from the mercenary monster!"

'"Give me the will, Miss Fairweather," I said; and, with a look that seemed to run through me, the girl handed me the paper.

'"Destroy it—I command you!" were the last words of Mrs. Hart as I turned to the door; and, with an assurance that her wishes should be obeyed, I closed it behind me.

'But they were not obeyed. Scarcely had I gained my own room, and sat down upon my bed, in a strange whirl of thoughts, when Miss Fairweather opened the door, and, without excuse, walked into the room. She was like a madwoman. The scarlet of rage burned in her face, and her eyes sparkled with unearthly, or rather devilish lustre.

'"Edward Marsh," she cried, "I'll give you five hundred pounds for that will!"

'There was temptation for a man that loved money as I did; and had as little hope of obtaining it.

'"Where is the money?" was my reply, or question.

'"In the house—you shall have it in your hands in five minutes. Decide!"

'"Without any further service?"

'"Excepting that you leave the house at once, and the country within twelve hours."

'And the upshot, as you will guess, was, that Miss Fairweather had the will, and I was possessor of five hundred pounds within ten minutes.

'I give you my word that until the money was buttoned up in my pocket and I had, in accordance with my promise, packed up a few articles in a valise and left the house in the darkness of night—it was not until I stood outside in the grounds and felt the cool night breeze blowing on my face, and saw the well-known lighted window of my poor mistress's room bright in the dark face of the house, that a sense of reality seemed to flash into my brain.

'"Good God! what is that woman sending me off this way for?" I thought. "I have done no wrong, to run away like a thief in this manner. The will can do her no good, if the old lady keeps her threat of making a new one in the morning. In the morning?"

'Something like that flashed across me, and then I dashed down my valise, and rushed back to the house I had left.

'You know it was late by that time; it must have been getting toward one in the morning. Some considerable time had elapsed since Miss Fairweather had locked the door behind what she supposed to be my departing steps; and the remembrance of all this drew big drops of sweat from my face and hurried my pace to a window, through which I had often effected an unknown and late entrance into the house. When I had crawled in and listened for sounds, as I stood in the dark passage I fancied I heard groans echo down the stairs. Good God, how my heart beat, and how I trembled, as if every nerve was unstrung!

'I scarcely took any precautions to lighten my steps as I flew upstairs and gained Mrs. Hart's dressing room, and the spot from whence I had witnessed the scene about the will. Never shall I forget the sight I saw through the chinks of that door. Upon the carpet, in front of the bed, lay my poor mistress, and over her was stooping that young devil, Emma Fairweather. The girl had her benefactor by the throat and had just dealt her a crushing blow on the gray head with a short iron bar that I recognised as having been in my pantry. I did not stay to look more. I flew downstairs, and got out into the bloodless air, as if the avenger of the innocent were behind me.'

'What for?' cried Bynon, 'Surely, as a man, you might have struck one blow to save the poor old woman!'

'Oh, it was too late! I saw that; and a terror I could not describe gained possession of me. I saw the wretched criminal's scheme at last. She had determined to fulfil her threat, and manage that my flight should seem the evidence of murder; and I felt that, should I remain, she would in some manner bring it home to me. I have lived

THE HART MURDER

the life of a dog since. Good God, how I have suffered!'

'And you returned?'

'I never left the colonies, and when public opinion began to exonerate me, and place the guilt at the right door, I felt as if I breathed once more. You know the rest.'

'No we don't. What became of all the jewellery and plate belonging to Mrs. Hart?'

'As I live, I don't know. I had nothing to do with one pennyweight of it. Ask Emma Fairweather that question.'

'Where shall we ask it, Marsh?' I inquired, quietly removing the handcuffs from the trembling man's wrists. 'Where shall we find Emma Fairweather, that we may ask her that question?'

'As heaven will judge me, I don't know! I traced her to a Labour Office in Melbourne and found she had taken a situation up here. If the new housekeeper is not she, I am at fault.'

'Had Fairweather any elderly friend who might be her accomplice—any person she visited when at Mrs. Hart's, or who visited her there?'

'Not that I know of.'

'What is your object in tracking the murderess?' I inquired.

'More money,' was the reply, as if he felt ashamed of it.

As I sat still there, after Bynon had taken Marsh quietly towards the camp, it would be difficult to separate and analyse the thoughts that ran riot in my brain. I had no doubt whatever that Mrs. Bell had some deep interest in both murderess and murder; and some strange conviction that she was the girl's mother forced itself upon me.

Yet there had been no mother accredited to Emma Fairweather; on the contrary, her mother had been reputed dead for many years. It was all a puzzler to me, but I was determined to unriddle it.

To have seen us, as a family party, occupying the same room at Illancarra that afternoon, one would little have dreamed of the fearful interests involved in my watch of the quiet housekeeper. Not a fold of dress, not a hair of the dark, smooth hair that rested so lowly and peacefully over her brows, not a movement of her eyelashes but was marked by me. If she observed my watch, she made no sign; but she seemed to be deeply engrossed with her book, or her own thoughts, and her face was paler, if possible, than that of the hour-dead corpse.

Miss Crawford sat on her usual couch, and her eye often met mine in its wander towards the silent Mrs. Bell. So strangely unaccountable was her quick, and, it seemed to me, angry observance of the housekeeper that I found myself beginning to watch the Squire's daughter instead of my original object of suspicion.

THE HART MURDER

Miss Mary's crochet needle glistened, and her steel beads sparkled as she passed them through her fingers, but her eye sparkled still more as it rested on me for one instant full of meaning.

'What on earth does the girl mean?' I thought, as my eye dilated with wonder. 'There's something extraordinary up, or my name's not Mark.'

Suddenly Miss Mary lifted her novel, and, with a pencil that hung at her watch-chain wrote some words upon a bit of paper she tore from its cover. Having done so, she looked first at the housekeeper, then at me. Mrs. Bell was observing nothing, if one might judge from her appearance, and the young lady dropped the paper upon the carpet, on the other side of her, and pointed to it with her finger while looking at me.

You may believe in my surprise. To possess myself of that scrap of paper it was necessary to make some plausible excuse. What was it to be?

'Are you reading that book. Miss Crawford?' I asked, with a pretended yawn.

'No. You are welcome to it, if you choose; it's a stupid thing.'

And I got up and crossed the floor to take the volume.

That young lady was no fool. Her pocket handkerchief lay upon the coveted paper.

'Allow me,' I said, picking it up and restoring it to her with a bow, and at the same time seizing the paper.

I returned to my seat, and turned over the leaves of Miss Mary's book. I dared not examine my prize until I was certain that Mrs. Bell did not observe my movements. Good heavens! I have had love letters in my time, but I declare I never valued one so much, or craved to possess myself of its contents, as I did that bit of worn paper pencilled by Mary Crawford.

At last I read it. Read it you, and fancy my feelings of humiliation.

'*You* a detective! Bah! That woman is young, and she wears a wig!'

That is what Miss Mary wrote, and the words stunned me.

My face grew scarlet, from what cause it would be difficult to define. I looked first at Miss Crawford, calmly clicking and counting her beads, and then at Mrs. Bell. I next rose from my seat, and then I calmed myself by a strong effort, and re-seated myself.

Wore a wig, and was young! Yes, I was a detective, and no mistake! If ever I felt ashamed of myself, in the whole course of my police career, I did at that moment. Young! Of course she was; and had I been blind? Why, the woman's eyelashes were as fair as flax!

THE HART MURDER

She was thin. No wonder; the murderer's conscience cannot conduce to plumpness. And the low forehead! Bah! I had been a fool, and all the honour of this detection belonged to Mary Crawford.

I stood upon my feet and noisily took my handcuffs from their usual resting place, and with them in my hands, advanced to Miss Mary and laid them in her lap. She understood me, and smilingly looked up in my face; and that was the girl I had thought a nonentity.

'Pray, excuse my rudeness,' she said, 'and accept my sovereign permission to make proper use of them.'

And she handed me the bright handcuffs. Very odd, indeed, they looked in the fair hands of a pure girl.

I turned to Mrs. Bell. She sat in her seat, with dilated nostrils and with wild eyes, watching the scene between Miss Crawford and myself which I have described. She seemed helpless and dumb as I walked up to her and clasped the nerveless wrists with those cold bracelets.

'Emma Fairweather, I arrest you, in the name of the Queen, for the murder of Mrs. Hart!'

And it was done!

She fell back in her seat, and with so piteous an imbecility in her face, that I had nearly forgotten she was a murderess. Miss Mary did not forget it, though and gathered up her beads from her lap and left the room. Her absence seemed to relieve the wretched woman. She looked up at me as if at once acknowledging her position.

'It is so sudden,' she murmured.

'Not so sudden as your murder of your benefactress,' I was heartless enough to say. 'That peep—which you drugged me to get—at my *Gazette* told you that Edward Marsh was on your track.'

Her face lighted up with fury again at the mention of the man's name.

'I'd give my life to kill that wretch!' she screamed, frantically bending over her manacled hands until her disguising hair fell over her face.

'Wretched being, think of your own frightful sins,' I urged, 'for the sake of your outraged Maker, rather beg His forgiveness. The man you wish to kill is innocent, and the blood of an old helpless woman is on your hands. Lord have mercy upon you.'

I don't remember that the hardness of a criminal ever affected me as did hers. To the last she was incorrigible, and died a felon's death scoffing at repentance to the very last instant of her existence. Bynon and I shared that five hundred, but the only part of it I could prevail upon Miss Mary to accept was a handsome pair of gold bracelets,

THE HART MURDER

prettily formed in imitation of a pair of handcuffs, and bearing the motto, in fine diamonds, 'To the fair detective, in memory of August 15th, 1860.'

First published in the *Australian Journal*, October 1870, as part of the *Detective's Album* serial, under the byline 'W.W.'

NOTES

1 *O.H.M.S.*: On Her Majesty's Service.
2 *soft sawder*: sweet talk, flattery.
3 *land o' cakes*: i.e., Scotland, the land of oat-cakes
4 *evanishing*: evanescing, fading away.
5 *an inmate of the Yarra Bend*: Yarra Bend Asylum, which was located near the junction of Merri Creek and the Yarra River, in what is now the inner Melbourne suburb of Fairfield.
6 *facing*: possibly an editorial mistranscription of 'tracing'?
7 *gammoning*: pretending.

THE CONVICT'S REVENGE

I always look back with pleasure to the times when I used to be stationed in the bush, far from the greedy, grasping, false excitement of a town life, and often at a considerable distance from even the small imitation of city vices which a 'township' of half a dozen houses presented. Pretty spots were often chosen for our camp, for the very simple reason that in some districts it would have been impossible to have selected one that was not pretty; but the one to which I am about to lead you was the very pleasantest in situation of any I can recall during my long career as a policeman in these colonies.

The station was called Coondarra Police Station, from the name of the district in which it was erected, and over which we were supposed to keep watch and ward. I say 'supposed' advisedly, for excepting when especially called on, which event but rarely happened, we scarcely left the camp but for our own amusement. There were some rare fine plains in Coondarra, and our most especial recreation was kangaroo hunting. There were only two of us stationed at Coondarra, and my mate, whose name was Pyne Rollington, was half-crazy with relation to that sport, and kept a couple of hounds, which were almost invariably the subject of barter or sale whenever he could get an opportunity of indulging his caprice and love of change.

I don't know whether or not you have had an opportunity of remarking that in the early days at least, almost every member of the mounted police force was well born and educated. Many of them were the remains of the old cadets, and to get into the cadet force was at one time considered rather a desirable thing. How much the anxiety to don their nice uniform had to do with the numbers of good-looking and very young fellows who gladly permitted themselves to be enrolled as mounted cadets, I cannot say; but the fact remained, and gentlemen bred and born, and very young gentlemen too, formed the greater proportion of the force.

And among the mounted troopers of the present day are still to be found many men who, from the advantages of birth and education, might have hoped to fill positions in a higher grade of society; but the old prestige of the cadet hangs no longer around the trooper of today, and the admission of many less favoured individuals has been the means of lowering the status of the mounted police to something more assimilated with that of their foot brethren.

THE CONVICT'S REVENGE

I have entered into this explanation simply to make you comprehend how it was that I had a young and rather aristocratical mate at Coondarra in Pyne Rollington. He was the son of a clergyman of the Church of England, and having become smitten with the gold fever, determined on coming to Victoria, in spite of all the entreaties and persuasions of his family. Accomplishing his purpose of gaining his father's reluctant consent at length, he was consigned to a merchant friend in Melbourne, who induced him to join the cadets under the supposition that the position was a much better one than it really was; however, the gold-fields were dull, and Pyne, to tell the honest truth, was rather lazily inclined and he preferred, on a close encounter, to ride in a saddle in a pretty uniform to picking and shovelling in hard ground, and so he became a cadet.

Just before the force was abolished, though, and at the period of my story, Pyne Rollington had merged into a mounted trooper, with a determined dislike to police duty, and a determined fondness for such field sports as the colony afforded him. The principal of these was, of course, kangaroo hunting; and to kangaroo hunting and the breeding and purchase of kangaroo hounds in a state of pupdom he devoted the energies and time which her Majesty's ten shillings and sixpence per day failed to secure on behalf of her loving subjects in the district of Coondarra.

He was a handsome young chap was Pyne; about twenty-two, with glossy fair wavy hair, blue eyes, and aristocratic-looking aquiline, although rather delicate and feminine features.[1] He was one of the very laziest fellows, too, that ever crossed a horse; and except in the one line of kangaroo business, it was almost impossible to get him off the broad of his back on his bed. He would lie for hours on the hot summer days, alternately snoozing and reading some novel that he procured, Lord knows how, and it took one of my determined fits to make him do his fair share of camp work. But for all that, Pyne was one of those harmless chaps that are always liked, and I liked my mate in spite of his lazy and useless proclivities.

Days, and weeks, and months passed pleasantly with myself at Coondarra. I had my books too, although they were of a different calibre to those patronised by my mate Pyne; and although I did occasionally accompany Pyne and some kindred spirit in one of their hunting expeditions, I did not neglect my duty, and my patrol to township or around to each of the neighbouring stations was not neglected.

It was on a February afternoon that I occupied the camp alone, Pyne having left in the early morning for a raid on the kangaroos at some miles distance. It was a hot hazy afternoon, when the air trembled

THE CONVICT'S REVENGE

in the fiery sun and the glitter of the creek was unpleasant to see; only under the shade of the huge box trees we had left standing around the camp was the heat at all endurable, and there, at full length on the shaded grass, I watched the sun gradually fall, until at last he crept under the drooping branches of my shelter and forced me to rise.

Coondarra Police Station looked strangely pretty at the edge of that broad undulating plain, where the tall peppermint and drooping box trees threw long shadows on the grass. The green loneliness around it, the tortuous course of the creek where the tall sedges grew, and whose banks were clustered thick with young gum and green wattle bushes; the far away outline of blue hill and sweeping forest, with not a sign else of man's habitation, made a strange and yet not unlovely contrast with the panelled wooden walls and iron roofs of the police barracks. I might have been unconsciously noticing all this for the thousandth time, when I heard the dull thuds of a galloping horse's feet on the firm grass, and a few moments after perceived a horseman rapidly approaching the station.

As the horse bore its rider nearer, I recognised him as a sort of handy man, or stable help, I had seen during my occasional visits, in a professional way, to Coondarra Station. I only knew him as 'Black Bob,' which he was known by in the neighbourhood, and I was aware that he had been for some considerable time in the employ of Mr. Rath, the owner of the station in question. Before I had much time to speculate upon his probable business at the camp, the man had pulled up within a few yards of me, and commenced to speak rapidly and to the point.

'Look here, mate,' he said, 'I'm an old hand, I am, and you know me over at the station, and I hope I'll never come to split on mates and turn informer; but Rath and his folk have been d—— kind to me, and I'm d—— if I can stand by and lend a hand to seeing them wronged, and so I'm off. That's how it is, you see.'

'But I don't see at all,' I answered, observing the man's anxious watch all over the plain as he spoke. 'You'll have to tell me something more before I see anything, mate.'

'I'm a goin' to,' he said, 'but I'm d——ly afraid some one may be on the look out, and if that's so, I'm a dead man. All I've got to say is, that there's going to be mischief over at Rath's to-night, and I advise you to warn them and keep a bright look out. That's all I've got to say, for I'm off. I never thought it could come on me like this, but I *can't* stand by to see it done, and I *can't* split on old chums, and so I'll bolt for it. Good-bye, mate. I'm riding my own horse, as any one at Rath's will tell you. And mind to-night, don't let them sleep at the station'; and, putting spurs in his fresh and spirited animal, Black Bob,

THE CONVICT'S REVENGE

a rough and determined-looking customer, darted from my side, and was almost across the plain before I had half understood the drift of his strange warning.

And yet, as far as it went, it was plain enough; there was to be 'mischief' of some sort perpetrated by some old hand chums of his at Rath's station, and it was my bounden duty to give them the warning I had myself received. I was in a pickle. It was between four and five o'clock, and I had barely time to reach the station before sundown; and yet I did not expect Pyne back before the time I ought to be at the homestead. It would never do for me to wait his return, so there was nothing for it but to leave a note of instructions for him, and start.

And so I entered the barrack-room, and hastily scribbled on a scrap of paper words to the following effect: — 'Come to Coondarra station at once. I have received information that something dangerous is to be up there to-night. Well armed.' Leaving these lines in a conspicuous place on the table, I went out and saddled my horse, and was soon in full swing for the homestead.

But the rapidity of my animal's progress did not prevent me from wondering of what nature the danger to Rath's station might consist; for, strange to say, I did not doubt the genuineness of Black Bob's warning for one moment. He was too evidently in earnest, and too evidently afraid of being seen in communication with me; and, besides, what object could the man have in giving me a useless trip to Rath's — a trip which, to a chap so idle and isolated as I was at Coondarra, could only be looked on in the light of a pleasant ride.

I knew but little of the Raths, although I had been for a considerable time stationed in its vicinity. My visits there had been principally for the purpose of procuring forage for the camp; but I knew that I had seen and spoken to every member of the family, and that it consisted only of three individuals. Rath and his wife were plain but shrewd people, who had been fortunate enough to work their way upwards from a very humble position in life, and they had given the benefit of their success to their only daughter in an education that had only taken effect by making her fancy herself too superior an article altogether for the society of her own parents.

You will perceive that Ann Rath had not, during my few opportunities of observing her, made a favourable impression on me; and I readily acknowledge that such was the case. She was dark and tall, and well enough looking as girls go, but she had a haughty and unbecoming manner, and a way of treating you as if she considered you immeasurably her inferior; and such a way is not, in either man or woman, a way likely to win friends. And now, as you know almost as

THE CONVICT'S REVENGE

much of the family at the station, I shall dismount at the door of the homestead, and, having fastened my horse to a hook in the verandah pillar, enter, and introduce you more personally to each of them.

Very rarely indeed will you find the doors of a homestead in the green bush shut while the sun shines—never, indeed, unless the weather is unfavourable; and so I entered the hall, and rapped with the handle of my whip at the front door. In a moment Rath himself made his appearance from a room on the right and, requesting my entrance, although with some surprise evident in his countenance, preceded me into the apartment, where were seated both Mrs. and Miss Rath.

The mother was seated, stiffly and upright, on a chair near the window. She was an old-fashioned looking old woman, and attired in very homely garb. She was busily engaged in knitting a rough woollen sock, and the huge worsted ball from which her fingers were rapidly weaving it lay on a clean checked apron that guarded her cotton dress. The daughter lounged in a large arm-chair at another window, with a cheap novel in her hand, and her bold black eyes met mine inquiringly as her father ushered me into the room. Mr. Rath had himself been, apparently, reading the newspaper that lay upon the centre table, and which he instinctively took up again even as he was about to open his mouth and inquire my business. He was a short, thin, wiry little man, with a keen black eye like his daughter's, and a shrewd, careful expression of countenance.

'In the first place, Mr. Rath, be good enough to order my horse under cover immediately. It is perhaps better that he should not be seen and recognised at your door.'

Rath laid down the paper at once and went to give the necessary orders; he was doubtless observant enough to see that I had some good reasons for the wish I expressed.

Not so Miss Rath. She appeared inclined to be impertinent.

'What odds is it who sees a policeman's horse at Coondarra?' she asked, laying down her book upon her knee, and looking at me rather disdainfully. 'What is your business here today, sir?'

'That I shall explain to your father,' I replied, tartly enough I dare say. 'Suffice it to say, it is not with Miss Rath.'

'Oh!' the young lady exclaimed, looking daggers at me; but whatever further attack she might have made upon me was prevented by the entrance of Mr. Rath.

'I have received some rather strange information concerning your place this evening, Mr. Rath,' I said, 'and I have lost no time in coming over to give you the benefit of it, and do what I can for you. Is Black Bob about your place now?'

143

THE CONVICT'S REVENGE

'Well, I sent for him just now, and Jim tells me that he has taken his horse out of the paddock, and gone. It seems he told the lad he was off for good, and I can't understand it, for we haven't had a word of complaint.'

'Well, he rode over to the camp this evening and told me that there was going to be mischief at your homestead to-night. From what I could gather, some old mates of his were in it; and as he would neither split on them or help to see you wronged, he has bolted. Have you any enemies, or any idea what sort of danger you might have to fear from them?'

A strange look passed from one to the other of the trio—a look of doubt and terror. Mrs. Rath's knitting fell from her hands to her lap, her daughter sat upright in her chair, and the novel fell to the floor unheeded, while, after a terror-stricken, as it seemed to me, pause, the old man himself darted to a side table, and consulted a book, which I observed to be an almanac, with finger that trembled as he turned over the rustling leaves. At last he lifted up his head, and looking his wife in the face, nodded.

'Is he really out?' inquired Ann Rath, rising to her feet and looking frightened, and consequently more womanly than I had yet seen her.

'Yes, a fortnight ago,' answered Rath unsteadily.

'Perhaps you had better explain to me, Mr. Rath,' I suggested, 'I am in the dark, and time is precious.'

'Yes, I'd better tell you all about it, but we may be frightened about nothing after all. Sit down sir,' and I did so, while Miss Rath followed my example, and the old woman resumed her knitting.

'A year and a half ago,' commenced the squatter, 'a young chap on horseback came to Coondarra, looking for work. He was a gentleman-looking sort of a chap, and indeed I believe he was a gentleman as far as rearing went, though he didn't act like one in the long run. He said he had only just come to the colony, and as I never was any hand at writing, and the like of that, I took him on as clerk and overseer. Well we got on first-rate, although he was a sulky black fellow when the fit was on him, until Ann came home, and he took it into his wise head to fall over head and ears in love with her.'

At this portion of her father's story Miss Rath thought it proper to lift her novel between me and her face, but she let it drop fast enough again at the old man's next insinuation.

'That is to say he gammoned to take a fancy to her, for of course it is well known that Ann is an only child, and that she won't be left penniless; but I don't believe the fellow cared for her no more—no more than I do for that poker, and—'

'Indeed you're quite mistaken, father,' broke in the young lady,

144

THE CONVICT'S REVENGE

'I'm very sure.'

'And I'm very sure that we've no time to waste over such non-sense,' I interrupted, 'go on, sir.'

'At any rate he proposed to Ann and did his best to get round the soft side of her; but she, as might have been expected from her boarding-school manners, insulted the lad and made an enemy of him for life, for if ever there was a revengeful vindictive chap in this world, John Conway was one.'

'But that wasn't all. I had trusted him pretty well by this time and used to send him to the bank regularly, in shearing time or the like of that, to get cheques cashed; and one day he coolly forged my name to a bill for a hundred and twenty pounds. But luckily for me, the bank clerk of Tooma suspected all was not right, and although he cashed the cheque, he had the young chap followed by the police, and he was arrested here at Coondarra.'

'He went down on his knees here to Ann, I believe, though I didn't see him, and begged of her to ask me to let him off. He said the disgrace would ruin him for ever, and kill his father if he heard it. I never heard a word of this, though, until it was all over; if I had, I believe I would have tried hard to get him off, but he was black and hardened-looking to me, and Ann there was as hard as him, and she gave evidence against him that settled the case; at any rate, between us we got him twelve months on the roads.'[2]

'And not half enough for him either!' said Mrs. Rath, for the first time opening her mouth since my arrival.

'But what has all this to do with Black Bob's story?' I asked.

'Oh, I'm not done yet. Before he was taken to gaol he was brought into this room handcuffed, and he stood there just by the table, with his manacled wrists resting on it. Ann was standing by the window there, very near where she is sitting now, and he swore the most dread-ful oath that after he was released he would live only to be revenged on her. I'll not forget him in a hurry, just before the troopers dragged him away! he lifted up his fastened arms and shouted at Annie, "I'll bring you lower than ever a woman was brought on this earth, I swear it by ——! Your pride shall be rolled out of you in the dirt, and by the lowest scum of the earth."

'He was a very handsome young chap,' observed Mrs. Rath, pick-ing up a dropped stitch very philosophically.

I looked at the girl who had been the subject of these terrible threats, and saw that every drop of blood seemed to have faded from her face; her frame, too, was trembling, and her whole aspect denoted a dreadful fear.

THE CONVICT'S REVENGE

'And this Conway's time is served then? do you think it is some attack, or intended attack, of his, that Black Bob hinted at?'

'Goodness knows; to tell the truth I never gave his bounce[3] a thought until you told us of the warning. But Black Bob I'd depend my life on, though he is an old hand, for he's been a good and trustworthy servant for two years. What do you think of it, Ann?'

'I don't know what to think. Like you, I never troubled about what he said until now. What are we to do?'

This question was partially addressed to me, but I made no direct reply to it. 'How many men have you about the homestead?' I asked of Rath.

'Not one'; he answered in a tone of consternation, 'only that lad Jim; and the home flock are not coming in to night either, for I told big Jerry to hurdle them at Spring Flat hut. Good Lord, what can we do? If any attack should take place there is not a man within five miles. Where's your other chap?'

'He's away from the camp, but I left a note for him that will bring him over as soon as he comes back.'

'I should like to go away,' said Miss Rath, rising from her seat and holding on by the back of the chair she had occupied. 'I should like to go to Tooma at once, father?'

Mr. Rath looked at the girl with unfeigned astonishment. 'Afraid!' he exclaimed, 'Well I wouldn't have believed it. But what harm can come to you here? Can't four of us—there will be four of us, counting Jim—can't four men keep you all safe in a stone house? Faugh, girl! I'm ashamed of you.'

Ann Rath fell into her seat again, and it seemed to me from perfect incapacity to stand any longer on her feet; and once there she burst into tears. 'Oh, you don't know him as well as I do,' she cried, 'John Conway is capable of any revenge; and I certainly did treat his presumption in the manner it deserved.'

'Yes, you were always an impudent slut,' the nonentity of a mother coolly observed, drawing another roll of wool off her ball.

Now I had little sympathy with the ordinarily bouncible[4] young lady, but I would, under the circumstances, gladly have seen her in safety miles away from Coondarra had it been possible, but I dared not advise such a measure.

'It is rapidly approaching dusk, Miss Rath,' I said, 'and Tooma is nine miles from this spot. If it is as we fear, and young Conway is about to attack the homestead to-night, he and his mates are most probably lying in wait in the neighbourhood at this moment. To send you out on the fleetest horse would be almost a certain way to throw you into

THE CONVICT'S REVENGE

their hands. So I think you are far safer where you are.'

'Do you really think it is probable that Conway will try to be revenged on us?' she asked anxiously.

'Not knowing the man at all, I can hardly give an opinion,' I said. 'If he is determined and vindictive, and really feels the disgrace that his sentence will attach to him through life, and blames you rather than his own conduct for that sentence, nothing would be easier than for him to organise a party in such a place as a gaol. There he will meet with the very worst characters the colony can produce, and such men are only too ready to assist any project in which revenge is the motive of the leader, and plunder that of his band. But we have no time to lose, sir, let us go out and see what measures we had better take, although I should say there was but little danger of any attack until you are supposed to have retired to rest.'

All we could do was easily done. As soon as darkness had fairly set in, all the windows were barricaded, and the doors locked and barred. We made the two female servants take up their quarters in the principal building from which the offices were entirely detached, and we collected and loaded all the firearms Mr. Rath could boast of; but as the night wore on and Pyne did not put in an appearance, I began to be seriously discomposed; for what could we do did the attackers come in numbers; two men and a useless boy—for such indeed was Jim—who could not even load a gun and was shaking with fear.

I had taken the precaution to 'plant' my horse, so that an inspection of the stable might not discover him. After he had been fed, I took him down to the creek, which was almost close to the back of the offices, and having watered him, tied him under a sheltering and hiding wattle bush. I knew I could trust him to be quiet there for almost any length of time, and so was easy as to the means of locomotion in case of necessity.

Mrs. Rath went to bed as usual, and as little put about concerning what was going on around her as anyone could possibly be. As she lighted her bedroom candle, she favoured us generally with her opinion, that we were all fools; and me, personally, with the information that she'd advise me not to interfere with her knitting and worsted on the table there or she'd let me know, and then she walked off and left us in peace. As for Ann Rath, she sat upright and stony-looking on the sofa near us, and no persuasions would induce her to join her mother.

'Even in the event of any men breaking in,' I said, half a dozen times, 'this is the very worst place for you to be; you are just in their way, where the first that comes can seize you.'

'With you and father by?' she questioned.

THE CONVICT'S REVENGE

'We might manage two or three, but the fourth would be sufficient for you, Miss Ann.'

'I shall *not* go.'

'Very well,' and so ended my attempt to influence this obstinate girl, who was yet a coward to her very heart.

At ten o'clock, all the lights, save that in Mrs. Rath's bedroom, were extinguished. She would *not* put hers out—no, that she wouldn't—until Rath came to bed, an old fool, that he was, like his father before him, and so it remained burning; but as the shutters were closed, we hoped it might not be observed from the outside. I took the precaution, however, to have a stable lamp kept burning in a half-closed cupboard in the room we occupied, which could be brought into use at any moment; and my own dark lantern I had alight and attached to my belt in the usual manner.

I don't think I ever spent a more wretched hour than that which elapsed after everything was still in Coondarra homestead that night; yet it was not my own position that occasioned my uneasiness, but that of my mate Pyne. I was in misery about him, and dreaded every moment to hear the gallop of his horse, and the shot, perhaps, which would terminate his young life. Of course it was a certainty that, if Black Bob's story was true, the intended outragers were in the vicinity, at any rate by that time, and in coming to obey my call, Pyne would be rushing into the very jaws of destruction. How I prayed heaven that his horse might have gone lame, or his favourite dog Spring got ripped open by an old-man's kick, and that he might be camped under a gum tree ten miles off, without either a blanket or a bit to eat. But my prayers were ineffectual, for within fifty yards of me was Pyne himself at that moment.

I daresay it was eleven o'clock, and there we were sitting in the darkness as silently as if we were dumb, when I heard a rattle like that of stones on glass, somewhere at the back of the house. We had every inner door open, so that the least sound from any part of the house might be heard more easily, and as this rattle was apparent, I rose to my feet quietly.

'It's at the buttery window,' whispered Ann Rath, tremulously.

'Most likely my mate wanting admittance,' I answered in the same tone; 'and I pray God it is,' I added to myself, as I stole on tiptoe in the direction of the sound. When I reached the small pantry sort of place indicated by Miss Rath, I cautiously turned on my lantern, and at the same moment, almost, a stone was thrown violently at the small window over my head, breaking a pane of glass to pieces and falling at my feet.

THE CONVICT'S REVENGE

I stooped down to examine the missive, and at once perceived that it was rolled in a bit of paper. You may be sure I lost no time in going away from the dangerous vicinity of the window, and examining the paper so unexpectedly received. I recognised at once a line or two in Pyne's handwriting, traced apparently in haste and with difficulty; and I could not doubt the genuine nature of the note, for it was written on a leaf from a small note book, the dandy nature of which I had often chaffed him about.

'You needn't be afraid of any attack,' it said, 'the mob are gone; but for God's sake come out to me quickly—I'm bleeding to death down behind the stable.—PYNE ROLLINGTON.'

When I look back to this episode in my police career, I candidly own to you that I'm ashamed of myself. My affection for Pyne was so great, and my anxiety at that moment so much excited on his behalf, that Coondarra and its residents gave me scarce a thought. Enough that the mob were gone, and that they had left my poor young mate lying bleeding to death. I stayed neither to wonder at what had caused their flight, or by what means Pyne's communication had reached me, I simply opened the door and, forgetting everything, rushed in the direction of the creek, where was the spot indicated by Pyne. Nay I did not even stop to catch the door behind me; was not Pyne dying, dead perhaps by this time?

I had reached my horse, who welcomed me with a whinny, when a smothered shout reached me from the opposite bank of the creek.

'Go back, Mark! I'm a prisoner! It's all a trap!' and then a sharp pistol crack and silence. Good God! they were murdering Pyne, and in a minute I was on my horse's back like a madman. Fortunately he was a good swimmer, and soon scrambled up the opposite bank. What was I to do there? It was pitch dark and as silent as the night breeze would permit the bush to be.

'Pyne!' I shouted at the top of my voice, and the echoes of Coondarra answered, 'Pyne.' 'Pyne!' I repeated, heedless, and indeed thoughtless of my own danger, and I listened while my panting animal trembled under me; but there was no reply, until a second after shrieks and shots and horrible noises that awoke me to a sense of the folly of which I had been guilty, came from the homestead, and once more I spurred my horse into the creek and dismounting in the yard, rushed to the door from which I had effected my departure. But there was not now a sound to be heard, not *one* after all the hideous screams of a moment or two before.

I think I was half-crazy just then; I walked as a man in a dream, dreaming all the time though of Pyne—my fair-haired young mate—who was murdered. I felt the wall of the passage, as I groped toward the room where I had left Rath and his daughter; but my thoughts were in the bush all the time, and it was a mechanical movement that turned on my dark lantern as I reached the door.

It was open, and there was nobody there, at least nobody that I could see on my first entrance. The table was overturned, the curtains were torn and hanging in shreds from the windows. There was a heavy smoke in the room, and a sharp smell of gunpowder; and there was a black crape mask lying upon the floor. That was all I saw at the first step, but my next brought me in view of old Rath, stretched on the ground insensible.

Almost at the same instant that this object met my horrified eyes, a shock head was protruded from under the valance of the old-fashioned sofa, and the lad Jim's face came in view, every feature expressing terror and dismay.

'What has happened?' I cried. 'Come, out of that and tell, you coward! What has happened?—where is Miss Rath?'

'Oh, they took her off!' exclaimed the lad, emerging, fearfully; 'and the master's killed—oh, Lord!'

While he was slowly extricating himself from his hiding-place I had raised the old man partially, and finding about him no wound, save a contusion on the head, I proceeded to try and recover him from what was, fortunately, only the insensibility produced by a blow. In this I had the satisfaction of succeeding, and, with the assistance of the lad, had just lifted him to the sofa, when a strange figure appeared at the door.

It was Mrs. Rath, in a most singular costume, with her chamber candle in her hand, and a cap with voluminous borders upon her head.

'A pack of fools!' she said, snuffily. 'What are you shooting and firing for, and skirling like idiots? And the table and my knitting!—eh, what's the matter?'

She had just caught sight of her husband's death-like face, and some idea of trouble seemed at last to strike her selfishness.

'Where's Ann?' she asked, looking from one to the other of us helplessly—'where's Ann, Jim?'

'Oh, the bushrangers have taken her away!' answered Jim, looking at the door fearfully.

'Tell us all about it,' I said, as I lifted Mr. Rath up once more, and administered a few drops of spirits, of which I had found a bottle in the cupboard, 'and be quick about it, for I must be off.'

'Yes, yes, follow them!' exclaimed the old man weakly.

'Well?' I cried sharply to the lad.

THE CONVICT'S REVENGE

'They rushed in, four on 'em, a minute after you left,' he said, 'an' all of 'em had black things on their faces. I runned under the sofa while two on 'em wor draggin' at Miss Ann, with every screech out of her you might hear a mile off. The master he fired five or six shots at 'em, till one chap knocked him down with the butt end of his pistol.'

'What sort of men were they? Would you know them again?'

'Oh, Lord, one on 'em, when they had gagged Miss Ann, dashed off his hat and his mask, and asked her if he'd kept his word, an' what did she think of herself now. He was like a wild beast he was; an' God help Miss Ann.'

'It was John Conway,' groaned old Rath, while Mrs. Rath dropped her candlestick, fell against the wall, and, after sliding down it slowly, dropped helplessly on the floor.

I let her lie there. God knows I was no more fit to attend to her at that moment than was the man who was slowly recovering on the sofa.

'I can do nothing till daylight,' I said, sitting down despairingly; 'there is no earthly use in my going in the dark I don't know where. And my mate, poor Pyne, most likely murdered by the wretches! Oh, may heaven curse them!'

And so I sat until day could not be far from breaking, and not a word was spoken by either the squatter or myself. Jim, indeed, less interested, had time to observe the bottle from which I had administered to Mr. Rath, and, as an excuse for his own libation, or perhaps from real pity, he poured out a glass, and carried it to the helpless nonentity on the floor. She drank it mechanically, looked in his face, but did not speak. It seemed as if the very spirit of silence had sealed up the lips of every soul in the room.

At length day did break, and I was startled by a loud neigh from my own horse. I had left him in the yard, as I have mentioned, and I could have sworn to his well-known voice; but the utterance of that neigh betokened a strange presence of his own species, and snatching up the revolver I had laid on the arm of the sofa, I hastily left the room and went to see what it was.

Reaching the back door, and looking out, I saw my own horse standing at the door of the stable, where he had doubtless been making himself at home; but his ears were pricked up, and his full eyes were fixed on an object that quickly drew my attention from the faithful animal. Entering into the yard by the wide gate that was used as a cart entrance was a horse, who, evidently at his own free will, carried upon his back the most pitiable object, and yet my heart bounded at the sight of it, for some premonition of the truth made itself felt by me at once.

It was a man who sat, or rather lay, upon the animal's back, for he

THE CONVICT'S REVENGE

lay forward in the saddle, and held on with his arms round the animal's neck. Every movement of the horse, gentle as his noble instinct made it, swayed the helpless body on his back, and down the shoulder of the animal was dripping a red stream, broad, and well defined on his coat, which happened to be gray.

I ran forward at once to support the poor wretch, who, in another few moments, must have fallen from his position from sheer weakness, and as I did so I shouted loudly for Jim, who made his appearance, and came to my assistance with very considerable hesitation. However, he helped me to carry the man into the stable, where we laid him on a heap of hay in a corner, and then I proceeded to search for his wounds, having despatched the lad for the brandy bottle to the house.

The wretch had three bullets either in or through him. One had passed through the fleshy part of his neck; another appeared to be buried in his shoulder, while a third had smashed the fingers of his left hand in a most pitiable manner.

By the time Jim returned, the terrified servant women made their appearance from their room in the attic, and I succeeded in procuring linen to bind up his wounds. A glass of brandy much revived him, and he was able to reply to my questions. As for the poor horse, who had served him so well at need, he had found his way into the stable, and was quietly munching the hay from a rack in one of the stalls.

'Yes, I'm one of 'em,' the stranger said, and a villainous-looking wretch he was, in spite of his weakness and pallor; 'and John Conway put these bullets into me. May —— —— him! He left me for dead in the bush, but if I *had* been dead, I'd have got up to be revenged on him for this job!'

'Tell me about it as quietly as you can,' I said, 'and don't excite yourself. But before you say another word, tell me is Pyne, the young trooper, my mate, is he dead?'

'Not he, there's not a hair turned on him yet, but he wouldn't hold his d—— tongue, wanting to give you warning; so they gagged him and took him off to the cave. Oh, we didn't want no traps;[5] it was the girl we came for, and the cash.'

'And you got the girl?'

'Yes, Conway's got her safe enough, —— him! But he wouldn't wait for us to get the swag; and when I swore I'd go back again and get it on my own hook, he turned round and put the bullets in me. I thought I was done for as I fell on the grass, but after a bit I managed to crawl into the saddle; and, by ——, I'll pay him for it!'

There is no use in giving you this wretch's story, word for word, as I can explain it myself with far less circumlocution. According to his

THE CONVICT'S REVENGE

statement, which was afterwards found correct on the whole, Conway had organised a party to assist him in his revenge, while still serving his time on the roads. All he claimed for his share was the girl, for whom the informer swore he had vowed a terrible fate, and his assistants were to have all the plunder, of which they were informed there was plenty at Coondarra. One of the villains had been an old mate of Black Bob's, who had been communicated with, but not placed much dependence on, from his evident disinclination to harm an employer who had treated him kindly.

At this stage of the wounded man's statement came its greatest interest for me.

'I was put on to watch Black Bob,' he continued, 'and was not a hundred yards away when he gave you the information at the camp. I watched you off, and then coolly got into the station and found your note to your mate on the table. Nothing was easier after that than to nab him as he came home, and it was with a revolver at his ear that we made him write you that note which I threw in the window to you. If he hadn't tried to give you warning over the creek that time last night, we wouldn't ha' took him with us, but he was —— near getting scragged[6] then.'

By the time the man had, with the assistance of the brandy, got to this point of his relation, Mr. Rath, looking ill indeed, but much recovered, joined us.

'And now,' I said, 'for your information, and I'm off to help out your revenge at once.'

'Mind, I'm Queen's evidence,' he cried, trying to sit up. 'By ——, I'll live to see him hanged yet! You'll find Conway not a mile from this spot. We'd a fine plant there. Do you know a gully that runs right through Coondarra range, where a bit of a creek creeps out and runs into this here creek?'

'Of course I do,' I said; 'but that's not a creek—it's a spring, that rises under the range. Pyne and I have drank at it twenty times on our way to Spring Flat.'

'Oh, much you know about it!' the man said. 'It runs right through the range, I say, and it's our entrance into one of the finest plants in the colony. But take your time, mate, for my pals, d—— 'em, won't stir out of it this day; they've got plenty of grub and grog in the cave, and Conway's girl, and they're as drunk as blazes by this time!'

My future proceedings will, however, explain the remainder of the wounded informer's directions, and in half an hour I had mounted my horse and was on my way to discover the cave where John Conway had taken up his quarters, and from whence I hoped to rescue Pyne

THE CONVICT'S REVENGE

and Rath's daughter. I own that I was far more anxious about my young mate than about the girl, although it may seem heartless to say so; still, I shuddered when I thought of the fate she was most likely to meet at the hands of such inhuman monsters.

The hope of rescuing his daughter almost cured Mr. Rath; and after hastily swallowing some breakfast, we parted in front of the homestead — he to organise a party of friends to join me at an indicated spot, and, I to make myself acquainted with the convicts' hiding-place with as much secrecy as I could; so that, once in force, we might lose no time attacking them from the best point. The informer almost fainted with his exertions to give me unmistakable instructions as to my best means of proceeding, so anxious was he to be revenged on the leader who had repaid his assistance with an attempt at his life.

And so I started. Such a lovely morning it was, with the dew glittering upon every blade of grass so heavily that my horse's hoofs left traces behind as though they had fallen upon fine snow, and hanging upon every leaf and branch in such abundance, that showers fell upon my head as the chirping green parrot hopped from spray to spray. Strange to know that over this very sward where the dew now glittered in the pure morning sun rays, and under those fresh green branches, full of birds' sweet twittering, had but a few hours before passed the robber and the murderer, with the spoil of innocence and the blood of the victim on his red hands.

A very short space of time brought me to the entrance of the gully in question, and there I dismounted and carefully bestowed my horse behind a thick clump of trees and rocks. Cautiously then I proceeded to the spot from whence the stream indicated by the informer issued, and which, even as I neared it, I could yet scarcely believe to have travelled half a mile before it crept through the rocks and bushes on the face of the broken range. But had I wanted confirmation of the wretch's story even more than I did, it would have met me in an object that, as I watched the water trickle down the stones, slowly glided under my eyes.

That object was a fresh cork, with Hennessy's brand on it, and I thought I was dreaming when I saw it emerge, in a little eddy, from around the corner of a boulder, over which hung heavy pendant sprays of a glossy-leaved shrub. I thought I was dreaming, I say, but when I captured the tell-tale cork and smelt, even after its bath, the strong odour of spirits upon it, I felt that I was wide awake, and that Pyne would soon be free. 'They are drinking, as the fellow said,' I thought, 'and, thank heaven, their capture will be easy'; and then I cautiously pushed aside the bush, and stepped boldly behind it into the stream.

THE CONVICT'S REVENGE

For some little distance the way was confined and blocked up with fallen rocks and rich growth of underwood, that flourished wildly in the half light that penetrated the confined passage; but after a bit I came to a more open spot, which had been carefully described to me by my informer, and also following his instructions, I paused and listened.

And very easily indeed I heard the sounds for which I listened, for, proceeding apparently from the very bowels of the range on my left hand, I heard such a row as men will make who drink until they are lower than brutes, and are naturally the vilest and most depraved. Snatches of song, wild oaths and shouts, and, oh my God, such woman's screams at last, that my brain whirled, and I had to think of my poor lad Pyne, or I should have been mad enough to have dashed in among them single-handed, to my own certain destruction.

However, I remembered that Mr. Rath would lose no time in collecting his men, and that they would be awaiting me at the appointed spot before I had made myself sufficiently acquainted with the approaches to the cave; and so I aroused myself, and followed the course of the stream until I reached a particular rock which he had mentioned, and there I turned to the left and found myself only separated from the mouth of the cave by a cluster of thick bushes. Under these I cautiously crept, the noise inside, with the exception of the woman's screams, which had ceased, continuing, and found myself in a position which, had it been constructed for the very purpose of espionage, could not have been more adapted to my purpose.

It was before the mouth of the cave, I have said, but I do not think the word mouth descriptive of the entrance; which was a lofty arch-like opening, partially filled with broken rocks and water-worn boulders, that had evidently been dislodged by time from the heights above. My loophole of observation was one of the interstices between a rock and the sheltering bushes, and through it I had a full view of the interior of the cave.

It was tolerably spacious, and very lofty, and was littered with broken and empty bottles, saddles, and the scattered remains of several riotous meals. One man lay in the stupid sleep of intoxication. Another sat upon the ground supporting his back against the side of the cave; he had a bottle and pannikin between his legs, the latter grasped in his hand; and he was shouting at the top of his voice a beastly, obscene song. From the man's scarlet visage and unsteady movements, it was evident that he would soon be in the same condition as his mate. But these wretched objects attracted but little of my notice, they were but the subordinate figures of a horrible picture.

At the opposite side of the cave, leaned against the wall, a tall, dark-complexioned young man with the devil's brand under his lowering brow, if ever a man carried it. His face was flushed, his attire disordered; and he was gazing on an object at his feet with such a sneer around his lips as only a fiend could wear; that object was the wretched girl, Rath, and for one moment I forgot Pyne while noting the misery and despair of her attitude.

She was on the ground and had turned partially over on her face, with her arms clasped around her head and entangled amid her long hair, that fell disordered around on the floor. Her dress was torn into shreds, and the arms thus partially exposed, with which she tried to hide herself in the sand of the floor, as it were, were covered with blood and bruises. She did not utter a sound, and I might have feared or hoped that she was dead, but for the occasional convulsive movement of her chest against the ground that surged up every portion of her frame. God, how I longed to revenge her! But where was Pyne?

Nearer than I thought. When I was convinced that he was not in the cave, and dreaded the very worst, a heavy sigh almost close to me drew my attention to the rock, at the side of which was my opening. There I discovered in the shadow something like portions of a recumbent figure which was stretched directly against the very rock I speak of, only, of course, on the inside. My heart leaped with joy as I recognised the fair curls of my mate lying within a foot of my eye; and I determined to communicate with him at any hazard before I left to bring the avengers into this den of infamy.

'Oh, come!' cried the young devil, in whom I had recognised the convicted felon John Conway. 'Oh, come!' he cried, just as I made this discovery. 'Don't be hiding your face there all day. You ought to be d—— glad to have three such fine chaps waiting on you! Come, turn up!' And the wretch gave the unfortunate woman a kick which still further disarranged the tatters around her limbs.

But I did not listen or look. I took the chance to whisper to Pyne, 'Pyne?' I said, 'don't stir. It's me, Sinclair. Cheer up, you'll be free in half an hour. Are you all right?'

'Bruised and weak, that's all.'

'Thank God.'

'Oh, Mark!'

'What?'

'That wretched girl. Oh, my God, to live and see such things!'

'Hush! it is all over'; and after this short whispered conversation, I stole out once more, and, once free from the vicinity of the cave, dashed quickly through the stream, and into the gully. Five minutes more brought me to the spot where I had left my horse, and there,

THE CONVICT'S REVENGE

silent as the grave, I found Mr. Rath and ten men, each standing by his horse's head, and fully armed.

'Is it all right?' cried Rath. 'I was lucky in getting all these friends at Bedson's, and they will help us to the last drop of blood. Oh, tell me of my girl!'

Alas! I could not tell him better news than that she was alive; but it was satisfactory to be able to say that we should have no trouble in arresting the villains. 'In fact, we have only Conway to contend with,' I said. 'I beg of you, for mercy sake, not to let him escape. As for me, I shall leave the wretch to you, and get my poor mate out of harm. You, sir, I would advise to select the friends you may choose to carry your daughter from the cave.'

A few words arranged it all, though several of the men who had volunteered to assist Rath expressed their disappointment at missing a brush with the wretches. 'I should just like to have shot Conway down like a bullock,' said one huge fellow in a stockrider's dress. 'It would have been better than a hunt to have seen him kicking the last breath out of him.'

'Let him kick it out at the drop,' I said, and my sentiments appeared to coincide with the most of my followers.

Of course, ten men required to be more cautious in approaching the cave than one; but we did it in single file, and at last mustered within twelve yards of the entrance to the cave. There was not a sound within, save the clinking of a pannikin and a bottle, and I concluded that Conway was refreshing himself with another nobbler, and his mate had at last fallen asleep.

'Now for it!' I whispered. 'I'll lead; but mind, I'll leave him to you after the first surprise.'

'For heaven's sake, let me in first!' urged the big stockrider to whom I have alluded. 'I'd give a month's pay to get the first grip of that fellow!'

'But would you bargain for the first shot from his revolver?'

'I'll risk it.'

'All right, onward!'

A rush, a crash through the bushes, shouts and cries and oaths and blasphemy; shots reverberating in the cave and out on the range, and a terrible struggle between our stockrider and the desperate convict, Conway, All this while, I was cutting the ropes with which they had tied my poor mate. I carried him out in my arms and laid him near the stream, and then rushed back to find the struggle over, and the three men lying bound with their own bridles and tether ropes on the floor of the cave. Ann Rath was lying out on the grass, where one of the men

THE CONVICT'S REVENGE

had assisted her father to carry her, but it was only too evident that her last moments were approaching.

Conway was swearing most fearfully; oaths that sounded horribly even in my accustomed ear. Even our threat of gagging him only served to increase the wretch's determination; and his one great triumph was the condition to which he had reduced the proud girl who had consigned him to a gaol. All the details of the indignities she had endured at the hands of himself and his drunken mates were detailed in the spirit of a demon, until at length we were obliged in real earnest to fulfil our threat of gagging him.

A mournful procession it was to Coondarra after that scene in the cave. We carried our prisoners bound and thrown like dogs on horses volunteered for the purpose, to Tooma, where only was a safe lock-up in which to dispose of them; but a few of the neighbours accompanied poor Rath and his dying daughter to the station, and the girl I never saw again. She died before the trial of the convicts took place.

The informer lived long enough to give evidence against his mates, but nature eventually succumbed to his severe wounds. Conway was hung, hardened to the last; but his wretched companions escaped with imprisonment for life.

It is the portrait of this cold-blooded young criminal that is before me in my album as I write; yet it is pictured a fine, intelligent face, with a frank, noble look about it that, God only knows, but he might have carried to the grave, had Fate placed his young life under more propitious circumstances.

First published in the *Australian Journal*, November 1869, as part of the *Detective's Album* serial, under the byline 'W.W.'

NOTES

1 *He was a handsome young chap was Pyne*: Fortune's description of Pyne Rollington is similar to that of the young Percy Brett, her second husband.
2 *twelve months on the roads*: a typical sentence at the time involved hard labour on the roads (in and out of chains).
3 *bounce*: boast
4 *bouncible*: impudent
5 *traps*: police
6 *scragged*: throttled

OUR LAST CRUSHING

It was a famous one, and the memory of it is hanging around the old reef yet, independent of its tragical termination. The old residents there still tell new-comers about the last crushing from the Swede's claim, and of the magnificent lump of gold that was turned out of the retort at Webster's machine, where there was such excitement on the occasion as has never since been repeated there.

At the time I write of, there were but three of us in the party; and our claim had taken its name from the fact that it had originally belonged to two Swedes. One of these was still a partner, but the other had sold out long before our last crushing. The remaining one, whose name was August, was a gentlemanly, quiet, and hardworking fellow, and I dare say, one of the handsomest chaps within a radius of fifty miles. A most complete contrast was my other mate, a raw-boned, vulgar Scotchman, with some of the filthiest habits you could imagine, and one of the biggest lushingtons[1] on the reef to boot.

We had worked on that claim for more than two years; getting payable stone one crushing, and not the next; for I never saw more patchy ground than was round the McKinnon Diggings. But the ground was now literally worked out, at least we thought so, and we had made up our minds to sell out after this crushing.

We had about two hundred tons of stone; and it made a very pretty pile when we had carted it down from the reef to the machine yard and built it upon the layers of timber that had been laid down for the purpose of burning it. It was rather a strange sight to see it by night, after it had been burning long enough to set the whole body of the stuff aglow; but it was almost impossible to remain in the vicinity of the heap, so strong were the sulphurous and arsenical fumes that puffed from it in huge volumes of smoke. I am afraid that our Scotch mate, Jack, made it the excuse very often for visiting the grog shanty close by, for he used to swear that he tasted nothing but copper in his mouth from morning to night.

We were supposed to take it in turns, or shifts, as they call them, to watch by the kiln, and also during the crushing that followed its being burnt; but, depending so little as we did upon Jack, the most of the watching, and indeed, all the responsibility, rested upon August and myself. So we took it in turns; one relieving the other at stated intervals, while the one off duty went up to the tent on the reef, cooked

OUR LAST CRUSHING

the necessary 'tucker,' and slept his allowance in his sack-bottomed 'bunk.' There was one other duty to be divided, however, and that was the attendance upon a sick miner, who was camped quite close to us on the reef.

I must say a word or two about this chap, as he has some little to do with my story. His name was Adolph Rasch, and he was none other than the fourth mate who had, as I told you, sold out of the claim long previously. He was one of those impatient fellows who *can't* wait for anything, and the inconstant yield of the claim disgusted him; so he sold out and went to the Lachlan about twelve months before our last crushing, with the price of his share in his pockets, which he had taken out of ours combinedly. So that my share got to be a third instead of a fourth, and we managed to carry on the work without either hiring labour or selling a share.

Well, Adolph came back two or three months before we said good bye to the Swede's claim; but he came back not only penniless, but so broken in health and spirits that he was looked upon by the lot of us in the light of a dying man. Diggers are not wont to be uncharitable, and so it seemed only natural to my mates and myself to see Adolph in his old place on the reef, and to share our stores with him, although he was quite unable to make any return in labour for it. He managed to chop a log now and then, or to look after the firing or so during our absence sometimes, but, generally speaking, he lay in his bunk, and at last, appeared to either want the will, or power, or both, to get out of it at all.

I don't think he was a favourite with any of us. He was selfish and rather surly in his manner; but I hope we never acted toward him, at last, as if he might have been more grateful. He used to growl a little at times about his ill-luck, and regret that he had sold out of the claim; and I have seen a dark bitterness in his face when he stood by, as we landed some stone upon the surface in which you could see the gold well defined and heavy; but ordinarily he seemed to care for nothing, saving the one thing of being let alone.

Well, the weary time of crushing was over at last; and the amalgam was carefully closed up in the huge retort, and put over the furnace; but this happened to be done during my absence, as August had been on watch from twelve o'clock the previous night, and I was to relieve him at noon. Shortly before I left the reef, I looked in to see if Adolph wanted anything, and I found him in his bunk, and in the most excited state I ever remembered to have seen him; but almost his first words accounted to my satisfaction for the unusual brilliancy of his dark, sunken eyes and the red flush on his cheeks.

OUR LAST CRUSHING

'Jack has been here,' he said, lifting himself up, and pulling a bottle from behind his 'bunk.' 'The retort is on the fire, and it took four of them to put it on. Ah, ye're lucky chaps!'

'What have you got in the bottle?' I asked.

'A bottle of port wine,' he replied. 'Jack brought it to drink luck to the smelting. You must have a drop with me, Bill,' he added, 'for the sake of old mateship, although I'm not in this lot. You're going on your shift now, aren't you?'

'Yes. I expect poor August is pretty well knocked up,' and I took the drop of wine he handed me in his own pannikin, more for the fear of offending his touchiness than anything else, and then I said good bye, and went down to the machine.

It was an afternoon of great excitement that. I don't suppose there were half a dozen unoccupied persons on the diggings who didn't stroll to the machine yard for the chance of seeing the lump of gold when it came out of the retort; and much was the pleasantry occasioned thereby in the aforesaid grog shanty to which my estimable mate drew them every one, and 'shouted' until he hadn't a leg to stand upon. And when the gold grew tolerably cool, there were great attempts at 'hefting' it, some of the women especially taking great delight in lifting it, and carrying it a few yards, to prove their uncommon strength of muscle. I need not tell you to a pennyweight how heavy it really was, but its weight was over a thousand ounces, and it was a goodly sight for a thirds-shareholder's eye to look upon.

At last, as the sun went down, and darkness began to creep around, the curiosity-seekers dropped off in twos and threes, some to their homes, and others to their several night shifts; while not a few joined my silly mate, Jack, at the shanty, where sounds of laughter and song, such as it was, served to do away with any lonely feeling I might have experienced as the night grew older. When I relate to you the position I was in at midnight, any of you who have not been on the diggings during the gold-getting days, and have not had ocular demonstration of the careless way they had of doing things where gold was so plenty, may perhaps be inclined to discredit my story; but there are very many who will read this that can recall similar circumstances, and not a few who will remember the very events in which our gold played so conspicuous a part.

The crushing machine was situated at a distance of seven or eight hundred yards from the reef, and at a bend of the creek where had been formed a dam that threw back a broad sheet of water close under the huge, dark beams of the engine-room. On the night in question, the low moon mirrored herself there, and a dismal-sounding breeze

OUR LAST CRUSHING

rustled the young trees that surrounded the water with a green fringe. At midnight there was not a sound save that rustle, and the occasional shout of intoxication that came from the shanty a little behind.

It was rather a strange situation, you may suppose. The generally noisy crushing mill was silent and loomed up between me and the pale sky as the moon went down, a weird and gaunt-looking shadow. Some necessary repairs were to be done before the next 'lot' was commenced on; and meanwhile the workmen had dispersed to their several homes; even the watchman was not there, as the amalgam had of course been removed from the ripples, and there was nothing to watch but the lump of gold that lay at my feet, and that no one had any business with but our three selves. The manager had, it is true, offered, nay almost, insisted upon stopping with me; but, as I knew the poor fellow had already spent one sleepless night, I would not hear of it. His office and residence was not twenty yards from the furnace; and, promising to arouse him as soon as the gold was cold enough to be reduced for the purpose of smelting, I saw him enter his cottage, and shut the door behind him.

And so I was left alone. The furnace was almost in the centre of the large machine yard, which yard was simply a portion of enclosed bush, with many of the trees still flourishing within its fence. One of them had been cut down almost close to the furnace, and into its side had been inserted one of the spindles of a much-used grindstone, the other having the benefit of a post of its own; and against this stump I placed my back, as I sat down to watch my gold. I sat upon a sheet of iron, upon the very end of which rested the valuable proceeds of our retorting, and which was still warm with the heat communicated to it by the gold.

I yet remember many strange thoughts that whirled through my brain during the short time I remained conscious after the manager turned in. I calculated what the amount of my share would be to a pound, setting down the loss in smelting at a very low figure, you may depend. The gold looked so rich—how could it be very impure? Indeed, I recollect drawing a comparison between it and the yellow moon as it went down behind the line of trees beyond the dam, to which, either in apparent size or colour, it was not really unlike. And then, as the moon disappeared and its glittering track faded from the water, I watched the lights of the reef reflected in the inky-looking dam, and thought how cold and comfortless a dive it would be should some wretched being from the near shanty terminate his purposeless existence there.

And then, as it grew so dark that I could no longer see the water or the fringing trees that rustled so restlessly in the breeze, I brought my observation closer and looked at the dying embers in the open furnace before which I was seated. The steady, red glow was pleasant to look at only when a fresh breeze lifted the white ashes and scattered them wildly over me and my gold; and the breeze brought occasional sounds of orgies distressing even to think of from the shanty, where my mate wasted his money and his strength, until I wished heartily that it was morning, or that my more sensible mate, August, would come and keep watch with me.

Not that I dreamed of danger to the gold, only I was sleepy, and sensible of a loneliness to which I was ordinarily a stranger. Perhaps it was my very good fortune that made me impatient for its perfect consummation in ingots of gold, with the stamp of Webster's machine on them; at any rate, my last conscious act was to lay my hand upon the precious lump of metal, and assure myself that it was quite cool enough for the manager's process. I might have aroused him at that moment, but how could I, when now and then came so evidently to my ears the sound of his weary snore. And I blinked at the twinkling stars, and looked into the red embers, and listened to the sighing of the wind in the branches of huge gum-trees that waved between me and the stars—all the while with my hand on the warm gold—until I slept.

And it must have been for hours. When I wakened, the sun was beginning to flush the east; the birds were beginning to twitter in the branches, from beyond which the stars had disappeared, and—the gold was gone!

I was on my feet in a moment, but not at first in any alarm at my loss, of which I was not indeed conscious. I at once concluded that August had come down, and that the manager and he were engaged in smelting or in preparations for that process; and although there did not appear to be a soul about the yard, my first visit was to the forge, where they were in the habit of smelting. There was no one there; the bellows were still, the charcoal black, and the place silent; and with a first sentiment of fear I hastened toward the office and knocked loudly. There was an immediate reply, and in a few moments the manager joined me.

'What has been done with the gold?' I asked.

'The gold!'

The very expression of amazement on the man's face as he repeated my words was a sufficient answer, and I felt my very heart tremble within me with fear.

'The gold's gone,' I managed to articulate; 'and if any of you have been playing a lark, it's a blessed silly one, that's all.'

'I've never been awake since I turned in,' he said again; 'and you

OUR LAST CRUSHING

promised to call me when the gold was cool. I've had no hand in any larks, I assure you.'

'I don't suppose you have; but the gold's gone, and I've been asleep, and I know no more about it. I suppose I had better go and turn up Jack at the shanty; most likely it's one of his games.'

And we both went to the grog shop, and managed to arouse the inmates from their heavy slumbers. Jack was lying on a rough sort of sofa in the part of the premises devoted to drinking, and I was obliged to confess that his worst enemy could not suspect him of the power of carrying a thousand ounces of gold for fifty yards. He was helplessly intoxicated, so drunk that all my attempts to arouse him sufficiently to understand our loss were ineffectual.

The greatness of the calamity seemed to so completely overwhelm my faculties that had it not been for the more collected manager, I would have sat down and wondered idly. It seemed so entirely incomprehensible to me that the riches I had but a moment, as it were, before possessed should have vanished so completely as to have left the consciousness of its possession a haziness only. I cannot describe my feelings to you; bewilderedness was the principal of them, I think; and what happened afterwards, in the search for our gold, I look back upon still as a sort of dream, until the *denouement*, which I remember as a vivid and fearful reality.

I leave you to imagine the dismay of August, whom we found fruitlessly searching the yard on our return, and the ineffectual search and inquiry, in which we were joined by every unoccupied man on the reef. It was not a common event that such a weight of gold should be carried off under the owner's eye, as it were; nor could it have been so easy a task to carry it off, but that one must hope to find some trace as a guide. But there were no traces — not one. It appeared as if magic had been at work in the affair, and the strangest excitement prevailed about it in the neighbourhood. Weary in both body and mind, August and I reached our tent at night and sat down upon our bunks opposite to each other with blank looks into each other's eyes.

'What on earth's to be done?'

'Nothing,' replied my matter-of-fact mate. 'We have done all that men can do, and the police must do the rest. I don't believe we shall ever see a single pennyweight of it again.'

The opinion was too much my own to contradict, and I own to you that had it not been for very shame, I could have cried heartily; but the sight of my more resigned mate gravely cutting up a pipeful of tobacco at the other side of the table restrained me, and I set to work to kindle a fire and hang over the billy.

OUR LAST CRUSHING

'Have you seen Adolph today?' asked August, as he stooped for a bit of red stick to kindle his pipe.

'No.'

'Nor have I. I think I'll go in and see how he gets on; we have forgotten the poor fellow.'

But August soon returned to say that there was no appearance of our sick mate either in or about his tent. Now this was rather a strange circumstance, as he had not, to our knowledge, been away from his place for weeks. So considering it, we left as soon as we had our suppers, and made a round of inquiry about him. No one had seen Adolph, not a soul, nor had he been observed about his door as usual. Indeed, we ascertained that he had not been in his tent in the early morning, as one of the reefers had dropped in as he was passing to tell him of the lost gold.

'He had a bottle of wine from Jack yesterday,' I said to August as we turned into the track which led to the machine. 'I hope he hasn't got too much and tumbled down one of the old shafts.'

My mate was silent for some minutes, and then he said, abruptly, 'Do you think Adolph could *carry* that gold?'

'Good heavens! do you suspect *him* of the robbery?' I inquired. 'I don't think he could walk twenty yards under it.'

'I believe Adolph to be a thoroughly unprincipled man,' was the reply; 'and more, I believed a good deal of his late weakness was *gammon*.[2] I don't mean to say that the man was not ill, for that was evident, but he made the most of it, and of our liberality. I have observed his chagrin at our late success when he little thought it.'

It is strange how often one idea of another person will start a train of fresh ones in a listener's head; after August had spoken, twenty circumstances recalled themselves, all tending to the deceit and untrustworthiness of our late mate. The possibility of his being the robber once settled by us, we reached the probability as a matter of course, long before we stood upon the spot near the furnace where I had slept, and from whence our gold had been stolen.

'I wonder if there is any drug which can be administered to take effect a stated number of hours afterwards?' I said to August as we entered the manager's office—'Adolph was very anxious for me to have that port wine yesterday afternoon, and I slept strangely.'

'The police have made no discovery yet,' said the manager, who had a worried and anxious look, as a man who must be partially implicated in so strange an affair, 'and I am sorry to say, they don't appear at all sanguine. By the way, you left your pipe near the furnace last night, or rather this morning'; and as he spoke, he took the article from the shelf

OUR LAST CRUSHING

above his head, where he kept his crucibles.

'I don't smoke,' I replied, taking the pipe from his hand and looking carelessly at it—'Is it yours, August?'

'No.'

'Well, I found it by the stump there, and I thought it must belong to you; but doubtless an owner will turn up for it.'

'I don't think it,' said my taciturn mate, in so strange a tone that I looked more carefully at the pipe, and at once recognised it as a favourite one of Adolph's.

'Oh, that settles it beyond doubt!' I exclaimed. 'Adolph is the robber. We must go and give this fresh clue to the police at once,' and we started on that errand, after explaining to the manager our suspicions of our late mate, now almost turned to certainties. The fact of the pipe lying there seemed so natural to us, who knew that Adolph was in the almost invariable habit of carrying his in the front of his shirt; what indeed could be more likely than that it had dropped from there while he stooped to lift the gold from my side?

I spare you the details of our doings at the camp, and of the restless, anxious night which we both passed. With sunrise we were down once more at the machine yard, and were examining closely for tracks of the missing Adolph. The deserted lead of some old alluvial diggings ran directly outside one side of the machine fence, and not a score yards from it; and at the other side of the lead, the bush scattered its old trees, and laid its darker shadows. Once across the lead with his stolen gold, then, and Adolph would be almost safe from pursuit, could we find his footmarks, or anything to guide us.

'He would doubtless carry such a weight the shortest distance possible,' said the manager. 'I should strike a line from the stump to the nearest point of bush, and then you will not be far off his track.'

We did so. The holes were very close on that line; some of them were girdled with tufts of grass, and others fallen in and leaving wide, shapeless gaps, instead of the well-defined shafts the diggers had left years before. I could fancy that by night the danger in crossing that lead would not be mythical, for in the broad daylight it required circumspection to choose a foothold in many places.

I had not half-crossed the lead, where I was carefully examining every foot of path for the chance of finding a footmark, when a call from August changed the direction of my progress. 'There are tracks here, and recent ones,' he said; 'and there—see over by that hole— marks, what are they?'

We went to see. They were slips at the edge of a less-fallen-in shaft than the others.

OUR LAST CRUSHING

'They are very like the marks something would leave in slipping into the hole. O Lord!' This last exclamation was drawn from me by the object upon which my eyes rested as I looked over the broken edge of the shaft, where my mate and the manager soon stood by my side and looked also. Looking as we were for tracks of the missing man, so little did we expect to find him as we did, that it was seconds before our tongues were loosened to comment upon the fearful sight.

At the bottom of the hole, about twenty feet from the surface, lay our late mate, Adolph. The body—for it was impossible the man could be living in such an unnatural position—lay upon its face, so cramped up in the narrow shaft that the legs from the knees were bent backward, and the head was bent so backward also that the crown was on a level with the back. Thus the upper portion of the half-upturned face could be seen from the surface; a face so white that it was evidently that of a dead man: but hiding the back, or rather crown, of the head was a small sack of some sort, and the sack was not empty.

You will doubtless guess what that sack contained. When the body was lifted, the neck was found to be broken and the back of the skull fractured by the weight of the gold he had apparently carried on his shoulder. There were many surmises as to Adolph's intention in crossing the lead, but there were few who doubted that he was on his way to 'plant' the gold in the bush, and return to his tent before he could be missed from it. One false step in the dark had precipitated him into eternity, and the object of his crime had been the means of his punishment. So it was that we recovered the gold of our last crushing, and we were glad when it found its way into the crucibles and lost the ruddy hue that the wretched Adolph's blood had left upon its side.

First published in the *Australian Journal*, September 1869, under the byline 'Waif Wander.'

NOTES

1 *lushington*: an alcoholic
2 *gammon*: pretence

THE STOLEN DEED

The case of which I am about to give you my recollections was a most complicated one, and one which engaged both my watchfulness and curiosity to their greatest extent. The chief events occurred in one of our largest towns, and in one of the finest houses in its most aristocratic quarter.

I was put into it in the usual way. Our chief handed me a note one morning, with an intimation that I had better attend to its contents. The following is that note—

'Mrs. Garrand will be glad to have a detective sent at once to Elwood House on duty. The matter she will explain to the officer personally.'

The note was written in a clear spirited hand, and on crested and monogrammed best cream laid note; and it had also the faintest suspicion of a perfume strong enough to have withstood its passage through various hands to our office. All that, however, did not secure it any better treatment than being dropped into my pocket, where it might air its aristocracy with the companionship of cigar shreds and some few stale biscuit crumbs, suggestive of a Bohemian existence enjoyed by the owner of the pocket in *my* coat.

Now, the business of a detective lies more among such people as the Garrands than an outsider would be apt to think; but in this particular instance it so happened that I knew very little about the family bearing that name; my first step there must be to make myself as well acquainted with their affairs as the short time at my disposal would permit. We have ways and means of doing such things, however, available at a moment's notice, and in a very short time I was up in the facts concerning the Garrands, with which I now make you intimate.

Some years previous, Mr. Garrand had been a wealthy merchant of fifty years and a widower with an almost grown up family of two or three sons and daughters. Almost simultaneously with his retiring from business on a handsome income he contracted another alliance (I had much rather have said married another woman, but that, you see, would have set me down at once to be as low as my profession) and, in a year or two was obliged to be consigned to a private asylum—according to the dictum of a medical examiner, a hopeless lunatic.

If I have put those two events in a too close juxtaposition, believe me I had no ulterior motive but that the fact really so happened.

THE STOLEN DEED

Poor Mr. Garrand was not the first man who married and went mad; but, on the other hand, a good many have gone mad before they went through that ceremony that begins with 'dearly beloved' and ends with 'amazement.' So to anyone drawing too hasty conclusions from either of these facts, I would in all humility recommend a study of the old national motto, *Honi soit qui, &c., &c.*

But fate seemed against Mr. Garrand in many ways; for after his marriage, and previous to his lunacy developing itself, he lost all his children save his eldest son Robert, who was at the time I was called to Elwood House a young man of twenty-five, with a comfortable income of his own inherited from his mother, though he still resided under the same roof as his father's present wife.

Fortified with this slight knowledge of their family matters, I presented myself at the almost palatial House of Elwood, and was instantly admitted to Mrs. Garrand's presence. I had taken the precaution to send in my name as 'Mr. Brown, from the office,' but the lady had, no doubt, guessed my business.

Mrs. Garrand was seated at a writing-table almost covered with papers, although she was richly attired in a style more suited to a drawing-room. She was what would be termed a fine woman, about forty perhaps, with a splendid figure and upright carriage, a profusion of dark hair dressed in the mode, and an aristocratic face with clear-cut features and a keen dark eye. I saw all this at a glance, and I saw, too, that she was very pale, and that her white hand trembled as she pointed me to a chair, until the diamonds on it scintillated like sparks of green fire.

'You are from the detective office, I presume?'

I bowed.

'I thought so; pray be seated while I tell you the business on which I require your assistance. I have lost a valuable document from this spot on the table,' she went on, placing a finger as she spoke on a particular spot not very far from her left hand. 'I had taken it from that old desk to refresh my memory with its contents, and hadn't finished reading it ten minutes when it was gone.'

'When was this?' I asked.

'It was last night, late—eleven o'clock, I should say. However, I did not feel so much alarmed last night, as I had been thinking deeply and fancied it so impossible for the paper to have disappeared that I thought I must have unconsciously pushed it among some of these others. So I locked up the room that nothing might be disturbed and this morning made a thorough search; the result being that the paper is gone.'

I looked around the room for the purpose of making myself acquainted with the position of things. The writing-table was almost opposite one of the French windows, and Mrs. Garrand sat with her face to it, doubtless for convenience of light, for view there was none, save the wreathing greenery of the piazza. There was but one door of entrance to the room, and it was behind the lady.

The window was slightly open as I looked, and I got up and opened it wider. The piazza ran right and left to each corner of the house, round which it went, I had no doubt, although I could not satisfy myself of the immaterial fact from where I stood. At the extreme right was a clustered mass of white jasmine, covered with star-like blossoms and surging out invisible perfume that reached me even inside the window. To the left, not six paces from the window, was a pagoda-like gimcrack of a little dog-kennel, out of which popped a little ill-tempered terrier as soon as I put my head outside and nearly exploded himself with yelping viciously at me.

'You see how impossible it would have been for any one to have entered that way,' Mrs. Garrand said, rising and following me to the window. 'That little dog would not permit the silent passage of a mouse.'

I turned inside again and glanced over the table. Tossed among the papers was a little wilted branch of jasmine with a bunch of the perfumed blossoms on it; most evidently it had not been gathered that morning—it was too much faded, and its appearance suggested one of the questions I plied Mrs. Garrand with at this stage.

'Are you quite certain, to commence with, that the paper you miss is actually gone? Is it *impossible* that you have mislaid it?'

'Quite impossible, unless it has taken wings. I have searched every corner. There was no fire in the room, and no person but myself in it—to my knowledge,' she added, cautiously.

'And you never left the apartment until you missed the paper?' I asked, with my eyes resting on the spray of jasmine I have alluded to.

Her eyes followed mine as she answered, and a faint colour rose in her face as she lifted the withered flowers.

'I did leave the room, but had it not been for this, I should have forgotten about a moment's absence; I just stepped outside to the piazza, feeling the air close, and stood a second or two at the jasmine trellis. But if you will come with me you will see how impossible it would have been for anyone to take advantage of that.'

'Even a second's absence would have been enough for anyone to enter the door and lift a paper from that table,' I observed.

'Have I not told you the door was fastened? Being well aware of the

THE STOLEN DEED

value of the paper—to some of the inmates of this house,' she added, hesitatingly, 'I snibbed the door before opening the desk.'

'Now, see here,' she continued, as we went out through the window and the dog nearly choked himself with insane attempts to get at me, 'that dog would make just as much noise if, excepting only two persons, any other one in the world were to venture here.'

'And those two exceptions?' I repeated.

'We will come to them presently,' she said, trailing her rich dress past me to the jasmine in question. 'Here is where I paused, and not, certainly, for more than five minutes.'

'As you stand now?'

'Precisely.'

'With your back, then, to the window?'

'Yes.'

She returned to the room again and resumed her seat at the table, while I also deposited myself on the chair I had previously occupied.

'And now about the two exceptions you spoke of, Mrs. Garrand?'

'The two exceptions are my stepson, Mr. Edward Garrand, and my lady companion, Miss Weston. Flora would not bark at either of them. I may add, however, that Miss Weston is not in town; she got my permission to visit some country friends a week ago.'

The inference was too obvious to escape anyone. Mrs. Garrand suspected her stepson of abstracting the missing document.

'About the paper itself?' I asked, after a moment's thought; 'of what description was it? And was the possession of it likely to benefit any person?'

'The document was a deed of gift,' she replied, 'made in my favour immediately after my marriage with Mr. Garrand, and it made over to me all the real estate he was at the time owner of. The possession of the paper could of course benefit no one, but the destruction or suppression of it would make a great difference in Mr. Edward Garrand's favour.'

She had evidently laid the loss at her stepson's door, one could read that without spectacles; but what I might or might not have said more in the matter at that time was interrupted by the opening of the door sharply and the entrance of a gentleman, young and distinguished enough to carry the name of Garrand, or any other name, with credit to himself and it.

He was a stranger to me, but I guessed rightly that he was Mr. Edward Garrand. He was tall and fair, with wavy light brown hair and handsome features that did not, however, wear a very attractive expression as he paused a little inside the door and looked keenly at his stepmother and myself.

THE STOLEN DEED

Mrs. Garrand's face grew hard as it hurried to him, and a sort of repressed flush went up partially into her cheeks as a sudden impulse seized her when the young gentlemen was about to go out again without speaking.

'A moment, if you please, was your business in the room in any way connected with a document, Mr. Edward?' she asked.

'With a document, madam?' he repeated sharply, turning round and looking at her haughtily. 'Certainly not. Why do you ask me such a question, pray?'

'Because I have lost one, and a valuable one,' she added, looking at him steadily.

'Perhaps you honour me by a suspicion that I have stolen it?' he said, with a sneer that curled a handsome lip as well as a dainty moustache.

She smiled—a cold sneering smile, too; and at the sight of it Mr. Edward's face flushed up with passion.

'What do you mean, Mrs. Garrand?' he asked angrily, taking a few steps that brought him directly opposite the lady's writing-table. 'Are you venturing to amuse yourself by ridiculing me, in the presence of a stranger, too?' and he looked towards me with a proud and resentful eye.

'No, sir, I am not indulging in ridicule or in jest, but simply stating a fact of which, indeed, I thought it just possible you might be already aware. I have lost a legal document of value to me—no other than the deed of gift bearing your poor father's signature shortly after his marriage with me. As for this gentleman, he is simply a detective, into whose hands I am placing my case with some faint hopes that I may recover my loss.'

Edward looked and listened while his stepmother spoke; and as she went on a fierce flush burned up his blood in his face. His eyes flashed angrily, his lips met in a powerful self-repression. Of course, I was watching him analytically; and such a mixture of passions held in strong check I never saw in a human face as I saw in his while Mrs. Garrand spoke those few words.

When she stopped the red had died out of his face—it was as though he absolutely, and by mere power of will, crushed down all outward evidence of his passion, but I saw his lips quiver as he opened them to speak in reply.

'You have lost the deed of gift signed by my poor father shortly after his marriage with you?' was what he said, repeating her word for word so far. 'Meaning, signed by my poor father *before* he went mad; and you have got a detective to find it. I need not tell you,

THE STOLEN DEED

madam, that I have always considered that deed as one of the most iniquitous ever signed, for you well know my sentiments on the subject: but I will say, for the information of the officer, and to make any use he may please of, that I am heartily glad the document *is* lost, and that I hope and will pray that it may never be found again. If it unfortunately *is*, I can only repeat, that I will move every legal engine to set it aside, as the act of a man who was *already* mad; for until he had the misfortune to come under your baneful influence, he was too good and kind a father to disinherit his own children for the sake of a heartless stranger. Those children are dead, it is too true, madam, but I am left to relieve his memory from the foul imputation cast upon his affection for his children when he signed that deed, and that I shall do by proving that he was already mad when he gave *you* his name.' Here he ceased, and with a slight inclination of his head to me, and a final look of scorn and almost hatred at Mrs. Garrand, walked haughtily from the room.

The woman was almost overwhelmed. The attack had been doubtless unexpected, and she had provoked it, but I felt almost a pity for her as I saw how deeply the young man's bitter words struck home. She half rose from her seat as he spoke and caught the edge of the table in a grip, as though to enable her to bear a fierce pain. Involuntarily, I thought of the lash, and the triangle, and the bitten bullet as I looked. Her lips moved stiffly as she attempted to speak, but could not, and she fell back again in her chair, with a face as white as the marble mantelpiece behind her.

When the door closed behind the young gentleman, she bent her face and pressed one hand on it for a moment—she was a proud woman, and bitter must have been her suffering and humiliations just then. When she removed the jewelled fingers and turned her rigid white face to me, it was hard and cold-looking, and the lips that parted to speak were blue as those of the long dead.

'I can't speak any more just now, Mr. — Mr. — but I think I have told you all. You had better go. Take what steps you think proper, and see me again.'

It was evident that she wished to be alone. No matter how we may fancy ourselves encased in the world's panoply of mannerism and propriety, there are moments when we *must* hide from it, to be miserable and natural. I seized my hat, and bowed myself out, with a mumble of something or other, meant to be polite, but which I daresay was entirely lost on the self-wrapped Mrs. Garrand.

Scarcely had I closed the door behind me when I was accosted by a servant, who told me that Mr. Garrand would be obliged if I would see him for a few moments in the library. The plot was thickening; of course, I would be only too happy to extend my sphere of observation in the household where valuable legal documents were lost, and I followed the attendant to the apartment in question.

The young man was pacing up and down unsteadily, and looked immeasurably amazed. His fine hair was disarranged, as from the rapid action of his hands; and a flush of excited feelings burned a deep spot in either cheek. All those signs denoted the fiery, impulsive temperament; but if ever a noble contour of head and forehead was to be trusted, Edward Garrand was no abstractor of either deeds or characters.

'If you can spare the time,' he said, placing a chair for me as the door closed behind the servant, 'pray be seated. I scarcely know what I want to say to you, but I feel that if I cannot discuss this abominable business with some one I must go mad.'

'It is a very strange affair, and doubtless a very annoying one to all concerned,' I ventured to observe.

'Do you think she has lost the paper at all?' he asked, stopping abruptly and seating himself in front of me.

The idea that the deed was not lost at all was a new one to me; and it puzzled me what positive reason had this man for asking such an odd question.

'Can you suggest any object she could have in pretending it to be lost?' I asked, instead of trying to answer the question.

'I can't at present—I am puzzling my brains over it. But that woman is cunning enough to form plans of wickedness beyond all ordinary precedent. By Jove! I have it,' he cried, 'she just wants to lay the odium of its abstraction at my door—she hates me enough for that. Confess now, she has tried to direct your suspicion against me,' he added, eagerly.

I smiled a little at the freshness of this young man, who seemed to expect information from me; and he saw the smile and understood it.

'I see, detectives, of all people, do not wear their hearts upon their sleeves for daws to peck at, and, by Jove, I *am* a jackdaw to expect anything out of *you*!'

'Of course, you can't expect water from a dry sponge,' I retorted. 'I know nothing, but it has become my business to find out. Perhaps you can help me—who knows?'

'Who, indeed. Well, in the first place, you can at least tell me how she *says* she lost that paper; for I still hold to it that she has it as safely as I have my dear mother's wedding ring, and that's the most valuable of my possessions.'

In a few words I related to him the facts as they had been told to

THE STOLEN DEED

me by Mrs. Garrand, adding, 'You see that the thief must have entered from the piazza.'

'There was no thief!' he interrupted, angrily.

'And as that little dog will only let you and some Miss Weston pass without attempting to explode himself, that either you or Miss Weston have abstracted the deed is no illogical conclusion. Now, will you tell me who and what is the said Miss Weston?'

'Miss Weston is Mrs. Garrand's companion; a sort of reduced lady, I believe, as such people generally are, and about thirty years of age, I should say. But I'd rather say no more about her; for in consequence of her intimate connection with Mrs. Garrand, I suppose, I detest the woman.'

'Does she detest you?'

'Good gracious, how can I tell! She daren't show it if she did, and she wouldn't if she could. She's a toady, born and bred, and knows her own interests too well to exhibit her feelings to their detriment.'

'Mrs. Garrand says that Miss Weston is not in town at present. I wish you could describe her appearance to me; or better, is there a carte of her in the house?'

'There positively is!' he cried, jumping up impulsively. 'Just stay a moment, I will try if the Fates will so far favour me as to permit me to become a thief in reality!' and he went out of the room.

Almost instantly he returned, jubilant, with a photo in his hand. 'I have been in luck,' he said, handing me the carte. 'I remembered having seen Miss Weston decorating the pages of an old album that lies in Mrs. Garrand's sitting-room. It is a good likeness.'

I looked at the portrait of an upright, prim, lady-like, and not ungraceful lady of a certain age, as the saying is, with a set smile in an ordinary-looking face, and a pair of the viciousest (if there is such a word) eyes as I ever saw in a woman's face. I put the photo in my pocket, with Mr. Garrand's permission; thus making myself, as I told him, accessory after the fact, and rose to take my leave.

'How are you going to proceed?' he asked, quite forgetting that he had called himself a jackdaw but a few minutes previously, for having expected any information from me.

'I will try and get a look at the fair companion,' I replied.

'You think she had something to do with it? I don't. I tell you that it is as safe under lock and key in Mrs. Garrand's keeping, as that photo in your pocket. You will let me know, won't you?'

'Certainly,' I said, and went out, feeling a greater interest in Edward Garrand than I had believed myself capable of feeling for one of his class.

176

Well, it was a complicated concern altogether. I fairly came to that conclusion as I thought the matter over on my way back. Mrs. Garrand said she had lost a paper worth some hundreds per annum to her, and plainly insinuated that her stepson had abstracted it. Mr. Garrand was positive that the deed was not lost at all, but that she pretended it was, out of some spite to himself. What conclusion was I to draw myself, thinking it over calmly, as a judge between them?

I couldn't decide. I simply left the opinion I must eventually form in abeyance. My safest way would be to set a watch on Mrs. Garrand herself, in order to discover if she was in earnest in requiring my services; and I was determined to have a look at Miss Weston.

If anyone had required me to give any reason for my suspicion against that fair lady, I should have found it impossible to do so. I didn't like the look of her pictured face, it is true, and I felt certain that what is called 'the devil of a temper' lurked behind those wicked-looking eyes; but what had that to do with Mrs. Garrand's deed of gift? What possible object could the possession of it be to Miss Weston?'

All my ingenuity of thought could find but two. Which was most likely to be the true one, if she was really the guilty party? She might have received some never-to-be-forgotten slight from her mistress, and be determined on revenge; or had she formed one of those violent, unreasoning passions that foolish women so often form out of their sphere for Edward Garrand, and from some wild hope of influencing him by benefit, have abstracted the paper that made him so much poorer than he ought to be?

I might have gone on asking myself these questions, with greater or less irreverence until now, had not chance, as it has so often done, stood my friend. I lived in Carlton at that time and was making my way toward my home about dinner-time, when at the gate of a small cottage garden opening to the foot-way I came plump on a lady dressed in rustling black silk and carrying something like a portfolio in her hand.

She passed out and turned to fasten the gate behind her, and still I stared and paused until she had turned the corner of the street. There could be no doubt about it; it was Miss Weston. Features might resemble, but expression never deceives—and that stereotyped smile, and those dangerous eyes, belonged only to Mrs. Garrand's companion.

Here was truly a stroke of luck! I opened the gate she had passed through and went up to the door of the cottage it belonged to; for the woman who resided in it was quite an acquaintance of mine. We have many acquaintances, and *all* of them of rather a seedy class, or they wouldn't be acquaintances of ours, you know, for we make them simply to be useful, and we don't find 'fiz-gigs'[1] among the Upper Ten.[2]

THE STOLEN DEED

And yet, when the few friends we possess, weighing in the balance of some emergency and finding us wanting in the delicacy or courtesy of a gentleman, they are disappointed, forsooth, as if one could touch pitch, not to say live and breathe among it for years, and not carry about some sensible emanation of its perfume!

But all this by the way, because the owner, or rather resident of that cottage had been known to me for years as a most amiable woman who was open to treat for information possessed 'for a consideration.' I didn't even wait for the ceremony of knocking, but turned the handle and walked in. Mrs. Gorman was busy in her kitchen at the back and made a great phrase of delight on my entrance. She hadn't seen me for an age, and wasn't I looking well—younger than ever. Well! she declared, and all that sort of thing, which I cut short.

'Look here, Mrs. G., who is that lady I met coming out of your place just now?

'Oh, a *real* lady, Mr. Sinclair; not one of your sort at all! She's here from the country since Saturday was a week, and I'm sorry to say I am to lose her in a couple of days.'

'Her name?' I asked.

'Miss Weston. She seems to have plenty of money but though honest as the day, is, I think, rather close with it for a lady.'

'Who's in the little back-room now?'

'No one but Anna. Miss Weston has the front.'

'Well, clear Anna out before evening, do you hear. I want that little back room. I'm a new young man lodger you've got, do you understand, Mrs. G., and my name—let me see, is Jones.'

'Good lawk, Mr. Sinclair! sure you can't have anything against Miss Weston!'

'Of course not, I've fallen over head and ears in love with her. A perfect case of love at first sight, you see.'

'Ha ha! well it's no business of mine. All right, the room will be ready for you in an hour.'

'When do you expect the lady back?'

'She nearly always comes in and has her tea at six, and she very seldom goes out again of an evening. Once or twice she had a gentleman call, but he didn't stop long—looked like a parson, or something that way.'

'Oh! well, I'll be here in the evening, so for the present goodbye, amiable Mrs. G.'

I was quite fidgety about Miss Weston and felt actually afraid to lose sight of Mrs. Gorman's, lest I should lose track of her and the excellent opportunity chance had thrown in my way. I hung about

THE STOLEN DEED

until I saw the companion re-enter the lodgings, and satisfied myself that she was settled for the night, ere I ventured home to refresh the inner man and attend to some matters necessary, before I devoted myself to my new attraction.

It was about seven o'clock when Mrs. G. ushered me into the little back room, with a sly twist of her thumb towards the front apartment, as an indication that Miss Weston was 'at home.' I went in and shut the door behind me, and took a look round the little crib, that was rather familiar to me, I do assure you. I had done a little D. business there before, and I knew every inch of the premises, particularly the partition wall between me and the fair companion at that moment.

Though, 'between you and me and the post,' it was not a partition *wall* at all, but a very flimsy division, lath and plaster on the parlour side, and simply papered lining on mine. I had a spyhole arranged in it long previous to my acquaintance with Mrs. Garrand, and it served me in good stead now.

On the wall at my side was a rubbishing coloured engraving, containing an almost unlimited quantity of awfully contrasting primary colours, and representing what—heaven knows, at least I don't. I took this handsome 'work of art' from the wall, greatly to the detriment of its rickety wooden frame, and lifting up a piece of loose paper, clapped my eye to the hole behind it, and saw the amiable Miss Weston!

I had made my peep-hole scientifically, I do assure you. A roll of paper formed a telescopic guide to the centre of a huge flower on the paper in the front room, and there was only one corner of the apartment into which I could not see.

When I first began my espionage on Miss Weston, she was seated in an arm-chair near the table, and evidently in deep thought. If ever I had been silly enough to think that lady possessed of a good temper or an amiable disposition, after one look at her eyes, the sight of her countenance as she sat there in fancied freedom from observation, would have opened my eyes.

She had a frown on her face that might have terrified a red Indian (though why a red Indian should be more difficult to terrify than a blue one or a yellow one, or a green one, is one of those questions to which I am open for replies, written in good English, from all parts of the world) and she was looking down at the carpet with those disagreeable eyes of hers, in a manner dangerous to the carpet's continuity as a whole. On the table by her side was the identical portfolio-looking thing I had observed her carrying in the afternoon, and her hand was resting on it as she sat.

I do not think the conclusion that she was thinking of something

THE STOLEN DEED

connected with the said portfolio was an illogical one to make, and I immediately and incontinently became possessed with an anxiety to get hold of that document-containing article; but how was my wish to become an accomplished fact? There could be no doubt that it was desirable, in the interest of my object; for in some way or other it would surely contain a hint of Miss Weston's movements, and so help me to form a conclusion as to her guilt or otherwise in the matter of the deed. I was determined to have that portfolio.

As I looked, and so thought, the lady lifted up her eyes and turned them as well as herself to the table, where she drew the writing-case to her, opened it, and became immersed in some documents it contained. I was aggravated beyond measure, looking at her there, with my fingers twitching to get hold of those papers, and a wall as well as a locked door between us. What was I to do? I left her there, and went out to consult my Mrs. G.

I carefully replaced my magnificent coloured print on the wall, and went out, to find the landlady alone in her own particular corner of the establishment, which was simply the kitchen. She was at her tea; and I sat down, congratulating myself on the absence of her inevitable daughter 'Anna.'[3]

'Mrs. G.,' I said, 'that delightful young old lady in there has a portfolio, and I must have it.'

'Good lawk, Mr. Sinclair.'

'My name is Jones, madam.'

'Well, Mr. Jones, then, but how do you know she's got such a thing?'

'Didn't I see it in her hand when I met her at the gate this afternoon.'

'Oh,' said Mrs. G., in delightful ignorance of my hole in the wall, of which I hoped she would remain in ignorance unto further notice.

'Well, how am I to get it? or rather, how are you to get it for me?'

'Me!'

'Yes, you. You don't want me to go into your lady lodger's room in the middle of the night, do you? Although; I daresay, I could do that if I was pushed.'

'Oh, I don't doubt you! but I can easily get you that thing you want for a few minutes, as luck would have it; but what good would it be to you, for she always keeps it locked, and the key on her watch-chain?'

'I must chance being able to open it, that's all. But how is the getting of it so easy?'

'Miss Weston has a bad cold, you see, and she asked me to let her have a basin of gruel after she was in bed to-night.'

'With a dash in it,' I interpolated.

THE STOLEN DEED

'Oh, you wicked man! Well I can go in after she's in bed to ask if she's ready for the gruel, and slip that writing thing out to you; but you can only have it while I am getting the gruel, you know.'

'Be as long as you can getting it, then,' I intimated, and returned to my back room.

I am very certain that Miss Weston, in her palmiest days, never had an admirer who longed half so much for a meeting with her as I did for the time she was to get her gruel, and I passed the time in tormenting the life of Mrs. G. by inquiries as to the state of forwardness of that delectable compound, and a watch on the young old lady herself through my unprincipled peep-hole. She sat at that table thinking in profundity, and occasionally scribbling a bit, until my patience was fairly worn out; but at last she shut the portfolio, locked it with a key attached to her watch-chain and placed it on a side table at my side of the house.

Then I discreetly retired, and devoted myself to a study of the work of art as represented by the splendid assortment of glaring colours between me and my coveted prize.

At last Mrs. G. went in for orders, and I started up and made for the door. I had already set the lamp on the cleared table, conveniently, with everything I thought likely to assist me in my burglary of the portfolio. My penknife was lying open at the sharpest blade, for into that sacred enclosure I was bound to be at all consequences. There was my dear Mrs. G.'s step! she was at my door, and the portfolio in my ready hand!

I instantly carried it to the lamp and discovered to my intense relief, that it was only one of those ordinary morocco things with a lock more for ornament than use; nothing was easier than to slip the narrow blade of my penknife behind the flimsy bit of iron doing duty as a bolt, push it back, and lo! the secrets of Miss Weston's private writing-case lay bare before the eyes of a disreputable D.

What were they? I turned them out indiscriminately on the table, my hand literally trembling with excitement and some faint hope of seeing a parchment deed among them. I lifted them one by one, with a rapid glance assuring myself of their unanimous contents before I returned them to the portfolio, one by one to the last, which I dashed in with a most unbecoming expletive at Miss Weston and her portfolio too.

'The old fool!' I was impolite enough to mutter, 'if I had my way of it, I'd make such women stocking-knitters in ordinary to Pentridge.'

Of course you want to know what were the documents that disappointed me so much. Well, they were neither more nor less than 'effusions' of Miss Weston's 'muse'—poetry (save the mark!) of the

THE STOLEN DEED

style classed by a literary friend of mine, not troubled with sentiment, under the head of 'mush and milk.' I should give you an extract or two that remains 'indelibly impressed upon the tablet of my memory' (that's the favourite style isn't it?), only that I have already done the fair poetess sufficient injury, and do not want to deprive her of a 'standard volume' of the value of one guinea, bound in blue morocco and the brightest of gold, and 'suitably inscribed.'

In short, from the magic words 'competitive' marked in one corner of one fairly copied string of verses, I concluded that the gentle companion was to become a competitor for the prize offered by the proprietors of the AUSTRALIAN JOURNAL; and being pretty well acquainted with the paying style of literature of the present day, I feel certain she will win it.[4] The lines commenced 'Lost love among the breathing lilies,' and ended with something about 'a soul in sweetness dying,' or 'sighing,' I'm not sure which, but you will know when you see them printed.

I didn't wait to fasten the lock again, I assure you, leaving the lady to account for it as the fruits of her own carelessness, but I shoved it into Mrs. G.'s hand as she came carrying the basin of gruel that, if my nose was to be trusted, undoubtedly *had* a 'dash' in it; and then I was about to seize my hat and bolt from the house in disgust when I saw a scrap of something like paper lying on the table where I had upset Miss Weston's 'effusions.'

I say something like paper, because it was not paper. I made a dart at it for examination, and found the scrap, of about a quarter of a superficial inch in size, was a bit of parchment. My hopes rose to the clouds again. What was Miss Weston doing with parchment? Some legal document had certainly been in the portfolio at all events.

I turned it over and over, and made as much examination of it as though I expected to discover some almost invisible hieroglyphics denoting its name and origin; but discovered nothing, only that it was a sort of three-cornered bit, partially torn, and that freshly, and partially seemingly gnawed. You may be sure it was safely consigned to my pocket-book, and with it a memo of a visit to Mrs. Garrand early on the following morning.

I went home, leaving Miss Weston to the combined effects of her gruel and its 'dash,' and slept myself the sleep of the just. But I called again at Mrs. G.'s in the morning, on my way to Mrs. Garrand's.

I was astonished to find that the companion had already left the house; but my delight was fully commensurate with my astonishment. I knew that I could hardly expect to be favoured with an interview at Elwood House before the mistress was in all probability out of her

THE STOLEN DEED

chamber: and I determined to take advantage of this grand chance to thoroughly search that of Miss Weston.

Mrs. G. was aghast. I turned Miss Weston's pockets inside out, while the landlady followed me, trying to make them straight again; I shook her petticoats and upset every article of furniture in the room in a vain search for the missing document. There was no portmanteau to aggravate me with its lock, only a carpet-bag, open and nearly empty, which had doubtless contained the clothing now scattered through the room. I did not spare the bed, the blankets, the mattress, the curtains. I disturbed the fair dame's toilette arrangements and spilt a lot of pearl-powder over my black coat in overturning the cover for a hiding-place; under every bit of untacked carpet I poked my fingers, and around every worn hole in the same, but I was unsuccessful—there was no sign of a paper anywhere.

'Whatever *are* you hunting for?' Mrs. G. would iterate and reiterate every now and then between her efforts at restoration, keeping her eye out the window in terror of the lodger's return. 'What in the name of mercy are you chasing after?'

'A paper,' I said at last, as I paused in disappointment and looked around for a new idea.

'A paper—good lawk! What sort of paper?'

'A love letter,' I cried. 'Don't you see I am suffering agonies of jealousy from the heartless conduct of that arch-deceiver, the fair and false Miss Belinda Araminta Weston.'

'Belinda Araminta! Is that her name? Well, a sweet pretty name it is too.'

'A sweet pretty name indeed,' and I made a dart at a torn bit of paper on the wall that I fancied had escaped my preceding search; but all in vain. If Miss Weston had the deed, she had not hidden it in her lodgings.

And I was not sure that she had it at all. Perhaps I was jumping at a wrong conclusion after all. She certainly was not in the country, as her mistress understood her to be, and that looked as if some scheme was on hand; but a far simpler object than the one I had suspected her of, would account for that little bit of duplicity. Perhaps the composition of that sweet 'effusion,' or, but less likely, the proximity of a lover; and then I remembered all at once the parson-like visitor mentioned by Mrs. G.

I must make that unknown gentleman's acquaintance. Was he in reality a lover of Miss Weston, or an accomplice in the deed business? Had that literary lady consigned the precious paper to his care, or was I, for suspecting the lady at all, an unmitigated ass?

THE STOLEN DEED

These interesting questions remained unanswered when I reached Elwood House, and was, as 'Mr. Brown from the office,' readily admitted to the presence of Mrs. Garrand. That lady looked pale and careworn but as haughty as ever; and the anxiety with which she accosted me I felt certain had nothing simulated in it.

'Have you any tidings for me?'

'Nothing decided, madam. I came simply to ask you a question relating to the paper on which the deed was written?'

'It was not paper, it was parchment. Unfortunately, I kept the deed itself by me, instead of a copy. If I had taken my lawyer's advice when it was drawn, it would have now been safe in his office.'

'I only wanted to ask if the paper or parchment was perfect, or in any way damaged or torn?'

'You have got some clue!' she said, with agitation. 'You have seen it. Tell me at once, is it not so?'

'I assure you that I have *not*, Mrs. Garrand. I have not set eyes on it or heard a single word about it. Nevertheless, I have a reason for asking you the question I have put.'

'I had been in the habit of keeping some valuable documents in a private drawer, the lost deed among the number. I had not unlocked that drawer for many months, when I had occasion to do so for some papers when it was found necessary to restrain Mr. Garrand, and I found the mice had made an entrance at the back and nibbled a good many of the corners of the deed in question; one corner was gnawed, and a bit nearly, but not quite, detached.'

'I think I have seen that bit, Mrs. Garrand. Now please ask me no questions, for I cannot reply to them, everything being suspicion with me as yet. As soon as I have really anything to tell, I will come and tell you.'

'You saw my stepson the last time you were here,' she said, in a low, hard tone, and with a hot flush in her cheeks. 'You were in the library with him, and I can put two and two together as well as any detective in the world! Well, I can wait.'

How determined she was to convict her husband's son—this hard, cold woman of the world. I had not a sympathy with her, but was bound to do my duty for all that.

At this moment Mrs. Garrand's eye fell upon her writing-table, near which she was seated, and she lifted several letters that lay upon it.

'I have not opened my letters yet,' she said, 'will you excuse me? I see a note from Miss Weston here, and I am anxious to know when she returns, as I am sure she would be of invaluable assistance to me in this affair, she is so clever and acute.'

'She is coming back almost immediately,' she added, when she had run over the note.

'Where is Miss Weston at present?' I asked.

'Somewhere in the Beechworth district, I think, or at Wodonga,' she added, looking at the post-mark on the envelope.

'Come,' thinks I to myself, 'it is evidently no such simple matter as a lover or competitive poem that makes our sweet Miss Weston so anxious to be considered in the country'; but I had no time to follow the idea any farther when an exclamation from the lady drew my attention as she handed me another letter she had opened.

It was an odd-looking concern altogether, written on a dirty scrap of paper in a cramped-looking hand, and exhibited some curious specimens of spelling. Here it is, with errors (?) in spelling corrected for your easier perusal:

'Mrs. Garrand has lost a paper about property that will take some money out of her pocket. If she is willing to pay handsome for the information, I can tell her how she will get it back again without any trouble. Meet the writer to-night in the willow-walk at the Fitzroy Gardens, at eight o'clock. No use dodging, or news won't be forthcoming.'

'Good gracious! what do you think of that?' cried Mrs. Garrand, for once astonished out of her mannerism.

I thought a good many things about it, but had no idea of confiding them to her.

'What am I to do about it? There must be something genuine in it, for not a creature knows of my loss but you and Mr. Edward Garrand. Perhaps it is a trap—perhaps they want to murder me, and so settle the matter of the deed for ever,' and her face paled under the idea.

'Oh, it's nothing of the sort,' I replied, rising to leave. 'You need not trouble any further about it, for I will meet this writer myself, and find out all about it. You will permit me to keep this precious document?'

'Certainly. Good morning.' And I scraped myself out, with the best imitation of a bow of which I was capable.

I was not, however, so easily to escape. As I passed out of the morning room, and closed the door behind me, I heard the last notes of a heavy peal at some bell and had not reached the hall before a message from Mr. Edward overtook me—'Would I please . . . the library,' &c., and, of course, I went to see the young gentleman, who must have set some one on the watch to be at all aware of my presence in the house.

He was standing waiting as I was ushered into the room, and he held an open letter in his hand.

THE STOLEN DEED

'I am so glad you came just now,' he began at once, 'for here's something addressed to me about that woman's deed, and I just want you to see if I am right or not in my certainty that all this was planned to throw odium on me,' and he handed me the letter.

It was in the same hand and style altogether as that I had in my pocket, just received by Mrs. Garrand, and offered, in language too plain to be misunderstood, the deed to Mr. Edward for a sum of money commensurate with its value to him. It also appointed a place of meeting and an hour, only on the following evening.

'Well, are you satisfied now? Can you not see plainly that they hope I will jump at the offer, and convict myself by openly trading for the possession of a paper that does not belong to me? I tell you,' he added, with a flushed face and angry eye, 'there is not one being breathing who would insult me by even such a suspicion but that woman!'

The tone in which he alluded to his stepmother as 'that woman,' told plainly how unutterably beneath contempt she was in his estimation; and even at that moment I could not help contrasting his open detestation with the form-screened hatred of Mrs. Garrand for him. He was invariably alluded to as 'Mr. Edward Garrand,' and in a tone of cold courtesy, while every effort was directed toward turning indirectly my suspicions on him alone. How infinitely superior was the woman in anything like *finesse* or duplicity.

'Well!' he cried, impatiently; and in reply I handed him Mrs. Garrand's note for perusal.

'Oh, it's all a blind!' he ejaculated, after having read it. 'Nothing would convince me that the deed is not safe in that woman's possession.'

'And I am as convinced that she has really lost it,' I observed.

'If she has,' he cried, impulsively, 'I pray God she may never again find it!' Then his face blazed scarlet at recognising something in his own words that jarred on his delicacy of feeling, and he hastily added: 'My wish is from no selfish motive, I beg you to believe, but I feel as if she was the robber of the dead in holding property that, had they lived, should have rightfully devolved to them. As it is, I would rather see it sold to build a hospital or a church than that it should enrich Mrs. Garrand.'

Well, it would hardly have done for me to echo the wish aloud, but I felt it, nevertheless, even while leaving him to take steps towards recovering the deed for his enemy, Mrs. Garrand.

On my way to town I was occupied entirely by the subject of this unknown correspondent of Elwood House. I wondered if Miss Weston would probably venture on such a dangerous step as that of lying, and, by the very same post, to treat with both parties to whom

186

the paper was valuable, with the evident intention of making the best possible bargain. I had no idea myself that she, who ought to have known Edward Garrand's character so much better than I had had an opportunity of doing, would think him capable of accepting or in any way profiting by the offer made him, for I could have laid my right hand as a pledge that he would spurn a dishonourable action as though it were a viper. One thing, however, was certain; whoever had the deed was well acquainted with the domestic disunion between Mr. Edward Garrand and his stepmother, or they would not have risked exposing their game to the likelihood of the two letters being compared.

I had other fish to fry, and didn't go near Mrs. G. and her fair lodger until toward evening, and then I learned to my delight that the clerical friend was closeted with the companion. I was not long before I had my eye at the wall and the satisfaction of seeing just opposite, and seated with his face in full view, the gent in question.

I had almost said that Mrs. G.'s idea of a man like a 'parson' and mine must differ very much, but I recollected in time that there are in these go-ahead days a vast variety of the parson species. If a parson usually apparels himself in black (as, indeed, I believe he generally does), and has a fiery face, and a pair of bleared eyes, and several patches of some sort of eruption on his neck and cheeks, and the air of a spirit-soaker generally, then Mrs. G. was right, and Miss Weston's visitor emphatically resembled a parson. And, indeed, when I come to think over the subject, I saw one not very long ago in a country pulpit bearing a very great resemblance to the said visitor. I may add he does not mount that rostrum now, having found the elevation dangerous—periodically.

Miss Weston and the stranger were in close and seemingly confidential conversation, but not a word of it could I catch; if they were not actually whispering, they were at least speaking in so low a tone that not even a mumble penetrated my aperture in the wall. Nor did he stay long after I began my espionage, nodding his head at parting with a familiarity that denoted great intimacy and an utter absence of all ceremony.

It was now seven o'clock; and as I had decided on meeting the writer of the note to Mrs. Garrand personally, it was time for me to be making my preparations. It was an almost certainty that a person of such proclivities as the one who could become a party to the abstraction of a deed, and try to make money by selling it to the highest bidder, would recognise the police force in general, and the detective force in particular, as his personal foes, and know every one of them by 'head mark.'[5] I did not want to be recognised, hence the necessity for a disguise, and I went to my friend Mrs. G. for it.

THE STOLEN DEED

'Mrs. G., my darling, I want a loan of your black silk gown, with petticoats to match, and that splendid new bonnet I saw you sporting at chapel last Sunday.'

'Good lawk, Mr. Sinclair! whatever would you be wanting with my black silk? But you're joking.'

'Devil a joke, then, Mrs. G. What would I be wanting of them, is it? Well, I want to put them on, and go to the theatre. Oh, you needn't look so glum about it; I'll take the best care of them, and if I do any damage, I promise you brand-new ones in their place. Mind and give me a nice petticoat now, and you'll see how dainty I'll hold up the silk to show it—they won't notice my feet in the dark.'

Miss Weston was still in her room, and must have felt very curious to understand the meaning of Mrs. G.'s muffled laughter in my apartment as she attired me in her finery, for just as I was stepping out carefully, my dress rustling and the landlady in convulsions of merriment, the door opened and the companion looked out.

I made her a profound curtsey and went on as well as I could in the unaccustomed garments, but was glad when the front door was closed behind me and I was at liberty to move naturally, at least as the confounded petticoats would permit me; and having hailed the first passing cab, I was soon set down in the vicinity of the gardens and proceeded to the place of assignation.

Many an anxious lover and loveress has repaired to the Willow Walk of the Fitzroy Gardens as a place of meeting in the long ago days, before it became the haunt of the low and vile, and a dangerous spot for any respectable person to stray in after nightfall; but I doubt if any of them ever approached it with such curiosity and interest as I did on that night. The post-office clock tolled out eight as I entered its northern end, and I walked a good bit down its shadowed way without seeing a creature or hearing anything but the rustle of Mrs. G.'s best black silk.

I didn't feel at all at home in my bothering petticoats, and after waiting for full ten minutes alone began to think the letter had been a hoax, and to wish myself at home. Indeed, I began to take it into serious consideration to make a swag of Mrs. G.'s finery and go home in my own clothes, only the bonnet, or rather the want of a hat, puzzled me; and besides, I was not sure by any means that I could manage the pin department, in which the lady appeared an adept as she attired me in her own finery. What would have been the ultimate result I cannot tell you, for at that moment I heard an approaching step on the gravel, and being near a lamp, I paused in order to have the benefit of the light in scanning the coming stranger.

THE STOLEN DEED

It was a woman, and to all appearance an elderly one, dressed in shabby mourning and by no means as stylish-looking as myself. This person paused on approaching me, and as I turned expectantly toward her, ventured to inquire,

'Are you expecting to meet anyone here, ma'am?'

'I am,' I answered.

'Might I ask about what is it?'

'About Elwood House, and about a paper,' I replied.

'That's all right,' was the answer. 'You're not the lady yourself, are you?'

'You surely aren't silly enough to fancy that the lady you allude to would come here to meet a stranger at this time of night, and alone? No; I am only an intimate friend, sent to see what you have to propose in the matter. Of course, it is money you want!'

'Of course.'

'Well, what's your price? There's no use wasting time over it, and I don't care about being here a lone woman, all by myself, much longer.'

And here I rustled my skirts, with a deftness that, I thought, must impose on anyone as to my sex.

The shabby old woman paused before replying; and keeping myself under the lamp, and near enough to be in its shadow, I tried to get a good look at my opponent. The said old woman had her eyes keenly fixed on me as I spoke, and with something of a suspicion in them; but there was something else than a suspicion in them—there was a look that seemed so familiar as to quite startle me.

Where had I seen those keenly piercing, dark eyes, with the wicked expression and the cold glitter in them? By George, they were Miss Weston's! Yet they could not be; it would have been almost impossible for her to have got herself up and reached the rendezvous since I had the pleasure of bowing to her at Mrs. G.'s door.

At the moment this certainty struck me, the woman turned her head slightly, as if in consideration of her reply to my question, and I saw something else. Under, or, rather behind, the old strings of her black bonnet, a patch of some skin disease that made me look at the face again when it was turned to me. Oh yes, take off the cap and the bonnet, and there was Miss Weston's visitor—red face, inflamed eyelids, eruption, and all. My eyes were quite opened!

He was some relation of the fair companion, doubtless. I could trace, even in the swollen features, a resemblance to the aristocratic and literary lady. A brother, in all probability, and, indeed, so it turned out to be.

'Well?' I questioned, as the would-be woman turned toward me

189

THE STOLEN DEED

again, 'are you ready to put a figure on it?'

'Can't you say what Mrs. Garrand would be likely to offer?' was the answer query.

'No, I can't.'

'Well, I'm not a principal, but an agent. It will be better for us to arrange another meeting and come prepared with terms.'

'That you may hear from Mr. Edward,' thinks I, but I *said*, 'All right,' for I heard a young voice whistling as the owner of it came tramping along the walk under the willows, and I had been waiting for it.

In a few seconds Jemmy Dace, for it was he, made his appearance and gave me a comical wink as he passed, pulling one hand out of his pocket to 'take a lunar' with his thumb at his nose behind my unconscious companion as he passed; and then, knowing all was safe, I bid my friend good-night, promising faithfully to see 'her' again soon, and meaning to more than keep my word to the letter.

Jemmy Dace was a gem among the Melbourne *gamins* and devoted to my service as long as he was appreciated, that is, well paid; and it was a sight for sore eyes to see him on the track of someone I had set him to watch. I daresay he was fifteen years old, but he didn't look twelve, and was the cheekiest young vagabone[6] that ever smoked a cigar, with his hat on one side and his hands in his breeches pockets. I have admired that fellow many a time, and predicted a career for him. The inimitable way in which he will set up his pug nose and chaff anyone that tries to get illegal information from him; or the owl-like visage he will assume to deceive when necessary, will be worth money to him when he gets among us, as he will one day, or my name's not Sinclair.

So you will understand that I had set Jemmy to watch our correspondent until he was planted; and I hurried back to Mrs. G.'s to get rid of my feminine toggery and get my hat in readiness to meet Jemmy at the appointed corner.

He was there when I reached it, with his back against the lamppost, his hands in his pockets, and whistling 'She's a pal o' mine' with an ear-piercing shrillness.

'Blow me!' he cried, as soon as he saw me, 'if the old 'ooman[7] didn't bring me right here — lodgin' at Mother Snell's'; and he pulled out one hand and twisted his thumb over his shoulder. 'And I'm blest if it's a woman at all,' he added, with a comical grimace. 'I saw a man's trousers as she hopped upstairs. There you are — that's you. I'm off.'

And having pocketed his douceur with a wink, he disappeared like a flash of light.

THE STOLEN DEED

I walked up the lane to 'Mother Snell's,' opened the door, and entered. The hall was in darkness, but I had seen a light in the front room window, and knowing that it was Mrs. Snell's principal lodger's room, I ventured on it by chance. Seizing the handle of the door, I found it unlocked and boldly walked in, and was fully repaid for my impudence.

Sitting in a chair, or, rather, lounging in one just opposite to me, was my friend Miss Weston's visitor—eyes, carbuncles, fiery face, and all; he had got rid of his feminine disguise, with the exception of the black skirt that clung round his boots as he lolled back at his ease, smoking a clay pipe. When he saw, as he thought, a stranger staring at him, the pipe dropped from his mouth; and then I saw, by the white fear that spread over his face, that he had recognised the D.

He tried to get up, but the petticoats got entangled with his legs, and he fell back again, while I walked in and fastened the door behind me.

'Don't disturb yourself, Mr. Weston,' I began, guessing the name. 'I have caught you in deshabille, I see; new-fashioned style of dressing-gown, I suppose. Now, you needn't say too much, unless you like, for I'm come for you about that deed.'

'What deed?' he stammered. 'I know nothing about deeds. And who the devil are you? What do you want, bouncing in on a gentleman in this way?'

'You know very well who I am, my amiable friend; but, as a matter of courtesy, I inform you that I am Detective Sinclair at present. A little bit ago I was a very nice old lady meeting a very seedy old woman in the Willow Walk. Now, you perceive, your game's up. Are you going to give up that deed?'

'I tell you I know nothing of deeds, or of Willow Walks either!' he cried, angrily.

'Of course you don't,' I replied, pointing at the petticoats. 'Are you going to give up that deed?'

'I know nothing about it,' he answered, doggedly.

'All right, Mr. Weston,' and opening the door I admitted A314,[8] with Jemmy Dace grinning behind him, and gave the crestfallen plotter into custody to be marched off to durance vile, while I thoroughly searched his late lodging for some trace of the stolen document.

There was none, and I was completely nonplussed; for although my interest in Edward Garrand had made me hope that the deed might never be recovered, a professional feeling inherent in my detective nature made me hate to be baffled when I was really doing my best. However, there was nothing to be done now but to sleep on it, and commence fresh in the morning.

THE STOLEN DEED

And the morning brought me a very urgent note from Mr. E. Garrand, directed to the office, and which was put into my hand as I presented myself there at the usual hour. In it he requested me to go to him at once, as he wished particularly to see me.

I started as soon as duty would permit, and saw, as I entered the house, a carriage and pair waiting at the door. I inquired for Mr. Edward at once, fearing that Mrs. Garrand would pounce upon me before I saw him, and was led at once to his room.

He was dressed, and ready to go out; his gloves on, and his hat in his hand.

'I want you to go with me at once,' he said, 'the carriage is waiting, and I can explain as we go.'

No sooner said than done—in a few moments we were being whirled rapidly, where, I knew not.

'I am taking you to see my father,' he said. 'I have a communication from him that has puzzled me, but I think the deed has turned up in a very strange place. He has requested me to go and see him at once, and to take a witness with me. As the matter seems to concern this troublesome and iniquitous deed, I thought you would be the best one I could select.'

I was surprised, but silently so, and kept wondering all the way what could have turned up to bring the poor old gentleman into the affair. It was not long, however, before we stopped at a private residence a little way in the country, where Edward Garrand had secured his afflicted father comfortable rooms and kindly attendance, with the strict supervision that his state required.

We found the old gentleman reclining very comfortably in a handsome cushioned chair, enveloped in a rich Indian dressing-gown. He was a fine-looking, white-haired old man, without a trace of his disease about him, save a restlessness of manner and eye that were sometimes entirely laid aside, and at others increased to something approaching the dangerous excitement of settled and incurable mania. On this occasion, however, he was perfectly calm, the document in his hand having doubtless recalled his memory of old times and faces, and some of his old settled purpose.

'Glad to see you, Edward—very glad to see you. Ah! this is Mr. Sinclair; be good enough to take a seat. Oh, I am indeed— much better, much better, I assure you, Edward, especially since this has been placed in my hands,' and he lifted the paper in his hand to call attention to it.

'And what is that, may I ask, my dear father?'

'You may, my son; you have a right to ask, and a right to receive an answer, for your interests are deeply concerned in it. This, my dear

THE STOLEN DEED

boy, is the deed of gift which in my days of folly I was silly enough to make in the present Mrs. Garrand's favour, and by which I did a gross injustice to my children. Mr. — Sinclair, I think you said, Edward? — Mr. Sinclair, would you kindly use the poker to that fire; it seems inclined to be stubborn this morning.'

Then he watched the blaze, I looked, and seemed going to relapse into forgetfulness, when his son recalled his attention.

'Ah, yes; thank you, Edward. It was for this I wanted you and the friend you have selected as a witness.' Here he waved the document again. 'Miss Weston kindly called on me last night — very late last night, indeed — it was so late that only by the merest chance in the world I was up. Well, that lady, who has always been very kind and attentive to me, indeed, explained the matter of this deed to me so thoroughly, and laid my own foolishness so plainly before me in having it drawn in the present Mrs. Garrand's favour, that I am astounded I did not perceive it at the time.'

'Miss Weston!' exclaimed Mr. Edward — 'Miss Weston brought you that deed!'

'Yes,' the elder gentlemen went on, in a sort of self-satisfied way that seemed painful to his son. 'Miss Weston has always been very kind to me, and I know the present Mrs. Garrand has not, by any means, treated her well. But let me complete this subject while I can think of it. You know, Edward,' he went on again, solemnly, 'they have decided that I am not of sound mind, and sometimes I do think my memory fails me, but if I *am*, my weakness of brain began before I made this deed. You know yourself, my son, that any will I might wish to make *now* would be null and void, even if I was in reality as sound in mind as you are yourself. You know this, Edward?'

The young man's face grew red up to the roots of his hair; he saw, as well as I did, that his father had some unexpected idea in his head, no doubt put there by Miss Weston, connected with the document so strangely lost, and feeling his own deep interest in it, felt the delicacy of his position. If his father asked his advice, what should he say? If he gave the deed into his charge, what should he do?

Something like these questions ran in Edward Garrand's head as his father spoke, but he tried to answer as calmly as he could, 'I do know it, father.'

'Yes,' continued the old gentleman, very lucidly for one in his state of mind, but with a growing excitement that could be traced in the red spot gathering in each worn cheek and in the clutch with which he held the document. 'Yes, the present Mrs. Garrand, with her inimitable self-appreciation, would take care to render null and void any attempt

THE STOLEN DEED

of mine to deprive her of what my insanity deprived my children of; I am, in the eye of the law, a cipher. I have no voice in the disposal of property over which I have lost the capacity to preside. I can make no will—I can sign no deeds! but I can destroy them,' he added, rising with such quick action that the folds of his dressing-gown flew out behind him, and cramming the deed into the very centre of the fire I had just broken into a glow.

'And that is how I do it!' he said, seizing the poker and stabbing it furiously through the parchment, as though he was giving his enemy a fatal sword thrust. 'In that way, do I render null and void the present Mrs. Garrand's claims on my real estate!'

I started forward to satisfy myself that it was really the precious deed blazing away there before I ventured to sing jubilate, and managed to see by the strong light of the consuming blaze that it was truly, in spite of poor Mr. Garrand brandishing the poker at me to keep me off from what he thought an attempt at rescue. As for Edward he grew as pale as death, and then went up to his poor old father, just in time to let the white head rest on his shoulders as the old man burst into tears.

I went out and left them, retaining enough of prudence to pick off the coals two or three scraps of the document that had escaped the course of the poker and fallen to the back of the black coal; one of these scraps was the corner from which the bit in my pocketbook had been torn, and it bore the remains of Mr. Garrand's signature.

I had the pleasure of taking at least the remains of the deed to Mrs. Garrand, and of relating to her my version of the manner in which her husband had destroyed it. She felt it awfully, and was wounded in pride and pocket both, and doubtless felt cause to regret her haughty treatment of her companion, who had retaliated so bitterly upon her.

Miss Weston must have 'vamoosed' the very night she gave the deed into Mr. Garrand's hands. When she found that her accomplice was imprisoned, and that her own share in the business was likely to be made public, she at least revenged herself for many slights of her employer. I do not suppose, however, that she will have gone so far as to be unable to claim her prize for the poem I had impudence enough to peruse before it became the property of the public. Her brother was liberated and also 'vamoosed'; and we don't seem to care much whether he ever turns up again or not.

And now I wind up this story of facts by a bit of news that I know will please my readers. Mr. Garrand the elder is so much better that the doctors have recommended his return to home and society.

Jemmy Dace has some acquaintance of his own in the stables at Elwood House, and he tells me that the old gentleman is beginning to

THE STOLEN DEED

make them all fly round there, not excepting the haughty lady herself; and I have great hopes that he will live to make a dozen wills yet, without any danger of Mrs. Garrand trying to set them aside as the testaments of a man of unsound mind.

First published in the *Australian Journal*, August 1875, as part of the *Detective's Album* serial, under the byline 'W.W.'

NOTES

1 *fizgigs*: informers.
2 *the Upper Ten*: the upper circles of society, the ruling class.
3 *her inevitable daughter 'Anna'*: meaning that Anna (not her real name) was a prostitute living at Mrs. G's, and therefore easier for a policeman to have evicted.
4 *a competitor for the prize offered by the . . . AUSTRALIAN JOURNAL*: There's an in-joke here. Mary Fortune had herself entered the *Australian Journal*'s poetry competition under a pseudonym—and won it.
5 *head mark*: facial features.
6 *the cheekiest young vagabone*: the description of Jemmy Dace here fits that of Fortune's son George. *Vagabone* is an archaic form of vagabond.
7 *'ooman*: woman (Irish dialect).
8 *A314*: i.e. a police constable (his helmet would have displayed his serial number).

KILLED IN THE SHAFT

How strange it is to be sitting here, with one's feet on a carpet, and crimson curtains shutting out the night, recalling tales of the deep sinking[1] of long-ago days and the many hardships we had to endure. 'Many a time and oft,' as I lay back in my easy chair of an evening and close my eyes, dreamily to listen to the soft notes of the piano, or the subdued prattle of my own prettily dressed children, seated in corners or grouped on the carpet, I recall the old times with a strange feeling that it could never have been. Something like the memory of a confused dream it is now, and yet it is the memory of a dream from which we sigh to have awakened.

We were so happy in those old digging times. When Charlie Crawford, Harry Borthick, and I were mates in that claim at the Green Hills, I don't think there were happier chaps in the whole colony, until the events began to cloud our horizon which ended so tragically for at least two of our number. We worked hard, it is true, but we worked each for himself, and at the beck of no master; and what a difference does that simple fact make in the strength of the most willing muscles in the world.

It is fourteen years ago this very month since the time I write of, and our tent was pitched on a green rise but a little distance from our claim. How well I remember that camping ground, and tent, and how often do I actually crave to exchange our brick walls and comfortably fitted rooms for the old free life and its canvas home! I can remember every seam in that tent, and the patches so carefully placed by our useful mate, Harry, on the places where the rough ridge-pole wore it into holes. I recollect the corner where the sun used to first show his round, dazing face through the duck, that looked so white among the green bushes; and I remember as well as if it were yesterday how glad I used to be to get out of my bunk and hide from him under the trees, with the green grass for my bed, when mine was not the day shift. No, all the gold that we ever drew from the earth's hiding places would never buy anything like the happiness of those old days.

At Green Hills our tent was a tolerably large one, and was furnished in the usual way. Three 'bunks' occupied the sides and one end, the opening used as a door the other. Between the bunks was a space of about five feet, and in centre of that stood our table. Many a laugh we had at Harry when the green saplins he had planted in our floor to

KILLED IN THE SHAFT

serve as legs for the empty gin case, which formed the top of our table, began to sprout and eventually send out strong green gum shoots; but I don't believe one of us would have pulled off a leaf for half an ounce of gold, and we began be quite proud of the natural wreaths that were soon twined around the battered gin case.

Charlie Crawford was a mate any man must have loved and been proud of. He was a gentleman born and bred, and never once got into the coarse habits so easily adopted by less refined diggers. Charlie's tea might be drunk out of a pannikin, but that pannikin shone like silver, and I was always glad when it was his cooking week, feeling as I did more confidence in his scrupulous cleanliness than I did in my own.

Charlie's bunk, too, was a crying reproof to both Harry and myself on occasions. He should have been a military man should Charlie, so large was his order bump, and so natural seemed every kind of regulation and discipline to come to him. Never did you see his blankets tossed carelessly upon his bunk or even spread neatly upon it, save in the evenings, for when they were not sunning themselves on a near bush, they were folded carefully and laid upon the foot of his bed; and it was a common laugh among our friendly deep sinkers to declare that any blind man could choose the Doctor's bunk from among our three.

That's what they used to call him—'The Doctor.' He had been studying medicine ere the gold fever seized him; and left a comfortable home and competency to carry back a fortune. It was time enough when he got back, he used to say, and he did not neglect to prosecute his studies even in our rude tent. Under his bunk was a case half filled with medical works, over which he would pore for hours after we were in bed, when work was not pressing or suspended.

I can shut my eyes now and see him, as I have hundreds of times seen him within those calico walls—his long fair hair scattered upon a pillow cover, so white that it might have been washed in his English home, and the candle stuck in a sardine-tin full of mud, drawn as close to him as the vicinity of the table would permit. I often lay and watched him, and wondered at his eager search after his chosen profession. He was so young that I fancied some fair girl at home must be interested in those dry studies to make them so determinedly prosecuted; but I was wrong, as events proved. Charlie had left no first love behind him.

He was handsome, too, this hard-working student—as handsome as a picture. If there was any effeminacy in the delicately moulded features, the fair skin, and the deep blue eyes of Charlie Crawford, it was amply counteracted by the determined and self-possessed curve of his proud lips. We had seen him, too, in situations that called out the latent fire and bravery of his character; and his courage had never been

KILLED IN THE SHAFT

found wanting at a moment when it was needed. That there are many such moments in the life of a deep sinker, I need not tell any of you who have been diggers.

In describing Harry Borthick, I must lay before your mental vision a very different picture. He was rather below the middle size and a very good-looking young fellow, with the unmistakeable free and easy bearing and saucy roll of the thoroughbred sailor. His complexion was dark enough to agree wonderfully with the blackest hair and the crispest curls and the keenest black eyes I ever saw in the world. He was particularly well made, too, dressed himself picturesquely in something of the old sea style, and altogether was as pleasant a companion for a man in a mood for rough enjoyment as you can imagine.

Not an intellectual one, by any means. Harry's whole appearance spoke of a social grade so inferior to that of Charlie Crawford that no contrast could be greater than between the several airs of the two young men. I don't think Harry Borthick could spell half a dozen words of three syllables, while his calligraphy was a work of time and trouble. But he was a much older digger than either of us, and invaluable to us as being up to all the strange management of deep sinking, wet and dry, and perfectly *au fait* in 'timbering,' etc.; so that while as a companion he was anything but an acquisition to Charlie or myself, during working hours he was able to hold his own with any man on the hills.

At the time this, my story, begins, our neighbourhood—I mean the neighbourhood of our tent—assumed quite a new aspect. Had the 'gutter' followed the path it might reasonably be expected to follow, indeed, the story would never have been written; but it did not. One morning, on turning out, we were much astonished to see the small red flag with the big white G on it some three hundred yards nearer to our tent, the gutter having displayed its erratic intention of turning round upon itself, to the great disappointment of many claim-holders and to the great delight of many others.

If you have been on the deep sinking at all, I need scarcely tell you the effect of this change on the part of the gutter. The original 'street' became suddenly deserted, and a new one was formed or forming within fifty yards of our residence. It was a grievous blow to both Charlie and I at first. Instead of our quiet evenings for talk or study, night began to be made hideous by the shouts and laughter of intoxicated men who frequented the stores, or the deafening stamping of half-mad dancers who patronised the saloons. I dare say we would have shifted had it not been that a new glory dawned upon the horizon of Charlie's hitherto calm existence.

KILLED IN THE SHAFT

On a green and level spot opposite to the opening of our tent a new store was pitched, and in due course of time was finished and opened. A short time served to show that the diggers intended to largely patronize it, not a small part of the said patronage being undoubtedly due to the fair face of Deborah Raine.

Deborah Raine was the storekeeper's only daughter and a girl of about twenty years. If one had searched the world for the greatest possible contrast, in appearance and character, to our mate Charlie Crawford, their choice might have fallen upon this girl. She was dark complexioned as a half-caste, tall and graceful, and with eyes and hair of the very darkest hue. She carried her head as proudly as a queen and there was something more than pride in the firm curve of her full lips. Deborah's was not a face or an air to win many friends; but that she was magnificently handsome, her worst enemy could not deny.

It need scarcely be added that, at a time when young ladies were the exception rather than the rule on the diggings, Miss Raine should not be many weeks on the Green Hills before she was besieged with suitors. That there were many of them who surrounded her as a simple amusement for their leisure moments, or to indulge a natural tendency to flirtation, is not to be doubted; but more than one was deeply in earnest, and you will imagine what a break in the union of our simple house was made when the fact that my two mates were rivals in that quarter became patent.

I never could understand how or what was the attraction exhibited by Deborah Raine for my refined and intellectual mate, Charlie Crawford. There was nothing coarse in the nature of the young student, and the mere possession of beauty in face or person could never alone have won the heart of my favourite mate. Not that there was anything vulgarly repellant in the manners or language of the storekeeper's daughter, but there was a great want of what sentimental ladies call 'soul'—a want exhibited in every word she uttered. Miss Raine was, in short, a young lady possessed of a very considerable share of vanity, a tolerably fine person, and a most vindictive and obstinate temper; at least that is the conclusion I came to after a sufficient acquaintance to warrant any conclusion at all.

Believing so, you will then understand with what real pain I discovered that Charlie was becoming perfectly infatuated with a girl so unworthy of his homage. I fancied at first that I must be dreaming when I imagined the attraction that drew him away from his books until the latter grew thickly covered with dust. From my bunk, where I often threw myself after my day's labours were over, I could see straight into the store opposite, which was furnished with the usual

KILLED IN THE SHAFT

wide door of those early days; and there would my mate's graceful figure—graceful even in the rough attire of the deep sinker—hang over the counter by the hour, until his constant attendance on the storekeeper's daughter became a subject of 'chaff' among the less fortunate suitors of the young lady.

For that he *was* fortunate soon became evident to any interested observer; but there was one of the most interested the last, as is often the case, to see a fact that so vitally concerned himself. From the very first arrival of the Raines, Harry, our mate, had devoted himself to Deborah; and that he was terribly in earnest, events only proved too well. With all the energetic wooing of a fiery temperament, he devoted himself and every moment of his spare time to an earnest attempt to win the hand of Deborah Raine, while Charlie looked quietly on, yet made the girl's heart so thoroughly his own that she faced a scaffold for his sake.

Under these circumstances, all the old comfort of our home life disappeared. Charlie was too much of a gentleman to exhibit anything like jealousy of our mate Harry; and, besides, he was the successful one, and could afford to smile at the evident, although suppressed, ill will of his rival.

If I had less interest in the event, I should have been amused at the different effects produced by the master passion upon my two mates, and the different methods they took of exhibiting its effects. Our claim was one of the most fortunate ones on the Hills, and a good portion of Harry's dividends were expended in presents to Miss Raine. That she accepted these presents, and laughed at the giver, was one of the facts that so lowered her in my estimation; but she did so, and while she did, Harry would not believe his own eyes as to our Charlie's greater success.

The latter presented no valuable brooches or rings to his beloved. Sometimes he rambled up the hill among the old granite boulders and gathered sprays of the lovely purple sarsaparilla, which would be twined among Deborah's black tresses for days after; or the delicate little feathery wild flowers from the same grey source would be seen, carefully attended, in a large glass behind the counter. I and many others knew where those flowers came from, and who gathered them; but no jewellery—save one simple turquoise ring—appeared on the person of Deborah Raine which had passed through the hands of my mate Charlie.

It is needless to particularise the discomfort occasioned between our hitherto contented trio by this state of things. Little passed between us in the way of ordinary conversation, and at last it was impossible

KILLED IN THE SHAFT

to observe Harry's manner toward Charlie without being convinced that he nursed the most vicious feelings toward him. Charlie, in reality, considered and felt himself so far above our mate, in a social point of view, that the idea of lowering himself by openly quarrelling would, I dare say, have been angrily denied; but it was impossible for a young man of his temperament not to offend his rival every hour in the day by an exhibition of jubilant happiness that made him one of the most joyous workers on the Hills.

One afternoon, when a heavy rain rendered our working almost impossible, I was lying on my bunk reading the weekly paper, while Harry was engaged in mending some of his working attire—a job which his old sailor training rendered him quite an adept at. From both his position and mine the door of the opposite store was visible, and inside it, talking to Deborah Raine, was our handsome Charlie.

Some of the most intense glances of hatred I saw Harry cast over the way, from under brows that seemed growing into a deeper scowl every passing day. Truth to say, I was beginning to dread an explosion between my two mates, and left them as little alone as I possibly could. The time for it had, however, arrived upon that afternoon, and it was preceded by the appearance of Charlie emerging from the store and walking rapidly across to our tent.

To one who knew him so well as I did, it was more than apparent that something had grievously disturbed him. He looked angry but stern, and I saw his fingers nervously clenching and unclenching as he walked in and placed himself at the opposite side of the table from that at which Harry was working.

'I have a few words to say to you, Harry,' he said firmly, 'and I say them here in the presence of our mutual mate, that no misconstruction may be put upon them. We have been working together now for some time, and working very comfortably together, as it has appeared to me, until—until within the last few weeks, when we have been unfortunate enough, in one sense, to become rivals for the love of one woman.'

Here Charlie's cheeks became suffused like a young girl's, while Harry went on with his work as though he had no ears. But I could see the dilated nostrils, and the awful rage that grew hard around his set lips; and I rose hastily from my recumbent position, trembling for the result.

'Had that woman chosen you, Harry, I might have carried a sore heart, but my sorrow would have been my own,' Charlie went on, more hurriedly; 'but she has not—she has made her choice, and you know it. In spite of that fact, you have insulted her by a repetition of addresses that are odious to her; and to put a stop to it at once and

KILLED IN THE SHAFT

for ever, she has commissioned me to tell you publicly that she will become my wife as soon as this claim of ours is worked out.'

It was an old jumper Harry was mending, and at this part of Charlie's communication he laid it methodically behind him on his bunk, rising at the same time to his feet and looking, for the first time since he had been addressed, in the face of our mate.

'Have you said your say, Charlie Crawford?' he asked, leaning his two hands on the table and putting a face pallid with passion across it to within a foot of his rival's.

'I have,' answered Charlie; 'and I hope I have said it so plainly that it need not be repeated.'

'Very well. Now, listen to me; I'll speak plain enough, too. If you live for six hundred years, you'll *never* have Deborah Raine for a wife. Remember that now, or if you forget, ask our mate there to remind you of my words.'

And out of the tent went Harry, and directly over to Raine's store.

In those few words there was certainly nothing of threatening to alarm, but I could not forget the expression of that man's face as he said them. He was white as paper, and there was an intensity of passion and determination in the glare of his eyes, and in the concentrated tones of his voice, that haunted me.

'Charlie, my boy, that's a dangerous fellow,' I said; 'and I am getting quite frightened that he will try to be revenged on you in some way. Pray, tell Miss Raine to be careful where she goes, or by whom she is accompanied. In a man such as Harry, a feeling that prompts to jealous revenge is to be dreaded.'

'My dear fellow, Deborah will be my wife in one month, and it is my present, as well as future, privilege to protect her,' replied he, smiling. 'I can make many excuses for Harry, feeling as I do myself; but even out of pity for his disappointment, I cannot permit her to be annoyed by his perseverance.'

After this explosion there was a still more marked separation of our triple party. Except for the most necessary matters, not a word was exchanged between the rivals. On Harry's part, the determined silence was attributable to the simple fact that he hated my mate Charlie for his greater success and could not bear to see the happy love-light that illumined his countenance; but his manner was guarded in the extreme, and even I began to half think that he began to be aware of the folly of his exploded anger, and to try and overcome his expressed affection for our Charlie's betrothed.

As for Charlie himself, he avoided any unnecessary intercourse with our disappointed mate, more out of respect for the disappointment

KILLED IN THE SHAFT

and its effects than anything else. But he was at that time so little in the tent, save at sleeping hours, that their silence toward one another was less noticeable.

We had a fourth mate in our claim who did not live with us, and whose name it is needless to mention in connection with this story. On the night when the fearful interest of this true tale culminates, this fourth mate and myself were to relieve Harry and Charlie at twelve o'clock, and I dare say it wanted no more than a quarter of that hour when I left the tent, billy in hand, and proceeded toward our claim, which was not far distant.

The moon was in her second quarter, but in consequence of a rather overcast sky the light was barely sufficient to reveal objects in an indistinct manner. Such a digging as the Green Hills presented a strange appearance at midnight in those days, and I never left the tent at such an hour without feeling a strange dreariness overpowering me—a feeling which has increased a hundred-fold since the night of which I write.

Along the side of the hill, and scattered over the flat beyond, gleamed hundreds of white patches, indicating the localities of many calico and canvas-roofed diggers' tents. In some of them, where men were returning from their claims or preparing to relieve their mates in the shaft, lights burned brightly and made huge-seeming lanterns of the little unlined homes. Down the street, too, where larger erections of canvas spread aspiring roofs in the fitful moonlight, open doors might be seen, inviting the tired worker to refreshment, or the joint sounds of laughter and music from a dancing saloon far up the street endeavoured to entice the wearied miner from his necessary rest.

Between the street and the 'lead,' many clusters of green saplins and undergrowth of various kinds still ornamented the unprofitable flat; and beyond these rose prominently the several working claims, with their 'logged-up' shafts and elevated windlass frames. Each of these stood high above the level of the surrounding ground, and on many of them, relieved strongly against the low pale sky, I could see the dark figures of men winding up the stuff, some silently, and others with measured songs that echoed far and wide over the hills.

One of these rude songs I have heard many and many a time since, but never without the sound recalling that night, so bitterly engraved in my memory. It was sung by some mates who had followed a sea life, doubtless, and became afterwards adopted by many a digger at his midnight work.

As I approached our claim on that evening, the roll of the rude voices came to me from the other end of the lead, mingled with the sighing of a lonely night breeze, and the rustling of darkly outlined and densely shaded bushes, that have been commingled in my memory with one other sound ever since.

I heard that other sound just as I put my foot upon the first clay step to climb up to the elevated windlass, and the strange sound almost froze me to the spot, with my foot suspended, to seek the second step. It was the dull reverberation of some heavy body falling down the shaft; and then a silence so intense that the chorus from the far-off diggers seemed hideous and interrupting.

My pause was but for a second, but during that second there was more than sufficient time to fear horrible things. I knew that Charlie would be down below, and I also knew that nothing harmless could have fallen down those one hundred and forty-four feet of sinking. Was it the bucket unloosed from the patent hook? or was it—heavens! I dare not think. In a moment I stood far enough up to place my head on a level with the windlass, and the first object I saw was the form of Harry leaning over the shaft and holding by one hand to the windlass, in attitude that denoted the most intent listening.

Never shall I forget that scene, or my terrified thoughts as I looked upon it. The dark frame and barrel of the windlass standing out in bold relief against the pale horizon, and the outline of Harry's silent figure bending in that listening attitude over the shaft. I could not—I dare not think, but one bound placed me by my mate's side, with the question, 'Good God, what is that, Harry? What has fallen down the shaft?'

'The block,' he answered, hoarsely, lifting his white face from its bending posture, and I could hear him draw a long, half-stifled breath as that of a fainting man recovering consciousness.

We used only one bucket in hauling up stuff in our shaft, and the block was a heavy junk of timber of a counterbalancing weight, which attached to the other end of the rope and travelled down the shaft as the bucket ascended, and *vice versa*.

'The block!' I exclaimed, fearfully. 'In the name of all that's pitiful, how did that get off?'

'Don't you see that the rope's broken?' he said, pointing to the empty windlass barrel.

'And I'll tell you how it was broken,' cried a voice behind Harry. 'If you've not murdered that poor fellow below, may God never forgive me my sins! Oh! you needn't look at me, mate! I've been on the claim this last half hour, and I saw you kick the block off the top of the shaft, as sure as my name's Arthur Crosse! But this is no time to talk—we want a new rope and help. I'll bring Bray's party in a minute.'

KILLED IN THE SHAFT

I felt sick and faint, and as if the subject of a horrible nightmare. My God, was our Charlie lying down there, a crunched and mangled corpse? Should I never again see the handsome and intellectual face lighted up with a smile I had often thought the very sweetest in the world, or hear his musical voice rippling in a laugh like the sound of sunlit waters? or—O God! was that a groan that came up to my sickened ear as I bent over the dark, cavernous shaft?

'Charlie! Charlie! oh, for the love and charity of heaven, speak, if you can!' But there came back no answer. 'Charlie! Charlie!' Alas there was no longer a Charlie, and the groan that broke the hideous silence was from my own trembling lips.

Ere I lifted up my head and looked Harry in the face, I felt the great drops of cold sweat leaving my forehead and dropping down the dark shaft. Even then—even at that moment of terror, I followed their fall and wondered if they would fall upon the face of my dying mate, and if, in the half consciousness of death, he would fancy them Deborah's tears! Had I felt certain of Harry's guilt at that instant, and one word would have avenged my prized mate, I could not have spoken it—I was completely unmanned.

As I raised myself, with despair tugging at my heartstrings and the sounds of voices and rapidly approaching steps in my ears, I got one look at Harry's face. It was rigid, and full of a white horror that flickered restlessly over it as the pale light came and went between the passing clouds. Even as the murderer of my Charlie I pitied him. Surely such a memory was punishment enough for any crime! He must have read my thoughts in my eyes; at least he looked like it, as he stared at me wildly and grasped the standards of the windlass in a crushing grip, as if he would obliterate them and memory together.

'So help me God!' he almost shrieked, 'I did not do it so! The block caught on the edge of the platform, and I pushed it off—and—and—O Lord!' He could say no more, but staggered behind our friends who hurried to the rescue.

Scarcely a word was uttered during the hurried preparations for descending the shaft. One of the number had been already despatched for a doctor, and half a dozen others were busy putting their own windlass ropes on to our barrel, and in attaching a bucket in which to descend. In a few moments everything was ready, and only a man to descend was wanting.

Knowing our close friendship, every eye was turned to me, while the empty bucket waited, and two of the men had taken possession of the cranks. The right was tacitly conceded to me, but I could not do it; my very knees were trembling under me, and I could not have held on

KILLED IN THE SHAFT

to the rope had my poor Charlie's life been depending on me.

'I cannot do it, mates,' I said, 'every nerve in my body is shaking—I am quite helpless.'

'I'll go down,' said our fourth mate, a strong and energetic man, and the same who had declared the falling of the block not to be accidental; and in a few seconds he was provided with matches and a lantern, and placing his foot in the bucket, was soon rapidly descending to discover the terrible certainty.

What fearful moments of suspense were those that followed! The hard breathing of the men as they bent over the mouth of the shaft and listened with strained ears, and the turning of the windlass handles as the rope slowly uncoiled from the barrel, was all the sound that broke the near stillness. But even then the chorus of the Deep Sinker's song floated down the lead and brought, to me at least, a crushing sense that there were joyous hearts not far away, while I awaited the certainty of a death that could never be effaced from memory.

I heard and saw all the rest in a sort of dream. I saw Harry Borthick standing back from the group of men, as one who dared have nothing in common with them, and saw strange looks bandied from one or another of our sympathising mates and friends to the silent man who had done the terrible deed. I saw the windlass cease to revolve, and the rope slacken, and then I *heard* a silence so terrible to endure that I prayed God Almighty to put an end to either it or my consciousness before it became too dreadful to bear and live.

'If any of you have a couple of strong scarves, throw them down.'

The voice came up the shaft solemnly as a death-warrant. Oh, of course, we all knew what that meant!

'Is he dead?' someone asked that was stronger than I.

'Quite dead.'

There are times when I hear those two words in the night watches, and they awake me from sound sleeps in which I have dreamed of my mate Charlie. Doubtless, I have repeated them myself as the refrain of a most sad memory, but they always sound hollow to me, as did that voice coming up with that deep horror in it that lay in the bottom of the shaft.

Scarves and handkerchiefs were thrown to the worker down below, and I caught myself hoping that he would not let them fall rudely on that face. Soon the 'Haul away' of our fourth mate came re-verberating up the perpendicular tunnel, and the windlass barrel once more revolved to the sturdy exertions of two friends. Those fearful ascending moments! But at last, the worst—the very worst—was at the surface.

KILLED IN THE SHAFT

With one foot in the bucket and both hands grasping the rope, our mate at last emerged from the shaft. Between both arms he supported the helpless form of our dead Charlie. He had tied the body to his own with the scarves with which he had been furnished, and our mate's poor bruised head lay heavily on the living man's shoulder, so close to his face that the fair hair of the dead mingled with the rough, dark locks of our kind-hearted mate.

'Oh, Charlie, Charlie!' It was all I could say, and all I felt, too, as I held him in my arms while busy hands undid the lashings, and set the living man free. It was some satisfaction to hold him there and feel his dead weight, and let his poor inert head be pillowed on my breast, knowing as I did that it could not have lain near the heart of a truer friend. If I had been a woman, perhaps I should have wept bitterly even then, but there are groans and silences that are far more bitter than tears.

We carried him to our own tent. In those days inquests were often held in the temporary homes of those who died suddenly, and it was a sad sight to see him lying so placidly on his own bed, with a sweet peace on his lips, and closed eyes that would never more open to earth.

Such a catastrophe was sure to be noised abroad in a very short time. Who told Deborah Raine I never knew; but far earlier than usual the store was opened, and the first face I saw behind the counter was hers.

When I went over to get a glass of spirits—which my shattered nerves stood sadly in need of—she was standing at one end of the shop listening to the comments of a cluster of men as to the accident and its result. One of those men was our mate Harry Borthick, and I could see from his more assured manner that our suspicion of foul play was not general. He had been taking a glass or two, evidently, and his face was flushed, while his restless eyes followed every movement of Deborah Raine.

I was astonished at the singular calmness of my dead mate's betrothed, but that the calmness was only external, and very hard to retain, was apparent in her twitching lips, and the strong heavings of a chest that seemed trying to burst from confinement. There was a fierce wildness in her eyes, too, that frightened me, and I should fifty times over rather have seen her weep than maintain that hard, calm exterior.

Anxious to get back to my watch, I whispered my wishes to her, glad of an opportunity to draw her attention from a subject that must have been so painful to her; and she turned to the counter to place a bottle of brandy near my hand.

'S—— ,' she said, looking me steadily in the face with such a determination in her black eyes as I could not describe, 'I am going straight over to see Charlie. You needn't say one word against it now, for I'll tell you I'll see him once more if every man, woman and child on the Hills should oppose me.

'If you are so determined, and can endure so painful a scene,' I said, 'of course, I can say no more: but I beg of you to avoid such a memory as must remain indelible for a life-time.'

'Nothing shall prevent me,' she iterated, pouring herself out a glass of wine, and swallowing it at a draught. 'You will know my reasons after. Harry, come here.'

This call was addressed to my mate Borthick, who stood at a little distance, gazing at the woman in whose affections the dead man had rivalled him; and I confess to the most profound astonishment as the words were uttered. There was such a strange softness in Deborah's voice as she called Harry, and so pleadingly her eyes rested on him, that I found my heart firing up with jealousy for the memory of my dead Charlie. Was she going to actually smile upon the man who was suspected of foul play against the life of him who was to have been her husband, even before his remains were covered in the grave? Such women *had* been—was Deborah Raine one of them?

Such a triumphant light flashed into Harry's face as he came close to the counter and eagerly listened to the girl's words.

'I am going over to see Charlie, Harry,' she said—and there the words seemed to freeze in her throat and half choke her—'and I—I should like you to come, too. Will you?'

Little need of the question—he would have followed her to his own grave.

'If I could only get over this,' she murmured, as she took a tumbler from behind her and half filled it from the bottle on the counter. 'If one little half hour were only over, I could sleep. Drink that, Harry, and let us go. You too,' she added, looking at me, and then watching my mate lifting the tumbler to his lips and draining the contents.

When the last drop had disappeared, Deborah lifted her hands to her head and laughed a low, pleasant-sounding laugh. I shall never forget her appearance at that moment. In memory, doubtless, of the sad event that had made her a widow ere she was a wife, she had attired herself in black from head to foot, and her face was, in contrast, whiter than a shroud. With her hands pressed on her forehead and her uplifted arms—with closed eyes and that pleased smile on her lips, I did not know what to think of her. A swift idea that she was losing her senses made me pity the girl and follow her rapid footsteps out of the store door and across the green flat to our sorrow-stricken tent.

KILLED IN THE SHAFT

'Quick!' she cried, seizing Harry, who seemed lagging behind, by the arm. 'I am in such a hurry, S——. Come—oh, come quickly.'

Only two men kept watch by Charlie. One of them was a stranger, the other, he whom I have made known to you as our fourth mate. Deborah's engagement to Charlie was well enough known to prevent her visit much astonishing these men, and on her entrance they rose and quietly left the tent.

The girl stood at the opening of the tent and, with a rigid face, signed to Harry and myself to proceed inside before her. No sooner had we done so, however, than she bounded inside, like a panther on his foe, and stood between the corpse and Harry, as wild and inspired-looking as a prophetess or a maniac. Her eyes flashed wildly—her form seemed to dilate and grow majestic under the influence of some feeling we knew nothing of.

Charlie was covered with one of his own blankets, poor fellow, and as Deborah stood there and pointed with one finger toward the shrouded form of her dead lover, with the other to the figure of Harry Borthick, I noticed that the face of the latter was white as Charlie's scrupulously clean blanket. He staggered, too, as my eyes rested on him, and a spasm of pain gathered up his features into an agony that needed no explanatory words. Falling heavily back into his bed, he sat grasping the table with both hands, and staring with fearful eyes at the woman for whose sake he had undone himself.

There was a repetition of that low, pleasant laugh we had heard in the store, and Deborah threw back the covering from Charlie's calm, dead face. Stooping down her lips to his, she kissed them with a woman's passionate fondness, and then she turned again to Harry Borthick.

'You have fulfilled your threat, Harry Borthick,' she said, as one speaks a religious truth. 'Do you remember it? You swore that before he should be my husband, you would crush the life out of him like a dog. And I have kept *my* promise. Do you remember that? Ha! you feel it, don't you? You are dying! Here, in sight of your victim, you are dying by *my* hand. I told you if anything happened to my Charlie at your hands, I should pursue you to the ends of the earth, but I would be revenged. I am revenged! Charlie *is* avenged!'

Before I could start forward to interfere, Harry Borthick had fallen back dead, opposite the bed on which lay the body of his rival.

Force had to be used before Deborah could be separated from the body of her lover. Twining her arms around him and pillowing her head on his cold bosom, she remained silent to all persuasions. At length her father discovered that reason had fled, and until the end of her short life she remained a harmless maniac. She had poisoned Harry

KILLED IN THE SHAFT

with prussic acid, administered in the brandy she had given him ere we left the store.

Years have passed since that episode in my Deep Sinking experiences, but the memory of it remains fresh, and connected with the name of Charlie, to this day.

First published in the *Australian Journal*, April 1871, under the byline 'Waif Wander.'

NOTES

1 Buninyong, in western Victoria, where this story is set, was not a goldrush where the gold was found easily, on the surface. Here it lay underground in a *lead* or *gutter*, in alluvial deposits that followed ancient watercourses which had trapped and concentrated the gold. Extracting it required *deep sinking*: miners dug shafts and created tunnels shored up with timber and lit with candles. The stuff (dirt) had to be brought to the surface in buckets, by means of windlasses, for the gold to be extracted. The course of the gutter was marked by 'the small red flag with the big white G' described later in this story; following it was a matter of guesswork. As the lead progressed, the *street*—the tent housing and associated businesses of the rush—packed up and followed its course, lest it be left behind.

BRIDGET'S LOCKET

I

It was the last night the passengers hoped to spend on board the *Seabird*; for, after a long and tedious voyage, she had dropped anchor in Hobson's Bay. One might think that after spending so many nights on board the vessel, this last one should seem as nothing to them, but it was not so; to most of them the hours appeared of double length while they waited for morning so near a shore upon which they could not land.

Two of the female passengers sat together on the bulwarks to which they had climbed, and were straining their eyes to try and make out what sort of country this land which was to be their new home was. The sun had set away behind Williamstown, but the red glow was still there and lay like a shadow of blood on the placid waters of our bay.

'So it has come to an end at last,' said the elder of the two women, 'and now there are only a few hours between you and your idol, eh, Bridget?'

'God forbid I should make an idol of anyone,' ejaculated the young girl fervently, 'sure, 'tis no harm to love me own husband.'

'Your own husband,' the other returned with a sneer, 'are you so sure of him, Bridget McDermot?'

'Sure of him! Is it Michael you are talking of? You don't under-stand, Miss Webster—'

'My name is Jane—don't Miss me,' the other interrupted shortly.

'Well, Jane, then—of course, I'm sure of Michael—am n't I married to him?'

'You are so innocent, my poor child,' murmured Jane Webster, half to herself, 'and it seems a pity to try and disturb your confidence in a man from whom you have been parted for three years. Does it never strike you that he may have met some one he liked better than you since you saw him last?'

'Like better than me? Me, his wife! Dear Jane, how can you talk like that?' And as if to assure herself that she did not share in the trea-sonable fears of her companion, the honest young Irish wife drew a locket from her bosom and kissed it.

'There! What do you call that but worship, Bridget McDermot, mumbling over the picture of a man's face like a simpleton as you are?

BRIDGET'S LOCKET

Let me tell you, now that we part so soon, that I was once as big a fool about a man as you, and—and he deceived me.'

'Maybe he wasn't your husband, Jane?' the young wife said in a low voice.

'He was my husband as fast as ever the minister who christened us could make him, and he deserted me for another woman. Is it any wonder that I have no faith in man?'

'No, perhaps not; but you must not judge Michael by the bad man who behaved wrong to you, Jane. Michael is not like him.'

'He is like him. It was his extraordinary likeness to my villain which made me doubt him. Oh, don't look so frightened, you foolish child. I am not going to put in a claim to your precious man. Mine would be 12 or 14 years older than Michael McDermot. No, the likeness is in the evil look of his eyes, the low formation of his forehead, the cruel shape of his mouth, the brutal squareness of his jaws. See—' And she drew the locket from Bridget's now trembling lingers and opened it to point at the pictured face—'could anything but the folly of a woman's love see anything but evil in that face?'

'He is my husband, and I love him dearly,' was the gentle reply as Bridget recovered her treasure and hid it in her breast. 'I am not learned like you, Jane, and I can't speak grand words, but I feel all the same and I trust Michael. God didn't make everyone handsome, and I never thought Michael a beauty, but I know he loves me. We were poor when we married, and he would have brought me with him if we had the money. Now he has sent for me, thank God, and we will part no more.'

'He has sent for you? Yes, when you had money to give him! Was there any word of sending for you until you told him of your uncle's legacy? Why, he did not even let you know where he was, and you had to advertise for his address. You told me all this yourself, Bridget—you know you did.'

'Yes, Jane, I did; but how can you draw bad out of that? If Michael was so poor all along that he couldn't send the money for me, why wouldn't he be glad to have me come when I had the money myself?'

'I know, child, that I am too ready to look at the evil side of everything—I know it well,' Jane Webster said repeatedly, as she stooped to kiss the honest rosy young face beside her; 'but I have liked and trusted you more than I have done any one of my kind since evil days fell upon me, and I tremble for your happiness. May God have you in his keeping, my good and gentle Bridget.'

'And you too, dear Jane. But don't be afraid for me—if you knew how happy I am! It seems to me that I am dreaming when I think that

BRIDGET'S LOCKET

in a few hours I'll see my husband once more! Oh, if my little baby had lived, wouldn't this have been the happy day!'

'Heaven grant you happiness, child. I start for my sister's by rail tomorrow, and if you write to me at the post-office, Birra, I will get your letter, and answer it. You don't know where your husband's place is yet, Bridget?'

'No, but please God I will know tomorrow.'

'You will write then; and now let us go to bed and try to rest. Kiss me good-bye, my child; in the hurry of disembarking we may not have another opportunity.'

The two women embraced for the last time and went below; nor did they meet again, for when at an early hour Jane Webster hurried on deck, the boat which Michael McDermot had sent for his wife was being rowed away. Not once did the happy and excited girl look back to wave her hand to her late shipmates, for she was gazing eagerly onward toward the landing-place, where a man's figure was visible, standing and watching the approaching boat.

The happiest woman in the whole wide world was Bridget McDermot as the evening of that same day was drawing on and she sat beside her husband in the trap he told her he had borrowed to meet her in town. Her rather ordinary face was nearly beautiful with the light of love in her eyes and the smile of happiness on her lips. She sat close to Michael's side, holding his arm so lovingly with both clasping hands, and looking into his face ever and anon to read his thoughts there as she fondly hoped.

But McDermot's face was not one so easily to be read as poor Bridget fondly believed. He was a powerful young fellow of seven or eight and twenty, with a low brow and deep set eyes too near his small, thin nose. All the lower part of his face was covered by a heavy sandy-hued beard, and his hair was coarse and of the lightest shade of brown. The hands with which he urged the fine horse he drove were strong and knotted in the joints, and his feet, though with a good pair of boots on them, looked huge and ill shapen. If there had been anyone to see they must have wondered at the choice the young Irish girl had made, for his face had a natural scowl imprinted on it, while hers wore the sweetness and light of a summer sunbeam.

But there was no one to see, and no one to hear the happy prattle of the young wife, nor in truth did Michael McDermot seem to enjoy it much.

'You are greatly changed, Michael, darlin',' she said to him as they entered a bit of bush through which their rough road led them, 'you used to be so full of fun and now I can hardly get a word out of you.'

BRIDGET'S LOCKET

'I've had hard times of it since I left the ould world, Bridget.'

'Yes, darlin', I know. But don't call me Bridget, Michael, asthore[1] — you used to always call me 'Bride' or 'Bridie,' and no one has even called me Bride once.'

'We are childer no longer, Bride.'

'No, Michael, we are better; we are loving man and wife for ever and for ever.'

She turned to look up into his face as she uttered the fond words, and wondered. Was it the shadow of the great, strange trees that made him look so dark? Was it the chill of the words that made his arm tremble under her loving hands?

'Are you cold, Michael, asthore?'

'It is chilly here, in the damp bush,' he said shortly.

'And it is lovely, too, isn't it? The road, I mean. We haven't met a soul since we left that bridge. We have come a good bit now, Michael?'

'About twenty miles, Bridie.'

'Will you go much farther?'

'No, I think we'll camp down by the creek—it's about a mile from this. I don't want to overdrive my neighbour's horse, and he'll go fresh home if he gets a good spell to-night. It will be something new for you to camp out in the bush, Bridie.'

'It'll be splendid! and with you, darling. Oh, I'm too happy, too happy, Michael! If only we had our baby alive!'

McDermot set his teeth, and ground an oath between them as he turned the horse's head into the bush. It was like a grand gentleman's park that was near her Irish home, this Australian bush, to poor Bridget, and her expressions of admiration of the ferns and grasses they soon found themselves among, by the half-hidden creek side, were unbounded. It was such delight to bound from the vehicle and help Michael to unharness the horse, and to gather sticks according to his instructions, while he led the animal to the water. That Bride was a very girl again, with a heaven she had only dreamed of around her upon earth.

'You have forgotten nothing, darling?' she cried, as the bush fire blazed up against the log, and the billy was hung over to boil, while Michael produced from a 'tucker box' materials for a meal, which promised, to the poor unsophisticated girl, a perfect banquet.

The supper was eaten and apparently enjoyed by both, and as the obscurity of night crept deeper into the bush the logs blazed up merrily, illuminated with great tongues of flame the weird-looking trees around them and patches of the deep creek among the tall reeds and bordering ferns.

BRIDGET'S LOCKET

They had talked of home and the neighbours of old days; of the uncle in America who so unexpectedly remembered the sister's child he had never seen. The notes which represented Bridget's little fortune now lay snugly in McDermot's pocketbook, for it had been their first object when the young wife landed to present her draft at the bank and get it cashed.

'We will put it in our own bank above,' Michael had said, 'and in your own name, Bridie; so you can lend me a couple o' pounds when I'm hard up!'

And she had laughed merrily, saying it was all his, and she wanted no name to it but Michael's.

'And now my Bridie must be tired, and I'll show you how we camp out in the bush. Put the things away in the box, asthore, while I spread the tarpaulin over the cart.'

That was poor Bride's first initiation into the mysteries of bush life, and her last! While McDermot went to bring in the horse to where he had placed some feed for him, the poor girl arranged the blankets he had bought with her own money into a rough but comfortable bed, and when he came back he looked under the tarpaulin and saw that she was asleep.

He did not seem surprised, nor did he seem to fear awakening her, for he made a good deal of noise in dragging big lumps of timber to pile on the already great fire which was blazing up against the logs. Perhaps he was afraid of the night dew for his young wife, though the cart, with the drooping tarpaulin over it, was at a considerable distance from the fire, or perhaps he felt the loneliness of the deep bush now that his lively companion was asleep, and there was a sort of comfort in the vicinity of a crackling fire.

What sort of face had Michael McDermot on this the first night of having his young and innocent wife by his side in this new land? A face which, never at any time prepossessing, had now the darkness of death in it. He sat on a log beyond the shrouded cart, with his pipe in his unheeding lips, until it roused him from his hellish thoughts by dropping to the ground and hiding itself among the grass, where it remained unsought. The moon was rising red and round beyond the creek, and he stared as if fascinated by the blood-red orb. Was he thinking of the deed her light should shine on ere long, or seeing in her awful hue the shadow of his approaching crime?

It was a night so perfectly still that behind him, in the shadows into which we dared not peer, the wretched being fancied he could hear a snake rustling among the grass; and, indeed, it might be so, for some little bell-birds which were nestling on the branches far above his

BRIDGET'S LOCKET

head twittered uneasily as if half-conscious of an enemy's presence. A blood-red mist blinded the man for a moment, and there was such a strange pang in the region of his heart that his hand went suddenly to the spot and he felt Bridget's roll of notes.

The very touch of them seemed to recover the villain, and he rose to his feet. Moving cautiously now down to the border of the creek, he pulled back a handful of the tall rushes and peered into the silent water; then he shook himself, as if its chill had touched him, and returned to the fire.

The wood had burned fiercely, and there was now a great glow of embers, such as might be made for the smelting of ore. The man seemed to hesitate; but at last he decided, and, stooping over the box he had left ready by the wheel of the cart, he drew from it a new and heavy tomahawk, which he hefted anxiously as though fearing it was too light.

What was he going to do with that tomahawk that he stooped and so cautiously drew up the tarpaulin? Was it to let the moonlight fall on the girl's sleeping face that he did that? Bridget was lying in a peaceful sleep, fully dressed, and with a happy smile round the red lips, through which the regular breath came so softly, and her fingers were clasped round the locket that contained the portrait of her idol. Ah sleeper, awake! if it is not even now too late. The image you have bowed your young heart and soul to is not the gold you deemed it, but the foulest dross of hell!

As the moonrays fell upon the peaceful face of the trusting girl-wife, the rays also glittered on the chain of the locket she held near her lips. It was the first time he had noticed it, and laying the weapon down beside him, he knelt on the grass, and gently as his rough hands could disentangled the embossed silver from Bridget's relaxed fingers. It was a more difficult task to unfasten the clasp, but he accomplished it, and gathering chain and locket in his hand, he pushed them into his pocket; and then, as he seized the weapon in the grip of a murderer, a dark cloud stole over the moon's face, and the reeds down by the creek rustled in a moaning breeze that sounded sad as the wail of a mother over the grave of her firstborn.

II

'Well Jane, and what do you think of us now?' was the question asked by Jane Webster's married sister on the morning after her arrival at

BRIDGET'S LOCKET

Birra. Jane was standing a little in front of the farmhouse door, among the tall hollyhocks and old-fashioned flowers, whose commingled perfume reminded her of the hour she did not regret.

'It is strange to you of course,' Mrs. Allen went on, 'but the country round here is considered very fine, and now that the railway comes within ten miles of us no end of summer visitors come up to look at our mountains.'

'No wonder, Ellen, they are very grand, but are you never lonely here? I can see only three houses round you, at least nearer than Birra. That's Birra over there under the hill, isn't it?'

'Yes, you could scarcely see it when we met you last night. Oh no, I have no time to be lonely, Jane. What with the cows and the children and the men—bless you, I am as busy as a bee all day. I wish you were a houseworker instead of a dressmaker; you'd be a greater help to me.'

'I can be a help to you as it is. By the way, you told me I'd be sure to get plenty of work in the neighbourhood. Are you still of the same opinion?'

'Of course I am! Why, ever so many have been expecting you, and are keeping dresses for you. I believe in my heart that Mrs. Connor has a month's work waiting for you.'

'Who is Mrs. Connor?'

'Our nearest neighbour. Do you see that stone house in the trees? That is the Connors'. They're Irish, but good neighbours. Mrs. Connor is rather uppish, and fond of dress and gaiety, but it is hardly to be wondered at. They have no children, and Connor himself is fond of company and very lively. But you'll see them all at the races tomorrow, and you must put on your most fashionable dress, for every eye will be on you—the dressmaker just out from England, you know!' and the merry woman laughed heartily as she drew her sister in to breakfast.

Jane Webster was no longer young. She was nearly forty. Her features were well formed, but there was a hard expression about the thin lips which scarcely ever smiled, and a dim look about the blue eyes which hinted at many tears. To strangers she was silent and cold, and even those who, knowing the hard sorrow of her life, made allowances for her variable moods, found her at times very trying.

Jane had no wish to present herself to the gaze of the good people of Birra. But her sister and family seemed to set such value on the yearly races that she sensibly determined on making the best of her circumstances and going without demur.

'It is fortunate that I made my new dress with a view to its being a sort of bush advertisement,' she said to Mrs. Allen, 'though it couldn't be on a worse block. I was never intended to serve in a dressmaker's

BRIDGET'S LOCKET

showroom,' and she was right. She looked stiff and respectable in the well-draped dress of fawn cashmere she attired herself in, but there was none of the style which another figure would have imparted to it.

To those who have seen a country race meeting I need not describe that of Birra. It was to the hard-working farmers around the one event of the year, and they with their families made it a regular day of enjoyment.

Almost every well-to-do farmer anywhere near a township in Australia owns a trap of some sort and drives proudly in it to church or chapel, or even along the public road, to see and be seen by the neighbours; but on the race day it is that the waggon or spring cart puts its best foot foremost, so to speak, resplendent with the newest dresses and millinery of the jolly owners.

For a little after the Allen's trap had drawn up but a little distance from the centre of attractions to many—viz., the refreshment booth— Jane Webster looked around her in silence at the unaccustomed scene. They were early, but so apparently was every one else; and while dozens of horses rested in peace, tied to the nearest fence, their riders clustered like bees round the counter of the booth, and made bets in loud, eager tones as they set their empty glasses down.

'I wonder whatever's come over Connor?' Allen said to his wife, as she was mixing his horse's feed in the cloth slung between the shafts.

'In what way?' asked Mrs. Allen.

'Why, look at him. Wouldn't you think he was going to be hanged tomorrow? And he's already got more drink than is good for him. John Rowan was telling me only this morning that Connor's a changed man since he went to town, though, by all accounts, he went to get money which was left him.'

'Money left him? That oughtn't to make him down-hearted, eh, Jane? It's the woman's husband I was talking to you about who has all the work for you, you know. That's he standing against the booth there.'

'With the dark clothes on and the whip in his hand?'

'Yes, Jane.'

Jane gazed in silence; but if her sister had not been occupied with some new interest she must have seen the more than strange look which developed in Jane Webster's eyes, nor will the reader wonder when I say that she had recognised in Michael Connor the husband poor Bridget had crossed the ocean to join, and whose miniature in the silver locket she had worn so faithfully near her heart.

'Is it that man with the red beard? He is talking now to a man on horseback. Is that Mr. Connor?'

BRIDGET'S LOCKET

'Yes, Jane, and here comes Mrs. Connor herself. She has seen you, and now don't be stiff with her like a good woman, for she is one of the best hearted poor things in the world if she takes a liking for anyone.'

Stiff with her? Stiff with the woman who was occupying Bridget's place openly before the world! Stiff with the pleasant, jolly young wife who came to her with outstretched hand and a beaming face to welcome Mrs. Allen's sister to Birra.

'I am gladder to see you than the races, Miss Webster,' she cried, 'though the races are very well in their way, and no end of fun when things go right. But just look at my gown. I'm ashamed of the old-fashioned thing; even old Mrs. Crowdy has got one on of a newer make! When will you be able to come to me? Ah don't say you're not rested yet! Sure I don't care how long you take over 'em if you'll only begin at me new gowns!'

Jane did not know what she murmured, her eyes were fixed sternly on Bridget's locket, which lay on the ample silken clad bosom of young Mrs. Connor; oh, it was it—she could have sworn to it among a thousand. What then had become of the girl her heart had gone out so strangely to during the long voyage in the *Seabird*?

Fortunately Mrs. Connor's attention was subtracted from Jane's countenance at that moment by the open admiration of Mrs. Allen for the mysteriously placed locket, and with a merry laugh of pleasure the young woman lifted it and touched the spring.

'Yes, Michael brought it to me from town. Wasn't it good of him? And they're all the fashion now, these chains and lockets. It's a good one, he tells me, but I'm no judge. Don't you think the likeness is good, Mrs. Allen? He had it by him, he says. It was taken a couple of years ago, but there isn't a bit of difference, only he has more beard now. Come here Michael,' and she beckoned to the moody-looking man who had just tossed off another glass at the booth.

He came slowly and with apparent carelessness toward his wife, and glanced sharply at Jane, whom he instantly recognised as a stranger. Ah, if he had guessed that the stiff-looking woman whose eyes met his so penetratingly held his life in the hollow of her hand, and would crush it as lightly as an eggshell, would he have spoken so bravely or kept up such a face to the people of Birra?

'I'm telling Mrs. Allen about the locket, Michael, and she says it's the picture of you, in spite of the beard. Do you know, Mrs. Allen, that if you look close you can see the scar at the corner of his mouth in the likeness? Well, that scar is under his great beard plain enough, though no one knows it but me—eh, Michael?' and she laughed merrily again, poor honest young woman, little thinking that every word was forging

BRIDGET'S LOCKET

a stronger link in the chain which was to bind her husband to death and herself to dishonour.

'What the mischief is up with you, Connor?' cried Farmer Allen as he let his hand fall heartily on Connor's shrinking shoulder. 'I've heard two or three talking about your low spirits since you came back from town.'

'I've got a —— bad cold—that's all. I wish people wouldn't bother their heads about my looks. What is it to them?'

He spoke so surlily that even his wife looked wonderingly at him; but he put it off with a laugh. 'The fact is, Allen, I did a very foolish thing, and it serves me blessed well right to pay for it.'

'What was it you did, Connor?'

'Camped out, I thought I'd make home that night; and so I would, but my horse fell lame. I camped at Howitt's Waterhole, and it seems the night air settled me.'

'He's too much coddled up since he was married!' the laughing wife cried; 'but I thought it was at Rae's Creek you told me you camped, Michael?'

'You dreamt it!' he said with an angry scowl at her, 'what the devil would I go to Rae's Creek for? Why, it is out of the straight road altogether.'

'So it is,' agreed Allen, 'you'd have to take the old road—it's nearly a deserted track now—to get to Rae's Creek. Well Connor, a cold that hangs on a fellow is a nasty thing, and you must try to rid of yours.'

'I can't get rid of it, my very bones are cold and trembling. I'm sure I've drunk nearly half a gallon of whisky already today, and my teeth are chattering yet.'

'Michael,' said Mrs. Connor introducing Jane, 'this is Mrs. Allen's sister, Miss Webster. She has just come out from England to set up dressmaking.'

'Just come out?' he asked quickly and with a suspicious look at Jane.

'Yes, I only landed three days ago.'

'In what ship?' His voice was almost inaudible as he asked the question.

'In the *John Marsh*.'

'Ah!'—the 'ah' was a long breath of relief.

Jane's sister looked at her in wonder, to get a frown that gave her a broad hint not to interfere.

'I was in town a couple of days ago,' Connor went on after a bit, 'and there was talk of an emigrant ship—the *Seabird*.'

'Yes, I heard of her,' Jane murmured.

BRIDGET'S LOCKET

But now great preparations for the first race distracted the men's attention, and Mrs. Allen got an opportunity to whisper, 'Jane, why did you give the wrong name of the ship?'

'I have my reasons, Ellen, and mind you just forget the right name for a while, and give John a hint to do the same.'

Jane Webster sat in the trap absorbed in thought, while the noise and excitement of cheering was going on around her. If she even saw the flying horses, it was as one might see them in a dream. Only one object had the least interest for her among all those around her, and that was the form of the man who was a living lie, and called himself by the name of Connor. From the moment she recognised his face she had doubted him—from the instant she saw Bridget's locket on his innocent wife's bosom she felt that he was a murderer. The fact of his having committed bigamy accounted for the deed, which might never have been committed had not the faithful Irish girl traced him so truly when she had money to enrich him with.

And now she, Jane, had her work before her. She would work, sleep, eat, and speak with only one object—to convict and punish the villain with the two names. She felt almost as if she had him already in her grip—the likeness, the scar his poor wife had told of, and the locket she had seen her young shipmate almost worship. All she had to do was to find out what he had done with his victim. He had undoubtedly taken her from the vessel—one of the girls who had come out in the *Seabird* with them had seen Bridget in a trap with, as she supposed, her husband. Was it his own trap—the very one his happy-looking wife was seated in at that moment, and had he made away with poor Bridget on the road?

On the road? He had camped out a night on the road, and his wife had fancied he told her, at Rae's Creek. That was out of the way, and on an old and unfrequented road. How anxiously he had asked the name of her ship, and how angrily he had denied having camped at Rae's Creek. Oh, he was guilty. Jane had not one doubt of it, she could even read it in his white face now that she knew it was fear which made his bones tremble, and had stricken the cold of death into his breast.

Something in this way Jane's thoughts ran until she aroused to find the races over, and horses being harnessed into traps. With a sudden determination she alighted and went among the people to Mrs. Connor's side.

'If you like I will go over to you tomorrow, Mrs. Connor?' Jane whispered; 'I can take over some patterns and look at your things.'

'Oh, thank you! how kind of you, Miss Webster. I will have everything ready, and make you as comfortable as ever I can.'

BRIDGET'S LOCKET

III

Jane was driven home with a sorrow for the living she had not calculated upon in avenging the dead. She was beginning to like this honest and good-hearted woman whom Michael McDermot had deceived. How she would have to break the happy heart in doing justice to poor Bridget! Yet it must be. It would be a crime to let the villain go unpunished for even a good woman's sake.

Jane Webster started for Mrs. Connor's on the following morning, hardly knowing what discovery she hoped to make. She wanted to be near Michael Connor, as he called himself, to watch the expression of his face and listen to his words. Perhaps she hoped he might unwittingly give her a clue to his own earlier conviction, enable her to find Bridget, if it was only to look upon her dead face before decay had time to do its work.

Mrs. Connor welcomed her into her large, comfortable kitchen with the most genuine warmth, and would hardly listen to Jane's assurances that she had already breakfasted. Satisfied of that fact, however, the kind Irish woman bustled her into the sitting room, from off which her own bedchamber opened, and seated her beside a perfect display of dress materials and trimmings.

'Michael is keeping his bed today,' she said, 'to try and sweat out the cold. He's been taking some doctor's stuff which makes him heavy and sleepy. I couldn't get any sense out of him he was so sound when I took in his breakfast. But at all events, we won't disturb him with the door shut.'

They talked of patterns and trimmings for an hour, and at last Jane decided on beginning to cut out her work. While helping her as well as she could, Mrs. Connor rattled on in her lively way, telling of her wedding gown—bringing it out indeed from her own room to show her the elegance of its material. She told innocently how devoted Michael had been to her from the first, and how she had never believed envious neighbours who hinted broadly that Michael had married her for her fortune. 'As if,' she added with a merry smile, which showed all her strong white teeth, 'as if I was so ugly that a young man couldn't take me for myself.'

'And you are nearly two years married?' Jane said, as she folded her pattern across Mrs. Connor's bed.

'Yes, nearly. I was disappointed,' she whispered archly, 'that no baby came. But I'll tell you a secret now, Miss Webster—you won't tell? I hope to see one of my own before Christmas. Good gracious! Are you ill, my dear?'

BRIDGET'S LOCKET

She had cause to ask. The material fell from Jane Webster's hands, and she sank into the seat behind her. Little did poor Mrs. Connor dream that it was the knowledge of her own expected happiness in being a mother which had so overcome the quiet dressmaker. Jane knew now that in bringing justice to the murderer's door there would be another innocent being to overwhelm with disgrace.

Pleading the unaccustomed heat as an excuse, Jane recovered herself and went on with her work. When it was so far advanced that the sewing machine was in requisition she proposed that no more should be done on that day as the noise might disturb Mr. Connor. The kindly woman readily agreed and went out to prepare some tea, leaving Jane to fold up and arrange the scattered material, &c.

Several times Jane Webster had heard a heavy snore from Connor's room during the morning, but now she listened vainly to hear it repeated. She had already observed that the partition was but papered wood, and now she had time to look for some opening through which she might observe the man's sleeping face. She had got a firmly fixed idea that his crime would be branded on it plainly when the mask he had to wear when awake had fallen off. She saw her hostess going past the window and knew she was going to the hen-house to get fresh eggs. Jane moved quickly across the parlour and put her eye to a crack between the boards, where the paper in drying had split.

She nearly cried out in consternation as she saw the face of Michael McDermot within a couple of feet of her. He seemed wide awake too, and to be staring at nothing, with wide, horrified and yet unspeculating eyes.

A sudden impulse seized the unpitying woman. Bending her lips to the narrow crack she whispered in slow distinct accents, 'Michael McDermot!' He started convulsively, and turned as if staring to see the dead standing at his elbow, but he seemed helpless to lift hand or foot—helpless from absolute terror. Jane saw the cold sweat grow out on his forehead in great drops, but she felt no pity for him—none.

'Michael McDermot! Where is your wife, Bridget?' Jane did not wait to see the effect of this second whisper through the partition; fearful of being suspected and her plans crossed, she slipped instantly from the room, and was in the garden when Mrs. Connor returned with the fresh white eggs in both plump hands.

They talked of the flowers and the vines a little, and then re-entered the house together. In the kitchen they were confronted by a tall, shrunken-looking being, who, with his tangled beard and dishevelled hair, looked wild as with incipient lunacy. He was dressed in shirt and

BRIDGET'S LOCKET

trousers alone, and his feet were bare. A cry of dismay arose on Mrs. Connor's red lips.

'Oh, Michael, dear, how ill you look! Go back to bed. Indeed, you are not fit to be out of it. Oh, do go to bed. You are feverish. I am sure you are! I must send for Dr. Tennant at once!'

'Stand back!' he shouted, as he pushed her aside, 'and let me see that woman. Who is she?'

'It is Miss Webster. Mrs. Allen's sister, you know, dear. I told you she was coming today. Don't you remember? Do go back to bed, Michael.'

'Was anyone in my room just now?'

'Not a soul, Michael. Who would be in your room but me, dear, and I was out getting eggs? We have just come in from the garden this minute.'

'There *was* some one in there—calling me! I heard 'em as plain as—plain as—. Oh, God, I'm going mad!' and clasping both hands on his head, he rushed back to his bedroom.

Jane had now no difficulty in getting away; for the poor young wife was distracted at her husband's condition. She sent a man on horseback for the doctor, and another for her own mother, who lived a few miles away, and Jane Webster walked to her sister's through the sunlit, green, growing leaves and grasses; feeling that she must have help and advice in her future proceedings against the man she knew to be a murderer.

From whom should she seek advice? Of whom should she make a confidant? The answer, in her own mind, was prompt. Her brother-in-law, John Allen, was the man. She had known him from boyhood—a thoughtful, trustworthy, and conscientious man. She would tell him the story at once.

Allen was at work up among the vines on the hill side and he was alone. When she had changed her dress and explained the reason of her return to her sister, she went up the vineyard to speak with her brother-in-law. The kindly man listened to her story with actual horror, and was at first inclined to doubt its truth.

'My dear Jane,' he said, looking into her face anxiously, 'You used to be a sensible woman long ago; none more so. But you have had enough of trouble to craze any woman. Is this awful idea not some kind of horrible dream?'

'No John—I wish it was. I wish that, even at the risk of being thought crazy, I could see my little Bridget's face before me there in life. I got to love the poor simple girl so much that she seemed almost a daughter to me, and her innocent blood is on that wretch's hands.

BRIDGET'S LOCKET

How could I be mistaken? He left Melbourne with her. He camped a night on the road and he came here without her.'

'But if this is so far true, my girl, Birra is the last place he would bring her to. He couldn't let the two women meet, you know. Well, he may have put her to live in some out-of-the-way place until he gets time to think.'

'And the likeness which my poor child would not have parted with, save with her life. Ah, John, if you had heard her tell, with proud happiness, how that locket was the first thing she bought out of her uncle's legacy. The likeness was only in a little black frame, and she was so happy to be able to hang it round her neck for aye! And now he has murdered her, the fiend, and hangs the child's trinket on another woman's breast.'

'A poor, deceived, kind-hearted woman, Jane. It will break her heart.'

'Yes, but all the same, poor Bridget must be avenged. Are you the man to counsel that I should let a murderer go free, John Allen?'

'God forbid, though it goes hard against the grain to have any hand in hanging him. What is it you want me to do, Jane?'

'I want you to take me to Rae's Creek by the old road. I want to find out where he camped that night, and see what he left there. No one need know our errand, not even Ellen. I can want some dressmaking things from the township.'

'All right. When shall we go?'

'Tomorrow at sunrise, if you can.'

'There is nothing to hinder me.'

And so it was arranged. Before night the news that Michael Connor was in a raging fever was all over the neighbourhood, and much sympathy was expressed with the poor wife. The doctor's comings and goings were watched, and many speculations were indulged in. But in spite of his good wife's urging, John Allen would not step over to inquire for the man he had promised to help on his way to the scaffold.

'It would be a merciful blessing from the Lord,' John murmured once during the evening, to his wife's dismay.

'What?' she cried.

'If he would die.'

Speechless for a few seconds from angry astonishment, Mrs. Allen at last burst out: 'I believe you are losing your senses, John Allen! I little thought to hear you talking that way of a neighbour; ay, and a good one! But if he hadn't a neighbour to regret him, hasn't he a wife; and can't her heart be broken as well as any other wife's heart? God help her!'

And John Allen puzzled his wife more by murmuring, 'Ay, indeed!'
But Jane understood the poor man's feelings only too well.

IV

The dew lay heavy on the long grass and sparkled bright on the broad vine leaves when Jane and Allen started on their expedition the next morning. The Englishman's heart was full of a sad unrest, and her lips quivered as they passed Connor's home, nestled amid its garden and vineyard. She felt she was going to sow desolation among the green corn and blight the pleasant vines—at least, as far as one innocent being is concerned—the unconscious wife of the criminal. Her brother-in-law, doubtless, felt affected in some similar way; for he turned his eyes away when they neared Connor's gate, and made his good horse increase his pace as if to escape from an unpleasant thing.

For five miles they drove in silence through the bush, with the grass-grown track winding in and out among the vales, and the birds in the branches overhead welcoming the sun with glad music. Then they had reached a spot where the track grew more indistinct, or seemed to separate into two less distinct ways.

Allen pulled up. 'We can turn right down to the creek here,' he said, 'but isn't it like looking for a needle in a bundle of hay, Jane? This belt of bush is five miles wide, and the creek runs right through it. How are we to know where he camped?'

'Strike Rae's Creek as soon as you can, John, and leave the rest to heaven. God will bring hidden murder to light.'

Allen turned his horse to the left, and walked him down among the patches of fairy growth and shaded green of the grass under the hundreds-of-years-old bush trees. With the eye of an experienced bushman, he was the first to detect a faint track which crossed in front of his horse's feet, and he pulled suddenly up and dismounted.

'Some wheels have passed here lately,' he said, 'though in the grass they are almost obliterated by the elasticity of the growing blades. But it is a strange place for a wheel track to be at all. You may as well get down, Jane. We had better follow this up.'

The track was very faint, and in many places almost indiscernible, the driver seeming to have picked out the highest and hardest parts of the grassy land, and to have avoided the damp spots where his horse's hoofs might have sunk. But Allen's eyes were keen, and he

BRIDGET'S LOCKET

declared that the wheel marks were those of such a vehicle as Michael Connor drove.

They followed them, Allen leading his cart down to the spot where Bridget had enjoyed her first and last meal camping in the Australian bush. Jane gazed round her with a queer feeling as if she had been touched with a cold hand, and Allen silently fastened his horse and looked around him.

'Some one has camped here, sure enough,' said he. 'There is where the cart stood. I see the mark of the shaft props. It's quite handy to the creek, you see, Jane, and the horse had been led to water down between those ferns and reeds.'

'They've had a deuce of a fire,' he added, looking at the heap of ashes by the charred log. 'What was that for now? We've had nothing but the warmest of nights this month back. They've had an idea of hiding the ashes, too, or that young sapling would not have been felled to fall right across the heap.'

He went to the butt of the sapling, a young tree about six inches in diameter, where it had been chopped from the root. As he stooped to draw it from the ashes he saw that it had been felled with an axe or tomahawk which had blood on it, for the wood was stained red. But he said nothing about it just then. He only dragged off the lightly branched young tree, disturbing and scattering as he did so the white, dead ashes.

A shriek was uttered by Jane Webster as a metal object, blackened by the fire and to which a scrap of some tough woollen material was attached, was tossed almost to her feet. Jane stooped and lifted it—her cheeks ghastly, her eyes wild and full of horror.

'Do you recognise that, Jane? You do. I see you do?' asked Allen.

'Yes, oh yes! It is a clasp which was on a rough wool jacket the poor girl used to wear on board. I could swear to it. See how peculiar the pattern is. Shamrocks intertwined. She was proud of it, poor thing. And look, John, it is firmly clasped yet. My God, he has murdered Bridget and burned her body! She wore this jacket when she left the *Seabird*.'

'No,' said Allen, as he raked abroad the ashes in a careful search, 'if it is so he has not destroyed the body here. There would be some remains of burnt bones. Jane, this a horrible job. I wish I had never begun it. We had far better put the affair into the hands of the police, as you have actually recognised a portion of the poor thing's dress here.'

She made no immediate reply; but with the bits of metal still in her fingers she raised her face and looked around her. It was as if she was asking the green fresh grass and the gray old trees to tell her the story of Bridget's cruel death, that she might avenge it on her murderer.

Did the green grass reply to her? As her eyes wandered round the fatal spot seeking some farther evidence against the cruel wretch, they lighted on an object half-hidden in the grass. She darted toward it and lifted it, coming back to Allen with it in one hand and the clasp still gripped in the other.

'It is a pipe, John,' she said handing it to him, 'and a peculiar one.'

'I have seen Connor smoking it a hundred times,' the man cried. 'Indeed I've smoked it myself. It belongs to him.' And the man was right. It was the pipe which had dropped from the murderer's lips as he sat on the log with the darkness behind him, and the glare of the great fire on his awful face.

'I have no doubt of the villain's guilt now,' said Allen, 'but I am sorry for the poor woman who believes herself his wife; and I will have no more to do with it. Let us go home, Jane, and let the police do the rest.'

'I cannot,' she said with determination. 'If he did not destroy the body by fire, he must have hidden or buried it somewhere about. He would never take away the poor girl after—after—'

Allen looked at the blood marks on the stump of the sapling, but said nothing, and Jane, with that clasp still held in her hand firmly as if it had been a talisman to guide her, stalked down to the creek.

She did not reach it where the horse had evidently been watered. Where the bank sloped down to the water, and indentations of shod hoofs were yet visible in the grass, she went obliquely through a deep border of thick-growing wattle and ferns, and to where the bank was steep, though not high, and an old fallen tree lay decaying and melancholy-looking, half on the bank and half down in the water which had once cherished its twisted roots.

Around that log the reeds grew strong and thick, and there was a little eddy in the water as the quiet current swept round the end of the slimy and rotting log. Jane saw or fancied that this current had bent the reeds back toward the log as if an arm had pushed them, but then a sudden inspiration seized her and, putting the fire-darkened clasp in her bosom, she gathered her attire more closely about her, and stepped boldly on to the fallen tree.

John Allen saw her, but did not interfere. He only stood and watched on the bank, wondering what discovery Jane had made. She had made none—as yet, but when she gained the end of the log she knelt down carefully upon it, grasping one of the prominent roots with one hand to steady her, and then stooping to drag back the reeds with the other.

BRIDGET'S LOCKET

It was the work of some moments; for there was no doubt that human force had been applied to bend those growing reeds, so that they should be held under the log to hide—what? The answer was there, lying still and awful when Jane succeeded in dragging away the rushes—an answer as loud as a thunder-clap, though it was spoken by the pale dead lips of the hapless Irish girl!

She was lying on her side in such a huddled and unnatural position that it was evident that her body had been forcibly pushed into its cramped position under the log, and it might have lain there packed and wedged in with the strong growing rushes and reeds until decay had done its work, had not Jane Webster's loving heart traced the murderer and his victim. One look only she gave at the awful crushed face, with the veil of water alone between her eyes and it; and then she tottered back along the log, glad of her brother-in law's offered support when she regained the bank.

Few words were needed on their hurried homeward journey. John Allen stopped near Connor's gate to let Jane alight, and while she made her way up to the farmhouse he drove on to the township to give information to the police. Jane's face was set and stern as she reached the kitchen door. Yet her lips trembled with sympathy as she saw an elderly woman sitting at the table with her head bowed on her arms, and bitter tears running from her swollen eyes.

The woman rose as Jane entered and seeing she was a stranger, set her a chair. 'You are some friend of Mrs. Connor's, and you have heard of our trouble; and oh, indeed, I am in sore trouble for my girl, for I am afraid her husband has taken leave of his senses for ever.'

'I am Mrs. Allen's sister,' Jane said pityingly, 'and heaven only knows how I pity you and yours, Mrs. Mahony. But I am come with evil tidings, which you must be strong to bear for your poor daughter's sake.'

'Evil tidings! there is nothing wrong at home? They were all well when I left! Oh——!'

'There is nothing wrong at your home, dear Mrs. Mahony. It is here, in this house, the evil is. Be strong now, for your poor innocent daughter's sake.'

'Go on!' the poor woman whispered, gazing at Jane with terrified eyes, 'what is it?'

'You must get Mrs. Connor away from this instantly; no matter what excuse you make. You must take her home with you, so that she is not here to see Connor arrested. The police will soon be here, and bad as it is to see him as he is, it would be worse for her to see him dragged to prison for a crime.'

BRIDGET'S LOCKET

'Dragged to prison for a crime!' repeated the poor mother, 'my daughter's husband dragged out of his own house—by the police, for—a crime!'

'Oh, yes it is only too true! I pray you, lose no time. Take me to her, and I will try to make some excuse for you to take her away before they come. My very heart is bleeding for the poor deceived girl!'

From the kitchen even Jane could hear the loud tones of McDermot's voice, and she went straight toward the bedroom, whose position she had become acquainted with on the previous day. The door between it and the sitting room was open, and Jane entered the bedroom boldly, followed by the frightened, nay horror-stricken, Mrs. Mahony. Connor or McDermot was partly dressed, and shrinking as far back on the bed as he could, in apparent terror, while his unhappy wife, poor soul, was bending toward and trying to pacify him with gentle words and touch.

She was prettily dressed, perhaps in honour of the doctor's visit, and the chain and locket she was so proud of, as her husband's last present, were round her neck, showing to advantage over the dark velvet of her bodice. She turned a pained face to her mother as she entered and laid her hand upon the locket as if to hide it from her husband's eyes.

'He wants the locket to break, mother! Oh, Miss Webster, I don't know what's come over my poor husband.'

'Take it off, I tell you!' shrieked the madman, 'she'll never rest till she gets it! Look at her standing there with the blood on her white face, just as if the water has not washed it off long ago! Give her the locket, and she will, perhaps, leave me in peace!'

The eyes of Jane followed the staring gaze of the murderer, and she seemed to see the shadow of a form bearing the semblance of the dead Irish girl. Closing her eyes with an effort to destroy what she believed to be an illusion of her own excited imagination, she opened them again to see the same white, pitying face of Bridget McDermot, and a small shadowy hand outstretched toward Mrs. Connor, as if claiming her own, even from her watery grave among the reeds of Rae's Creek.

As the vision seemed to fade, the locket and chain slowly slipped from Mrs. Connor's velvet bodice and fell with a rattle to the floor. Jane Webster put her foot softly on the glittering ornament while a shout of delight escaped from the murderer's parched lips.

'Bridget has taken it!' he exclaimed, 'she has got her own locket again. Now she will rest, and let me rest!'

'Take her away,' Jane whispered to the mother as she stooped to lift the chain, which had so strangely become unclasped. 'This is no place

BRIDGET'S LOCKET

for her'; and poor, kindly Mrs. Connor allowed herself to be led out like a helpless, half-stupefied child.

Jane Webster followed and locked the bedroom door behind her. The last glance she gave toward the bed showed her the murderer huddling himself up in the bed clothes as if relieved, and composing himself to sleep. Hastening to the kitchen to relieve the bewildered mother, she found Mrs. Connor sitting in a chair as if stunned. She went to her side and laid her strong hand firmly on the soft shoulder.

'Dear Mrs. Connor, you must get ready at once and accompany your good mother home; for I have brought bad news to you. The doctor says that a terribly infectious disease is developing in your husband, and he has ordered that the house is to be strictly isolated.'

'Oh, merciful Father! but they will let me stay with him—*me*, his own wife!'

'They will let no one stay with him but a professional attendant. The police will have the house in charge. Dear Mrs. Connor, let your mother get you ready to go while I go out to tell one of the men to harness up a conveyance. I am sure you are too sensible to stop until you have to be, perhaps rudely, forced out of your own house. You cannot fight against the law.'

'I will go; but, oh mother, come with me, I *must* see him once more—just once more!'

How could they say her nay? Jane softly unlocked the door, and saw it was as she had hoped. The man was asleep. Jane whispered to the poor wife not to arouse him from a sleep which might be of such benefit to him. Jane let the poor woman approach the bed, and gaze tearfully into the sleeping, white face. Tears for him! Tears for the wretch who had upon his guilty soul the innocent blood of a loving, trusting girl! Ay, tears, for even him!

Stern and unforgiving, for Bridget's sake, cool and hard, and silent, Jane Webster sat awaiting the myrmidons of the law who were to take the murderer in charge. She held the key of his room in her hand, and felt a sort of grim delight that even for a short space she only should be his gaoler. Time seemed to her to be annihilated, and passed by without being marked. She was going over every incident of the voyage with which the memory of faithful Bridget McDermot was connected. And then she came to the last hour they had spent together the night before landing, when she had vainly tried to shake the young wife's faith in a man whose pictured face seemed to her branded with evil.

Her sad thoughts were interrupted by the sound of approaching feet, and two policemen stood before her. She rose and silently handed them the key of Connor's door. They asked her some questions in a

BRIDGET'S LOCKET

low voice, and she gave them the chain and locket from her pocket. She told them that Mrs. Connor had gone home with her mother; and then, her work done until she was called to appear as a witness at the inquest to be held on poor Bridget's remains, she gathered her cloak around her, and prepared to go.

'Stop a minute Miss Webster,' one of the men said, 'do you think this man is in a condition to be moved?'

'The doctor would be a better judge,' she replied, 'he was asleep when his wife went in to see him for the last time. I should think he is suffering from overdrinking in trying to drown the memory of his crime.'

'And from all I hear, that's just what ails the villain. Come on Corbett, we must wait no longer or we won't be ready when the cart comes back from the creek.'

'Are they gone to Rae's Creek?' she asked, in trembling tones.

'Yes, to bring in the young woman's body, and we will take our prisoner to the lock-up in the same conveyance.'

A refinement of cruelty? As if one *could* be too cruel to a wretch like him.

The sudden and noisy unlocking of the door roused the murderer, and he sat up in bed with a sudden convulsive motion. His face had flushed during his uneasy sleep, but at sight of the men in uniform it paled to a ghastly, greenish hue. His lips moved, as if he tried to speak, but no words came from them.

'Get up!' said one of the constables roughly, as he seized the bedclothes and dragged them from the cowering wretch, 'you have to come with us. You are arrested for the murder of your wife, Bridget McDermot.'

'My—my wife!' he gasped, staring from one to the other, in horror.

'Yes, your wife. Get up man—though 'tis a shame to call you a man—get up or I'll drag you out.'

They *had* to drag him out bodily. He was struck helpless with fear, and the growing delirium which was prostrating him.

'Does he understand you, Mac?' asked the inferior constable, half-pityingly.

'As well as you do, the villain. I arrest you, Michael McDermot, alias Michael Connor, for the murder of your wife, Bridget McDermot; and mind, whatever you say will be taken down in evidence against you. Handcuff him, Corbett.'

They led him out of the house which had been his home, and down among the flowers a poor deceived woman had planted to make that home sweet for him. He passed them with a hangdog air and quick, wild glances at either side of him, as if he feared to see at his right hand or his left the face of the dead. At the gate were tied the horses of the mounted men who had arrested him, and a group of horrified-looking men were standing halfway between the gate and a double buggy, from which one seat had been removed, and which was in the middle of the road.

At the back of that buggy, covered with some dark woollen material through which moisture was soaking, lay an object which to glance at even in its shrouded condition made the strongest man there shudder. The policeman led McDermot to the cart and ordered him to mount the front seat, but he stood still gazing at the object in the waggon, until they had to drag him away and half lift, half push him to his seat between his two guards.

Even when seated he turned round to stare at the awful huddled-looking shape, until Mac, the least patient of the constables, got quite out of temper with the unhappy being.

'Show it to him! Damn it, show it to him! Pull off the blanket, and show him his work since he *will* have it so!

And the covering was partially withdrawn from the corpse of the murdered girl. As the terrible face came into view, with the fearful gap his tomahawk had made above the death-white brow, the prisoner tossed up his manacled hands as he rose from his seat. A shriek, so full of pain that it might well have been his last, pierced the air like a sharp knife.

'Bridget!' he cried, and before the men could hold him up he fell backward against the splashboard, and then rebounded to the men's feet; and leaving him lie there, they drove him insensible to the lock-up.

A few words now will close this tale of a heartless crime. McDermot was tried, convicted, and hanged for the murder of the helpless Bridget. Before his death he made a full confession of his crime, and recounted how it was done; but he never went the length of expressing sorrow for having committed it, and he never once uttered the name of the poor girl he had married under a false name, and while his lawful wife yet lived and loved him.

Perhaps it is as well to have to record that the woman known as Mrs. Connor did not survive her husband. She died at the birth of the baby she had built such living hopes on. It had been impossible to keep the truth wholly from her, and when she closed her eyes for the last time it was gladly to escape from a world which had no future for her and her babe, who was buried with her.

Jane Webster took much trouble to secure for Bridget's aged mother in Ireland the three hundred pounds which had cost her her young life;

BRIDGET'S LOCKET

but she succeeded, and still lives at Birra, within an easy walk of her favourite Bridget's grave.

First published in four instalments in the *Australian Town and Country Journal*, 27 November 1886, 4 December 1886, 11 December 1886, and 25 December 1886, under the byline 'W.W. ("Waif Wander"). Author of "The Detective's Album," &c.'

NOTES
1 *asthore*: a term of endearment, of Gaelic origin; literally, oh treasure.

CONSTABLE DYASON'S DEFEAT

Constable Dyason was 'a most efficient officer,' and an ornament to the force. He had a 'Milesian'[1] nose, a beautiful pair of glossy black whiskers, and a good-conduct stripe. Not to say that any of these possessions were at all uncommon, or conferred any particular distinction in themselves, but the man made them, you see, and not they the man.

There wasn't in the whole town, let alone his own particular beat, such a nose of consequence as that Milesian appendage of Constable Dyason's; it had an air with it, sir, that wanted seeing to believe in; for mortal man would never have believed without seeing that such an air of superiority and authority could be exhibited by any nose in the known world; and no wonder that, conscious of its own value, that nose had wings on it, as if it would fly far away, up to the regions beyond the contemplation of common human orbs.

And then Constable Dyason's whiskers! the binding of his helmet alone rivalled them in gloss, or the wig of a Special Pleader[2] in abundance. It was a sight worth looking at, I tell you, to see that valuable officer caressing those admirable whiskers with the white-gloved hand belonging to the arm on which the buckle of that good conduct stripe glistened; and surely never buckles, or buttons, or boots, did glisten and shine like those of Constable Dyason. Ill-natured people did say that he had an unfortunate wife somewhere handy, who did nothing but polish those boots and buttons and things, and waited till they were ornamenting the constable and his beat before she ventured to let her ready tears at his ill treatment fall and spot their gloss. But then people will say wicked things of each other, and more especially of constables so efficient as Constable Dyason.

One might wonder in what way he exhibited the efficiency of which the magistrates talked on the bench sometimes, but the one who ventured to do so would in all probability do it behind his back; and I don't think that in the whole of Fitzroy there was an individual hardy enough to smile in his presence, with the exception of George Lathorp and Sam Sherberry.

And, of course, these were boys. Boys! The constable would have assured you with a solemn shake of his head that no good would ever come across 'boys, wid the divil in 'em so hard that nothin' but the gallus would ever dr-rive it out of 'em.'

But, being as I am, and always was, very partial to boys and inclined to take their parts, even when I must acknowledge they scarcely deserve it, I must 'stick up' for George and Sam. They were both hard-working lads, apprenticed in the same shop, and nearly out of their apprenticeship. George Lathorp was the only son of a widow, and his father had been a gentleman; and Sam Sherberry was an honest and well-doing mechanic's son. I won't have either of them called 'larrikins,' though I must confess they were both fond of a stroll in the street after work, and would have given one of their ears at any time for a 'lark.'

Especially at Constable Dyason's expense, for they detested him, as boys somehow will detest constables, or anyone else who has 'a down' on them. It was war to the knife between these lads, and if they had known how they humiliated and annoyed him, they would have each been prouder than the legendary 'dog with two tails.'

'You are tired to-night, George,' said the rather prim Mrs. Lathorp—who was, however one of the best and fondest mothers in the world—'take off your boots, now, after your supper, and put on my old slippers; you'll rest better in them.'

'Tired, mother! why I'm fresher than a daisy! Sam's coming for me—we're going out for a stroll.'

'Now, George, dear.'

'Yes, mother, I know; but you can't expect a fellow to stick in always of an evening after being hard at it all day; it's only for a run, and you're going down to Mill's.'

'Only for a little; I shall not be long away.'

'Neither will we, mother. Here's Sam'; and seizing his hat, George was off like a shot.

'Well, where for tonight?' questioned Sam. 'I say, I saw that precious Dyason down at the Shamrock. It's his week on night duty. Let's go down and have a lark at him.'

'Faith, Sam, I'm half-afraid. He nearly had us that last night we got him down the lane shouting "police!" I wouldn't like to get into it, for mother's sake.'

'Into it! What can we get into for a lark? The idea of that heavy lump catching us! Why, you know very well that either of us could run to Sandridge while he'd be getting wind up to start!'

George laughed, and as he was only too ready, his friend easily persuaded him to join in the especial 'lark' he had mapped out for the benefit of Mr. Dyason.

The Shamrock hotel stood at a corner not very far from George Lathorp's home. The corner was formed by the junction of a side street with one of the principal thoroughfares. This side street was mainly private cottages, and not too well lighted; and in the darkest

CONSTABLE DYASON'S DEFEAT

spot between the hotel and a lamp post, the two conspirators planted themselves after having completed their sly arrangements.

'There he comes!' whispered Sam. 'Now, just watch the conceited strut of him! Wouldn't you think he was Lord Mayor, at least, or Inspector-General? His trousers are shining like my best Sunday shirt, when mother puts a candle end in the starch, and I'm blest if he hasn't white gloves on, and at night! Ain't I glad the street's muddy near the trough!'

'I wonder what the reason he sticks about the Shamrock so?' said George; 'I'm sure it's not a bit rowdy.'

'Don't you know? Gammon! Everyone in the street knows. It's the looking glass! Just you watch him; and now he'll saunter up, and what a glance he'll cast inside. Gammon at the bar, but it's his own self in the glass opposite the door he watches best.'

I must confess it looked very like the truth, although it was told by an enemy. Constable Dyason sauntered along the well-lighted thoroughfare, slowly and more slowly past the shop windows. He was spick and span, as if he had come newly brushed out of a freshly papered hat-box. His pants (let us be polite) shone like the well-ironed and starched linen that they were; and his buttons might have been diamonds of the first and finest water, they glittered so in the gaslight. There wasn't a fleck on his uniform, or a dull spot on his tight boots. Run, indeed. Now, could such a man be expected to run, in such admirable boots, I should like to know?

As Sam had predicted, Constable Dyason paused in front of the Shamrock door. There was a pretty barmaid there, but he never cast an eye that way, for he couldn't spare one: they were both too busily engaged in looking at himself in the opposite mirror. Well, it was a pleasant picture to look at, that handsome bobby with the Milesian nose, and the glossy whiskers and the shining buttons, and the tight boots, and—I give you my word on it—the big gold ring on his little finger of the ungloved hand that held the glove that belonged to it, and softly, not to say fondly, passed it over the shining and abundant whisker.

'Now, you see, he'll gammon to pass, but he can't; he'll just step back to have another look; he always does it, and then we'll have him.'

Sam was right; he did step back gingerly, and leaned his head back to get within sight once more of the beloved object; and as he did so a something tripped up the bright shining boots, and Constable Dyason found himself on the broad of his back in the dirt puddle at the Shamrock's water trough.

Certainly there is a deal of wickedness in the world, and very little sympathy with misfortune. It must have moved a heart of stone to

CONSTABLE DYASON'S DEFEAT

pity to see Constable Dyason's helmet rolling from his head into the gutter, and his 'illigant' whiskers daubed with mud, as he tried to struggle to his feet; but those wicked boys were harder than stone, and they laughed as if they had never laughed before and would never be able to laugh again; and Sam's perfect enjoyment of his lark had nearly undone him. When he saw poor Dyason's pitiable condition, he seized the end of the string which had caused the mischief, and giving it a strong tug to regain possession of it he stooped, so that his face came into the light, and the constable saw and recognised his enemy.

'You young riprobates!' he shrieked, as he crawled to his hands and knees, and thence to his feet. 'I see ye, and I know ye. This'll be the worst night's work ye iver put in!' and girding himself for the race, which means pulling up his defiled pantaloons, hatless, and almost breathless, he started in pursuit.

Sandridge, Sam said. It was exaggeration, doubtless, but an excusable one. The efficient officer was inclined to what our French friends call embonpoint, which, I take it, means, in plain English, fat; and long before he had got halfway up the dark street, the lads' flying footsteps had ceased to resound in his ears.

He puffed and panted and followed, however. Game to the backbone was Constable Dyason, and he had a bump as big as one of the potatoes of his own country on the back of his head to remind him of his duty! and he fulfilled it until his breath failed him and the corns under his tight boots caused him the sufferings of a martyr.

However, in a pitiable plight as regards his corporeal feelings, he at last reached Mrs. Lathorp's door, and made such an application with the knocker thereon that the whole neighbourhood was alarmed; and when it was at last opened, with a jerk, he roared and panted and gasped, 'Ye may as well come out! I know ye're here, yeah young shcamps, an' I'll have ye, if I have to drag the roof aff! Stand back, young 'ooman, an let me pass!'

The 'young 'ooman' was an extraordinary-looking figure—she had a round, coarse-looking face and a not over-clean nightcap, which was a very tight fit, tied on her round head. She had a great loose jacket, and very short petticoats, and a huge white apron tied round her broad waist.

'The missus ain't in,' she cried at first, and then 'Coo, it's the p'leece! It's the p'leece! Master George, Master George, it's the p'leece!'

'Shut your great mouth up an' stop screechin!' shrieked the angry constable. 'Let me in, I say! Master George, indads! I'll Master George him! Oh! here you are.'

240

CONSTABLE DYASON'S DEFEAT

Yes, here he was, indeed, coming coolly out of the parlour into the passage with his hair all standing anyhow on his head, his mother's slippers on his feet, and *The Herald* in his hand.

'Is the whole street a-fire, or the Yan Yean[3] burst again? Oh, it's you, Constable Dyason. Pray, what do you want here, kicking up such a disturbance?'

The mystified officer looked at George with his mouth as well as his eyes — for the unlimited coolness of the young chap staggered him.

'I want Sam Sherberry,' he said; 'and well you know what I want. All your gammon doesn't take me in. I'll swear you were out in the street just now, and that rascal Sam Sherberry ran in here.'

'Out in the street, me!' cried George, lifting his slippered right foot, and gazing at it admiringly. 'Upon my word, after that! Sam Sherberry, eh? Maybe you'd like to search the house, Mr. Dyason?'

'Search the house! For what, pray?'

This question proceeded from Mrs. Lathorp, who just entered her own door and, as she spoke, pushed her way past the fat constable. 'Pray, what does all this mean, George?'

'Oh, you'd better ask the gentleman, mother; he's been hammering at the door here until I thought the whole town was a-fire; and now he wants to search the house for Sam Sherberry. What do you want Sam Sherberry for, Mr. Dyason, may I inquire?'

'It is none of my business what he wants Sam Sherberry for,' said the precise widow, drawing herself up; 'but I'll see that this matter is inquired into by his superiors. Leave the house, sir! How dare you force yourself into my quiet house and bring disgrace on me among the neighbours?'

'And nearly frighten the servants into fits,' added George.

The said servant looked certainly as if something unusual was the matter with her, for she was squeezing herself along the wall of the narrow passage to get nearer the door and the constable, it seemed; and as the angry and disappointed man was drawing back over the threshold, so as to keep within the safe pale of the law, the said servant's fist came in such violent contact with Dyason's nose that he reeled back several paces and staggered into the gutter.

'I'll teach the villain manners,' she cried, 'trying to kiss a decent girl right in front of the missus's face.'

'Kiss you!' exclaimed the bewildered widow. 'How dare you, constable! This shall certainly be seen into. Shut the door instantly!' and the bang of that door rang through poor Dyason's sore head as if he had got another blow.

'George,' said his mother very seriously, 'I see there is something up. Will you explain to me, who is this girl, and what is she doing here? I hope, my son, that after the way you have been brought up'—but the poor woman proceeded no further. George was rolling on the sofa with his mother's slippers up in the air, in the agonies of irrepressible laughter, and the 'girl' had dragged her cap off and, with her petticoats held high in either hand, was performing a pas de seul[4] well known to the intimate acquaintances of Sam Sherberry.

'Mother,' said George, as soon as he was able, 'I forgot to tell you Mrs. Smith was here, and told me to ask you to step round a minute as soon as you came in.' And as he delivered this message, he lifted a corner of the blind to see the battered constable standing within the shadow of the next house railings, and he winked so hard a wink at Sam that his mother nearly caught him.

'Mrs. Smith, eh? I hope Jane's not worse. I'd better run round before I take off my things.'

'Well, I'll go with you mother, my oath. That beast of a Dyason might take it into his head to kiss you too if he saw you alone; he seems in a curious humour tonight.'

'Fie, George! How can you?' But she made no objection to her son's escort, and Sam was left alone until his friend should return; and what Sam did when they went out was to plant himself at the window with a bit of a blind in his hand to watch their progress—and this is what he saw.

Scarcely had the tall figure of George emerged from his own door, and turned itself up and down the street, as if to be certain that no one was about on watch, when Constable Dyason strode quickly towards them. Mrs. Lathorp, always glad of an excuse to have her beloved son's arm as a support, seized it, and was just beginning to step out on the pavement, when the constable rushed at them and seized the poor little woman by the back of the neck and shook her violently.

'No, you don't,' he hissed between his set teeth. 'I'm not such a fool as you think, Mr. Sam, and I know a real woman when I see one. Stand back you, Lathorp, or I'll brain you with this baton.'

But it wasn't likely that George would stand back when he had at last a legitimate opening for having it out with Constable Dyason. That worthy, keeping still a firm grip of Mrs. Lathorp's shawl and the back of her bonnet with one hand, flourished his baton around before George's face, quite regardless of the genuine sound of poor Mrs. Lathorp's shrieks, so convinced was he that it was Sam Sherberry trying to escape, still in the disguise of a girl.

George made short work of him; he tore the baton from his grasp and made heavy ruts in his fat body with it; and when the infuriated

CONSTABLE DYASON'S DEFEAT

constable let go of his prisoner and tried to defend himself, he threw the baton away and showed the constable so good a specimen of the art of self-defence, that when he lay on the broad of his back admiring the stars shortly after, he was quite unable to give the time of day to Sam Sherberry, who bent over him and tried to console him.

It was a day of fasting and humiliation with poor Dyason when he appeared before the Fitzroy bench of magistrates on a charge of attacking and maltreating and most shamefully insulting one of the most respectable and respected residents of that town. He was heavily fined and read a severe lecture by the old gentleman, who looked over his spectacles and shook his head at the constable, until the spectacles fell off and had to be recovered by the clerk of the court before the old gentleman could proceed.

'Your conduct, sir,' said he severely, 'is a disgrace to the coat you wear, and which, if my representations are attended to, you will wear no longer. Your personal appearance, sir, your bloated and sensual-looking—a—a—protuberance, sir; are a sufficient guarantee of your indulgence in the—a—a—pleasures of the table; but to have attacked a virtuous and respectable gentlewoman, sir, in Her Majesty's public street, sir, and under the protection of her lawful son, sir, you must have been as drunk as a pig! You may go down, sir!'

And poor Constable Dyason went down so very low that he has never appeared on the surface again, while his foes are triumphant. His portly form paces no more the broad payment he loved, and where wicked boys tend to try and trip him with traps of orange peel, and no more shall be reflected his stately form in the mirror of the Shamrock. George Lathorp declares he saw him once driving a disreputable old cab down Bourke-street but knowing, as we do, that gay young chap's proclivity to 'gas,' we may be permitted to doubt that statement.

First published as 'Sketches of the Force. Constable Dyason's Defeat' in the *Herald*, 1 January 1879, under the byline 'W.W.'

NOTES

1 *Milesian*: Irish (the reference is to the mythical ancestors of the Irish people, the 'sons of Míl').
2 *Special Pleader*: a historical legal functionary in the British courts.
3 *Yan Yean*: a reservoir north of Melbourne, the oldest water supply for the city.
4 *pas de seul*: in classical ballet, a solo dance.

THE PHANTOM HEARSE

Many of my readers will have observed that many 'corner' shops, whatever their location, are known by the names of their owners.

The one I am going to introduce you to was literally a corner shop, and the individuality of the man who kept it had obscured the very name of the street. You never heard his shop called the corner shop; it was 'Jones'' or 'old Jones',' and the corner at which it stood was, and is, 'Jones' Corner.'

I introduce Jones and his place of business to you on one sunny afternoon in March, when Lumsden, the new 'bobby,' was airing his dignity in taking a survey of this particular part of a beat that was quite new to him. Indeed, all beats were new to the young man, who had only just been 'called in,' though his name had been on the list of applicants for police employment for a good while. Lumsden was an especially raw recruit, and as full of an idea of his own importance as raw police recruits generally are.

He was standing on the pavement engaged in a condescending conversation with a sharp-looking resident named Jack Turner, a man of forty, perhaps, and of a small, wiry build. Turner had been relating to Lumsden a legend of the neighbourhood, about which the policeman was disposed to air his superior knowledge.

'And do you tell me, now, that there are live people hereabouts so ignorant as to believe that kind of a yarn?' he asked, with a smile that puffed his fat cheeks out till they met the collar of his jumper.

'Plenty of 'em; why, a man can't help believin' what he sees with his own eyes.'

'And have you seen it?'

'Yes, I have, and many more'n me; but if you want to hear all about it just ask old Jones—*he* knows the story from the beginning.'

Perhaps Lumsden would not have condescended to exhibit his curiosity to old Jones or anyone else if he had not been provided with a convenient excuse. He was standing in front of Turner's door, and the corner shop was obliquely opposite when a man came to the door of the shop and, with his face turned back, indulged in some pretty strong language that was apparently addressed to old Jones himself.

'Who is that?' asked Lumsden of his new acquaintance.

'It's a chap that lives down the lane behind here. Jerry Swipes they calls him; him and old Jones are always having rows.'

THE PHANTOM HEARSE

'What about?'

'Goodness knows. Jerry is in the old man's debt, I fancy, and it's hard to get any money out of Swipes.'

'Jerry Swipes? Is that the man's real name?'

'Blest if I can tell you, but it *may* be a nickname, for he is a regular swipe[1] and no mistake.'

While Lumsden had been gaining this information, Jerry—a tall, slouching figure with a sandy face and a long, sharp nose—had been roaring his uncomplimentary remarks to old Jones, who now came to the door of his shop with a red and angry face, as Swipes edged up the street toward the lane.

'Don't let me catch you inside my shop again!' shouted the old man as he shook his fist after Jerry; 'as sure as I do I'll give you in charge! You're nothing but a sneakin' thief—that's what you are!'

'I'll ram them words down your old throat one o' these days!' shrieked Jerry, as he reached the end of his lane. 'Police, is it? By gar, it'll be police with yourself first! You'll give me a glass of whisky next time I call? Eh, old man!' and the dirty unkempt-looking mortal disappeared into the mouth of the unsavoury right of way.

Old Jones' vituperation stopped as suddenly as Jerry disappeared, and such a look of fear came into the twinkling eyes under his penthouse,[2] ragged eyebrows that even Lumsden observed it, and Turner had to turn away his face to hide the grin of enjoyment that overspread his parchment-dried visage; but he controlled himself to remark ere he entered his door—

'Now is your time to go and ask old Jones about the phantom funeral, and you will be sure to hear all about this quarrel with Jerry.'

Lumsden took the hint, and marching across the narrow street was at Jones' almost as soon as the old man had got behind his counter again.

Jones' had all the characteristics of a thriving corner shop, with a little extra dirt and untidiness into the bargain. It was so small that the counter on two sides left but little space for the use of customers, that small space being further curtailed by 'stock' in the form of boxes of soap, bags of potatoes, rice, oatmeal and sugar. The narrow shelves were laden with fly-marked packages, and boxes and bottles of great variety; and the space that ought to be empty under the ceiling was hung with brooms, brushes, clothes-lines, and tinware, the original brightness of which was dimmed by age and smoke. Into this confined emporium Constable Lumsden stepped, meeting old Jones' suspicious eyes as that worthy very unceremoniously resumed his usual seat behind the counter, placed his spectacles astride his nose, and with a

THE PHANTOM HEARSE

sharp rustle shook out the morning paper on his knee.

'Good day to you,' said the young policeman as he looked curiously around him.

'Good day it is; what can I serve you with?'

'Serve? Oh, nothing, I heard some strong language at your door just now and came in to see what it was all about.'

Old Jones gave his paper an angry rustle as he answered—'If you come in here to know what's the matter every time I get cheek from a customer you'll not be able to do much in the other parts of your beat.'

'The cheek wasn't all on the customer's side this time. I heard you calling the man a thief, and in the open street. That's something in my line, you'll allow?'

'And so he is a thief,' cried old Jones, angrily; 'he's the biggest loafer in Melbourne. He never comes near the shop only when he wants to shake[3] a plug of tobacco or a pipe.'

'What did he shake today?'

'When I want to lay a charge against him I'll take it up to the sergeant,' said old Jones, expecting that it would shut up the officious young trap.[4] But it had very little effect on Constable Lumsden, who was, fortunately for himself, not very thin-skinned.

'Ah! two might play at visiting the sergeant. If Jerry Swipes went up himself he has a very good charge against you, and me for a witness. It's again' the laws to call a man a thief in the open street.'

'I can prove it.'

'If you could prove it twice over, all the same the law won't allow you to do it; and I'd advise you to give him that glass of whiskey he seems to expect from you the next time you get the chance.'

At this second allusion to the whiskey, old Jones once more grew white under Lumsden's observing eyes, and his knobby, hard hands shook so that they rustled the paper he held. Seeing this repeated agitation at the allusion to spirits, Lumsden took it into his head that drink was sold 'on the sly' at Jones', and he determined to keep a close watch on the place in future.

The old man made no immediate reply to Lumsden's advice about the treatment of his enemy, Jerry. He was considering within himself that it would, perhaps, be better for his own interests that he should take a different tone with the new policeman. The independent sharpness of Lumsden was a new experience at the Corner, the last man on the beat having been an old, steady-going policeman, who duly considered Mr. Jones' status in the neighbourhood and was friendly accordingly. Old Jones would have liked to twist the impertinent young constable's neck, but he tried to do the amiable instead—a very

THE PHANTOM HEARSE

difficult matter for the crusty old man.

'The fact is my temper's wore out with them sort of customers,' he said, with a sigh at his amiability. 'It's a very low neighbourhood, especially down Long's-lane, and it's getting lower every day. They get a few things from you, then they get into your books somehow, in spite of you, and they wind up with dropping in to steal when they think your back's turned.'

'A bad business,' returned Lumsden, but without the least intonation of sympathy. 'What does that fellow you were jawing to do for a living?'

'Jerry Swipes? Ah! he'd be puzzled to tell you. He hires a truck, and pretends to attend to the markets and that. I've heard of him rag and bottle gathering, but it's all a blind.'

'You've been a long time in the neighbourhood, I suppose?' asked Lumsden, as failing anything else in view, he took a pinch out of the oatmeal bag, and began to munch it.

'I've been nigh on thirty year in this house and this shop, and if anyone knows the neighbourhood I ought to.'

'Ye—es, I suppose so,' was the slow and evidently absent reply; 'and that reminds me; I've been told some ridiculous yarn about the ghost of a hearse that appears about here. Can you tell me anything about it?'

'There's nothing ridiculous about it, young man; it's only too true that the Phantom Funeral, as people have got to call it, is often seen in S—— and O—— street. I've seen it often, and I know how it began. There isn't a man in C—— can tell you as much as I can about it.'

Old Jones' air had quite undergone a change when his favourite topic came to be dwelt on; the paper was cast aside, and he rose from the old arm-chair. He took off his old, greasy felt hat, and ran his fingers through his stubby grey hair until it stood nearly straight up, and then he replaced the hat and 'ahem—ed,' as he looked inquiringly towards Lumsden.

'I'd like to hear the story,' said the latter, as he looked out of the door to see there was no 'duty' staring him in the face, and then leaned easily against the heap of bags, as he listened to old Jones.

'It's getting on for twelve years ago now since that hearse was first seen, and people always said it was because Sam Brown was carried out of No. 9 in the dead of the night and taken to the morgue, without common decency, in a dray. Sam was murdered or committed suicide—it was never actually decided which—and from that day to this the hearse haunts the place as a sort of revenge on the neighbours that they didn't pay more respect to his remains.'

THE PHANTOM HEARSE

'But that's trash,' said Lumsden. 'How could a dead man set a hearse to haunt a neighbourhood? I don't believe a word of it.'

'I've heard a many say that, as grew white to hear the hearse mentioned within less than a year after,' returned old Jones solemnly. 'It's the scoffers as see it, and it's not lucky to see it.'

'Not lucky?'

'No. If a man sees it—as you may when you're on night duty—the best thing he can do is to turn his back and walk away from it. There has never been a man foolhardy enough to watch it but he died within the year.'

'But you've seen it often, you say?'

'Aye, by chance. One night a woman was very bad down Long's-lane there, and she wasn't expected to live over the night. I got quite nervous like, and couldn't sleep. It was a bright moonlight, and about two o'clock in the morning I saw a slow shadow cross the blind of my window there. Before I had time to think, I was out on the floor and had the curtain in my hand, for I thought it was the "Phantom Hearse." It was. I saw it for a moment moving slowly past, and I dropped the blind quick, and got into bed again.'

'What was it like?' asked Lumsden.

'Like a plain, low, box-hearse, all black, and with one black horse in it. Sometimes there is a driver, and sometimes a man in black walks at the horse's head. It makes no sound, and is like a dream.'

'By George, I'd make a nightmare of it!' cried the young trap. 'Do you mean to tell me that no man has ever had the courage to walk up to the thing and grip it?'

'No man has ever been foolhardy enough to go straight to his deathbed that way,' was the serious answer.

But the unbelieving policeman laughed aloud as he raised himself and went toward the door, saying lightly—

'Well, here's one man that'll take the first chance of *feeling* what that ghostly machine is made of, at all events. Good gracious! To think people believe such yarns as that!'

As soon as Lumsden had left the shop Jones's face fell, and he muttered uneasily to himself as he stood by the counter, with his hands upon it, and an anxious look in his scowling face. He was not at any time a pleasant picture, that old Jones of the corner shop, but he looked absolutely repellant as he stood muttering to himself, with his ragged eyebrows almost met in an anxious scowl.

A few minutes later the old man, dashing the old greasy hat under the counter, began to divest himself of his rag of a coat, leaving the shop by the back as he did so. He went through a very slovenly kitchen, and

THE PHANTOM HEARSE

to the verandah at the back of it, where an old, meanly attired woman was washing in a wooden tub that seemed almost as old as herself. She looked up with a frightened air as Jones shouted at her—

'Margery!'

'Yes, master.'

'Leave that washing, and get on a clean apron. I'm going out; you'll have to mind the shop.'

'Yes, master'; and the thin, trembling arms were being hastily wiped in her wet apron as she was hurrying away.

'Stop. I want to speak to you.'

She stopped instantly, and humbly turned an apparently vacant face towards him.

'You've got to watch that boy—that's *your* business, you know. Don't *you* go trying to serve, or you'll poison someone, but keep your eyes *sharp* on Con. You hear?'

It would be queer if she didn't hear, for the man was roaring at the top of his voice, and at every emphasized word the poor old creature jumped.

'I hear. I'll watch him well.'

'I'll leave nothing in the till; and, *mind,* see that there's something in it when I come back. Give no *credit*. Do you hear?'

'Yes, master. I'll let nothing go without the money.'

'And *count* it before you let the things go out of your hands.'

'Yes, master.'

While Jones had been giving these instructions he had been making a pretence of a wash in the old woman's far from pure suds, and when he dismissed her with a nod he seized a grimy old towel, and rubbed his face with it. It seemed as if Jones was in an awful hurry, for he had not finished with the towel when he had crossed the littered yard, and was giving some more orders to a sharp-looking boy of about thirteen who had been occupied in washing bottles in a dilapidated shed.

'Con!'

'Yes, sir!'

'I'm going out for an hour or so, and the old woman is to mind the shop; *you* keep your eye on her.'

'Yes, sir.'

'Let her sit in the chair and count the money. Do you serve, and mind don't give ONE PENNY OF CREDIT!'

'Very well, sir.'

'And watch the old woman well; see that she doesn't get slipping a penny now and then into some corner of her gown. I've known her do it afore.'

THE PHANTOM HEARSE

'I'll watch her close, sir.'

'That's right. And see you keep account of every penn'orth you let go.'

'I'll be very careful, sir.'

Ten minutes afterward old Jones was scuttling away down the street pretty easy in his mind, because he had put in practice his favourite receipt for keeping people honest. 'Set one to watch the other!' he would say, 'that's the way to do it! You don't want no detectives if you set one to watch the other!'

Very few would have recognised the two happy faces that beamed behind old Jones' counter that afternoon to be those of the stupid, hopeless-looking old woman who was previously slopping grimy rags at the back, and the half-discontented one of the boy who had listened with such outward respect to a master he both disliked and despised.

The old woman, who was no other than old Jones' lawful wife, sat in Jones' chair stiffly and upright, with her hands folded on a clean white apron and a broad-bordered, starched muslin cap on her unsteady head. Her withered old face was beaming with pride and delight, and with an air of dignity that was pitiful when one knew its short-lived nature. The one happiness of poor old Mrs. Jones was in being permitted to play at keeping shop, for it was only play after all, Con doing in reality whatever was necessary in the small sales. Con was very busy just now wiping down the counter and 'tidying up things a bit,' as he was wont to call it, when speaking to Mrs. Jones.

'Isn't this fine!' cried the gratified old creature with a child's unreasoning delight. 'If the master would go away oftener and let us keep shop, Con, wouldn't it be nice.'

'It would,' answered the boy with some decision, 'but no sich luck. Some old men die, but the likes of *him* never dies.'

'I wish he would die,' Mrs. Jones said in a deep whisper to the lad. 'I'm allays a-wishing it. If he did there would be no one to knock me about, and I would sit in the shop allays. I wish that dead-hearse would stop right under his window some night, I do!'

'Did you ever see the dead-hearse, Mrs. Jones?' questioned the boy as he ceased rubbing at the counter, and looked at the old woman curiously.

'I did,' she replied, with an energetic nod that set her wide cap-frills bobbing. 'I seed it one night last March. The master he woke me up to see it. It was passing the window and stopped opposite Grinder's. Mrs. Grinder she died next day but one. That's the reason I wouldn't never sleep in that front room again; and, besides, the master he was allays a-knockin' me about for snorin'. I don't snore. *He* does.'

THE PHANTOM HEARSE

'Aye! Jones wanted to get you out of his room, missis, and he wasn't short of an excuse. *I* know!'

This unexpected remark was made by no other than Jerry Swipes, whose lanky figure had entered the shop unobserved in the deep interest attached to the 'dead-hearse,' as poor old Mrs. Jones called it. Con stared at the man, but Mrs. Jones was on her dignity and, bridling, asked what business it was of Jerry Swipes?

'None, missis, none whatsomever, only no man as is a man likes to see a lawful wife med a slave of and beat when another woman—but it's none of my business. Con, hand me a threepenny plug and a pipe.'

'You don't know what you're talking of, Jerry Swipes!' cried Mrs. Jones, with angry suspicion. 'It was my own doins as made me go to sleep in the back room.'

'Was it? Oh, then, maybe you knows what Jones does of a night since you left. If ye doesn't, jest watch him, and you'll see, that's all.'

Listening open-mouthed to these strange words of the disreputable customer, Con had mechanically laid the required articles on the counter. In an instant the tobacco and pipe were transferred to Jerry's pocket, and his ragged ulster wrapped over them.

'Put 'em down, me boy,' he said, with a leer, as he made for the door. 'Me credit's always good with Mr. Jones. Yes, missis, that's what *I* say—watch him an' you'll know.'

'Oh, Mrs. Jones, he's never paid for 'em!' cried Con. 'The master'll kill us!'

'Watch him an' you'll know,' murmured the old woman, on whom Jerry's words appeared to have made a strange impression. She was staring at the door out of which Jerry had just passed, with her brows bent together and a queer, thoughtful look in her faded eyes that puzzled the boy.

'Please, Mrs. Jones,' reiterated Con, 'that Swipes took the pipe and baccy without paying for it. What'll we do? The master'll kill us.'

'Watch him and you'll know,' again murmured the completely absorbed old woman; 'and it's true. He *used* to go somewheres at night. I've missed him.'

Fortunately for Con's peace of mind at this moment, there entered two legitimate customers, who put a few shillings in the till and distracted Mrs. Jones' thoughts again. It was painful even to the boy to see her pluming herself in the chair and feeling so proud and happy, when it was so certain that at the first sound of her master's harsh voice she would drop into the cringing, half-stupid slave who seemed to have no idea beyond the avoidance, by unselfish service, of the kicks and thumps the brute was in the habit of bestowing on

THE PHANTOM HEARSE

her whenever he wanted some object to explode his temper on.

By this time Constable Lumsden had worked round his beat, and was in the vicinity of Jones' Corner again. As he was about to pass the door he looked in, and seeing only the boy and the half-idiotic face of an old woman behind the counter, he changed his mind and entered. Mrs. Jones bridled immediately. The poor old creature had a very exaggerated idea of a policeman's importance, and being a woman, was not, perhaps, insensible to the young chap's ruddy and healthy-looking face. Con was not so sure of Lumsden. He had a town boy's detestation of all bobbies, big and little, young and old, and would just as soon have seen a big brown snake wandering into the shop as that young man in blue.

'Is Jones at home?' asked Lumsden.

'No, sir, he's gone out on business. This is Mrs. Jones.'

'Yes,' she nodded, proudly, as she smoothed down the white apron with both trembling hands, 'I'm keeping shop. I'd like to keep shop every day.'

'Would you?' Lumsden asked, with a suspicious look into the child-ish-looking face, for the constable was not quite sure whether she was laughing at him or was in reality half-witted. But he was soon at his ease, for it was impossible to doubt the want of intellect so plainly pictured in the vacant, withered features. 'I suppose, now, you sell everything here?'

'Yes,' she answered proudly, 'everythink.'

'I was just wishing for a glass of something,' Lumsden said, in a low tone, as he glanced towards the quiet street. 'There's no one about; I'll take a glass of spirits, please,' and he quietly laid a shilling on the counter.

'Oh, we don't keep no drink here, sir,' quickly returned Con, as he pushed back the shilling, for which the unconscious old woman's hand was already outstretched.

'I wasn't talking to you,' snapped the constable. 'Are you Jones' son?'

'No, sir, I'm only hired; but I've been with them a good while.'

'You're too precious sharp,' Lumsden said, with a frown that he believed sufficient to overcome the sharpest youngster in the city.

'Missis, can't you sell me a glass of something?'

'The master takes a glass often,' she mumbled, 'but he never gives me none. I don't know where he keeps his bottle; s'pect it's in the front room. Master allays locks the front room when he goes out.'

'Hum, give me sixpen'orth of lollies,[5] boy'; and the discontented constable pushed back the shilling, on which the old woman's eyes were fixed greedily.

THE PHANTOM HEARSE

Con weighed the lollies, and was graciously presented with some of them for his own use.

'Did you ever see this ghost of a hearse that haunts this neighbourhood?' asked Lumsden of the lad, as he decided that the old woman was not worth talking to.

'No, sir, *I* never did, but Mrs. Jones has seen it. Haven't you, Mrs. Jones?'

'Seen the dead-hearse? I should think so. Ha! there's allays someone dies when that comes. I wish 'twould stop right *there* tonight,' and she pointed a shaky finger straight out of the shop door to the empty street, on which the afternoon sun was shining warmly. And then, as if the subject brought back to her memory Jerry Swipes' words, she repeated them to herself, with her brows again tangled into a thoughtful frown—'Jest you watch him, and you'll see.'

'What is she muttering?'

'Oh, nothing of any consequence, sir; she's talking to herself half the time.'

'Um! a little queer, eh?'

'A little, sir.'

'Did you never see the old chap sell a glass, now?' asked the clever new policeman, and Con's naturally rosy face grew crimson.

If there is one thing more despised than another by even the lowest Melbourne lad it is an 'informer.' In this case Con had nothing to tell, but it insulted him that it should be supposed possible that he *would* tell, even if he knew anything.

Lumsden saw the boy's increase of colour, and it increased his suspicions.

'No,' Con answered—without the 'sir' this time, you will observe—'nor I never see no spirits of any kind about, even for Mr. Jones' own drinkin'. If he keeps any it must be, as Mrs. Jones says, in his own room, that's mostly always locked.'

The mention of her name aroused the old woman from an unusual absorption in thought, and she repeated over and over again—'Yes, Con, in his own room; allays in his own room.'

In a very discontented mood Lumsden strolled out to the pavement again, munching his lollies as he went; and it so happened that Jerry Swipes at that moment appeared at the corner of the lane, and, after a sharp look up and down the empty street, beckoned to the policeman. Lumsden was inclined to stand on his dignity, and let the drunken-looking fellow come over to him if he wanted him; but all at once he remembered that this was the man old Jones had been abusing, and thinking of the probability of retaliation, he put his dignity in his

THE PHANTOM HEARSE

pocket with the lollies, and crossed the narrow street.

'Just come down here a few steps, constable; I want to speak to ye.'

Lumsden followed the speaker a few yards, and then stopped. The lane was most uninviting to all senses, and two or three red-faced, loud-voiced women were in front of some old wooden cottages farther down gossiping, amid the noise of screaming babies and quarrelling children.

'If you have anything private to say, there's no need of going any further—there's nothing but a dead wall here.'

'It's the fence of Turner's wood yard,' returned Jerry, 'and I guess you're right. We can speak low, and, besides, there's no one in the yard—I saw Turner go out five minutes ago.'

'Well? what is your business?'

'Are you game now to go halves in an informin' business?' asked Jerry, cunningly, in reply to this question.

'Informin'? Is it about old Jones?' was the sharp return.

'The very man.'

'By Jove, I suspected it!' cried Lumsden, as he stooped and slapped his leg in thorough enjoyment. 'Game? I should think so!' And then a sharp suspicion crossed his mind, and made Lumsden look steadily into the bloated face with the sharp nose.

'If you are on the look-out for a reward, how is it you don't try to keep it all to yourself?' he asked.

'D'ye think I'd ever get it if I hadn't someone decent to back me up?' Jerry asked, cunningly. 'I couldn't take him in if single-handed—I'd want help; and if I was the respectablest man in Melbourne there wouldn't be a conviction without the worm.'

'Without the worm? What do you mean? What are you talking about?'

'I'm talking about a *still*—didn't you know it afore?'

The low whistle that gave expression to Lumsden's surprise was so prolonged that Jerry cut it short with a 'Hush.'

'I thought it was sly grog-selling!' he exclaimed. 'I noticed the effect your mention of the glass of whiskey had on Jones a while ago, and I thought it was sly grog-selling. But a still! By Jove! are you sure, man?'

'As sure as that there fence is made o' palin',' was the answer, as Swipes put his hand on Turner's fence; 'an' now just wait a minnit till I'll see if Turner's back.'

He stepped on a stone as he was speaking, and craned his long neck in an examination of the wood-yard.

'No, he's not at home yet, for the back door's shut an' the barrow's not there. Come now, let us settle about it. It must be done to-night, for I gave him a good many hints today, an' he may be frightened.'

THE PHANTOM HEARSE

'He's gone out?' said Lumsden.

'Yes, and I am afraid he's gone to try and get rid of the plant somehow, for he must have customers for the spirits somewhere, and they're bound to help him. The best thing that you and me can do is to go up to the sergeant at once, and lay our claim to the reward.'

There was a little more talk about it, and when it was over they separated, so as to avoid suspicion; appointing, however, a time when they were to meet at the police office in the presence of the sergeant.

Old Jones came home very shortly after, in one of his worst humours. At the first glimpse of his face in the doorway all the brightness fell from that of the poor old wife, who hobbled humbly to the back, leaving Con to face 'the master'; and Con did so with more confidence than usual, for there was some money in the till, and he had some news to tell Jones that might make him think less of Jerry having outwitted him in the matter of the pipe and tobacco.

'Well! Everything at sixes and sevens, I suppose?' Jones asked, with a furious look around the shop. The man *wanted* something to swear at, for his blood was boiling within him.

'No, sir. Everything's all right in the shop; only' — the boy hastened to add, ere Jones had time to explode — 'that there young bobby's been here, sir.'

'Again! What the deuce did he want?'

'I'm afraid he was after no good, master,' replied Con, as he shook his head sagely. 'He tried to get a glass of spirits out of the mistress and me; actually put the money on the counter for it.'

'What!'

'Yes, indeed, sir. He gammoned[6] that he knew drink was sold here but when he could get nothing out of us he bought sixpen'orth of lollies and went away.'

Jones absolutely turned grey with apprehension as he stared at the boy.

'You are sure you didn't tell the villain anything?'

'I had nothing to tell him, sir.'

'That's true, Con — of course, you had nothing to tell him. You may go out and finish them bottles now.'

Jones fell into his old arm-chair behind the counter dumbfounded. He felt that he was caught in a trap and didn't know where to seek help. He had taken off his best hat, and held the old, greasy one in his hands, looking at it in a queer, bewildered way, when a man entered with an active step. It was Turner, the small, sharp, dark man that kept the wood-yard.

'How many hundred of wood will I bring you over, Jones?' he

THE PHANTOM HEARSE

asked, as he bent over toward the old man with a strange grin on his face.

'Not one!' shouted old Jones, as the blood rushed into his face, and his eyes flashed under their overhanging brows. He had got someone to vent his rage on at last—'Not one; and I'll never take another from you—you swindling rascal. The last was green messmate.'[7]

'Hush, hush, Jones! you have no idea what a mess you're in. I've come to give you a bit of neighbourly help, for both Jerry Swipes and the new bobby'll be down on you in a brace of shakes.'

'Jerry Swipes! The new bobby! Oh, curse them.'

But, even as the words fell from his lips, they trembled, and he put on his old hat in a hopeless way very unusual with him.

'Yes, and there's no time to waste. Jerry has been watching you by nights, it seems, and he's found out all about the still. He's told Lumsden, and they've gone up to the sergeant and agreeing to share the reward for informing between them.'

'Oh, Lord, what'll I do?' groaned the old man.

'That's what I'm come to tell you. I have the horse ready in the cart and the wood in it. I'm going to bring it into the yard, and you'll pack all your whisky into it, as well as the whole still, if we can manage it, and I'll drive 'em off before the informers come.'

'Where will you take 'em?' Jones asked, doubtfully.

'Where they'll be safe. Never you mind so long as they don't get 'em *here*.'

'But what are you doin' it for? I never was friends with you, Bill Turner. What are you so willin' to do this for?'

'No! you old screw, you never *was* friends with me! I don't owe you so much as a thank you for one neighbourly act! What am I a-doin' of it for? What a darned fool you are to ask! I'm a-doing it for what I can make out of it, of course! Do you think I'm a fool to do it for nothing? I'll save you a fifty-pound fine and the loss of your stock, never fear; but I'll ask for my pay when the job's done!'

Strange to say this assertion, though it touched the weakest part of old Jones (the region of his pocket) convinced him of Turner's sincerity, and before many minutes had elapsed the woodman's cart was in the old storekeeper's yard. Jones sent Con and Mrs. Jones into the shop while a new load was packed into the bottom of the conveyance and covered with a layer of wood that made all, as Turner declared, 'look quite natural.'

Few could have guessed in what a state of excitement old Jones had lately been, had they looked into the shop after Turner's departure and seen him, spectacles on nose, apparently absorbed in the paper; at least,

THE PHANTOM HEARSE

Jerry Swipes didn't guess it when he entered with a wicked grin on his dirty visage, and with Constable Lumsden at his heels.

'I hope I don't intrude, Mister Jones,' sneered Jerry, who had evidently managed an extra glass somewhere. 'Allow me to introduce me friend, Constable Lumsden.'

'Stash that!' cried Lumsden angrily, as he pushed Jerry out of his way very unceremoniously and advanced to the counter. 'I'm here on duty, Jones. We have received information that you are carrying on a sort of private distillery here in contravention to the laws, and we're here to search the premises.'

'Search, and be hanged to you!' was the very unexpected reply; 'but by the heavens above me if that drunken thief comes inside my private premises I'll brain him—so help me!'

'Will you?' retorted the pot-valiant Swipes. 'Maybe two could play at that game; though if it comes to brains it's very little you'd have to let out. Stand back, Lumsden, and let me blacken that old villain's eyes.'

'If you don't keep quiet, Swipes, I'll put you out myself,' was all the comfort the angry man got from his unwilling companion, who went on to Jones—

'You may as well let us in peacefully, Jones. There's two constables in the back yard by this time, and there's no earthly use offering any resistance.'

'I'm offering no resistance; didn't I tell you to search? There's the door open; but I say again if that informer crosses that threshold I'll fell him.'

'Oh! I'm an informer, eh? D'ye hear that, Lumsden? By George, the old fool is giving himself away. It seems there's something to inform on, eh?'

'Hold your jaw, Swipes. You had better go round to the back; there's no use having any unnecessary row.' And the young policeman went behind the counter to the door that old Jones was still holding open with shaking hands.

Jerry, finding himself in a minority, did as Lumsden had suggested, and went round to the yard, cursing Jones all the way.

Jones immediately shut the shop door and barred it behind him, going out then after the young policeman to see what disturbance they would make among his household gods.

That part of the household gods represented by poor Mrs. Jones was in such a state of bewildered surprise at the advent of two strange men in blue entering her slovenly kitchen that the entrance of another from the shop-way added nothing to her confusion. Lumsden, as befitting the fact that he was co-informer, took the lead in what followed, his first action being to proceed towards Jones' own bedroom, and order it to be opened.

'My information is that the door of a cellar opens in a closet of this room,' he said, importantly, 'and that in that cellar is the still.'

Without a word Jones unlocked the door and flung it open. At this moment Jerry Swipes, fortified by the presence of so many policemen, advanced to push his way into Jones' room, and without another word of warning the old man, who had been a pugilist in his young days, lifted his fist and struck Swipes so heavily between the eyes that the half-drunk man fell to the floor almost as if he had been shot.

'I had a right to do it,' cried Jones; 'I warned him. I put no hindrance in the way of the police, but that man I'll not let cross my threshold. Clear out o' this, or I'll let you have it double.'

Jerry, who was picking himself up with difficulty, turned to go, but as he did he uttered a threat that was remembered against him afterwards.

'Do you see them?' he asked, pointing to the drops of blood on the floor; 'you drew 'em from my face, but by heaven I'll let every drop out of your heart for 'em!' and he staggered blindly out to the yard.

It is unnecessary to enter into particulars of the unsuccessful search made by the constables of Jones' cellar and premises generally—there was nothing whatever criminating discovered. The unsuspected load Turner had taken had removed everything immediately connected with the still, save some empty hop-pockets and sugar bags, and a suspiciously smelling keg. Jones enjoyed the discomfiture of Lumsden, as indeed did his fellow constables, who were, like all the world, jealous of a neighbour's good fortune.

'I'm sorry for your disappointment, gentlemen,' said Jones, with a derisive grin; 'but you see it is not always well to depend on information received from a low scoundrel. Howsomever, as I'm sorry to see Mr. Lumsden look so down in the mouth, I don't mind giving him a glass of very good whiskey I happen to have here by me.'

'Hang you, and your whiskey too!' was the young man's not over civil reply to this kind offer, and in a few moments the police, accompanied by the terribly disappointed Jerry, had all cleared out by the back way. To say that Jerry was disappointed is putting it very weakly—he evinced his feelings in such threats at Jones, and indeed, at the police, who had, he fancied, cheated him in some way or another, that Lumsden was within an ace of marching him off to the lock-up.

Lumsden was quite as much disappointed as the informer, though he was able to control his feelings a little better. So convinced was he

THE PHANTOM HEARSE

that Jones had been warned and cleared his cellar out, that he determined on doing duty on his own account that night. That is, instead of going to bed or to amuse himself after his patrol was over, after dinner he returned to his beat to watch Jones' Corner.

He did not get to his beat till about eleven o'clock, believing that whatever illegal thing might be done on the old man's premises would not be attempted before that hour. He had acquainted the constable on duty of his intention, so that his movements should be taken no notice of, and he chose as his place of watch the entrance to a narrow right of way opposite old Jones' back yard.

When he took up his post there was a light in the shop, though it was shut, but all was darkness at the back. Jones was not the man to let his wife and Con sit up burning candles for nothing. After about half an hour's watch Lumsden saw the light disappear from the shop, and in a few minutes a man crossed the yard stealthily, opened Jones' gate noiselessly, and slipped round the corner of the street where the door of the shop was. Lumsden was curious, and followed him to the corner. There he saw a small, lithe figure dart across the moonlit street and enter Turner's wood-yard. Lumsden went back to his station, wondering what Turner was doing there at that time of night; and just then the town clock was striking twelve.

It was quite another hour before he saw anything else at Jones'. Then a slinking figure crept along in the shadow of the houses, and deftly climbing Jones' high fence, dropped inside. The young constable recognised Jerry Swipes instantly, and guessed at once that the low scoundrel was on the same self-imposed duty as himself, viz, watching old Jones, with the hope of making some discovery of a fresh plant. It was about half an hour before Jerry left the yard, and it was chiming the half hour after one as he dropped out into the street again, and ran down the lane.

Another half hour, and Lumsden saw a light appear for a moment in the kitchen window. The light was very indistinct, for the window was under the back verandah, where Mrs. Jones did her poor washing; but it was distinct enough for Mr. Lumsden to see it twice—once when it seemed to come and go away again, and once more when it reappeared, and seemed to be suddenly put out. Believing that Jones was rambling about the place making a bestowal of some illegal machinery, Lumsden was about to climb the fence for a nearer watch when he saw something that changed his mind with a strange suddenness. The young man had heard no noise, but he felt, as it were, that there was something moving in his vicinity. Turning involuntarily, he saw, coming down the street, full in the moonlight, what seemed to be the

260

THE PHANTOM HEARSE

shadow of a hearse. A sort of fear crept upon him for a moment, but he recovered himself speedily, remembering his jibes at the 'dead hearse' that very day, and his determination to prove its mortal and tangible nature.

The thing passed him—the shadow of a hearse—and turned Jones' Corner noiselessly. It appeared to Lumsden's eyes just as Jones had described it, a plain, box-like hearse with a cover shaped like a sarcophagus. The shape of a black horse drew it, and the shape of a man in black, with long black crape weepers hanging down from his hat behind, sat in front and held the shadowy reins. There is not one among the very wisest of us without some hidden superstition, however we may to try to deceive ourselves about the fact; and young Lumsden felt a queer, cold creeping up his back in spite of his declared unbelief in the 'Phantom Hearse.'

No sooner had it turned the corner, and was out of sight, however, but he pulled himself together and hurried after it, determined to see the affair through. He had not far to go. I have said the thing turned the corner. It had barely done so; when Lumsden reached the front of the shop he saw the hearse standing in front of the window he knew belonged to Jones' bedroom, the vehicle and horse still and soundless, the man sitting on his box as if carved out of black marble.

One moment the young man hesitated, for he was only mortal, but then he strode on toward the hearse, his steps making a loud noise on the moonlit pavement. His heart was beating quickly, but he did not stop until he was so near that by putting out his hand he should have been able to touch the hearse. He *put* it out, and touched nothing! He moved a little nearer, and tried again. Still there was nothing tangible, but he heard a terrible moan that seemed to come from the interior of the ghostly vehicle, and started back. When he looked again the whole thing had disappeared. There was nothing in the whole length of the street, but the moonlight lying upon pavement and roadway!

Constable Lumsden stared for some minutes and then, being, as I have already said, only mortal he turned quickly, and sought the companionship of his fellow policeman, whose step he fortunately heard at that moment echoing down a neighbouring cross-street. The constable on the beat that night was an elderly man, and he did not laugh at Lumsden's story.

'I've heard of it often,' he said, thoughtfully, 'but I never saw it, and I don't want to. They say it is a sure sign of death in the house where it stops. It was at Jones', you say?'

'Yes, but was it there at all? I wonder if I could fancy it all?'

'You ought to be the best judge of that yourself; but that the hearse

THE PHANTOM HEARSE

has been seen there's no manner of doubt. I've been on this beat over eight years, and I've heard of the hearse a dozen times and more.'

'Well, whether or not I imagined the hearse, I'm certain the sound was real.'

'What sound?'

'Why, the awful groan I heard. It made my blood creep.'

'You'd better go and get a sleep,' said Cooney, 'or you'll not be fit for duty tomorrow.'

And the young man took his advice, the sight of the 'Phantom Hearse' having cured him of all the interest he had lately felt in 'still-hunting.'

Lumsden lodged with Cooney, who was a married man with a family, and it seemed to the young man that he had not been asleep ten minutes when he was wakened by a rough shake. Cooney was standing by the side of his bed with something in his rugged face that roused Lumsden at once.

'What is it?' he asked.

'It's murder, that's what it is. Get up at once, and be puttin' on your clothes while I tell you. You'll get no chance of pocketing that fifty pounds now. Old Jones was found dead in his bed this morning.'

'Good heavens! Who found him?'

'That little chap, Con, who lives there. It seems he had to call Jones every morning before he opened the shop at seven o'clock, and this morning when he went, he found the old man so sound asleep that nothing but the last trump will waken him. The boy ran to tell me, and before Smith relieved me the whole neighbourhood was in a commotion.'

'What time is it now?'

'Near nine. Hurry out and get your breakfast. Didn't you tell me you saw Jerry Swipes climbing over Jones' fence last night?'

'Yes.'

And then a sudden recollection of the terrible threat Jerry had made against the old man after he was struck down recurred to Lumsden.

'How was he murdered?'

'Stabbed in the breast, or rather stomach, by some sharp instrument. He appears to have been lying on his back asleep, from what the doctor says, and was found in a pool of his own blood. By Jove, Jerry seems to have kept his word. He swore he would let every drop out of the old man's heart, and it looks as if he'd done it.'

'You think it was Jerry?'

'Can there be a doubt of it after what you saw? At all events, I went straight to his tumble-down shanty and arrested him on suspicion.'

THE PHANTOM HEARSE

'How did he take it?'

'Like a man stupid—as indeed he was with the effects of his yesterday's drink. There was blood on his clothes, too; but he denies the murder, of course.'

'Does he deny he was in Jones' yard this morning?'

'No; he owns to it. He says he went in hopes of finding the old man in the cellar. It seems there's some crack in the wall he can see through. Come now; if you've done breakfast we'll be off down and see what we can find out. You can question the boy this time.'

We can understand the deep interest of Lumsden in this case. It was his first in the force, and the matter of the suspected illicit work in Jones' place, together with his own intimate connection with it as co-informer, made the whole affair of importance to him. And there was what he had seen last night, too—that solemn hearse that had stood for a few moments at the dead man's house. He could never again disbelieve in apparitions as long as he lived.

Talking the case over, the two men walked quickly to Jones' Corner. The shop was shut, except that one shutter had been taken off to light it, and there, in pitiful state, sat Mrs. Jones, with her one decent dress—a black stuff—on, and a white apron she had actually that morning washed and ironed spread under her folded hands. Her withered old face was deathly as ashes, her cap borders scarcely seeming more blanched in colour. Looking at her for a moment, as she stared straight before her into the dim shop, among the confusion of boxes and bags, it seemed to Lumsden as if her little share of sense had been stricken out by the shock, to leave her but one remove from an idiot.

It was not so with poor Con. He had wept until his eyes were like boiled gooseberries, and there was a look of terror in them as they seemed to wander against his will to that awful closed door. He was sitting in the yard, on a box, when Lumsden appeared, and welcomed the young man, though he *was* a policeman.

'Tell me all about it,' Lumsden said, as he leaned against the fence by the boy. 'It was you found him this morning, wasn't it?'

'Oh! yes, sir. I haven't got over it yet. I'll *never* get over it.'

'Oh! you will; never fear of that. When did you see Jones last—I mean alive?'

'I didn't see him after I went to bed about nine, sir, but I heard him, off and on, for a long time. Someone had taken the key out of his bedroom door; he blamed the police for it, I think. At all events he couldn't find it, and went on awful. I fell asleep after a while, and then when I wakened up I heard him saying, "Goodnight, Turner," and someone came out the back door.'

263

THE PHANTOM HEARSE

'Where do you sleep, Con?'

'In that little skillion room[8] at this end of the verandah; Mrs. Jones sleeps in the other one, only hers opens into the kitchen and my room doesn't.'

Lumsden considered a moment. If Con had heard Turner so plainly, how was it he had not heard Jerry Swipes so shortly after? And there was that light he had twice seen in the kitchen—who had carried that?

'You heard nothing after that, Con?'

'Nothing, sir; I fell asleep again, and never wakened till mornin' when Mrs. Jones called me.'

'Oh, *she* called you, did she?'

'She always calls me; Mrs. Jones is up by daylight, but the master wouldn't let her call him—I had to do it about seven. I always knocked and he was easy wakened, but this morning I knocked and knocked, and got no answer. Then I remembered about the key being lost, and I opened the door quietly and called again. I could see the bed then and guessed something was wrong, and I went a little nearer—oh—' and Con covered his face with a shudder.

'What did the old woman do when you told her?'

'She only looked stupid, and stared at me, and then when she appeared to understand, she said—"Yes; that she would put on her apron and mind the shop"; and there she's sat ever since.'

'Con, there was someone moving about the place with a light at two o'clock this morning—I saw it in the kitchen window myself. Do you think it could have been Jones?

'More likely Mrs. Jones, sir; she's often awandering about the kitchen at night, and she seemed very unsettled when I went to bed last night.'

Having got all the information he could out of the lad, Lumsden went in to see the terrible object in the guarded and darkened room, and then to visit the poor old woman, who sat in state, 'minding the shop,' while her murdered husband lay within a few yards of her. If the young policeman had any hopes of getting information out of her respecting the light he had seen in the kitchen, he lost them ere he had been speaking to her five minutes.

'This is a sad business for you, Mrs. Jones,' said the young man in a low, sympathetic tone. 'Have you no neighbour that would come and sit with you?'

'He would never let me have no neighbours,' she answered woodenly, as if a machine were speaking. 'I'm minding the shop. Why doesn't Con come in? I want Con.'

'I'll make him come in presently. Mrs. Jones, was it you that had a

THE PHANTOM HEARSE

light in the kitchen at two o'clock this morning?'

The sudden way she turned her fishy eyes on him set the young man wondering, and her unexpected reply startled him.

'There was no lights, only dead-lights, and the Dead Hearse was there. I heard 'em say it. It was all quite true. Watch him, and you'll find out.'

Lumsden remembered that she had used those very words when he was in the shop yesterday, but he did not know that it was Jerry who had originally said them, and that they had made a terrible impression on the poor, ill-treated old creature.

'Do you think that you'll keep on the shop now that the old man is gone?' the young constable asked, out of curiosity as to her reply, and finding nothing better to say.

'Yes. I'll allays mind the shop now—allays—me and Con, me with a clean cap and a white apron; and no one'll beat me and knock me about.'

The old woman's eyes now glowed with an almost fierce pleasure; she drew up her head and wagged it at Lumsden in an alarming manner as she spoke. He drew back, scarcely knowing whether to be shocked at her apparent insensibility or not, when Cooney appeared behind him in the doorway.

'I wish we could find that key, Lumsden,' he said, not observing the old woman; 'it's very awkward not to be able to lock the body in.'

'I've got no key,' almost shrieked Mrs. Jones, as she stood up and faced the speaker; 'why don't you take him away? Tell the Dead Hearse to come and take him away, quick!' and she almost fell into the old chair again, trembling and shaking all over.

'She's not even half-witted,' Lumsden said. 'What on earth will become of her? Do you think the old man was any way well in?'

'I don't know,' replied Cooney, who was closely observing the old creature, who sat shaking in her chair. All at once she got up and, muttering some indistinct words, tottered away into the kitchen, and from it to her own room, and they heard her locking the door behind her.

'Have you heard anything fresh?' inquired Lumsden of Cooney, who was staring after Mrs. Jones in an odd way.

'I've been talking to the doctor. He says that when he was called here this morning Jones had been dead five or six hours. Do you remember what you said last night about that groan you heard, Lumsden? You said *it* was real, at any rate, and so it was. It was about that time, or a little before, that he got his death stab. And you know the weapon has not been found, Lumsden. Whoever had that light you saw last night

THE PHANTOM HEARSE

knows something of the murder.'

'You have changed your mind about it's being Jerry, then?'

'I don't know; he might have come back again—went for a knife, perhaps. But several of his neighbours are ready to swear that the blood on his clothes was on it yesterday—he sells rabbits sometimes, it appears. And another thing—the doctor says the weapon must have been an unusual one—long and narrow, and sharp at the sides—such a wound as is in his breast could not be made by even an ordinary carving knife. I am going to make a very thorough search of the premises. Con?'

'Yes, sir.'

The two constables had been passing through the kitchen while Cooney was speaking, and when Con was called they were standing under the verandah between the two skillion rooms.

'Con?' questioned Cooney, 'the old man has been killed with a long, narrow kind of knife, the doctor says; do you know of anything about the house answering that description?'

'A long, narrow knife?' repeated the boy, thoughtfully; 'master used to have an old thing like that—I think he used it in the cellar. I saw him sharpening it on the grindstone yesterday morning—it was rusty, and had a black handle.'

'You haven't seen it since?'

'No, sir.'

'What are you driving at, Cooney? Is it very likely the murderer would find and leave his weapon on the premises?'

'I'm going to have a hunt for it, at any rate.'

Lumsden went out of the yard and across to Turner's, for he had a mind for a talk with the woodman about his visit to Jones last night. He found Turner very busy sawing in his yard, but with such a serious face that it was evident the murder of his neighbour had affected him greatly.

'Yes,' he said, as he sat down on a wood heap and wiped his face with the loose sleeve of his shirt, 'I'm awfully cut up about it, though Jones was not a man any of his neighbours cared for; but, you see, I must have been the last man that talked to him before he was killed.'

'It *was* you I saw last night, then?'

'Oh, yes, it was me; and it's a good job the boy heard the old man bidding me good-night, or I might have been suspected myself. I went over to get paid for a little job I'd been doing for him.'

'Clearing out the still, maybe?' Lumsden asked, suspiciously.

'Nonsense; not that I'll deny the old man *did* once work a private still in his cellar, for he owned as much to me last night. And I want

THE PHANTOM HEARSE

to tell you something else. They say you saw that "Phantom Hearse" last night?'

'Yes, I saw it,' was the short answer.

'Well, Jones told me a queer story about that last night. He said that he would never again have anything to do with illicit distilling—he was getting too old, and the Dead Hearse he had encouraged such talk about all these years was nothing but the conveyance that used to come for the whiskey now and again. Some man was in the secret with him, it seemed, and they had a black cover, and so on, made for the cart, so as to frighten people.'

'I'll take my oath!' cried Lumsden, angrily, as Turner concluded, 'that what I saw last night was no real conveyance. I went as close to it as I am to you, and I put out my hand twice to try to touch it, but I had only air in my grip. And how could a natural thing disappear from under my very eyes when there wasn't a thing from end to end of the street but moonlight like day?'

Turner smiled as he remembered that this defender of the supernatural had only yesterday scouted the very idea of a ghostly appearance, but he only said—

''Tis impossible to account for these things, but there's an old saying that "mocking is catching." It may have been the real thing last night, as a sort of warning for people not to imitate the dead. Have ye found any kind of clue to the murderer?'

'Swipes is arrested, you know.'

'Oh *he* never did it, no more than I did; he's low and drunken and foul-tongued, is Jerry, but he wouldn't spill blood.'

'Who do you think did, then?'

'Ah, constable, if I had any suspicions I'd keep 'em to myself. It's rather a dangerous thing to accuse an innocent person; but I'll go so far as to say that I think both the lost key of the old man's door and the knife that killed him never left his own home.'

And Turner turned to his work again.

Turner's opinion that the lost key and murderous weapon were in the corner house renewed the young policeman's interest in it, and he returned to see the result of Cooney's careful search.

'I haven't left a corner hardly,' said Cooney, in reply to his question, 'and Con has been helping me. We've found nothing bearing on the murder. Con, go and try if you can get the old lady out of her room. Say she's wanted in the shop; that'll fetch her, I think.'

'Cooney, are you going to search her room?'

'Yes.'

'You have some suspicions?'

THE PHANTOM HEARSE

'I can't answer you now—follow me and you will see. I must get into that room by hook or by crook. Won't she come out, Con?'

'She won't answer at all,' replied the boy, who was knocking at the door in the kitchen.

Cooney went round to the small window of the skillion room— there was a coarse curtain over it, but perceiving that it was simply hung on hinges and opened outwards, the experienced constable drew it open, and was master of the situation. Lifting the curtain aside, he saw Mrs. Jones sitting on a box opposite to him, quite immobile. It appeared as if extraordinary emotion of some sort had frozen into helplessness every bit of brain power of which the poor old creature was possessed.

'Mrs. Jones, there's half a dozen customers in the shop—don't you hear Con calling you? Open the door and let him in.'

She got up mechanically, still keeping her eyes fixed on Cooney, who was leaning in the open window, but she seemed glued to the spot where she stood, and kept her hands behind her in such a strange way that the policeman decided on active measures, and he had bounded through the open window and was standing before the now trembling old creature in a moment.

Cooney's first act was to open the door, and then, having Lumsden and Con as witnesses, he put a hand on Mrs. Jones' arm and drew her forward. The instant she was touched, her hands dropped to her sides, and there was a sound of something falling.

Lying on the floor behind her were the key of her dead husband's door and the long, rusty weapon the unfortunate man had sharpened for his own murder.

'I thought it was something this way,' said Cooney, as he stooped for the articles. 'God help her; she's not accountable. How did you come to kill the old man, missis?'

'It was quite true,' she said, stonily. 'Watch him and you'll see. I must go and mind the shop.'

Past the horrified Con she staggered, and her shaking hands groped before her as one in the dark. Opposite the door leading into the shop she paused unsteadily, looking toward that of the death chamber, which was on her right hand. Then she turned to the right, opened the door of the darkened room, and glided in. All this time the men and boy were watching and following her. When the poor old creature crossed the threshold she put out her hands in an attitude of entreaty, as though to the dead, and, falling on her knees by the bedside, her face sank to the reddened coverlid, over which her outstretched hands lay. She spoke no word—not even a moan passed her lips, and when

THE PHANTOM HEARSE

Cooney had waited vainly for a moment or two, thinking to hear some word of prayer or entreaty, he stepped forward quickly and raised her face. She was dead.

'So best,' he murmured, 'she's gone to keep shop in comfort in the "big city." I'll never believe she knew what she was doing.'

'It seems to me a matter of impossibility that an arm like that could strike such a blow,' muttered Lumsden.

'She struck through no bones, and the way the man was lying made it an easy job. I've been hearing something from Con that made all plain to me. It seems that Jerry Swipes told her to watch the old man yesterday. The fool was only amusing himself trying to excite the poor old creature's jealousy, but a fool's words often makes the devil's opening. It was she that took the key of the door, so that Jones could not lock himself in, and the devil laid that long knife handy to her. May God have mercy on her soul!'

'And maybe that's more than was said for the man she murdered,' Lumsden discontentedly remarked.

'Maybe he doesn't want it so bad. At all events he had no blood on his hands.'

No more need be said, save that never from that day to this has the 'Phantom Hearse' been seen near Jones' Corner.

First published in the *Australian Journal*, September 1889, as part of the *Detective's Album* serial, under the byline 'W.W.'

NOTES

1 *swipe*: a thief.
2 *penthouse*: overhanging (from the original meaning of penthouse: a lean-to structure or overhang roof on the side of a house.)
3 *shake*: steal.
4 *trap*: policeman.
5 *lollies*: boiled sweets (UK), hard candy (US).
6 *gammoned*: pretended.
7 *green messmate*: unseasoned eucalyptus wood.
8 *skillion room*: a lean-to structure attached to the side of a building.

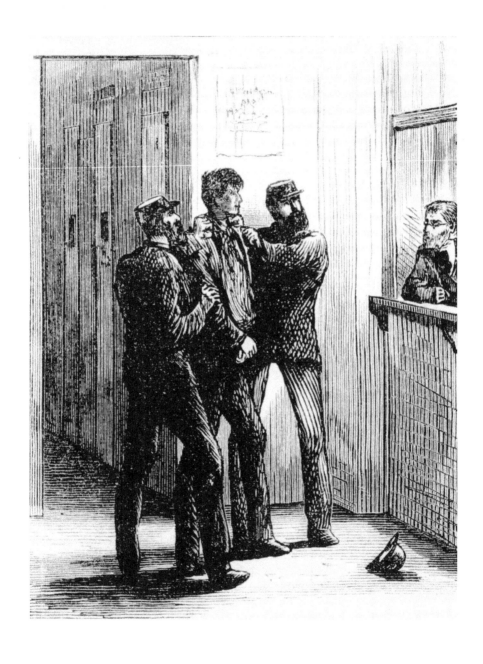

THE PRISON BRAND

At about noon, one dull and showery day in early summer, a man came out of the Detective Office, then in Swanston-street, and stood, hesitatingly, near the door. He might have been any age from thirty to thirty-five and was of good figure, though his worn-looking face was stamped with the brand that so often puzzles the uninitiated. He was dressed in what had once been a good tweed suit but was now old-fashioned in make, and wrinkled, as if it had been unworn and closely packed for a long time.

As he came to the street and looked wistfully and hesitatingly up and down while his hard hands twitched, as if helplessly, a spruce figure came sharply to the door also and, standing opposite the first man, looked keenly at him from under prominent brows. Such a contrast was this second man to the first! Clean-shaved, glossy-haired rotund of stomach and puffy of face; well clad, and with the air of a man whose bed was soft and whose dinner was plentiful and tasty; his white fingers, jingling among the loose silver in his breeches pockets, suggested pomposity and a banking account. Ah! released prisoner, Gerald Moore, what have you in common with Senior Detective Charles Sneakem?

'I suppose the air feels rather fresh to you out here, Moore?' the detective said, with a grin.

'No,' answered the man, as he moved a little away and looked steadily at his questioner, 'not just now.'

'Maybe you're a bit strange and down on your luck, eh? There's not many of your old pals left now. It's a short life and a merry one with your sort mostly, you know. And none of them have met you? Come, old man, have you any money to start you?'

The late prisoner moved a little farther away, and the shade of a flush mounted to his dark cheek, but he made no reply.

'If you hadn't been always such a bull-headed chap, things would not have gone so hard with you,' the D. went on, a little angrily. 'Don't be a fool, Moore.'

'I was always a fool. Why should I change now?' the other returned sullenly, as a dangerously bright pair of intelligent eyes met the D.'s bloodshot ones steadily.

'Ha, ha! that's good! But I suppose it's true, too. *Your* sort ain't to be changed, even by ten years' quod. But don't be a fool, Moore. Take a few friendly shillings to get you a bite and a bed till you can borrow

THE PRISON BRAND

a jemmy!' and the officer held out his hand with a few coins on its soft, warm palm.

Moore looked at the coins and again at the giver—a hard, steady look—as he answered—

'If I was dying of starvation I couldn't touch *your* money, Sneakem. A jemmy? Well, yes, I'd rather get it *that* way. I'd be risking ten more years maybe, but at all events it wouldn't be a bloodhound's pay.'

'Curse your pride and your cheek!' angrily cried Sneakem, as he returned the money to his pocket; 'and take my word for it, I'll give you another ten before you're a month older!'

Moore smiled—a queer smile, that puzzled even the astute Sneakem—and then he turned with the air of a man at drill and walked sharply away down the street, amid a noise and a bustle of town life that dazed him. Free, was he? or was he dreaming only of freedom in that narrow cell that had coffined him for so many years of his young life? Was it really over? Was he free in truth? Free at last! but what was he to do with that freedom now he had got it?

The last time, after a sentence that had been as death to him, he had gone straight back to the slums and the associates of old, and had been what he called *driven* back into the old life. Was he going to do that now? No! At least, not without a fight with starvation in the country first. There were blue hills to the left there, far away from the tempting haunts of busy men; he would go straight to those blue hills and see if the soil would give him work and food.

The man was still in a strange, dreamy mood when he was suddenly awakened to a full consciousness of a danger barely escaped. With a roar and a scream and a rush, a train passed him so closely that the wind of its transit made him shiver. He was standing upon the down line, while the up train had just gone by; but in the same instant that the late prisoner recognised his own awful escape, he saw, tearing down towards the crossing on which he stood, a horse that was evidently a runaway, with a white-faced young gentleman tugging vainly at the bridle of the clenched bit.

In the same moment that Moore saw this approaching runaway and the set fear in the rider's young face, he saw a down train so close that almost certain collision between it and the horse was imminent. A fierce strength darted into the poor fellow's muscles as he flung himself before the approaching engine and, seizing the horse by the head, by a mighty power drove him back upon his haunches. For an instant, as the horse exerted his powerful strength and tried to wrest himself from the mad hold of the man, those who stared horror-stricken from the windows of the train feared yet for the apparently doomed animal and

THE PRISON BRAND

his rider; but the train had passed, and on the very edge of the track stood the unhurt rider, while Moore still held the now half-subdued and wholly frightened animal.

'I hope you are not hurt, sir?' the late prisoner asked when he had conquered, and was able to see to the young fellow he had saved.

'No!' was the awe-stricken reply; 'but, oh! I have been very near death; and I owe my life to you!'

'Thank God!' muttered the man.

'Yes, thank God! Oh, I thank Thee sincerely, Thou mighty and merciful Father for sending this man to my help this day!'

The young gentleman had taken off his hat reverently as he addressed his thanks to Heaven. Moore gazed at him wonderingly.

'The horse is quiet now, sir; will you please take the bridle. I must go.'

'Go! Where?' the young fellow said, as he turned his frank, handsome face to his deliverer. 'Are you in such haste that you cannot wait to be thanked? Why, man, I'm full of gratitude to you, and couldn't thank you enough if I talked until tomorrow! You will come with me, won't you?'

'Go with you, sir? Where?'

'Home! Maybe *you* would not be so excited over an escape from a terrible death; but then, perhaps'—and the musical voice grew low and pitiful—'perhaps you have not so much to lose?'

'I have nothing to lose,' Moore replied, in a low voice, as he turned away and began to softly rub the animal's smooth neck with his rough hand.

'Poor chap! Come with me. See, I'm all of a shake yet! You will help me to lead that old rascal of a horse back to the stable? unless, indeed, your own business—'

'I have no business, sir. I will take the horse home for you—indeed, I should be glad to earn the price of a bed by doing it, if you please.'

'The price of a bed!'

The young man could say no more; his heart was full and his voice choked, and he laid his white hand on Moore's shoulder, as if in a caress.

And he kept the hand there, though the muscles under it instinctively shrunk and shivered, as though to throw it off. Moore glanced sideways at his companion and saw the immaculate riding-dress, the gold-mounted whip, the dainty and glossy boots, the lithe and graceful figure, crowned with glossy, fair curls and a noble-looking face, handsome enough for an Adonis.

'Sir,' said he, 'don't walk with your hand on me.'

'Why?'

273

THE PRISON BRAND

'I am not fit. It is not proper for such as you. I would shame you if I was known.'

A bright flush burned in the young man's face as he drew himself up and moved nearer to Moore.

'If you were the—the hangman I am not cad enough to be ashamed of the man who has just saved my life!'

'You have come very near it, sir. I am not the hangman, but I belong to his sort. I have just been released from Pentridge, after serving a long sentence.'

'Poor fellow!' the young man made answer, in such a tone of pity as touched Moore's heart. 'Yet I am selfish enough to be glad that you are in a position to allow me to be your friend. Give me your hand. You are young yet; you will do better.'

Moore turned away, and laid his face on the arm that rested against the horse's side.

Godfrey Cardross awkwardly looked away, and wiped his eyes with his perfumed cambric, while Gerald Moore dashed his tears away with a rough, brown hand as he raised himself.

'It is something so new to me, sir,' he said—'the sympathy and pity, I mean—yet it is harder still to say in return for it, "God bless you!"'

Godfrey, in reply, only pressed with his warm hand the no longer shrinking shoulder on which it still lay; then he began to speak lightly of his horse, so as to give his companion time to recover himself.

'I hardly know what came over the old villain; but I mustn't call him names, for I may have been to blame myself in some way. I know I was thinking of anything save the poor old chap when he started to run away and at last got the bit between his teeth. I daresay something frightened him that I didn't observe. And is it any wonder I was preoccupied, eh? Why, I'm to be married tomorrow.'

'Married tomorrow!' Moore repeated in wonder, as he looked wistfully in the young face.

'Yes. You think me too young, don't you?' the young man merrily asked. 'Everyone does; but I'm not so young as I look. It's the fair hair and happy heart, I think, for I'm nearly twenty-seven. So you see what I owe you, my dear fellow—to be married to the girl I have long loved, and who loves me with all her heart, tomorrow, and but for your bravery I should be on a stretcher now—dead and broken to pieces! I can never repay you!'

'Hush, sir; you pain me.'

'Well, I won't. Here we are. Now, come on in without any drawback or hesitation. With the exception of servants, there is no one at home but me. John, take the horse into the stable and be good to him,

THE PRISON BRAND

though he would have killed me but for this friend of mine. Here we are in my own private den. Sit down, and feel you are with a friend.'

The ex-convict seated himself in the comfortable chair to which his host gently pushed him, and as if still in that dream which seemed somehow to cling to him looked at the unfamiliar objects around him, that so strongly contrasted with his late quarters.

'Come,' said Godfrey Cardross, 'here is something to eat. Come and help me, for in spite of my fright I'm as hungry as a hunter!'

Moore made a good meal, for after his long experience of hard, coarse fare, very welcome were the good things set before him with a generous hand; and when the tray was removed and the young men were again alone, Godfrey drew his chair nearer and busied himself with a generosity that was part of his nature in trying to set Moore at his ease.

With his handsome, fair face all aglow, and his big, grey eyes alight with kindly feeling, he told the burglar the story of his love.

'It was that which saved me, Gerald. Now I know your name you must let me call you by it,' he went on, when he had told of what seemed to him a wild and hopeless youth. 'It was Emeline's pure trust in me that stopped me just as I was breaking my mother's heart. Her—my darling's—people were awfully against it, and no wonder, for I belonged to a very fast set; but she would not say me nay. "Godfrey will change for *my* sake," she always said; and I did, thank God, and we are to be married tomorrow!'

A couple of hours later the ex-burglar left the home of his benefactor, and he was clad in a decenter suit than the one that had lain so long in the prisoners' store at Pentridge. There was some money in his purse, too, and he had promised to write to his new friend from the country township he was going to.

'I will send you my address when I have shown myself sincere in my professions of reform, sir,' he said, as they parted; 'and you may see me sooner than you think for.'

'At Carramdown? Is that where you're going?' the young fellow asked, eagerly, as he still gripped Moore's hand. 'That is where we are to spend our honeymoon. But you don't want to tell yet? Well, never mind; I shall know soon, for you have promised. And now, once more, God bless you, Gerald! I will never forget that I owe you my life!'

Rob Forsyth didn't look a very old man, or a very frail one either, as he sat on the verandah of his old farm house near Carramdown that evening, though he was always called 'Old Forsyth,' or 'Old Rob Forsyth,' behind his back, but his sixty years' wrinkles were deepened

THE PRISON BRAND

by the expression of a nasty, ingrained temper of discontent and a miserliness that made even necessary expenditure almost painful to him.

The orchard in front of the old house was thriving and giving promise of a good return, and the stack-yard was not yet empty of last year's harvest yield. Cows dotted the low pasture lands, and horses munched their feed not far from the unyoked carts, yet the old man's dress was shabby enough for a pauper's, the very sleeves of his coat showing hanging shreds when he lifted his arms.

Forsyth was talking to a tall, powerful-looking young man, in his shirt-sleeves, and with his broad, old hat driven low over his eyes. This was James Bram, to whom Forsyth had let his land on shares a couple of years ago, and there had been evidently some unpleasantness on that subject between the two men.

'I'm no in wi' your plans at all, man,' Forsyth was saying doggedly, 'and this year finishes me wi' them. Fac' is, I'm a ruined man wi' your mind No. 1 ways, and I'll hae nae mair o't.'

'What do you mean by my No. 1 ways, Mr. Forsyth?' Bram asked sulkily, as he fixed his small, deep-set eyes on the old man's face; 'there hasn't been better crops in Carramdown since I farmed the land on shares.'

'Yer right there! Oh, I'm no denyin' it! There's been crops, ay, and siller[1] for them, only it's no got into *my* pocket! An' what do I mean by No. 1 ways, ye're askin' me? Fegs, ye're no blate, James Bram! Well ye ken that I mean ye've looked out so well for yoursel that you haven't had an eye to my just interests. But nae mair words the noo, my lad—I've said that the neist reckonin' atween you and me'll be the last. But wha hev we here?'

The sudden question was asked by the appearance of a swagman who had unlatched the garden gate and was coming up the walk towards the door. The swagman was young and comfortably dressed, and such of his face as could be seen was much browned with the sun.

'Good-evening,' the stranger said as he dropped his blankets from his shoulder. 'Could I get accommodation here for the night?'

'This isn't a public house,' Bram answered disagreeably, 'and the township isn't a mile off.'

'If it isn't a public house, James Bram,' old Forsyth put in, as he turned an angry face on his partner, 'at all events it isn't *your* house to put anyone in or out of it! The house is mine; I'm master here.'

'I didn't say it wasn't,' was the surly retort; 'only I never knew you to give a man a bed or a bite free yet.'

'I can pay for what I get,' the new-comer put in quietly.

'You are welcome to stay,' Forsyth said decidedly. 'I take instructions

THE PRISON BRAND

as to my doin's from neither man nor woman, and I'm glad to get a chance o' a crack wi' someone that's likely to hae brains in 'is heed. Sit ye doon and rest ye, freen'.'

With an ominous scowl on his face Bram went into the house, and left the two seated.

'Are ye seekin' work?' questioned Forsyth, with a sharp look at the stranger.

'Yes, I'd be glad to get a job, sir.'

'Ay! But, ye see, it's the wrong time. It's no hairst yet, and there's little doin'. There's many bits o' jobs aboot that a man might turn his mind to, if I had the farm in my ain haund; but as it is, I'm tributin' like—workin' the land on shares. Ye see, I'm no sae young as I was, and canna pit my ain back tilt as I used.'

'You have no family at home?' questioned the swagman in a low tone.

'Neither at home nor abroad,' was the short answer as, with a suspicious look, the old man turned his head away. 'I've had a wife and children, like other men, but they're a' deid.'

'You have one alive, have you not?'

This question was in even a lower tone than the last, yet old Rob Forsyth heard it plainly enough, though he returned a thundering 'What!' as he angrily scowled at the traveller.

'You have a son alive—a son who has been a disgrace and a heart-break to you. I have brought a message to you from him.' A sort of spasm passed over the old Scotchman's wrinkled face, and his knotted hands gripped the arms of his chair hard. It seemed to the anxious stranger as if Forsyth was for a little incapable of speech, but when he could he said sneeringly, though with a visible tremble in his voice—

'Asses hae long lugs.[2] Might I speer[3] o' ye whaur ye met with ony ane claimin' kin wi' me?'

'In the prison at Pentridge, from which I have just come myself—at least, only a few days ago.'

'Ye're no blate to tell't. Gad, the warld's gone ding! A decent man would hae thoot to maybe *hide* he'd been in sich a place as that ye name!'

'You asked me, and how could I give you the message I promised without telling where I got it? The man who was once your son was very anxious that you should get it. And no wonder; he was born under this roof, he told me. I have heard him speak a hundred times of that old apple tree yonder, where he used to sit when a child with his mother and play with old Rover.'

The old man's face grew scarlet and then blanched again. He rose to his feet, tremblingly, and then sank back again as he gasped—

277

THE PRISON BRAND

'The dog! how dare he! And you, you accursed gaol-bird, how dare you to cart to a man's own doorstep the shame he had tried to cover up wi' the years that made his hair grey? I have no son! There isna a drop of my bluid in the veins of an accursed thief! What do you want here, ye spyin' hound?' he added furiously, as a window behind him cautiously opened, and the greedy face of James Bram appeared behind it. 'Who gave *you* a right to go into my rooms to listen and watch?'

'I think it was needless to wait for an excuse when I heard you quarrelling with a tramp,' replied Bram sulkily. 'When you talked of gaol-birds how was I to know that you didn't want a helping hand?'

'And you came past the open door to offer it through the window? Faugh! Go back to your ain preemises, and tak your dirty curiosity with you, James Bram!'

The fury of old Forsyth had exhausted him and, as he ceased to speak to Bram, he fell back in his chair and closed his eyes. The young traveller had risen, and with trembling hands and humiliated, white, hopeless face, was arranging his swag. As he threw the swag over his shoulder, Forsyth opened his eyes, and they met the pitiful ones of the stranger.

'You are right to go,' said the old man, bitterly; 'I want none o' your sort here.'

The stranger moistened his dry lips with his tongue; it seemed hard to speak. 'You will not send one word to him?' he asked, pleadingly. 'Remember his long punishment; he has been there for nine long years.'

'If my wish was studied he should be there until his hair was as grey as mine ain—nay, he should be there for ever!'

'God forgive you!'

The swagman turned and went slowly down the path; he did not look back except for a moment as he closed the gate behind him. Old Forsyth watched the retreating figure, and when the trees on the road-side shut it from view, he bent his face to his hands and moaned. He was a hard old man, but he had a heart for all that, and his curses had made it sore.

James Bram was very angry at the names he had been called by his partner, and that before a stranger, too, but there was no one save old Ann to complain to, and she was so deaf that the prospect of inviting her sympathy was not encouraging. When he had his supper he took his hat and went off for his usual evening visit to the township.

Constable Whatmough was standing just outside the public house door, and it suited Bram to tell his story to him.

'I've just had a bit of a word or two with the old man,' he said, 'and as it seems something in your line, constable, I may as well mention it.'

THE PRISON BRAND

'Something in my line, eh?'

'Yes, I should say so. A well-dressed sort of a tramp, with a swag, got up to Forsyth's a bit ago, and hearing the old man cursing and rowing at him when I was going to get my supper, I thought I'd better see what was up. I heard the old fellow call the man a gaol-bird and say he'd have none of his sort about the place, but all the thanks I got was a lot of bad names to myself.'

'A gaol-bird, eh?' asked Whatmough.

'Yes. If the old man didn't know him, he knew something of him, evidently, for he talked of a nine years' sentence, and in good English, too—a sure sign Forsyth is mad angry. When he's in a good humour he always speaks broad Scotch.'

'I've heard that old Forsyth had a son that got into trouble,' mused the constable.

'So have I, but it's a thing no one dare name to him. The son was a bad lot ever since his boyhood, if all that's said is true.'

'So I've heard. Well, I'll look over the *Gazette* and see if there's any long-sentenced men out of Pentridge lately. Hallo! who have we here?'

'That must be the new married couple from Broadbush, I should say.'

'What? Young Mr. Cardross?'

'Yes; he's a barrister, you know, and Broadbush belongs to his father, the judge. Lucky young dog, eh? They say he's married a fortune, too, and that Broadbush has been done up no end for them.'

'Yes,' murmured the constable absently, as the carriage whirled past, affording a glimpse of two happy young faces. 'Ah, that's them, is it? I've been away a couple of days, you know.'

'It would be rather awkward if the merry burglars should interrupt the honeymoon, wouldn't it, Whatmough?' laughed big, slouching Bram cunningly; 'it might perhaps be worth your while to keep your eye on that swagman I was telling you of, eh?'

'Has he left Forsyth's?'

'Oh yes, the old man chased him off, but I saw nothing of him coming down, so he's maybe headed towards Prout's.'

'Do you sleep at Forsyth's, Bram?'

'Me? No! I never left the old hut on the back farm. Me and old Joe camp together.'

'And Forsyth is alone?'

'No. Jim, the ploughman, sleeps in the stable, and old Ann Cummings in the house. Oh, I don't think the old man keeps anything on the premises to be robbed of—he's too cute for that.'

279

THE PRISON BRAND

The young man who had met with such an unfavourable reception at Forsyth's was none other than Gerald Moore, and he walked quickly away from the gate, with a great bitterness at his heart. He had known the sorrows that certainly follow in the train of sin in their hardest and most cruel form, for with the crimes of his years he had, perhaps unfortunately for himself, retained yet something of a naturally sensitive nature. Let it not be wondered at, then, that this man, fresh from the hardening experiences of a prison life, turned into the bush and, sitting down upon his swag in the lonely depths of the greenland, wept silently but not the less bitterly.

Is Satan a real personality, exercising a direct influence over the affairs of man? Could it be that this poor soul—about to escape, as it seemed, from the coils of the old serpent, whose name is sin—was to be the victim of an evil influence that had followed the poor young fellow even to this quiet haunt, where no evil might be supposed to lurk? Moore had sat there long enough to partially recover himself from his bitter disappointment. Noting the lateness of the hour, he was rising to go, when a man who had been for some little time watching him crawled out from the undergrowth and greeted him joyously.

'By gad! this is luck. If I had my choice of every man in Victoria, I would have asked for you! What devil sent you here?' And the speaker's hand fell heavily on Moore's shoulder.

The young man started, and his face clouded. He recognised the unwelcome face as that of one to whom he had owed no little of his life's evil influence, and who had been released from prison but a few weeks before himself. The encounter was far from a welcome one to Moore, but he was careful at first not to exhibit his feeling.

'Why, Dan, is it you?—a strange place to meet. What lay are you on here?'

'A blessed poor one, Bob'—Moore's nickname with his old associates. 'Me and Martin has been mostly starving since we got out.'

'Martin! Is *he* here?'

'Yes; we came out together. Town got a bit hot for us. Well, as I said, we've been out of luck, but just dropped on a grand chance where another man's wanting. It *was* the devil sent you here.'

'I don't think so, Dan, for I'm not on, anyhow.'

'Not on!'

'No; I'm sick of the thing, and mean to try to live decently. That last sentence made me swear to give it best.'

The man called Dan laughed loudly and harshly, and the lines and seams which a criminal life stamps almost indelibly on a man's face seemed to become more marked and repulsive.

THE PRISON BRAND

'If anyone had told me that Ger. Moore would have been the man to show the white feather, I'd have laughed at him,' he said; 'and, by George, it sounds funny!'

'Oh, what's the use of talking!' Moore said, helplessly. 'My mind is made up. I'll put my hands into no sort of trouble—never more. And having told you so much, I had better be moving.'

'In the name of all the saints, Moore, what has come over you? Just listen. There is a chance to make a regular haul, and not a bobby or a D. within miles! Why, man, we can share enough to clear out of the country and *then*, if you like, talk of turning over a new leaf. The place is within a mile of where we sit, and is chock full of valuables, with not a soul to guard it but a new married man that's too much taken up with his honeymoon to sit up o' nights watching for burglars. It would be a shame—a cursed shame—to lose such a chance.'

'A new married man?' repeated Moore strangely, as he looked toward the other's face, now getting dim in the dusk. 'His honeymoon, did you say?'

'By George! yes. It's at Broadbush—Judge Cardross' station place, and the son has just come up with his bride. They've brought no end of jewellery and presents, and half an hour's pluck will do it.'

Moore had already risen in preparation for his intended departure when the name of the burglar's intended victim fell on his astounded ear. What was he to do for the best? How save his new and generous friend, while also saving from themselves these miserable old accomplices in crime?

'Dan,' he said, hoarsely, 'you mustn't do this.'

'Mustn't do what?'

'Rob Broadbush. Listen to me. That young man you speak of—Godfrey Cardross—has lately been a good friend to me, and I couldn't go into anything against him without the darkest ingratitude.'

'You're a blamed fool,' the other said contemptuously; 'but if you are, it doesn't make us fools too. Martin and me must just do as well as we can by ourselves.'

Moore's temper rose, and he spoke hotly.

'But I say you shan't—do you hear? If I had been a wise man I should have gone on my way without saying a word, but I don't want to round on old pals. Don't drive me to it, Dan, but mind you, I swear that no harm shall go to Broadbush that I can prevent.'

'Oh! So you're ready for the informing line, eh? But I guess Martin will have a word to say to that.'

'That's what Martin has to say,' spoke the other ruffian, as he came up behind Moore and struck him a heavy blow in the head with a 'neddy.'[4]

281

THE PRISON BRAND

Moore fell without a groan.

'My Lord! you've killed him!' cried Dan, as he knelt beside the prostrate form.

'Well, and if I have, what else could I do? Did you want our last chance to be blown on by the white-livered informer? I've been listening for a minute or two, and, by heavens, if he had been my own brother the blow was his! Is he dead?'

'I'm afraid so,' Dan said, rising and turning his white face fearfully around. 'I hope to heaven no one saw you do it! I can't feel a bit of heart in him, Martin. I was never on for murder!'

'You always was a coward,' muttered the huge villain as, with an evil face, he stooped to examine his victim. 'No, there's no pulse as I can see; but he brought it on himself. Let us clear out o' this like winkin', Dan.'

And so poor Moore lay there while the darkness gathered and deepened in the silent bush—while the stars came out and winked wonderingly through the rustling branches. But he was not dead, though hours had passed before he opened his eyes and lifted his heavy head. 'Where was he?' was his first wonder, and then, with a thrill of horror, he remembered all. Was it too late? In his dazed and weak condition, would he be able to reach Broadbush?

Raising his hand to the wound on his head, he managed to bind it closely with his handkerchief and then, hiding his swag behind some bushes, he took the shortest way to Broadbush. And it would seem that he was no stranger to the country, for he proceeded as if the place were well known to him. At the creek he refreshed himself with a drink and by laving his brow and hands. And at last he reached the boundary fence of Broadbush, and crawled through it painfully. When he stood erect again he saw that the old moon was not far from the eastern horizon, and knew that it was not far from daybreak. 'I am too late!' the poor fellow groaned, and then all at once his pain and weakness from loss of blood overpowered him, and he fell prone on his face among the long grass by the fence.

An hour after sunrise on that morning, Constable Whatmough, having helped the man under him to secure in the lock-up a prisoner they had brought into the township in a conveyance belonging to Broadbush, walked quickly across the road and knocked sharply at Dr. Maxwell's door. The doctor was a bachelor, and rather fond of spending his evenings at the Shire Hotel, so there was an almost certainty of finding him in bed at that early hour.

This proved to be the case, but the policeman's summons roused him. Slipping back the lock, he admitted Whatmough and, leading him

THE PRISON BRAND

into the bedroom, began hastily to dress himself.

'It must be something pressing brought you over so early?' he questioned, as he drew on his second sock.

'It is that. Broadbush has been visited in the night by a pair of burgling villains, and young Mr. Cardross has had a severe tussle with one of them. I think you'd better go over and see him, though he makes light of his injuries.'

'Burglars! At Broadbush! Good Lord! what is this you tell me?'

'Mr. Cardross did not send for the police until daylight. He said that as the villains did not succeed in their intention of looting the place, there was no hurry in trying to arrest them.'

'Why, I'd have hunted the wretches down in the dark, if it had been possible!' cried the doctor. 'So they escaped, then?'

'We got one of them. He was lying insensible near one of the boundary fences; and one has got clear off, apparently. This fellow in the lock-up seems very bad, and most likely has a bullet in him somewhere, but he's sulky like, and will hardly speak.'

'A bullet! Who fired?'

'Mr. Cardross managed to discharge his pistol when one of the blackguards had him down, and the noise doubtless brought help. Mr. Cardross must have fainted, for he remembers nothing after he fired the shot. It all happened in the dining-room, about two o'clock this morning.'

The doctor, being now dressed, and having fortified himself with a 'nip,' followed the constable outside. When he got to the door, after ordering his horse, he saw James Bram riding up the road at full gallop, and dismounting when he reached the police station.

Dr. Maxwell strode across the road, and stood at the door while Bram spoke to Whatmough inside.

'Constable, and you, too, Dr. Maxwell, had better come out at once to Forsyth's.'

'What's wrong out there?'

'The old man is dead! Oh, Lord! What awful things are these! The old man has been murdered in his bed.'

'Murdered!'

Bram was white to ghastliness, and with his loose shirt sleeve tried to wipe the damp from his face.

'It's given me an awful turn—I don't think I'll ever get over it. I came down to breakfast at the usual time—we're fencing, Joe and me, out by the west paddock—and just as I went in the kitchen door, old Ann came out of the hall screeching like mad and crying that the master was dead. It was true enough, for I went in and looked, and an

THE PRISON BRAND

awful sight it was. The old man has been stabbed in the breast, and the bed is one mass of blood. Whatmough, *now* do you remember what I told you about that tramp?'

The trembling man asked the question so eagerly as to attract the doctor's notice.

'What tramp?' he asked. And Whatmough replied—

'It is the man we have in the lock-up. I knew him at once by Bram's description yesterday. So it seems the villains have been at Forsyth's before they went to Broadbush, and doubtless the old man has met his death trying to defend his property. Doctor, you had better come out to Forsyth's first.'

Accordingly, they rode rapidly in the direction of Forsyth's, while Bram went on towards the store, where he had to get some things needful to old Ann, he said.

When they reached the farm they found the old woman housekeeper out in the garden, her face white and rigid with anxiety and fear.

'I am afraid,' she cried to them. 'I am an old woman, and they had no business to all go away and leave me in the place with a murdered man. Heavens! how could I know but the murdering wretch might come back again and cut my throat, too?'

'You needn't be afraid of that, at all events,' Constable Whatmough said, 'for he is in the lock-up, safe and fast. Did you see him when he was here yesterday evening, Ann?'

'I got a look at him through the window, that was all; but I'd know him anywhere. A dark, murderin' lookin' chap he was, sure enough. And, oh! the poor master!'

They went inside, and soon Whatmough had the old woman busy getting hot water and flannels and spirits. There was a strange fuss over a dead man, old Ann thought. But Dr. Maxwell soon went on his way to Broadbush, leaving Whatmough in charge at the farm until his mate, the other constable, should come out to relieve him.

Whatmough sat on the verandah with the key of Mr. Forsyth's room in his pocket, and he remained there for nearly an hour before Bram rode through the slip-panel and round to the back. Presently the man came creeping round the house on tip-toe, as if afraid of wakening the dead, and he sat down on the step of the verandah near the policeman with a strange, rigid tension of face and body.

'Are you going to stop here, constable?' he asked, in a half whisper.

'Until Smith comes.'

'Will they move the body to the township for the inquest?

'I guess not. Will this make any difference to you, Bram?'

'To me?'

284

THE PRISON BRAND

'About the farming, I mean. You were on shares, weren't you?'

'Yes, but that's all on paper. No, it won't make any difference that way. I wonder who'll get the farm and the old man's money?'

'There's the son, you know; he'll get it if there's no will. Is there much money, do you think—I mean banked?'

'They say that Forsyth *didn't* bank. Old Ann says that he had regular plants about the house. The son, are you talking about? One of *his* pals did last night's work, you bet!'

'What makes you so sure?'

'Why, of course you know! You've got him in the lock-up, haven't you? Smith told me. Don't you remember I told you that the old man called him—the tramp I mean—a gaol-bird? Oh, the villain of a son wanted what the old man got, and they settled him for it. In the name of God, what's that?'

What had frightened the speaker so was a strange, muffled sound from the room behind them—the front room—in which the murdered man lay. Whatmough rose to his feet instantly and grasped the key in his pocket.

'I guess it's the cat got in there,' he muttered, as he hastened inside and entered the bedroom, from which he did not emerge for some minutes.

James Bram awaited him, and his face was awful in its horror, though his eyes were bloodshot, evidently the effects of drink.

'What was it?' he whispered.

'The cat, as I told you,' half-laughed the constable. 'I expect the animal is as much afraid of a dead man as you seem to be, Bram.'

'I never could stand death. It seems to me just awful to think that he's lying in there dead, and only last night he was sitting in that there chair, as cross and crusty as usual; but he was an old man.'

'Not so old, either. Do you think it's time for a man to be murdered when he comes to be sixty? That would be a funny kind of belief—at least to act upon. Is that your hut over there on the rise?'

'Yes, and I see Joe hanging round, waiting for me; but, somehow, I don't feel fit for much work today.'

He didn't look like it, certainly. Whatmough stood and watched the man as he slouched away in the direction of his hut, his shoulders bowed, his hands heavily swinging, his shuffling, big feet taking unsteady steps. He wore a pair of dark moleskins and a dark cotton shirt, one sleeve of which was unbuttoned, and swung loose as he swayed his hand; and a torn and soiled felt hat, that had once been grey was pressed low over a thick, untended crop of reddish hair that matched the huge, tangled whiskers.

THE PRISON BRAND

Two days after the raid of the burglars on Broadbush, Constable What-mough opened the door of his lock-up and let the hot afternoon sun stream into it for a little space. The prisoner sat on the floor, with one shoulder against the wooden wall and his face turned from the light. The whole attitude of the man was hopeless and dogged-looking, and when the heavy door creaked back, he turned toward it a face in which there was a painful hardness of expression, as well as a deepening of the lines which I have come to regard as the brand of a lawless life.

'You're going to have some visitors,' Whatmough said, somewhat sternly; 'and, though I don't suppose it's any use recommending you civility, if I was you I wouldn't make my case any worse by your usual dumb-devil manner.'

The prisoner laughed—a hard, forced laugh. 'You are going to exhibit the wild beast!' he sneered. 'Well, take care he doesn't devour your sight-seers.'

'I'm going to bring Mr. Cardross to identify you,' the constable said. 'You ought to be ashamed to look him in the face, for you nearly left him a dead man, you villain! He has not been able to come until today.'

'Mr. Cardross?' the prisoner repeated, and over his haggard face there rose a painful, red flush.

'Yes, and James Bram is coming, too, to see if you are the tramp the murder is blamed on'; and the door was clanged to again, with an echo that seemed to stun the unhappy prisoner. He bent his face in his hands and groaned pitifully.

Meanwhile, Godfrey Cardross had alighted at the door of the police station, and was met by Dr. Maxwell.

'I hope you haven't been imprudent in coming out too soon,' the latter said; 'you are very pale, Mr. Cardross. How does the arm feel?'

'Oh, it's nearly all right, doctor!' the young fellow, who looked wearied and worried, replied. 'I am troubled about these men more than anything else. I don't see what is the use of trying to hunt them down since they did not succeed in their object.'

'Oh, we must consider the public; your leniency would be only a selfish weakness.'

'I suppose so,' Godfrey returned, with a sigh.

'And there is a more serious matter hanging to it, you know,' Dr, Maxwell continued. 'There is that poor old man, who might have been struck down in cold blood without a moment's time to prepare for death—you know that it is supposed that this same man in the lock-up must have gone straight from Forsyth's to Broadbush.'

'But the old man has a chance of life yet, hasn't he?'

THE PRISON BRAND

'A chance—yes, but the intention was the same. It was a cruel thing; he had been stunned by a blow on the head before he was stabbed.'

'He has not regained consciousness?'

'No; but we have hopes that he will, and meantime, in the interests of justice—till he can name his would-be murderer—we are keeping the fact of his being yet alive a strict secret.'

'I understand.'

'You are certain you will be able to identify either of the burglars, Mr. Cardross?'

'Oh, positive! We have the gas at Broadbush, you know, and my first act on entering the dining-room was to turn it on. You never saw such consternation as the fellows exhibited. One of them fled through the window, and I believe it was in desperation only that the second closed with me. He was a tall, powerful man, and his very weight drove me down.'

'This man does not answer to that description, so it must be the one who fled. Here is Constable Whatmough now.'

'Will you come with me. Mr. Cardross, if you please?'

'I'd rather face the mouth of a cannon,' the young gentleman said, as he turned to go with the constable; 'it seems to me a horrible thing to make a sort of show of a helpless man in a cage, as if he were a wild beast.'

'He *is* a wild beast,' Whatmough returned as he looked curiously at Godfrey's troubled countenance. 'The criminal class don't have the feelings of decent people, Mr. Cardross; they're hardened to it. I hope this villain will not be too uncivil to you, but he's a nasty, sulky card.'

The door of the lock-up was once more opened, and, hesitatingly obeying Whatmough's hint, Godfrey Cardross passed into the cell.

The sun was shining so brightly outside that at first the place seemed to be in semi-darkness; but, when his eyes had got a little accustomed to the obscurity, he saw, standing within a few paces of him, a young man, with a death-pale face and some bloodstained bandages round his head. One moment the two looked into each other's eyes, and then a cry that was full of horror rang in the lock-up.

'Gerald! My God! Is it you?'

'Yes,' was the bitter answer; 'you see how vain a hope is for one that bears a prison brand, Mr. Cardross.'

'It is no vain hope! What do you mean? What brought you here? What mistake is this, Constable Whatmough? This man is my friend!' And the noble young fellow stepped forward and seized Moore's hand.

Moore gazed into the handsome, generous face, and his lips twitched as the tears filled his eyes.

287

THE PRISON BRAND

'You are taking the hand of a man accused not only of robbing you but of murdering his own father,' he said in a choking voice.

'Hush! How dare you? Accused, indeed! I say, what is this mistake, Whatmough? This man had nothing to do with the burglary at my place. He is not near so like any one of them as *you* are!'

'I hope it is not you who are making the mistake, sir. We arrested this man within a few yards of your place, wounded as you see him.'

'Wounded! How? It is not the man, or one of the men. If one of the burglars is wounded it will be with my pistol-bullet—he had no other wounds. At all events, this man is innocent, and you must give him his liberty.'

'I cannot do that, sir, for there is another charge against him.'

'Of murder—of parricide,' the prisoner said, in a cold, hard tone. 'Mr. Cardross, do not try to help me; it would be in vain. I am a branded man. Can any good thing come out of Pentridge? I am a robber and a murderer.'

'You see, sir, he doesn't even try to deny it!' cried Whatmough.

'Deny anything to a policeman!' Moore returned, with a look of the deepest scorn at the constable. 'Mr. Cardross, you had better go and leave me; I am a hopeless case.'

'I will never leave you, Gerald! I am as sure of your innocence as that I hold your hand in mine, and that you could, if you wished, give an explanation of the circumstances that seem now to point to your guilt. Is it not so, my poor friend?'

'I could explain to you, but to these paid creatures, whose trade is unbelief in anyone who is poor or has sinned, I would only waste my breath in doing so. But I thank you, sir, from the bottom of my heart for your belief in me, and you are right—I am as innocent of these charges as you are.'

'He lies!' a coarse voice here put in, as James Bram's face pushed itself between Whatmough and the door of the cell. 'That is the man that was quarrelling with Forsyth two nights ago. I can swear a dozen oaths on it! Take him up to the old man's corpse and make him touch it; that'll tell! Where I came from it's known that the corpse of a murdered man will bleed if the murderer lays a finger on it!'

'A very good idea indeed, Bram,' was the very unexpected remark which here came from Dr. Maxwell. He had come to the door of the lock-up, and was holding a bit of paper in his hand. 'Bring the prisoner up to the farm. Whatmough and Mr. Cardross will accompany us.'

'Ha, ha!' Bram sniggered, '*that* brings the villain to his bearings! I knew that would frighten him!' and he pointed toward the prisoner as he slouched away.

THE PRISON BRAND

At the mention of poor old Forsyth, Moore, still with his hand held in Godfrey's firm clasp, turned his head away and hid his face against the wall.

'Yes,' the doctor replied, to a question in an undertone from Whatmough, 'I've just had a note from Smith. I gave him strict orders to send me word if there was a change, and there is. I am going up instantly.'

'We will follow,' Cardross returned; 'and now, Whatmough, I want a word alone with my friend here.' Whatmough went out, and drew the door behind him.

A solemn stillness lay around the old farm-house when Dr. Maxwell alighted from his horse and joined Constable Smith on the verandah. The window of old Forsyth's room was open to the sunshine, and the curtain that shaded it slightly was moving softly to and fro in the sweet south breeze. As the medical man passed through the orchard under the heavily fruited old trees, with the strong sunshine casting leafy shadows on the grass beneath, the wheels that brought the other actors to the bedside of Farmer Forsyth stopped at the slip-panel on the main road.

'The old man has been conscious, then?' the doctor asked, as Smith moved to meet him.

'Yes; twice, as you expected, doctor; but he drops off again almost instantly.'

'Just so. The woman has been attentive with the nourishment I ordered?'

'Oh, yes; it has been administered faithfully. Has Bram been down with you?'

'Oh, yes; identifying the prisoner, of course. He has returned?'

'Prowling about the back—yes.'

'No suspicions?'

'Not one. Mrs. Cummings has never shown herself outside, and Bram's that afraid of the corpse that money wouldn't tempt him near that room!'

Ten minutes later the door of the old man's chamber was softly opened, and admitted Constable Whatmough, escorting Gerald Moore, who was closely followed by Cardross. The doctor was already in the room and was bending over the bed. The old farmer lay, still and blood-less-looking, with his hands and arms straight beside him, like the hands and arms of a dead man, and his eyes were closed as if in sleep. The doctor beckoned to Moore, who advanced to the bed, and, kneeling down by its side, gently took the old, white, thin hand in both of his.

The face of the poor prisoner was a piteous sight. Remorse and pain

THE PRISON BRAND

and pity were strongly expressed in his white lips and sorrowful eyes; and it would seem as if from the heart of the father to that of the son, through the gentle touch of the hard hands, a sympathetic chord must have been vivified, for suddenly Forsyth opened his eyes and turned them to his son's face.

'Poor Gerald!' the old father whispered. 'I was very hard on you. Forgive me!' and then, as his fingers weakly responded to Gerald's hand pressure, the old man's eyes closed again. There was a broad smile all over Dr. Maxwell's face as he lifted the patient's head gently and put a stimulant to his lips.

'Bring Bram here,' he said with a grin, 'and let him see the corpse bleed at the touch of the murderer!'

Whatmough left the room.

'Forsyth,' continued Dr. Maxwell, 'you have not been able to understand hitherto, but I think now, if you compose your thoughts a bit, you will be able to tell us who it was that assaulted you so cruelly. Do you understand me?'

'Yes.'

'We have a pretty good idea who it was already, but to clear an innocent man you had better speak.'

'Am I dying?'

'Please God, no; we have every hopes of saving you now, and your son will nurse you well, I know.'

'Gerald!' the poor old fellow murmured, as he once again turned his eyes to the prisoner.

At this moment James Bram crept into the roo   m—very unwillingly, as was evinced by his manner. The man was white as ashes, and Whatmough pressed in behind him. Gerald yet knelt by the bed, and now he had hidden his face on his father's hand, for the old man's weak eyes had re-closed.

'Arouse yourself for one moment, Forsyth,' whispered the doctor, 'and then you can rest as long as you like; just look up and try to identify the man who wounded you.'

Forsyth obeyed, and looking from one to another, his eyes fell on Bram.

'There is the man,' he said; 'he left me for dead to rob me. James Bram, give up the gold you stole to its rightful owner, my dear son here,' and the sick man's outstretched hand fell on Gerald's head.

Bram shrank back in horror, for to him it was as if the dead had spoken. Whatmough laughed as he handcuffed the villainous hands.

'The stolen gold is all right, Mr. Forsyth!' the constable explained. 'We have struck the murdering wretch's plant. I suspected him the very

THE PRISON BRAND

minute he brought me the news, for he had something awful in his eyes. Smith dogged him day and night, till he saw him trying to put the proceeds of his robbery in, as he thought, a safer place.'

Gerald Forsyth, as we now know him, stood up to grasp the offered hand of his faithful friend, young Cardross. 'May God bless you always, sir! In spite of the prison brand, you have been just to me.'

'You did something better for me when you saved me from a horrible death, Gerald. My dear fellow, you have a happy future before you, and we shall meet often, for you will never leave the old father now.'

'Never!'

Nor did he. Old Forsyth grew young again with his changed son as his right-hand man, and a more contented pair it would be hard to find—only on Gerald's face there always remained the melancholy of a sad remembrance. Cardross often brought his growing family to gather apples in the old orchard, and Gerald's face grew bright to see them, but he would hear no word of a marriage for himself.

'Years have only softened the hard prison brand in my own face,' he used to say to Godfrey, 'for I can see the well-known seamy lines of sin yet. Would it be right to plant the poison in the blood of children? Ah! sir, there are no worse hereditary curses than the curse of sin! And father is content. Just look at him now, laughing with your boys; yet I think too much of even them would weary him. I have never seen him unhappy since the day Bram was sentenced to death.'

'It was a pity that sentence was commuted,' Dr. Maxwell, who was one of the visitors to the farm that day, said dryly. 'But there's one comfort—the villain is strong and able; he'll live a long time to suffer.'

First published in the *Australian Journal*, December 1893, as part of the *Detective's Album* serial, under the byline 'W.W.'

NOTES

1 *siller*: (Scots) money (from silver).
2 *Asses hae long lugs*: Donkeys have long ears.
3 *speer*: (Scots) ask.
4 *neddy*: in this context, a cosh or blackjack.

AN AMATEUR DETECTIVE

It was during the time of the great influx of visitors to Melbourne, when our great Exhibition[1] was in full swing, that the Baron and Baroness Cugerna established themselves here, and our department began to be troubled by the robberies reported by present or late guests at Burro Lodge.

There could be no doubt of the baron's bona-fides as to his position and means, for he was well furnished with introductory letters to influential persons. An establishment was set up at Burro Lodge—a mansion in an aristocratic suburb—and soon the hospitalities offered by the baron and baroness to their new friends became a topic of the day.

It was said that the baron had come to Australia chiefly in search of health, though his medical man hinted that gout was the baron's chief ailment. When he appeared in public it was mostly in a handsome close carriage, with his own man in attendance, and his drives were usually in the direction of the —— Bank.

Our trouble concerning the Cugernas began with private complaints from guests who had missed one valuable or another during visits to Burro Lodge. It was the same story always—a ring, or a pin, or a brooch, or a bracelet had unaccountably disappeared. The losses were reported, but always with the proviso that the matter should in no way reach the ears of Baron Cugerna or the baroness. It was evident that visitors valued the privilege of the entree to Burro Lodge, and were unwilling to take action which might cause their hosts annoyance.

Superintendent Stanford felt greatly annoyed at the position we were placed in by this enforced secrecy. 'What is the use of reporting losses if they won't let us investigate on the premises?' he said; 'it's all rot! I don't care how great a bigwig he may be in Austria, Baron Cugerna is under our laws here, and we have a right to trace up a robbery where it is reported as having been committed, and I shall tell the Commissioner so the very next loss reported.'

He was thus enlarging one day when the mid-day post was delivered, and I was in the Super's private office taking notes of some departmental papers. 'Ha!' he cried, when he had read one of the epistles, 'the very thing I was talking about! Here's a summons from the baroness herself at last!'

AN AMATEUR DETECTIVE

Stanford threw the note across for my perusal. It was embossed with a coat of arms and 'Burro Lodge'; while below ran, in queer, crabbed characters — 'The Baroness Cugerna wishes a capable detective sent to her at once, and she trusts that a gentlemanly and intelligent officer may be sent, so that there may be no suspicion here that he belongs to the police.'

'Flattering, isn't it, Sinclair? The baroness seems to think that only in rare cases is there any possibility of a detective being taken for a gentleman! Will I pass muster, do you think?'

'You are going yourself, then?'

'Wouldn't lose the chance for a crown! Of course, I shall not let on that I have the honour of being a Super. Ta-ta!'

I looked after Stanford as he hailed and entered a hansom. We had reason to feel proud of him, for he was a splendid-looking fellow, who had served in the army and carried the old military air as if it had been born with him.

Burro Lodge was a large and handsome house in pretty, spacious grounds, and with a broad circular carriage drive leading up to the portico. Stanford left his hansom at the gate and walked up the portico steps and rang the doorbell. It was opened with promptitude by a footman in showy livery.

'I have an appointment with the Baroness Cugerna,' Stanford explained. 'Be good enough to inform her that I come in reply to her note.'

'Her excellency is expecting you; please follow me!'

Her excellency! Stanford, looking at the evidences of luxury he passed as he followed the man, began to think he was getting into rather unaccustomed society, and to feel even a greater curiosity about his interview with the as yet unknown baroness. He was ushered into an apartment furnished with the greatest elegance, where a lady was seated at what appeared to be breakfast, though it was very near our ordinary lunch hour.

Our Super often described the baroness as he saw her on that first time. A small-made woman in every way, with the abnormal activity of a restless nature looking out of a pair of small, sharp eyes that seemed to irradiate her face. Stanford always declared that the woman's eyes burned into a fellow as if she was 'determined to see through him.'

The woman was about forty and was dressed in most expensive dishabille. The breakfast table was furnished in valuable Sèvres and silver gilt, and the table drawn up to her brocaded easy-chair was a gem of marqueterie. The only thing wanting to a perfect aristocracy of appearance was 'the calm repose of Vere de Vere';[2] there was nothing

294

AN AMATEUR DETECTIVE

of that about the Baroness Cugerna; she was restless and volatile to a degree.

'Will you be seated?' she said, with a strong foreign accent, as she waved her hand to a chair at some little distance. 'You are from the detective office?'

Stanford answered in the affirmative as he drew the chair nearer and seated himself, the lady scanning him from head to foot with those piercing eyes of hers.

'You are a member of the detective force of this city?'

'I am, madam.'

'And if it should be approved, you will personally conduct the investigation I wish made?'

'Most likely.'

'Your appearance is more favourable than I had hoped.'

'A detective is supposed to be able to assume any appearance he wishes,' said Stanford.

'It is impossible for a man, no matter to what branch he may belong, to assume either the appearance or the manners of a gentleman unless he is one.'

Our Super acknowledged the compliment with a bow. 'I shall be glad to know what investigations you wish me to make?'

A sudden flash of anger shot from her eyes.

'I wish you to find out the villains who, under the name of guests in my house, are robbing and disgracing both me and my other guests! I know of the reports that have been made to your office!'

'May I enquire how you know that our department has heard of the matter you allude to?' Stanford coolly asked.

'I have heard through Sasson, the baron's personal attendant and major domo. I refer you to Sasson for the disgraceful particulars. It is humiliating to think that persons in our position should come round the world to be initiated into the methods practised by chevaliers d'industrie[3] in Melbourne!'

'You have thieves in Austria also, I presume, madam?' said Stanford, as he rose.

The baroness stared at him as she struck the silver gong on the table at her side. 'I presume there are, sir; but it remained for Australia to afford me any personal experience of such individuals. Send Sasson here,' she ordered the servant who answered her summons, and presently a most respectable-looking, well-dressed man of forty or so entered the room.

'Sasson, this gentleman is from the detective office here. You will inform him of the robberies. Do not forget that the baron wishes a reward to be offered'; and the baroness waved a dismissing hand that was covered with gems even at that hour in the morning.

Sasson, with a few low-spoken words of invitation, led the way to his private sitting-room, and, having closed the door, placed refreshments on the table. 'You found her excellency rather abrupt, I fear?' the man said; 'but it is her way—you must not mind her.'

Stanford smiled as he looked into the quiet face of Sasson. 'Oh! it's all in the way of business. Now, as my time is, or ought to be, valuable, I shall be glad if you will give me full particulars.'

'I will put it as shortly as I can. I have been aware for some time that visitors have lost valuables at the receptions here. You are aware of it also?'

'Yes; complaints have been made to us, and we have been privately trying to trace the lost property through pawnbrokers and that. But secrecy has always been insisted on.'

'Just so, and that is why the matter has not been made known to the baroness until now. Gentlemen who visit here often remain the night, and as my duty is to see that each guest is comfortable, I make a tour of the bedrooms when the guests are retiring. Once or twice I have been told of losses in confidence and have made search in the reception and card rooms for missing articles of jewellery. Last night, however, a country visitor—a Mr. Iverton—missed a purse containing a large sum of money, and he made such a fuss over it that I was obliged to tell the baroness. Hence her note to your office.'

'Mr. Iverton has not reported to us.'

'He is awaiting our action. The baroness is prepared to offer a reward of one hundred pounds for such information as may lead to the discovery—'

'Of the property?'

'No, of the thief. There can hardly be a doubt that these continued robberies have been committed by someone on the premises.'

'And you have no manner of suspicion?'

'None. I have been in the household of Baron Cugerna for some years, at first as personal attendant and now as major domo. In the latter capacity I have engaged and am responsible for the servants, most of whom we brought from Austria with us. I do not believe that one of them is dishonest.'

'You have actually no suspicions?'

'No; at least, I suppose that in a measure I suspect everyone. At first I did not believe but that the articles of jewellery and what not had been lost outside the house, but now I am obliged to own that they are missed in the card and billiard rooms. Mr. Iverton's purse

AN AMATEUR DETECTIVE

disappeared from his pocket as he was seated at the card table with the baron himself.'

'You are not an Austrian?' Stanford said; 'you speak English too well.'

'No; I am an Englishman, but have been abroad since early youth. Are you disposed to suspect me?' And Sasson smiled as he asked the question.

'"Suspect every man till you find him innocent,"' said our Superintendent. 'If you can give me the opportunity of attending one of your receptions, I think it probable that I may be able to lay my hand on the thief.'

'With your appearance nothing would be easier; but unless one was certain that a robbery would be committed on that very evening, what should you gain by attending?'

'If what is called a professional thief is in the business, and it was known that a detective was in the rooms, the fact would be sufficient to urge another attempt. My experience of the thieving fraternity is that they take a delight in committing crime under the very eyes of our best men. I know a criminal who is quite capable of robbing a constable from whom he might be pretending to ask for information in the street.'

Sasson shook his head. 'You will not elucidate the mystery so easily as you expect. If, however, you wish to make a trial in the house, I can arrange for you to come as a visitor.'

Stanford told me how matters stood when he returned to the office. He was in high glee when he talked the matter over with me that evening while he was dressing for the baron's 'reception.' Stanford and I occupied quarters in the same house, and I had the opportunity of watching his toilet and learning his plans and suspicions before he left.

'Between you and me and the post, Sinclair,' he said, 'I believe Sasson himself knows a good deal more about the affair than he is willing to admit.'

'Do you think he's the thief?' I asked.

'Hum; I don't go quite as far as that, though it is impossible to be certain at present. But I'm certain he's hiding, or trying to hide, something from me. And he needn't think he'll succeed, for I'll get it out of him if he's as deep as a well!'

'Don't be too clever, Stanford!' I laughed; 'pride goes before a fall!'

He gave me the 'look as good as a summons' that he was proverbial for and, being now fully dressed for Burro Lodge, took out his silver snuff box, of which he was particularly proud, and daintily helped himself to a pinch.

AN AMATEUR DETECTIVE

'You're a very good fellow in your way, Sinclair,' he said; 'but don't you get my paddy up to-night.'[4]

'I'll hear what you say when you come back,' I retorted; 'for I expect you will have bagged the thief long before the reception is over. If you like, I'll go and hang round the baron's gate on chance of an arrest, eh?'

He didn't condescend me an answer, but ran downstairs to his waiting cab, as fine and gentlemanly-looking a man as stood in the city of Melbourne that night.

Stanford went early, by arrangement, and was taken to the baron's own room and introduced by Sasson. Cugerna was an amiable-looking elderly gentleman who apparently took the world easily and looked upon a detective's appearance in his home as rather a good joke. 'I think madam is worrying herself altogether too much over these little affairs,' he said; 'but I am very much pleased to see you, Mr. Stanford;,and shall introduce you to our guests. Between ourselves, I don't believe the articles have been stolen at all, but lost outside or misplaced. Sasson, your arm?' And with the help of a stick the good man managed to reach his usual seat in one of the splendid reception-rooms, where Sasson placed his bandaged foot on a rest and threw a light silk drapery over it.

There were only a few gentlemen present on the baron's entrance, and to them he named Stanford in an easy way; but very soon there were many arrivals, and madam made her appearance. She glanced toward Stanford as she passed, but otherwise paid no attention to him.

The Superintendent seated himself near an occasional table, and watched the movements around him. Refreshments were being carried about by footmen; while others were drawing out and arranging card tables in another handsome room, that was only separated from the one in which the baron was by a high and wide, draped archway. There was a low buzz of conversation, and presently Stanford was himself addressed. 'Hallo! what are you doing here?'

The Super recognised the voice and the man; it was Charles Iverton, to whom Sasson had alluded as having made a fuss over the loss of his purse. Stanford had had some business dealings with him and replied lightly, 'I think it probable that I am here a good deal on your business, Mr. Iverton.'

'Ha! these foreigners have taken my warning, then? I told that major domo fellow that if something wasn't done toward recovering my property, I should put the affair in the hands of the police. Things have come to a pretty pass in Melbourne when a man can be robbed with impunity in the very drawing-rooms of a foreign adventurer.'

'It would be better for you to refrain from such personalities, at least while you are a guest under the gentleman's roof,' Stanford said, in a low tone. 'As to the bona-fides of Baron Cugerna there can be no possible doubt; the Consul for Austria is in the room at this moment.'

'I do not care if there were a dozen Consuls; there are thieves in the room, even if they have half a dozen ribbons at their button-holes. I am the last man to sit down quietly and lose forty-five pounds without a try to get it back.'

'When did you miss the purse?' the Superintendent asked.

'I was at a card table—that one at which your Consul is seating himself now—and I was playing with Joliffe—there is some heavy card-playing here, you must know. The purse was a morocco one, a sort of pocket-book affair, and there were four ten-pound notes, one five, and some silver in it. It was in my pocket when the game was made up, for I felt it when I sat down, and had to draw my coat-tail aside. I don't know what possessed me to be so careless as carry a purse to such places at all; a man can use his cheque-book for legitimate purposes. At all events, I felt for the purse shortly after, and it was gone.'

'Did you say anything at the time?'

'I went straight to that Sasson fellow and told him. He advised me to keep quiet till a search was made. I hope you will be able to give a good report of the matter.'

'I hope so.'

Iverton took himself and his sulky face to another part of the room, while Stanford joined Mr. Ratz, who was at that time Consul here for Austria.

'Have you heard that I am here on duty?' Stanford quietly asked.

'Yes; I received an intimation of it.'

'Do you think Iverton really lost the purse?'

'I have no doubt of it; his chagrin is genuine. He is a mean man, although a wealthy one.'

'I think there is no doubt that our host is what he pretends to be?'

'None whatever. The baron is one of our best-known Austrian noblemen.'

While the Consul was speaking, he had seated himself at the table near Stanford, and both had accepted coffee from one of the lightly stepping footmen. Stanford had previously indulged himself in a pinch from his valued box, and laid it on the velvet cover of the table while he drew his coffee toward him. As his hand released the dainty saucer and sought the snuff-box to replace it in his pocket, the box was gone!

Every muscle in Stanford's frame grew rigid. He couldn't believe it possible that he himself had been robbed by the villain of whom he was in search.

AN AMATEUR DETECTIVE

Mr. Ratz was sitting unconcernedly opposite to him, coffee cup and saucer in hand, and his eyes were apparently fixed on a woman who was winding her way easily among the card tables toward the baron's chair, near which the baroness stood. This woman was apparently an attendant, and was carrying a lace shawl over her arm. She was a tall and upright figure, stiffly dressed in black silk, and with a foreign-looking head-dress of white muslin and lace on her black hair.

The Superintendent stared as she placed the lace shawl round the lady's shoulders.

'Is that woman the baroness' attendant, Mr. Ratz?'

'Yes; her own maid. She came with them from Austria and is, I believe, a great favourite.'

'Did she pass near us just now?'

'Yes; why do you ask?'

'I fancied I heard a swish of silk.'

'I wondered what case you were thinking about.' Ratz returned laughingly, 'you looked so absorbed. I feel a bit drowsy myself. To a man who does not play, these receptions are dull, and the buzz of conversation is drowsily monotonous. I think I shall take my leave—there will soon be a break-up anyway.'

Stanford rose to leave also, his eyes still upon the group round the baron. The maid, having placed the lace over her mistress' shoulders, had glided away again, and as Stanford approached the host to make his conventional adieux, he was surprised at a sudden exhibition of graciousness on the lady's part.

'I fear you have spent but a dull evening,' she smiled; 'and I am sure you have had no success in your object. Would you like to try again? We are to have a sort of conversazione tomorrow evening in honour of the baron's birthday; I shall be pleased to have Sasson send you a card.'

Stanford got away as quickly as he could, and, beckoning to Sasson as he passed, waited in the hall for the major domo to join him.

'I only wanted to ask you a question, Mr, Sasson,' he said; 'who is the woman who just now fetched the baroness a shawl?'

'Her own maid, Katchin Gergoff.'

'Did you engage her? Has she been long in the service of the baroness?'

'No,' replied Sasson, hesitatingly; 'I only engage the servants. Miss Gergoff is not exactly in that class; she was engaged by the baroness herself about two years ago. I have fancied'—and Sasson looked keenly at the Superintendent—'that there may be some relationship between Gergoff and her excellency; there is a certain resemblance.'

300

AN AMATEUR DETECTIVE

'Yes; I have observed it. The baroness talks of sending me a card for a conversazione for tomorrow evening, Mr. Sasson, but you need not trouble; I shall not attend. By the way, who does your catering?'

'The Messrs. Denton, of Collins-street.'

When our Super that night returned from Burro Lodge I was waiting up for him. My first view of his face told me that something strange had occurred, and that not of a pleasant nature. Stanford sat down and stared at me.

'You have not succeeded?' I asked.

'No; I have been robbed myself.'

'What!'

'My snuff-box is gone; it was taken almost out of my hand in the very reception-room. But,' he added, with such an oath as rarely passed his lips, 'if the loss leads me to something I have in view, I shall be content. Sinclair, who do you think I saw to-night at Burro Lodge?'

'How can I guess?'

'Ina Cliff.'

'Good heaven! You don't say so? I'm afraid you must be mistaken; it's too good news to be true!'

'There is no mistake; it was that anointed villain of a woman, and none else. Oh, Lord! to think she should have ventured back to this ground in a little over five years.'

As soon as he calmed down, Stanford related the particulars of his evening at the Lodge, and we discussed his plans. Stanford had decided to put me on duty at the Lodge on the night following, and I was to act in conjunction with another man. I don't suppose such an idea had ever entered into the mind of an Australian detective before, for the man chosen by Stanford to go to Burro Lodge as my assistant was well known as the sharpest thief and cracksman[5] in Melbourne, by name Con Blaney.

'That is, if he will take the job,' added the Super; 'and I think he will for the novelty of the thing, as well as a chance of the reward. He is, fortunately, not in any sort of trouble just now, and I'll go to see him first thing in the morning.'

Ina Cliff, the woman to whom the Super had so uncomplimentarily referred, when in Melbourne had been the subject of much suspicion. Her first appearance here was as lady's maid to a French countess who had visited our State and who left Miss Cliff behind. A series of engagements followed, during which her various employers were victimised by the loss of jewellery or money. But nothing could be brought home to Cliff, though we had a good try for it, which she laughed at, until at last her star declined on the sudden death of her most recent mistress,

AN AMATEUR DETECTIVE

a lady of eccentricity and wealth named Melton. Mrs. Melton had been found dead in bed, with a phial that had contained poison clasped in her hand. The maid, Ina Cliff, who slept in another part of the house, stated that she only discovered the body when it was stiff and cold. She was arrested on suspicion of having poisoned her infirm mistress, but we were unable to secure a conviction, and shortly after the trial she left the country.

Two years afterwards, a young man who had many times been convicted of burglary, and was then serving an eighteen-months' sentence, was set at liberty and paid a visit to the detective office with the information that he had been in Mrs. Melton's house, intent on robbery, on the night of her death. He stated that he had been hidden in the room when Cliff administered the contents of the phial to her employer. When he found the old lady was dead, the intended robber was so fearful that he should himself be suspected of the murder that he got away as quickly as possible, and held his tongue.

When this late information reached the police, Cliff was traced to Hamburg, but there she seemed to have melted into air. Now, after some five years, she turns up again as maid and companion to the Baroness Cugerna of Austria.

On the following morning Stanford went early on his odd errand. Knowing well the haunts of criminals, the Super had no difficulty in finding Con Blaney. Stanford went in his usual attire, and his advent in the unsavoury locality created much curiosity, and perhaps consternation, among the habitues.

'Yes, Blaney's at old Mag's still,' one of the loungers replied to a question. 'What have you against him this time?'

'Nothing; I'm only paying him a morning call,' the Super answered with a smile.

'Gammon!' retorted the man, with a sneer, as he turned his back on the officer; 'you're not a man as gets out of bed early in the day to do a fellow a good turn.'

The door of old Mag's frowsy dwelling being ajar, Stanford pushed it open and went through to the kitchen, where Mag was washing up some breakfast things.

'I want to see Con Blaney; is he up yet? Oh, you needn't look so grief-stricken. I have no charge against him. I only want to ask him a question.'

'He's in his room upstairs. Of course, he'll be glad to have the honour of a visit from you, Mr. Stanford; you were always a friend to Con, you know.'

The Superintendent laughed at this cut at his having tried hard to

AN AMATEUR DETECTIVE

get a conviction against Con on the last charge preferred against him.

He was soon on the upper floor and in Blaney's room.

Con was lying on the outside of his bed, fully dressed with the exception of his coat, and engaged in reading a book. Con was a great reader, and not of foolish, sensational rubbish either. He was a well-made, slight-built chap of about thirty-two or three, with a strong, clean-shaved face and close-cut head of brown hair. His forehead was high and broad, his blue eyes well set; and though the suspicions scowl of the criminal was evident, it was an intelligent face, and when he laughed, showing his white, even teeth, was quite prepossessing.

He scowled as he looked up.

'I'd like to know what you want here, Mr. Stanford?' he said sharply; 'you haven't anything against me.'

'You are quite right so far as I am concerned,' Stanford replied, seating himself and drawing the chair nearer to Con. 'I have a favour to ask of you. I want you to help me out of a regular bog.'

Con jumped up, sat on his bed, and stared. 'It must be a queer bog that a cracksman is needed to help a police officer out of!' he said. 'But speak plainly; I'm no fool, Stanford, though I am a member of the criminal class.'

'It is because you are that I know you can help me, Con. You are not only one of the cleverest cracksmen in the colony, but you are one of the sharpest thieves in Melbourne.'

Con grinned good-humouredly. 'I've often thought I'd like to have a try for that grand snuff-box you're so proud of!' he said.

'That is exactly what I want you to do! I've been robbed of it, and I want you to get it back for me.' And Stanford then told the whole story relating to the disappearance of valuables from the guests at Burro Lodge, and the particulars relating to his own loss.

Con was evidently interested. 'We heard something of the Lodge business,' he said, 'and wondered what new hands could be at work in it. But, look here, Stanford, doesn't it seem a bit silly of you to set a man of my propensities at such work? Good lord! how could I be mixed up, and maybe handling articles of value, without having a go in at 'em on my own account? The idea is too funny.'

'The fact that I am willing to trust you shows that I may have a better opinion of you than you think, if I put you on honour to take no mean advantage of the chance I am willing to give you I know you will not break your word. Besides, there is the reward the baron will give—you shall have every penny of it if you succeed.'

'In getting back your snuff mull, eh?'

'No; that is a secondary consideration. I should certainly like to

AN AMATEUR DETECTIVE

recover it; but I would forfeit it ten times over to get that woman caught and punished.'

'Surely you have her safe already? As you have recognised her, all you have to do is to arrest her.'

'I haven't any charge against her at present; and I daren't risk a mistake. I might have made one. I have not even heard her speak. And if it is she, the colour of her hair is changed. If you will undertake to fox her, you will probably be more successful than we. No man in Melbourne ought to know Ina Cliff better than you.'

'Ugh!' and Con shuddered; 'I'll never forget that night in the old lady's room when I knew she was dead and that, if I was seen leaving the premises, I was certain to be hanged! I have it in for Cliff, I tell you, Stanford; and there's my hand on it that I'll do my best to bowl her out. You want me to go as assistant to Denton, the purveyor, eh?'

'I'll get you admission to the house that way, but if you find it necessary, you need not leave the baron's premises immediately after the supper. You are a handy chap at getting in or out of a window, Con, and Sinclair is going to be in the garden in case you should want help.'

Before Stanford left everything had been arranged.

I was not enamoured of my superior's extraordinary plan to elucidate the mystery at Burro Lodge. The idea of a partnership between a detective and a burglar seemed to me very unpromising.

Con duly attended at the baron's birthday reception, and industriously assisted in laying and arranging the tables, etc. He was an active chap, and made himself especially busy in carrying boxes, etc., from the purveyor's traps to the supper-room. While thus employed, he had opportunities of seeing both Sasson and 'Miss Gergoff,' and he found out what rooms were respectively occupied by the major domo and the woman; and when Denton's last trap had driven off, he remained behind in hiding, awaiting events.

Con had mixed among the domestics at the Lodge freely during the evening and heard many jealous remarks as to the favour shown by Sasson to her excellency's maid. They did not eat with the other servants, but were served in a sitting-room appropriated to their special use. It was in this room that Blaney hid himself, hoping to get some hint from the occupants' conversation.

'So the clever detective didn't put in an appearance this evening, after all?' the woman said, as she rose from the table.

'No,' returned Sasson, gloomily.

'And what do you think will be the next move, Mr. Sasson?' she asked, as she arranged her hair before the mantelpiece mirror.

'It will have to come to an end, Miss Gergoff,' Sasson returned, determinedly. 'I have made my mind up to it. I will keep my knowledge to myself no longer. You have presumed on your influence over me in the belief that I was too foolishly devoted to you to expose you. I may or I may not have been so at one time. You promised me that you would cease your thefts, but you have not done so. If you make an excuse, and leave the house to-night, I will hold my tongue; if you do not, I shall make a statement to the police tomorrow morning.'

From his hiding-place, Con Blaney could see the reflection of the woman's face in the mirror, and he always declared afterwards that never did a human visage so reflect the soul of a devil. It was only for a moment, however; when she turned to the major domo it was with a sad smile, that had a certain charm in it. 'I know I have been trying you too far, and you have been so kind and lenient with me. Well, it shall be as you say, my friend—I will leave the baroness. I go now to attend her toilet for the night, and I shall plead illness. If you will wait my return here, I shall then tell you what arrangements I have made, and say adieu?'

Sasson undertook to return to the room ere he made his rounds for the night. All the visitors had left or retired, and the servants were having a late meal downstairs. When the woman left Sasson, Con Blaney slipped unnoticed after her. She did not go to the baroness' room, but to her own.

Con was now puzzled how to proceed. When the woman entered her room, she locked the door, and in order to continue his watch, the young man was obliged to slip along a passage to a side door. Once outside, he was soon at Gergoff's window, that he had already arranged to suit his intentions of espial. Through the little opening he had made, Con could see all that passed in the woman's room.

The apartment was a plain, but comfortably furnished bedroom, and her first move was to draw the bed from the vicinity of the wall against which it was placed. No noise was made, the castors running easily on the carpeted floor. Fortunately for the watcher, the bedstead was at right angles with his eyes, so that when the lady's maid went behind it, Con's scrutiny was unobstructed. She lifted a corner of the carpet, stepped on a loose board, and when it tilted up, lifted a small but apparently heavy box from the space. This box she laid on the carpet and, kneeling down, unlocked it with a key that was attached to a chain round her neck. The light from the gas gleamed for a moment on many glittering things in the box, and so anxious was Con Blaney to get a sight of them that he inadvertently made a slight noise. The woman heard it, and turned a startled face toward the window.

But it was for a moment only. Evidently she put the noise down to

AN AMATEUR DETECTIVE

some trivial cause and returned to her search for some article, apparently at the bottom of the box. When she had found it, and arose from her knees, Con saw her face. It was the face of a woman possessed by a devil, made more white and ghastly by her dyed black hair. The treacherous eyes gleamed with the determination that had set her white teeth together and drawn her thin lips back from them, as the tiger does when about to rend his prey.

Held by an awful fear, Blaney watched her unfold the cloth that hid the article of which she had been in search, until the light gleamed on the steel blade of a slender dagger. When she closed and replaced the box, and pushed back the bed to its place, she held the weapon in her clenched hand, and once lifted it, as in the act to strike.

Con drew back from the window and looked in the shadows for the detective who was to have been there, but seeing no signs of him, and fearing he might be too late, he glided to the door from which he had silently emerged and as silently, but hurriedly, made his way toward the room in which Sasson was awaiting the woman's promised return.

Con always said that Satan was undoubtedly working for his own that night. In his hurry, he took a wrong turning that delayed him for perhaps five minutes, and when he at last reached the major domo's door, it was open, and the room in darkness. Cautiously feeling his way, trying to resume his hiding-place behind the curtains so as to hear exactly what further passed between Sasson and the woman, the burglar stumbled over some object that lay prone on the carpet, and in falling he struck his head against the marble base of the mantelpiece and became unconscious.

The noise of his fall called the attention of some passing servant. Lights were obtained, and Con was found lying partly across the yet warm body of Sasson.

When Con opened his eyes, he was being dragged by a constable into a sitting posture. His hands and shirt-cuffs were covered with blood, and he saw horrified faces round him, and the murdered man on the floor near him.

'In the name of God, where am I?' Con asked, desperately, as he stared at the awful hands he held out before him. 'What has happened?'

'I am afraid you know that best yourself,' replied the constable; 'come, get up on your feet!' But it was soon seen that the prisoner was unable to obey the mandate, he had again relapsed into unconsciousness.

'He must be hurt some way,' said Constable Johns.

'Leave him till the doctor comes. Sinnot, do you know this man?'

'Of course I do; it's Con Blaney, the burglar.'

AN AMATEUR DETECTIVE

'I thought so. He's been at his old game, and the gentleman has made a fight for it, and got the worst of it. Now, you folk, get away out o' this! There's no occasion to disturb the family; the police will be here all the rest of the night'

My own share in the doings of the night of the tragedy was a small one. I mingled with the servants and the caterer's men, and moved about among the guests, my eyes and ears on the alert, but I saw nothing that helped to a solution of the Burro Lodge robberies, and only learned of Sasson's murder and Con's arrest as the police were taking the burglar away in a cab.

I went home hurriedly, knowing that Stanford would be waiting up for me, eager to know the anticipated success of his protege.

'Well, Sinclair? Well? How has Con got on? Is he coming to report, and bringing back my snuff-box?'

Stanford spoke laughingly, but as I dropped to a seat and stared at him, the laugh died out suddenly. 'What is wrong?' he asked.

'Blaney is arrested for the murder of Sasson.'

'Good God! murder! Sasson? Why should Con murder Sasson? Besides, Con is not a man to shed blood! — I don't believe a word of it!'

'Very well, I can't help that. The fellow may be innocent, but he is accused of it, and Sasson is undoubtedly dead.'

'Tell me all you know.' he said, shortly.

'Ha!' Stanford cried, as he started to his feet when I had finished, 'we have the woman, at any rate! Take my tip for it, Sinclair, Con is as innocent as you are. Ina Cliff is the murderer, if murder there was! Come on; I shall get the truth out of Con before I'm an hour older!'

The town clock was striking 2 a.m. as we presented ourselves to the lock-up keeper, and were admitted to the cell, where a bed had been hastily prepared for Blaney. 'He's pretty bad,' the officer said. 'but he refused to be taken to the hospital; says it's only a knock on the head he's got from a fall.'

Con was sitting on the edge of his bed as we entered, and was holding his bandaged head between his hands. When Stanford spoke to him, he lifted a white face, and said — 'A pretty job doing your work has got me into, Super Stanford!'

'You're not guilty, Blaney? I won't believe that.'

'No, I'm not guilty; but they'll hang me all the same,' he returned, bitterly. 'I'm a man with a bad record. I feel very dizzy and queer, and I had better tell you all I've found out before I get insensible again'; and he did so to Stanford's great satisfaction.

'Cheer up, Con; you'll get out of it all right! What you heard between the woman and Sasson shows a motive for the murder. We'll get

AN AMATEUR DETECTIVE

on the track of that dagger, too, and trace it home to her. You'll be back in your own bed before daylight I hope.'

'You are going to arrest her?' I asked, as we re-entered the cab.

'If I'm not too late. But I think the devil is so self-confident that, assured of Sasson's death without speaking, she has most likely gone to bed to sleep the sleep of the just.'

And so it proved, for we aroused the woman out of a sound sleep.

'Do not stand on any ceremony with us, Miss Cliff!' said Stanford, sarcastically; 'Sinclair and I are very old friends, you know. Allow me, to save you any inconvenience, to remove your bed before you make your toilet'; and the Superintendent seized the bedstead and set its castors rolling to the opposite side of the room.

The woman sat up, staring in consternation, while the carpet was lifted from her hiding-place and her precious box laid on the floor. When one by one the glittering jewels were revealed, she made no sign. When Stanford grabbed his valued snuff-box, she laughed hysterically; and when Sinclair held up the bloody cloth, to which she had again consigned the fatal dagger, she uttered a cry of terror, and fainted.

Con Blaney was removed to his own bed at old Mag's before the day broke. And I may here say of the said amateur D., Con Blaney, that he profitably acted upon his lately formed resolutions, and put the reward and his savings to good use in South Africa, where he settled down to a respectable and prosperous life.

It is greatly to be wished that others of our criminal class would profit by his example, and remember his last words to Stanford—'You are right, sir; a criminal life does not pay in either the long or the short run.'

Many will remember the trial of Ina Cliff, and her demeanour during its progress. While the case had been in preparation—and there were several remands—that she had dyed her hair was made evident, and the black-haired Austrian, Katchin Gergoff, stood palpably revealed as Ina Cliff.

She bore herself in the dock as a hardened and reckless creature. She refused to speak more than a mocking word or two. She laughed in the faces of pitying chaplains and salvationists, and it was not until she was led into her cell after the death sentence had been pronounced that her callousness left her. She wept and shrieked out her fear of death, threw herself on the floor of her cell, and refused to either eat or sleep; and the few who witnessed the last fearful moments of Ina Cliff will carry the shuddering memory with them to the end of life.

The baron provided the means for Cliff's legal defence—a circumstance which may have had no significance, for he was evidently a kindly-hearted old gentleman, but I learned nothing further in support of Sasson's suggestion that the maid and her mistress were in any way connected. The baron and baroness left Melbourne soon after the Exhibition closed.

First published in the *Australian Journal*, November 1906, as part of the *Detective's Album* serial, under the byline 'W.W.'

NOTES

1 *our great Exhibition*: In the second half of the 19th century, Melbourne was one of the richest cities in the world, thanks to the goldrush. It was an international trading city and had—it still has—a great rivalry with Sydney over the claim to be Australia's premier city. When Sydney hosted an exhibition in 1879, it was more of an agricultural show, while the Great Exhibition that Melbourne hosted in 1880–1881 was in the tradition of those held in London and Paris, and included arts, culture and technology.
2 *'the calm repose of Vere de Vere'*: the reference is to Tennyson's poem 'Lady Clara Vere de Vere' and its languid, cold-hearted protagonist. The relevant lines actually read, 'that repose which stamps the caste of Vere de Vere'; Fortune was perhaps recalling the poem from memory, and misquoting slightly as a result.
3 *chevalier d'industrie*: a thief or swindler, a pickpocket.
4 *don't you get my paddy up*: don't make me angry
5 *cracksman*: a safe-breaker or, more generally, a burglar.

A NOTE ON THE TEXT

These stories were scanned from the original texts as printed in the *Australian Journal* (all but two), the *Australian Town and Country Journal*, and the *Herald* newspaper. The publications had different editing guidelines, while the fifteen stories taken from the *Australian Journal* appeared over a period spanning forty years, during which the Australian language was evolving and the magazine's editorial practices along with it. As a result, there is considerable variation within the stories collected here with regard to spelling and, especially, punctuation. We have made minor adjustments to both in the interests of consistency and readability, as well as correcting obvious typographical errors.

ON THE ILLUSTRATIONS

The images are taken from publications of the period in which Mary Fortune was writing. Several are from the *Australian Journal*, which ran illustrations to accompany some articles and stories (though not any of the Fortune stories included here), and from similar magazines, all in the then conventional styles of wood engraving. Other, rather different, illustrations are from *Police News*, a shortlived newssheet (1875–77) devoted to coverage in words and (especially) pictures of crimes, accidents, and other calamities. It was the brainchild of Richard Egan Lee (one of Mary Fortune's former editors at the *Australian Journal*), who editorialized against political corruption and social injustice (especially against women), while encouraging his readers to send in their sketches of death and disaster to be turned, via his patent zincotype process and with the aid of a skilled engraver/platemaker, into the images that appeared in *Police News*. Many are crude, some quite sophisticated, and not a few are startlingly modern, even proto-Expressionist in style.

All illustrations courtesy of the State Library of Victoria.

22: *Wood's Point Road*, wood engraving, *Illustrated Australian News for Home Readers*, 31 December 1872. — 36: *Prince's Bridge by Moonlight*, wood engraving by Samuel Calvert, *Illustrated Australian News*, 13 March 1880. — 52: *View on the Sebastopol Lead, Ballaarat*, wood engraving, *Illustrated Melbourne News*, 2 January 1858. — 78: *A Seducer and His Victim*, photomechanical print, *Police News*, 7 April 1877. — 105: *The Rescue*, wood engraving, *Australian Journal*, 7 September 1867. — 112: *The Brighton Outrage*, photomechanical print, *Police News*, 14 April 1877. — 138: *Man Strapped to Horse*, photomechanical print, *Police News*, 14 April 1877. — 168: *Beatrice: Her Way Lay to Her Home through the Fitzroy Gardens*, wood engraving, *The Australasian*, 22 December 1888. — 196: *Goldgewinnung auf einem australischen Goldfeld*, chalk lithograph by Herman Deutsch, 1858. — 212: *Emigrants Embarking*, wood engraving, *Australasian Sketcher*, 18 December 1880. — 244: *Attempted Murder and Suicide by a Wife*, photomechanical print, *Police News*, 3 February 1877. — 270: *The Victorian Police, No. 3: The Watchhouse*, wood engraving, *Illustrated Australian News*, 6 November 1880. — 292: *'Mr. Pringle' in Gay Heber's Apartment*, wood engraving, *Australian Journal*, 1 December 1872.

www.ingramcontent.com/pod-product-compliance
Lightning Source LLC
Jackson TN
JSHW022302170225
79236JS00003B/5